SOUL
RAGING

SOUL RAGING

RONIE KENDIG

BETHANYHOUSE

a division of Baker Publishing Group
Minneapolis, Minnesota

Published by Bethany House Publishers
11400 Hampshire Avenue South
Bloomington, Minnesota 55438
www.bethanyhouse.com

Bethany House Publishers is a division of
Baker Publishing Group, Grand Rapids, Michigan

Printed in the United States of America

ISBN 978-0-7642-3189-6 (trade paper)
ISBN 978-0-7642-3783-6 (casebound)

This is a work of fiction. Names, characters, incidents, and dialogues are products of the author's imagination and are not to be construed as real. Any resemblance to actual events or persons, living or dead, is entirely coincidental.

Isaiah 45:1 is from the Holy Bible, New International Reader's Version®. NIrV®. Copyright © 1995, 1996, 1998, 2014 by Biblica, Inc.™ Used by permission of Zondervan. www.zondervan.com. The "NIrV" and "New International Reader's Version" are trademarks registered in the United States Patent and Trademark Office by Biblica, Inc.™

Isaiah 45:11–13 is from THE HOLY BIBLE, NEW INTERNATIONAL VERSION®, NIV® Copyright © 1973, 1978, 1984, 2011 by Biblica, Inc.® Used by permission. All rights reserved worldwide.

Cover design by Kirk DouPonce, DogEared Design

Author is represented by Steve Laube of the Steve Laube Agency.

20 21 22 23 24 25 26   7 6 5 4 3 2 1

Acknowledgments

Thank you to Elizabeth Perry Maddrey, PhD, for your help keeping Mercy Maddox tech-savvy, sexy, and in-the-know!

Also, special thanks to Carrie Stuart Parks for her inspiration with the Hieronymus Bosch painting and crafting another layer of intrigue for Leif with the panels.

Special thanks to Amory Cannon for her help with chip implants and toxins.

ego semperer ex profundis

Prologue

THREE WEEKS FROM NOW

"The devil was once an angel."

The gritted-out words hung in the stillness of the crippled bunker, and Dru Iliescu hesitated. Finally, he understood the meaning of the phrase "be careful who you trust."

Head angled toward the M4A1 tucked firmly into his shoulder, the operator was preternaturally relaxed, his finger resting with experienced calm along the guard. He had come to collect on a debt, repay a wrong done.

In Dru's periphery lay the grim scene of what had happened only minutes after he sprinted through the hatch. Bodies laid out. Red emergency lights spinning across pools of blood. Coiled tension tightened the posture of the other operators in black tac gear, their anger and weapons also trained on him. A firing squad. It was appropriate.

It didn't surprise Dru that he'd been found out. That truth had hurled itself all over this nightmare. As an agent, he'd done time in the field, worked in the shadows, lied straight to the face of many a friend and loved one. Done things he'd never repeat in civil company. Yet . . . he hadn't been prepared for this.

Palms up, Dru followed the business end of the M4A1 to

the man leveraging lethal force against him. He drew in a slow, even breath as he focused on the lead operator, whose face was hidden behind a balaclava. "Hear me out."

"No!" came an angry bark, the voice familiar. The anger familiar. "No more." He charged forward a step. "Down!" He motioned to the floor. "On your knees, or they'll be mopping your gray matter off the concrete."

Swallowing hard, Dru assessed his options—at least, he tried to. It was hard to think past his heartbeat and the staccato grunts of injured personnel in the corner, holding bloody wounds.

"Let's go, Ossi," muttered one of the balaclava-clad men. "Time's up. We got what we need to end this."

The code name wasn't necessary for Dru to know the man before him was Leif Metcalfe, but the confirmation gutted him. The kid had unnatural skills, had gone through things nobody should have to—and that told Dru not to break eye contact, not to make a wrong move, because Neiothen reaction time was fast and lethal.

He'd already failed Leif. But if he had a chance, if he could turn this . . .

How? They were watching him. He wasn't going to give them a reason to interfere. "Please—"

He flinched when Leif's finger flicked to the trigger as if itching to apply that subtle, dangerous pressure. But when Dru realized he was still standing and not bleeding out, he focused on Leif. On what had changed: his head angle. A simultaneous lift of his shoulder, spine arching. As if . . . he was in pain. Fighting it.

Growling, Leif tucked his chin. The heel of his hand thumped his temple.

Dru surged forward. A blur came from his right, and with it, pain exploded through his skull. Washed the world gray and buried him.

8

PART ONE

ONE

"Holy son . . . of a motherless . . . Caesar's goat and fudgesicles . . . on frick frack." Groaning through the hammering gong in his head, Barclay Purcell climbed onto all fours, the floor blurring and wobbling beneath him. He shook his head—only to spin his surroundings into a frenzy. Letting out a low moan as he wrangled the world back into its right-side-up position made his throat burn. He canted sideways.

"Cell!" Mercy caught and steadied him, then knelt beside him. "What happened?"

"He—"

"Where's Leif?"

"He . . ." The incident careened through his mind in a kaleidoscope of colors and realizations. "Sugar honey iced tea, my skull hurts." He slumped against the bed, head back as the team seemed to sense the 911 of this situation and crowded into the rear room of the CIA safe house.

"Where's Runt?" Culver Brown demanded, scowling.

Cell snorted. "Gone." He'd never forget that powerful arm coiling around his neck like a viper. The calm, even breaths against his ear a countdown that sent the world into nothingness. "He sleeper-holded me." A shake of his head reminded him not to do that. He touched his forehead. "He's probably long gone. How long was I out?"

11

Mercy shrugged. "You came back to talk with Runt about a half hour ago."

"Half—" Cell bit off his frustration. "And nobody came to check on us?"

"You're grown men," Mercy argued.

"Exactly. And how many men do you know who can talk for thirty minutes, especially Leif?"

Mercy arched an eyebrow in acquiescence. "I figured you two were working out something related to the Book of the Wars."

"Yeah," Cell grunted, struggling to his feet and giving Culver a nod of thanks when he assisted, "like the fact Leif is one of the Neiothen."

"Back that crack truck up," Culver said, pressing a hand to Cell's chest and pushing. As if to squash his words.

"*Hai*," Dai Saito chimed in. "Try that again—and choose your words and accusations carefully. This is our brother you're talking about."

"And it's my neck he choked!" When the scowls went unabated, Cell nodded, his own frustration over Leif's . . . whatever it was—he refused to call it a betrayal, though his pounding migraine begged to differ—hitting a tipping point. "I get it. I hear you." He pointed toward the living area and started that way. "But it's legit. Let me show you. But first, I need ibuprofen and a stiff drink."

"We don't have lemonade here," Culver taunted.

"Ha. You're a riot. Right now Atlas ain't got nothin' on the weight on my shoulders." Cell banked into the hall and headed to the kitchenette.

Iskra followed. "What were you talking to Leif about?"

"Seriously?" Cell said with a groan over his thumping skull. "What you're really asking is, 'What'd you do to upset him?'"

"Well, don't be rude. Give the lady an answer," Saito teased.

12

"Doing something like this"—Iskra motioned toward Cell—"is not normal for Leif." She had a fierce expression and a worse reputation, having gone from Viorica-the-notorious-assassin to Iskra Todorova, love interest of Leif Metcalfe, golden boy of team Reaper.

Why had Cell ever given the team *that* name? It suddenly seemed macabre and borderline prophetic.

"Right," Culver said. "He's never gone against his own—never will."

"Hello? Sleeper hold?" Cell indicated his neck. From the small fridge, he retrieved a bottled water. "Look, I didn't want to believe it either. Ever since I translated the first name from those scans Iskra brought us, I saw the signs. I've known but wanted to prove myself wrong."

"Wait." Baddar Amir Nawabi's accent deepened when he was agitated, and it took a lot to agitate the former Afghan commando, who'd seen much and done more. "You know Runt was bad guy, but not tell us?"

"Give me a sec." Gulping three ibuprofen, Cell powered up his computer and prayed to God he could salvage this nightmare.

Massaging the pain in his chest made him aware there wasn't a wound there. Well, maybe a few inches below his skin lay the ache of betrayal. He'd gone to Leif out of an earnest desire to help. The former Navy SEAL had been searching for answers surrounding a six-month gap of his life, and Cell wanted to help solve that puzzle. Sadly, he *had* found the missing intel—hard truths neither of them liked. It wasn't every day you told a friend *he* was the demon they'd been hunting. But they were friends . . . or so Cell had thought until an hour ago.

"Hey." Eyes soft, Mercy touched his shoulder. "It wasn't personal. He liked you."

Cell snorted. "No, he didn't." And that was the rub, wasn't

it? "To him, I was a punk comms specialist always up in his business."

"But he was your *friend*." Meaning radiated through her hazel eyes. "You know Leif wasn't a guy to bro-hug, but he'd protect you and—"

"Sleeper hold." He shrugged. "All I'm sayin'."

"He could've snapped your neck," Culver put in. "I can do that, too. Want me to show you?" The brawny guy, who'd attempted to become a country music icon with his swagger and deep voice, grinned through his reddish-blond beard.

"We have the same training, remember?"

"How did you know he was a Neiothen?" Iskra's calm demeanor couldn't mask the acid in her words. She had it going on a million ways from Sunday, but her dark expression said she wasn't surprised by this turn of the Leif.

"How'd *you* know?" he asked.

Put on the spot, most women would shift, glance around. Not her. Very little ruffled her Bulgarian-Turkish feathers. And he remembered right then her former profession before Leif had jumped out of a perfectly good chopper to save her.

"You said something about the first name you translated," Saito said, easing onto a chair. "Start there. Catch us up so we can brief Command, get back to base, and figure out what to do."

"We're *not* leaving without Leif." Mercy glanced at the others. "Right?"

"He has a thirty-minute lead," Culver noted, stroking his beard.

Baddar sighed, looking like Eeyore's cousin. "And he is very fast."

"Right—a Neiothen," Saito supplied with a slow nod, thinking. "So that half hour might as well be an hour, since he has superpowers."

"Enhanced abilities," Cell corrected, still rattled at the truth of what—*who* they were talking about. "At least, that's what we've sorted out so far. I don't have all the details, and I've been working very hard to keep what I know on the down-low so I don't get deep-sixed. Then there's the fact that I've been warned off digging into this."

"By?" A shadow flickered through Culver's eyes.

Cell probably shouldn't have mentioned that, because now he had to come clean about Dru's warning. But how could he do that without compromising intel?

A soft beeping from his laptop alerted him to an incoming call. "It's the director." His gut tightened.

Culver cursed, dropped back against a chair, and roughed his hands over his face.

"Answer it," Saito said. "He has to know at some point."

"But we should talk," Cell said. "*Before*—"

"We've got about a twenty-hour flight to debrief," Saito said, then nodded to the screen. "Do it."

Cell glanced at Iskra, knowing she'd been warned off, too. Or had she? He was suddenly questioning everything and everyone. Just as Leif had, no doubt. Reluctantly, he accepted the call.

Deputy Director Dru Iliescu appeared on the screen. "Reaper." His gaze narrowed. "Where's Leif?"

"Gone," Cell answered, expecting a deluge of questions and anger.

The director glowered for several long seconds. "How long?"

"Thirty minutes and change."

Iliescu slid a hand over his mouth. "Okay." He tightened his lips, shook his head. "We'll start the hunt. Get wheels-up, and we'll talk in the air."

Cell blinked when the transmission ended. What, no shouting? No long diatribe? That meant one thing: the situation was a lot worse than he realized.

TAIPEI, TAIWAN

"Ossi. Ossi. Two. One. Nine. Initiate rise. Rise. Rise."

Like a drill chewing steel, grating and shrieking, those nine words bored through Leif's skull. He'd been fine one second, ready to take down Carlyn Sienna Gilliam, then drowning in pain the next. Lost in indecision and confusion. Yet something in him had shifted with those words. A terrible haunting washed through his consciousness, as if a ghost of himself had somehow freed itself. Paced with him through that kid's amusement park and now infected his life.

Veins thrumming and head aching because of the code that had erupted from the loudspeakers, he'd missed the pivotal shot against ArC. And it hadn't bothered him. No . . . it had. Just not the way he'd expected.

Sitting in that safe house and acting like nothing was wrong, as if his brain hadn't been irrevocably altered, he'd felt an inordinate rage. An undoing. A million scorpions crawling beneath his skin, ready to strike. The buzzing had peaked while talking with Reaper, stirring his biggest fear that he'd go crazy and kill his friends.

Then Cell had called him on it, said he knew what was happening.

Restraint vanished. He hadn't wanted to hurt Cell, but he couldn't let them stop him. And staying meant being drugged, cuffed, and delivered back to Langley. A measure only taken if he resisted, but he would've. He'd been cuffed by the lack of answers for years. Too long had he left decisions to others.

No more. It was time to change that. Which meant shaking things up. Splitting from the complacency that had held him hostage.

In the black night, Leif sat on a rooftop, staring down at the safe house across the street that harbored his team.

16

No. They weren't his team. Not anymore. He scratched his jaw, wrestling with the betrayal that now sheathed his skin. They would see his actions differently. Only see that he'd acted against Cell.

What would Iskra think? She'd be many things—hurt, angry, confused—but not understanding. While she had the skills to stop him from leaving, it would've been the disappointment in her deep gaze and her frown that disabled him. He'd taken the coward's way out because he couldn't afford to get derailed.

He peered through the night and across Taipei to the amusement park, mulling over what had happened there. How was Devine? The memory of Lawe's raw howl when she'd been struck by the sniper bullet pushed Leif's gaze down. Made his conscience writhe.

"Pete! Pete! Peyton! Oh God—please, no! Coriolis is down! Repeat, Coriolis is down! I need immediate evac!"

Leif pinched the bridge of his nose. Because of him, she might've died. Probably had. The likelihood of surviving a sniper shot was slim at best. No doubt Lawe would hold Leif responsible and hunt him down.

On the street below, a black SUV glided to a stop at the safe house. Leif drew deeper into the shadows as Reaper filed out of the building and into the waiting vehicle. They wouldn't look around, wouldn't search the street for him, because they expected him to be long gone.

Which he should be. So why was he still here?

As the SUV swung back into traffic, he moved back against the concrete wall. A weight pushed him into a crouch. Cupped his hands over his face as his friends left.

". . . you were supposed to say that you didn't have any other options, that you were maybe scared . . . That's you. You're Ossi."

Rutger Hermanns had told Leif he was integral in the fight against ArC, but hearing this from a friend made him sick.

17

Forced him to process the truth in a new way. It explained a lot—the missing time, the inability to remember six months. His unnatural speed and ability to heal quickly. His lack of fear.

He shifted and, at the far end of the street, spotted the taillights of the team's SUV slipping away. It was like some massive symbol—all the good parts of his life being boxed up and shipped off. Like a soldier's body coming home to be buried, forgotten.

What was left?

A man he didn't know.

And yet . . . he wasn't bothered seeing them leave. Knowing they'd get on the jet and be home inside twenty-four hours, he felt . . . relieved.

Something dark inside him vied for dominance. He didn't want to face that monster, to become one who hunted and killed. If he was a Neiothen, it meant he was connected to the Armageddon Coalition. Essentially, he was the enemy.

He tugged out a phone and dialed.

"It is good to hear from you, Mr. Metcalfe."

"I'm ready."

TWO

Silence could be a weapon used against a person to extract tears and fears. But the twenty-plus-hour silence as the team trekked back to America made Iskra Todorova want to kill. They had intended to talk and plan, but less than an hour into the flight, Director Iliescu informed them the briefing would wait, that they were not to discuss anything until they gathered in the bunker.

She should have followed her instinct and gone after Leif. It was exactly what he had done for her when she was being kept by Hristoff Peychinovich. So what had held her back? What made her mute in his defense? Was this the type of friend—girlfriend—she was to him, a silent one?

Yet even with that mental flagellation, she kept her mouth and heart closed.

"Are we seriously going to sit here and not talk about this?" Culver groused from his seat.

Only the thin, conditioned air of the jet met his query.

"We suck," he muttered.

"It's a little late to do anything, now that we're thirty-three thousand feet in the air," Cell said. "Besides, he's back there."

"We have a day to get up to speed, maybe get ahead of it—"

"Ahead?" Cell scoffed. "Dude, we're so far behind, we might as well be the b—"

"I think," Mercy said in a strong, assertive voice, "that the best way to help Leif is *not* to do anything stupid. To think

19

through this, get as much intel as possible. Use this time on our own to brainstorm."

"Right, so I was thinking—"

"On. Our. Own," Mercy bit out.

"We *are* on our own," Culver shot back.

Appreciation slid through Iskra at the "misunderstanding" Culver used to his benefit, as well as his desire to throw himself into action. But *for* Leif? Or against him?

"No, I mean—"

"He know what you mean," Baddar said, touching Mercy's arm.

She hesitated, considering the red-haired man. "Leif needs us to be intelligent, not rash."

"I ain't got no rash," Culver teased, "but I do have an itch that wants to be scratched—my trigger finger."

"Exactly what we don't need!"

"What do you know about operations, HackerGirl?" Culver growled.

Weary of the bickering, Iskra pushed to her feet, strode to the back of the jet, and locked herself in the lavatory. They were a broken, crumbling team. Peyton and Adam were at Landstuhl Regional Medical Center and would return once she was stable, but in reality, the rest were all as broken.

Just like Iskra's brother, Leif had gone through the training and physiological alterations of a Neiothen. But Mitre, whom everyone else knew as Andreas or Andrew, was far more damaged. At least she thought so, after their encounter at Rutger Hermanns' estate, when her idealistic view of him had been unmercifully shredded, along with her very naïve, unrealistic hope that when she found him, she could save him. But Mitre believed he had been damaged in a way that left him good for one thing—combat. Fighting those who had done this to him, the notorious Armageddon Coalition.

Leif is with Mitre.

Of course. It made sense. At the amusement park, Mitre was there to help identify the final Neiothen. It was hard to comprehend that both her brother and the man she loved were part of a super-army referenced in the Book of the Wars of the Lord. She had fought hard and failed to get that ancient text from Hermanns several months ago in a salt mine in Israel.

She sighed. That confrontation seemed so long ago.

Unable to endure the lavatory smell any longer, she ducked into the galley for water.

"How are you?" came a soft voice from behind.

Uncapping the bottle, Iskra turned to the small table where Mercy sat, and searched for an answer. The hacker was the closest thing to a friend Iskra had since joining the team, but she still wanted to don her hardened shell and once again become Viorica. Go after Leif.

No. That life had been too hard for too long and too damaging to her soul. Viorica must remain in the past.

She shrugged at Mercy's question. "Sad, hurt." Angry. Powerless. "Maybe it's my fault."

"How can you even think that?"

"If I had worked harder to find the book, maybe he would not have felt the need to do this." Her words were empty of conviction, and when no response came, she saw the remonstration. The disbelief. "What?"

"So . . ." Mercy drew a leg up on the seat and hooked an arm around it. "You don't think he's"—she dipped her chin in meaning—"turned?"

Fire coursed through Iskra. "You so quickly betray your friends?"

"No!" Mercy wet her lips, glanced out of the galley toward the others, then back at Iskra. "It's just . . . the code we heard in the park was for *Leif*."

21

"But Mitr—Andrew used the resonance rifle in The Hague to counteract the chip."

"And you . . . you think it worked?"

"Of course it worked!" The futility of such a question and the eons she took to answer it made Iskra wonder. "If it had not, Leif would have betrayed us right there in the park."

Mercy peered through a knitted brow. "You're sure?"

Indignant and frustrated, Iskra could not continue this discussion. "Excuse me." She strode for the gangway.

"Wait, Iskra. Please. I only meant—"

"I know what you meant," she snapped, whirling around. "And if you all turn on him, then even if I am wrong, who is left to help him come back? How did you so quickly trade loyalty for . . . *this*!"

She stalked back to the restroom, the only place that afforded her solitude to think through this ordeal. Door locked, she thrust her fingers into her hair and stifled a scream. Hot, angry tears raced down her face, unbidden and unwanted. She did not want to cry, because that meant she had accepted this, and by accepting it, *she* had turned on Leif.

He had fought like nobody else for her and Taissia, her five-year-old daughter. He had raced all the way to Russia and literally knocked down doors to rescue them. Why had she not done more to help him?

With a shuddering breath, she pulled herself straight. Saw her reflection in the mirror. Dark hair and eyes. *What did he see in you?* A girl kept by a ruthless ArC operative, raped repeatedly, hard and bitter toward life and men. She had nearly killed *him* to accomplish her mission. Ciro Veratti's mission. All with the goal of freeing her daughter from a nightmare existence. When she failed to make that happen, he entered the game and changed everything. Changed *her*.

Hanging her head, she rubbed her neck and ached for him. She could not leave him like this, could not believe he was one of the dark souls ArC had altered with chemical infusions and a chip implant.

She refused to abandon him. Not now. Not ever.

Iskra pulled out her phone and swallowed as she found Mitre's number. Would he answer? Would he tell her if Leif was with him? She would never know if she did not try. She pressed TALK.

The phone rang several times, the noise grating against her nerves. She rubbed her temple. *Please, Mitre. Please answer.*

"Yes?" His clipped, sharp answer backed her breath into her lungs.

"Is he there?" Over the drone of the jet, it was hard to hear if he spoke. But she doubted she had missed a response. So. He would not respond to that. "Is he okay?"

"*Auf Wiedersehen.*"

"No, wait! Tell him I—"

A series of beeps and then emptiness filled her ears. She slammed the phone against the lavatory counter. "Curse you!" And yet there was no anger, because he *had* answered her. First by picking up the call, then by *not* expressing surprise or confusion at her questions. If he was not with Leif, he would have asked who she meant.

Unless he had anticipated the call, knew Leif would run, and denied assistance. Which was possible. Being a reformed Neiothen, Mitre no doubt felt the need to protect Leif from everyone. Including—no, *especially*—her.

MILAN, ITALY

"What happened?" Ciro Veratti told himself that eliminating everyone in this proverbial war room would show a significant lack of restraint. He must be better than that. "Where is he?" He looked to Dr. Sheng, one of the lead scientists on the

Netherwood project. His wife, a psychiatrist in America whom Ciro had recruited for practicality's sake, had very nearly betrayed her connection when Ossi inquired after Carsen Gilliam during his attempt to stop ArC. "You sent the initiation code with the high-frequency burst, yes?"

Sheng's eyes widened. "Yes, of course." He gave a cockeyed shrug. "Just like all the others."

"Sir." The colonel stood with his lackeys on the far side near three large suspended screens. "You should see this."

Why could the colonel not just deliver the information? Irritation scraped along Ciro's collarbone and up his neck until he clenched his teeth. He forced himself to cross the room, glowering at the officer.

"Go on, Flinn," the colonel said to the man in black tactical gear.

The sergeant shifted, darting a look at Ciro—who imagined putting an extra hole in his head—then indicated the wall screen. "At the amusement park, we noticed this man."

Ciro focused on the shape moving through the park, which really had been a brilliant location for the attack. *If* it had worked. But it hadn't. An unacceptable yet unalterable loss. Now they were down one integral asset, and he needed to remedy that before Risen went online. Still. One failure to multiple successes. He must pick his battles.

"What about him?"

The sergeant smiled. "He entered the park with a woman and later crossed paths with candidate Ossi at least four times. The third time, they lingered long enough to converse."

"But," Ciro said with more than a little frustration, "he's clever enough to avoid cameras, and the hat hides his face from satellites."

"Yes, sir." The smile didn't vanish.

"Has someone told you I'm a patient man?" Ciro asked calmly.

24

Straightening, the grunt refocused on the screen. "Our system is sophisticated enough that we don't need facial recs. By comparing him with known subjects like candidate Ossi, we can accurately assess his height and weight. In addition, we then use his gait and posture against known individuals." His gray eyes glinted. "Especially Neiothen."

Understanding dawned, making Ciro feel like a parent whose rebellious child had simply needed a firm hand to find their way in the world.

"As you can tell, sir, it appears to be—"

"I know who it is." Ciro could not keep the acid from his words. Thoughts churning, he knew his anger was wrongly directed. His gaze connected with the middle-aged woman he'd kept on too long, despite her many shortcomings. "You failed me, Ms. Lapaglia. Again."

Face ashen, she swallowed. "Sir?"

"Come, Chiara." He tucked his head as he started toward her, considering how to correct her many failures in this project. "Will you pretend you were not aware?" He sniffed a laugh. "I am not sure which would be worse—to admit you did not know or to admit you did."

Her gaze skittered between him and his right-hand man, Santo Greco, who mirrored Ciro's path around the room. Her chin and hands trembled. "Sir, I—"

"You were to monitor the whereabouts of Rutger Hermanns and his protégé at all times." Ciro stopped before her, studying her. Sensing the palpable tension in the room, noting the terrified silence despite the others working, doing what they should to bring Risen online.

"Yes, sir . . . ?" She wore an uncertain frown.

"Then why did you not report to me that Akin was at the amusement park?" His gaze met Santo's with the briefest of nods.

"Because—"

Thwat! The discharge of Santo's suppressed weapon shifted the electrically charged room and came with the splatter of blood and gray matter. Gasps followed the termination, but the busy thrum quickly resumed, everyone re-engaged in their work. As it should be.

Ciro glanced over his shoulder. "There are no excuses," he growled. "Not this close to the endgame." He flicked his attention to the colonel. "If your technology is so advanced, I should have been notified that Andreas Krestyanov was in that park. Our sniper could have eliminated a very big problem."

"Had we done that," someone asserted from a workstation in the middle of the room, "it would've alerted the Taiwanese president and possibly the entire American team."

Shock had nothing on the rage that surged through Ciro as he stared hard at Dr. Jennifer Malloy, the lead psychoanalyst, who dared counter him. It was under her supervision that Netherwood had been revamped. "Be glad, Dr. Malloy, that I still appreciate your work."

Her gaze was steady and unrepentant. "Thank you, sir."

He could not blame her, though he wanted to, because she was right. But killing that coldhearted operator was something he'd been itching to do. "Akin is a thorn in my side."

"Is it possible he removed his implant?" Dr. Malloy suggested.

"No." At least not as far as they knew. Ciro looked to Sheng for confirmation.

The scientist shook his head frantically. "No, not possible. The implants are too deeply embedded." He shrugged. "And with Akin, it has been implanted so long that neural paths have formed around it. Removing it would have severe cognitive repercussions, possibly even death."

Ciro focused on the colonel. "How are things going at the facility with the second generation?"

"On track. The major says the team has been running scenarios on the system for the last ten days, purging bugs." He nodded. "They'll be ready."

"They'd better be! We only have four weeks left."

With a grim expression, Santo approached and angled his shoulder toward him. "Hermanns is here."

Arching his eyebrow, Ciro mused that his pent-up frustration might find release today after all. "Show him to the conference room.".

"Abassi." Santo nodded to one of his men, who left to carry out the task.

At a terminal, Ciro pointed to the monitor. "Pull up our internal security feeds." On the screen, Abassi delivered Hermanns to the glassed-in room, offered him nothing—not even a glance—and left, locking the door. Did they have any of the gas they'd used against the Chinese minister? Hmm, perhaps it might contaminate this area as well. It would be a terrible inconvenience, but since they were pressed for time . . .

"Sir, perhaps a moment to clean up?" Santo suggested, indicating his jacket.

Ciro appraised his silk-blend suit, which now sported blood spots. Though repulsed, he decided it would be effective. "No." What better way to make his point to Rutger? He could endure being soiled awhile longer. He started for the door, and Santo hustled ahead to usher him into the hall. Two more guards fell in behind as he strode toward the conference room.

Santo flicked open the door.

Ciro smirked as he met his guest's gaze. "Rutger." He motioned Santo inside, taking far too much pleasure when Santo locked them in and made Rutger shift. "Imagine my surprise that you come to me."

The German hesitated for the briefest of seconds. "You always make us come to you." He glanced at Santo. "I see you're up to your old tricks, *ja*? If you cannot force people to do your bidding, kill them."

Ciro pursed his lips. "Tried and true." He slid his hands into his pockets. "Now, what reason have you to disturb our work?"

After a sigh, Rutger said, "It's Andreas—Akin."

Interesting. "What is?"

"He's . . ." Rutger wiped a hand over his mouth. "He's gone rogue."

Ciro barked a laugh. Was he supposed to believe this? "Clever."

The German frowned, shaking his head. "I don't—"

"No." Ciro moved to the window that overlooked the city. "You don't, do you? You *don't* understand what you are dealing with. *Who* you're dealing with."

"Ciro—"

"Andreas interrupted our work at the park." He eyed Rutger for signs of deception, worry, or surprise. Nothing but a blank façade beneath the graying goatee. "Now you tell me he is rogue."

Placid acknowledgment came in the form of a one-shouldered shrug. "I came as soon as I heard what happened."

"Mm." Ciro brushed at the blood on his jacket. "I just made an example of someone who had more excuses than loyalty." With a heaved breath, he squared himself. "Must I do it again?"

"Why do you not listen? He is *rogue*. I cannot track him anymore." Hermanns motioned frantically. "Surely you have detected this as well. I do not know how he did it, nor do I know if he is yet alive. You must intervene!"

Lies, lies, lies. Even were they not, Ciro could not eradicate this vermin from his organization. Through this pig the remnant of the Neiothen could be found and snuffed out, if he would bide his time. "Is this about Katrin? Still?"

"What?" Rutger's mouth hung nearly slack.

"Because I had her killed—are you thwarting this project to pay me back?"

"I came to tell you he is rogue and—"

"I would be very disappointed, Rutger." Ciro fisted a hand to his mouth. "You've been with me from the start. I hated what happened to your sister, but it was necessary. She would have destroyed everything. In fact, she did her best to ruin me and Netherwood."

"This is not about Katrin!" Rutger spat, his German accent thickening.

"Good." Ciro narrowed his eyes. "Because if I even think you defied me again, I will send you to meet her."

THREE

He had more problems than he'd thought, and that was saying something.

Rutger Hermanns stared at the vault, dumbstruck. While
still on the Learjet returning from his visit with Veratti, he
had received notification of a breach at his home. He could
not have fathomed . . . *this*. More than a dozen emergency
vehicles had already clogged the drive when his helicopter
delivered him from the airport. He had rushed straight into
his home and the daunting truth. Now he stood in the vault,
hand over his mouth, disbelieving.

"Is anything missing, sir?"

Rutger glanced around the fire- and natural-disaster-proof
room, with its feet-thick walls and triple-redundant security
measures. Tried to form words as he took in the empty fireproof boxes, steel drawers strewn across the floor, a shattered
Ming dynasty vase. . . .

"Sir?"

He twitched toward the *Polizist*, who watched him intently.
"Are you *blind*?" he asked, incredulous, waving around the
vault. "*Everything!* Everything is missing!"

"Of course." The reply was anything but repentant.

Rutger shook his head, absorbing the fact that his life's
work had vanished in one breach. One very well-informed
breach.

"Do you know who might have done this, Herr Hermanns?"

30

the officer asked. "Any reason you can think of that someone would break into this room, which"—his dull eyes scoured the empty walls and shelves—"looks fairly impenetrable?"

"Clearly not," Rutger growled, making a mental note to call the security company and demand a refund. "And yes, there are many who would want what was in this vault. Have you any idea the value of what was stolen?"

"No, I'm afraid I do not." He seemed lazy, bored. Why had he not asked for a list? Something about his tone, the odd gleam in his gaze, warned of trouble. Was he on ArC's payroll?

"What do you need from me? Information? A list, perhaps, of the stolen items? Would that not be helpful for you to do your job?"

The man smirked. "Of course, Herr Hermanns."

"Then why have you not asked for one?" Rutger gulped his annoyance in one lumpy swallow. A list would make no difference in uncovering the true reason behind this invasion. If the purpose had been the Book of the Wars of the Lord, the thieves had met with failure, because—mercifully—that was on loan to a certain young man.

Still. So much gone. *Mein Gott!* The loss—the incalculable loss.

"I must sit. If you need anything, my staff can assist." He left the vault, motioning to his butler. "Tea, please." He removed himself to the parlor and slumped into a chair.

Was this Veratti's doing? He had warned of repercussions. Rutger had gone to ArC to garner sympathy and turn their gazes away from himself when it came to blame for the failed attack against the children's park. Such a heartless place for an attack—so many children! Though Rutger had argued against that venue, ArC insisted on it to gain public attention. Show people that those against the coalition would not survive.

31

He did not doubt that he, too, would soon be among the dead. Because just as ArC would not cease in their mission, neither would he. His conscience refused to let him turn a blind eye any longer. Not after Katrin and that cruel, bitter night when he'd found her in the clock shop, bloody and dying. The days afterward, trying to keep her alive. Then keeping others alive.

"You must save them, Rutger. They did not deserve what we have done to them, what she intends to do with them."

"I cannot!" he whined. *"They will kill me!"*

"Then you condemn your soul."

His little sister had never been bigger than that night. She had sacrificed herself to interrupt a project so large and nefarious that the left hand—one scientist—didn't know what the right—another scientist—was doing. Katrin and her fiancé had put the puzzle pieces together too late, and yet too soon. Had she been smarter, a bit more sly . . .

"Bah!" Rutger grimaced at his own audacity. He who had waited years before finally taking action. Who cowered just yesterday before the man responsible. Granted, Netherwood, which spawned the Neiothen, had been the brainchild of someone else—Wilhelmina. He had not seen that coming either.

"You are getting old," he murmured to himself.

Now who held the key, the book? Perhaps it was good he failed so miserably, with Leif stealing the panel paintings from under his nose. He had tried to pacify another and protect Leif from the meanings of the panels.

"Herr Hermanns, you know these men?" an officer asked.

Rutger glanced at the door. Who would be visiting at such a time? The estate was tucked away from civilization for a reason. But then he saw the two men, and relief speared him. "Ah yes. *Danke.*"

He noted the way the officer took too much interest in

Andreas and Leif as they entered, both projecting the message to leave them alone. With an uncertain glance, the officer left the room.

Rutger huffed and leaned his head back, closing his eyes. "You had me worried."

"What happened here?" Andreas demanded.

"The vault was raided."

"By who?"

"Does it need to be asked?" Rutger pushed out of his chair, the old leather squawking in protest. He went to the serving bar and poured a glass of water. "I was with Veratti just last night." Gulping, he felt the liquid sliding into his enraged gut. "He threatened me."

Andreas gestured to Leif. "He knows about him?"

After another sip, Rutger returned to his high-backed chair and offered Leif the other. "So . . . you came."

The young man had a vise-grip on what was happening inside him and gave no response.

Rutger placed his water on a small table next to his chair, then reclined and folded his hands as he considered the young man. "Had someone not entered my home and come for the book . . ." He smiled. Then laughed. Shook a finger at Andreas. "Had I listened to you, it would have been here— and now, *pfft*!" He fluttered his fingers like flapping wings. "But you have it." He sharpened his focus on Leif. "Yes?"

"It's safe."

"You left it?" Rutger came out of his chair. "Have you any idea the—" The hard pale eyes challenging him registered. His anger bottomed out, and he lowered himself to the cushion again. "That was foolish."

"I want answers and needed a bargaining chip. It's why I'm here." Leif shrugged. "Right? Or maybe you don't have them either."

"My boy, did I say that?"

Jaw tightening, Leif looked at Andreas, who parked himself on the coffee table facing them.

"We have scans of every page, and you have the paintings. Yes?" Rutger prodded.

Again, no answer.

Though he understood the hesitation, it also annoyed him. Already so much had been handed to Leif in the hopes he would be . . . *more*. More responsive. More aggressive. "Do you recall what I said when you were here with your *Freundin*?"

"That I was Neiothen, that I had to stop what was happening."

"And yet you doubted."

Irritation slashed the impassive façade.

"Your actions at the amusement park—"

"I had to protect my friends."

"Friends." Rutger grunted. "You could have protected them by embracing what you are, what you were meant to be," he said, a growl pulling him forward. When he saw the ridge between Leif's eyebrows grow, he eased off. "When you doubt and fight it, that puts them at greater risk."

"One of my friends is down, possibly killed by an ArC sniper." Leif gave a cockeyed nod. "I wasn't even activated yet. Then they all saw me freeze and act like I'd lost my mind when that code blasted through the speakers, destabilizing me." He drew in several quick breaths. "Now my team thinks I'm a traitor."

"You *are* a traitor!" Rutger barked around a laugh, motioning to their surroundings. "You sit in the home of a man embroiled in ArC's sinister deeds. There will be no explanation or acceptable excuse. They will not understand, because they have not to this point, have they?"

Leif swallowed.

"They have doubted you, wondered about you, marveled

at you. But *accepted*?" He flung a hand in the air. "Bah! You get more loyalty from a dog."

Leif slowly rose, fists balled, nostrils flared. "If you aren't going to help me—"

"Help you?" Rutger charged to his feet. "What do you think this is? A spa? A vacation?" He thumped the young man's chest. "This isn't about you, you petulant little pup!"

It had not seemed possible for Leif to appear more rabid, but Rutger had clearly been wrong.

"I do not want your toe-dipping efforts as you skirt the danger, play it safe. *You* came here. We did not force you. We face a vicious dragon with ten rows of razor-sharp horns and teeth!" Spittle flew as Rutger raged through the room. "And we are poking that dragon with a searing-hot poker. There is no 'safe'!"

In his periphery, he noted Andreas closing the door. Oh yes. They had guests, did they not? Ah, well.

"Our days of playing it safe are long gone." He smoothed a hand over his goatee, then lifted a finger to the lone hope of the Neiothen. "Let me tell you a story about a young woman who was not yet thirty and had a revolutionary mind. What she determined to do, no one could stop her from accomplishing. Knowing her grandmother endured a concentration camp, she vowed to make it possible for men to fight, to be unafraid when they took a stand and confronted evil. Because of her brilliance, decades later there were advances in science and research that were once thought impossible.

"Then along came one who had much greed and deviousness, who caught the vision behind the dreams of this young woman. Thrilled to see her dream come alive, the young woman never saw the truth of her benefactor or the wicked barbs that embedded into her and the other scientists, poisoning them and their work. Perverting it!" His shout rang off the high ceilings. "When this brilliant young woman finally discovered the truth, she again put her ingenious mind to work." He tapped his temple and squinted. "She created a . . . response. A key! Because she knew that without an answer, there would be no end to how the wicked could corrupt and twist her brainchild." He slowed, his chest heaving, aching from the memory. "Though she succeeded, it came at a price—her own life."

Suddenly exhausted, Rutger returned to his chair, lifted his water, and took a sip.

"Real tale of woe." Leif shrugged. "It have a point?"

Rutger tossed the contents of his glass at him.

Water splashed Leif's face and shirt. He lunged upward.

Andreas leapt forward, shouldering between what would have been an expertly delivered punch and Rutger's face. "Easy, easy," he said, palms held out, ready to fight.

After several long, tense seconds, Leif stepped back.

Rutger had lost focus, his grief over Katrin fresh despite the years. Perhaps it was his failure rubbing that ache raw. "Veratti has long had me tethered, but I fear that rope is at its frayed ends. Very well. I will tell you what I know. Everything. What you do with that"—he could not help but snarl—"be on your head, your soul."

FOUR

STUTTGART, GERMANY

"Start with The Hague."

Those words directed Leif's attention to Andreas, who seemed just as ready as he was to move past Rutger's rage, which had come out of nowhere and made Leif reconsider his decision to step onto this dark path.

No, he wasn't second-guessing. There'd been no choice. Nobody was hand-delivering answers, so he had to dig them out on his own, and this man, connected to the enemy pitted against Leif, knew where to start.

Hermanns sent a sharp glare toward his protégé. "You push my hand."

"Sometimes it needs pushing," Andreas said without regret.

A heavy pause lingered. "As explained when you were here with his sister," Hermanns said, "Andreas was at The Hague to disrupt the chips implanted in the Neiothen. Including yours."

Leif nodded, then caught himself. "Hold up." He glanced between them. "If you disrupted the chip, why was I affected by that blast in Taipei?"

"That," Rutger said with a long sigh, "is a question we want answered as well."

Something about his expression unhinged what little confidence Leif had in these men. "So, what? You're just going around blasting people's heads with a frequency charge

37

without knowing what it does or doesn't do?" His heart thudded. "How do I know you didn't just fry it?"

"It is possible," Rutger conceded too easily, "that while we prevented the chip from igniting whatever training they hardwired into you, we did not completely undo the effectiveness of the implant itself."

That sucker punch stole his breath. "So you're telling me that at any minute, I could be their lapdog."

"We're telling you," Andreas said with an edge to his voice, "that we didn't design the implant, so the effectiveness of the resonance weapon is—at best—an educated guess. It has worked on all the others. A team has been working for years to counter the Netherwood project, but ArC is always at least one step ahead. As to why it was not one-hundred-percent effective with you . . ." He shrugged.

"What is there, what they know and are able to accomplish, will not change by us rambling about it," Rutger muttered. "However, there is something we should discuss that you will not like."

"I haven't liked anything you've said yet."

"You will like this less." Rutger exhaled loudly. "Until a month ago, the only people who knew I had the book and where it was are in this room." His eyes sparked with no small amount of accusation. "Who did you tell?"

Though Leif didn't appreciate where this was going, he had to keep an open mind, because truth had a way of hiding behind assumptions. "Two people." His gaze hit Andreas. "Iskra." And then back to Rutger. "And Iliescu."

"So one of them has betrayed you and, therefore, me."

Andreas grunted. "Or both."

Anger tightened Leif's muscles, but he balled it up. He couldn't afford to rule out anything at this stage of the game. "It's possible."

"But?"

"Both of them would come after me before they went after the book."

Hermanns' laugh barked through the private library. "If you believe that, you are a bigger fool than Andreas suggested." He shook his head. "No, to them, that book and stopping the wars is far more important than finding you."

There was only one person Leif could believe that about.

STERLING, VIRGINIA

In his luxury SUV, Dru Iliescu crammed into the early morning traffic, slogging east along Route 7. He accelerated, one vehicle behind and to the left of the Camaro, but kept his distance. His timing had to be perfect as he followed the sports car from the private school where children had been dropped off. Though the vehicle made no effort to lose him, Dru had a feeling he'd been spotted. As the light ahead turned red, he slid around a slow-moving minivan and dived back into his lane. He braked, coming to a stop alongside the Camaro. Keeping his gaze straight, he gauged his periphery and erased all doubt. He'd been seen.

Once the light turned green, he gunned it and zipped over two lanes, then took the turn-off lane, exiting onto Loudoun County Parkway. At the light, he banked right, then made another right at the next intersection, noting the Camaro swing into his rearview. He navigated the trendy shopping center, heading to the parking structure, and parked on the top level. He cut his engine and stepped out as the Camaro rumbled to a stop next to him and cut its engine.

The door opened, and if Dru hadn't known who he'd tailed, he could have easily mistaken this guy for Leif. Same blond hair and blue eyes, just a bit rougher around the edges and longer in the tooth.

"What's wrong?" Canyon Metcalfe demanded as he came toward him, hands balled at his sides. "I mean, that's what this is, right? Why you followed me to my kid's school and tagged me on the road." He jutted his jaw. "Whatever you wanted to tell me couldn't be overheard. So here we are. Talk."

How was Dru supposed to deliver this news? Instinct said he'd done everything he could, but he hadn't seen this coming. Leif had been a ticking bomb for the last year, especially since Iskra Todorova barged into his life.

"Where is he?" Canyon asked.

"I don't know," Dru admitted with a sigh.

Stretching his jaw, Canyon shook his head. Then he nodded, as if ready to take on the challenge. "Give it to me."

"They were on mission, dealing with a threat in Taiwan. We interdicted as necessary. ArC activated him, Canyon. The signal came over a loudspeaker. Someone on his team was injured, but the team exfil'd and returned to the safe house otherwise intact. Shortly after, Leif put one of his guys in a choke hold and fled."

Canyon stared at him—hard. Almost as if waiting for Dru to tell him this was a joke. He scratched the side of his temple, then roughed a hand over his mouth. "You said you wouldn't let this happen. And it did." Anger writhed through his hardened resolve. "What're you doing to get him back?"

Dru wanted to scoff. Wanted to bark that they both knew nobody could make Leif come back. But that wasn't good enough. "His team is returning now and—"

"I'll help."

"No." Dru couldn't have that. "I'm telling you only as a courtesy. You know the sensitive nature of what Leif's embroiled in. Now that he's rogue—"

"*Rogue?*"

"MIA," Dru hastily corrected, lifting a hand to placate the

former Green Beret. "That's his status until we know more. Regardless, we have to be extremely cautious."

He would make sure Leif's status remained Missing In Action to ensure nobody turned this against the former SEAL. What had been done to Leif, what he'd tried to undo for the last nearly half-dozen years—none of it had been his fault. He'd entered the program after many of his team died. A mission and friends Leif no longer remembered, thanks to the extensive Neiothen rewiring.

"You know I have connections," Canyon said, more than a little warning in his tone. "If my brother's not back in a week—"

"Your brother left of his own accord. What do you suggest—"

"Drug his butt and drag him back!" Canyon roared. "And if you don't, I will."

"It's not that simple." Dru shifted, and he saw a storm move into the eyes so like Leif's. "Please—hear me out."

"I'm hearing, Chief," Canyon retorted. "But I'm not hearing a lot of good. My brother is in trouble, and he might know it, might not. He trusted you to find the answers, to dig it up and set him free." His jaw muscle popped. "And you didn't do it." He cocked his head, his voice raw. "You. Didn't. Do it."

For every pound of suspicion, Dru had had only an ounce of proof. Never enough to bring down those responsible. Only enough to be dangerous—to himself and to those responsible, but mostly to Leif. Dru hated this. Hated what he'd had to do. When the truth hit the proverbial fans, Leif would bury him.

"You know what we're dealing with. The size of the brass and the power of the influence behind it means we're walking a tightrope. If we come out swinging without—" The det cord was in his hand, and he could either blow himself or Leif into oblivion. "I—"

"Enough," Canyon said, backing toward his car. "All this time, you've been the keeper of secrets, and it's gotten us nowhere. I've let you play that game. But no more. You know more than you've shared. The ball's in your court, Director." He pointed at Dru. "Find him. You have one week, or I'll muster every connection I have to bring you down and my brother home—alive."

RESTON, VIRGINIA

Being back in America without Leif was strange. The jet landed a full day after he vanished. Iskra understood why he'd done it. When Hristoff was hunting her, she felt safer and more confident on her own, pretending she didn't care about the child left in his care every time he sent her on a mission. It made sense that Leif would slip away without a word before anyone could stop him, because each of them surely would have.

When they entered his loft, her daughter ran to the industrial refrigerator, where he stocked yogurt drinks for her, but then Taissia paused. As if she, too, sensed the depressing gloom of his absence. "Where's Leif?"

"He is . . . working." Iskra veered to the coffee table and set down a small souvenir from the amusement park while Taissia chose a drink. "Okay, let's go. We're late for dinner with Tala and Mrs. Dani."

With a yogurt mustache, Taissia turned, eyes molten. "Are you leaving me again?"

"No," she lied, not having the emotional capital to deal with her daughter's distress on top of her own. "We are just having dinner. They were very nice to invite us over." But she knew Leif's older brother had questions. So did she. And she was not going to sit around and do nothing. Somehow, she guessed he knew that, too.

The drive was too short to prepare answers. Typically, she avoided encounters like this, but she had always sensed Canyon knew more about Leif's past than he had let on. So she would let him work her for information, and she would return the favor. She pocketed a small jamming device to ensure they weren't spied on.

In the driveway, Iskra eyed an unfamiliar car, and a steady uneasiness grew in the pit of her stomach. Who else was here?

She gripped Taissia's hand and strode up the front path. The door flung open, and an ever-rowdy Owen Metcalfe grinned before speeding back down the hall. "Mom, they're here!"

Taissia darted after him, heading toward Tala's bedroom.

Abandoned by her own daughter! Mustering internal fortitude, Iskra stepped inside and locked the door behind her.

Dani rounded the corner with a smile. "Hey," she said, waving toward the rear of the house. "Come on back. Canyon said he wanted to talk to you—he's in the living room. I have to get some packing done."

"A vacation?" Iskra asked, worried Dani was going to be unavailable.

"Ha," Dani said with a laugh. "I wish. Work trip—couple weeks."

Iskra's heart fell a little. This meant she had no babysitter for Taissia.

"I'd better get to it." Dani nodded toward the back of the house. "The guys are back there. Holler if you need me."

Guys. Was Leif here? Had he come back? Her heart stuttered at the thought, and she hurried in that direction.

A deep voice carried heavily through the house. Definitely not Leif.

In the living room, Canyon chatted with a slightly older

man. "Iskra." He came to his feet. "Glad you could come." He motioned to the older man. "This is my brother Stone. He's in town through the weekend."

Taller than Canyon and Leif, Stone was definitely a Metcalfe with those blue eyes and that intensity, but his blond hair was darker and shot through with red and silver. He was broad-shouldered and commanding as he angled toward her. "Iskra." He nodded. "Nice to meet you."

Shaking his hand, she smiled. While she might be conjuring trouble where there was none, it just seemed too thick with tension in here for this to be a casual get-together.

"I've heard a lot about you." Stone had a powerful presence that said he was used to being in control. "You were with Leif in Taiwan?"

Iskra snapped her gaze to Canyon. "You told him?"

"He's my brother, Leif's—"

"He's not cleared regarding this—"

"Iskra, listen."

"You just killed him!" she hissed, feeling a deep dread in the pit of her stomach.

"I think that's unfair," Stone said, his voice like rocks in a tin cup. "Not to mention quite an accusation against those who've known Leif his entire life."

"Perhaps you have been in the same family, but have you really known him?" She glanced between the brothers. "Because his action doesn't surprise me—"

"We didn't say it surprised u—"

"But what does surprise me is neither of you respecting that this is classified intel and discussing it where anyone can hear," she said, looking at Canyon. "Unless you've cleared this house and room somehow." Silence confirmed her concerns. She activated the jamming device she always kept with her.

"I know you care about Leif," Canyon said in a placating

tone, "so I'll shoot straight. I've given Iliescu one week to find Leif before we"—his gaze hit his brother—"interdict."

She drew up, stunned at his words. "Idiocy!" So much for bleeding him for information. What they knew wasn't worth the time.

"You're intelligent, Iskra. I've always known that, and it's one of the things Leif admired about you. Tell me you haven't questioned why Dru, the CIA Deputy Director of Operations, hasn't shared more intel."

She swallowed.

"Because he *does* have more intel."

Her pulse tripped over his words. "You know that?"

"Know? Yes. Prove?" He gave a cockeyed shake of his head. "I have a gut instinct that more is happening than we're being told, and I won't let my brother be a fatality of whatever maneuvering is involved."

"So you're just going to go out there and . . . what?"

"Find him. Bring him home." The Metcalfe men were clearly used to hitting life head on.

"Dead," she amended.

He scowled.

"Because that is what will happen if you go out there un-informed."

"Then inform us," Stone said, irritation in his posture.

"This is insane." She could not believe this. "This is about you—your egos."

"Or is it yours, Iskra?" Canyon squared his shoulders, and his brother anchored up next to him. "Do you think you're the only one who can help him? Why wouldn't you want every resource thrown at finding Leif?"

It was hard to breathe. "Because I know who we are up against. I have fought these people for years."

"And lost," Canyon challenged. "Each time, right? I mean,

that's why you're here in the States, with my brother, with Dru. Right?"

Her pulse hammered with indignation and rage.

"I'm not as uninformed as you might think," he said. "Stone and I didn't get to where we are in our careers by being arrogant or foolish. We're strategic, focused, and determined. I've been in black ops for as long as you've been an assassin, Iskra. I might not have gone up against the same men, but I've confronted similar men. But they're not my focus—Leif is. And I know he's important to you, too. You're here. You're angry. I respect that. Let's use it. You came with a purpose. So give it to me."

She drew her lips tight and huffed. "Your brother is strong, yes?"

Hesitating, Canyon gave a nod.

"Smart, intelligent. Patriotic."

Another nod. "One of the best."

"Leif is the best of all us Metcalfes put together," Stone added. "It's like our mother perfected the genes with each pregnancy."

"Then *that* is why you need to rethink whatever you have planned." She drew in a ragged breath, desperate to make them understand.

"He doesn't know what he's doing," Stone asserted. "He's being influenced by that thing in his head."

"You are a fool if you believe that." Iskra made herself calm down. "Think about it! You are his brothers. You know Leif. And these people convinced your very loyal, very patriotic brother to turn against his country, against what he believes in, his family and—"

"And you?" Canyon narrowed his eyes.

"This coalition should scare the arrogance out of you. I have seen what they do to people. My own brother—once a caring, generous person—no longer has the ability to care or empathize. Now he is a cold, hard killer." She hoped that truth landed as hard as she had thrown it. "Is that what you want for Leif?"

Canyon's phone rang. He glanced at the screen, then at her with a smirk as he answered it, putting it on speakerphone. "Director, how can I help you?"

"I have a way you can help find your brother."

FIVE

"All right, ladies and insurgents," Cell muttered through the comms. "I show you entering the fifth-floor access of the building. All clear."

When Dru said they had a tip on the technology connected to the Neiothen, the team had leapt at the chance. Well, by "team" Mercy meant Reaper's operators. Not her. She wasn't anxious to get back out there, with Peyton still in the hospital, fighting for her life, and Leif missing. Then Dru added Leif's brother to the mission, and it just got . . . weird. Canyon Metcalfe was down in the server room with his guys, fixing a broken AC unit and making sure nobody was alerted to her actions.

A richly attired Baddar strode down the corridor with his shoulders squared and head held high, flanked by Culver and Saito. Mercy glided forward as the man hurrying alongside her rattled on about their security measures and latest innovations in technology.

"I hope that is just the beginning of your efforts, Mr. Labonte, because that's kindergarten next to what I can do." She paused for emphasis. "We would not want to waste Mr. Hannan's time if you cannot promise greater protection than this."

"O–of course." Labonte skipped ahead a step and scrambled to an entrance.

"Sharp and ready," Cell said in her ear comms. "I show two men on the other side of the door."

48

Which swung open.

"Remember, Merc," Cell said, "get that USB on the laptop, and then y'all make like rabbits and hightail it outta there."

Nerves fried, Mercy couldn't understand why they'd insisted she do this. Sticking a USB in a slot didn't take a genius, and it was also more obvious. A more subtle approach would be to use Bluetooth. And even then, anyone on Reaper could've done this transfer. But then again, if trouble came, it'd be better for Reaper to be ready with weapons.

"If I'm not receiving your signal again in forty," Cell said, mentioning the time frame it should take Baddar to negotiate with Durrani International CEO Ayoubi Karzai, "then I'm activating backup."

He meant the tactical team, directed by Canyon, in the basement.

Either way, Mercy didn't like it. First, Baddar was a good commando, but he wasn't a negotiator. Second, there was a reason she had a "noncombat" designation attached to her profile. The idea of shooting her way out . . .

"Sir, here to meet with you are Mr. Hannan and his detail," the sniveling Labonte said, all but bowing as he entered the office decorated with a touch of distinctive Moorish decor. Just enough to lend an impression of the CEO's heritage to his place of business.

"Of course. Bring them in." In his midfifties, Ayoubi Karzai wore a black kurta, its buttoned front embroidered all the way up his torso and around the almost mandarin-style collar. His hair was more gray than black, and wavy. Thick. Much like Baddar's, though his wasn't gray. Beady eyes met them, a smile pinching their corners. "*Salaam*, friends."

Baddar's dark head bowed. "*Salaam alaikum.*"

Karzai opened his arms and moved toward Baddar as if ready to embrace. "*Ta sanga ye?*"

With that ever-ready smile, Baddar nodded to Durrani's

founder and spoke more in Pashto. Her itch to know what they were saying made it hard for Mercy not to shift on her feet. She slid her gaze to Culver and Saito, who had their hands loose at their sides, stance relaxed but ready. She didn't think the others spoke Pashto—and this was making her wish for Leif more than ever. While she knew there were cultural expectations to inquire after each other's health and families, she couldn't help but feel like Baddar's conversation with the CEO was going well beyond that.

The thing with the handsome Afghan was that he bore his heart in his eyes. Just a look at those dark, expressive orbs, and she knew what beat twelve to fourteen inches below. A flicker of annoyance hit them, and Mercy's pulse skipped a beat.

Karzai threw his head back and laughed, startling her and drawing a smile to Baddar's face as he joined the merriment, earning a slap on the back from the CEO. The foreign language seemed to morph into casual conversation as the two men moved to a seating area.

What was it like for Baddar to live in the U.S., among a population whose language and culture were so entirely different from his own? It must give him such relief to talk freely in his native tongue without fear of impediment or speaking the wrong word.

She had not given Baddar the credit he deserved. Pride stirred as she watched him navigate this negotiation with casual effort. As if he'd fallen into his element.

With Culver and Saito strategically situated—one next to Baddar for quick, hushed messages, and the other monitoring the door they'd just entered—Mercy perched on the edge of a chair that gave her a view of their profiles. The more she listened to their dialogue's unique rhythm, the more she realized Karzai was not all ease and confidence. The latter, yes, but there was something . . . stiff about him. It hadn't been there a moment ago.

She flicked a look at Baddar and saw irritation flash through his eyes. But as soon as she saw it, it was gone.

Karzai laughed, as did Baddar.

Maybe she'd imagined it, only . . . their laughs didn't . . . Then she saw that Baddar's smile was plastered on, performed. His gaze steady but telegraphing more than he spoke.

"T-minus thirty and counting," Cell commed.

Had it really been ten minutes already?

"Please." Karzai stood, switching to English and motioning Baddar toward a side door—a steel-reinforced room. "Come see what we can offer. I believe it will be worth your time."

Mercy came to her feet, uncertain this was a good thing, and peered up at Baddar, trying to Morse code her concern. He motioned to her, and she moved to his side without reservation.

His hand slipped to the small of her back. He pressed his lips to the soft spot near her ear and whispered, "Be ready." A shiver raced down her spine, an involuntary reaction to his warm breath and proximity, but also to the warning. Clearly, trouble waited.

Baddar nudged her forward but didn't leave much distance between them. She was glad, because now Cell and backup felt light-years away.

In the next room, Labonte rounded a table and smiled at them. "Here is the program I mentioned." He hefted a laptop from a side table and angled it toward Mercy. "The chips are RFID active, but we've added more complex . . ."

Yawn. RFID wasn't super sexy anymore, so his words were like some wicked sleep tonic. But seriously, how advanced could Durrani be if they were still fiddling with RFID?

In that case, the system shouldn't be too hard to hack. And Labonte, CIO of Durrani, should have security clearance for everything, right? She leaned closer to him, hoping to use charm as a distraction. He double-clicked an icon, and a new screen splashed over the monitor. She scanned it. "Looks pretty. But does it work?"

He grunted, accepting her challenge. Held the laptop in one hand and typed with the other. When it wobbled, Mercy steadied it for him and slipped the USB from her pocket. After one final tap, the program came to life.

"Oh," Mercy said with a bit of exaggeration. "Very nice." She arched an eyebrow. "May I?" She indicated the laptop, and he passed it to her. "Okay, maybe I'm starting to be impressed," she murmured and shifted aside, then whirled to face him, her hand surreptitiously inserting the USB. While he regaled her with his technical expertise of this program, she did her best to maintain a neutral yet interested expression.

"Okay, we're accessing," Cell said.

"Can I see the coding? This seems familiar. I might know the genius behind it." She wrinkled her nose.

"Seriously?" Karzai said. "You can do that?"

"Coding and spam, I know them, Mercy I am."

"Dr. Seuss!" he exclaimed with a laugh. "My daughter love him!"

They really were too easy. "Just as you recognize his style of writing, we do the same in my profession. There is always some madness to the method with coding."

"Do you not mean method to the madness?"

"Where's the fun in that?" Mercy refocused on the laptop and noticed the access light was still on. Hmm, taking longer than expected. Which meant a lot of data was being transferred. A flicker of nerves raced through her. What was going on?

"Is something wrong?" Labonte reached for the laptop with a concerned look.

"No." Mercy nearly choked. The light *still* glowed. What on earth had Dru put on this USB? "I just . . ." What was it? A virus? A Trojan? She would sear the living daylights out of him. Those could so easily be detected, especially with the firewalls in this system. Had Cell finished his magic?

"Slow is smooth," came the calm voice that had a tinge of Leif mixed with years of authority—Canyon. "Smooth is fast. Bees are buzzing."

"What does that even mean?" Cell said in the comms.

"Please." Labonte wagged his hand at the laptop.

"It means we move," Culver subvocalized, his back to Mercy.

As her mind processed the comms chatter, Mercy saw Labonte reach for the system. About to let him take it, she palmed the USB—and he snatched the laptop from her, knocking her hand.

She sucked in a breath—and coughed, perfectly timed to cover the sound of the USB hitting the floor.

Baddar was there, rattling in his native tongue, no doubt lodging an objection over Labonte's treatment of her.

But Karzai wasn't distracted. "What is that?" he demanded.

Oh no . . .

Saito slid between her and Labonte, shoving the laptop into the man's face and swiping his feet out from under him. In a blur, Culver dove for the doors, securing them while Baddar rushed at her and pulled her aside.

"Wait!" Karzai called. "Take me with you. Friend, please."

Baddar glanced back, nudging Mercy toward the door. "Samurai, go. Get her down."

When she realized what was happening, Mercy stopped short. "What? No!" She had no idea why Baddar would even think of bringing the Durrani CEO with them. "You can't—"

"Take her," Baddar barked at Saito, who caught her arm and pulled her toward the rear stairs. "This is dangerous," he said to Karzai. "If they learn you defected . . ."

"They will not. You will kidnap me, yes?"

After a moment's hesitation, Baddar inclined his head and motioned Karzai ahead.

When they moved into the stairwell, Mercy hurried down a few steps, still not sure about the change in plans. It was risky. They didn't know Karzai well enough. What if he was tagging along so they could be tracked?

"Coming down, plus one," Culver said into the comms.

"Negative," Canyon bit back.

"Yeah, I'm going with Midas on this one—bad call," Cell muttered, using Canyon's call sign. "Boss-man won't like this."

Mercy peered up toward the landing, where she saw two things almost simultaneously: Baddar's arm hooked Karzai's neck, choking his air off, and the door to the office bucking.

"Go!" Saito shouted at her. "Go go go."

Mercy flew down steps as fast as she could, her shoes clanging loudly.

Crack! Tsing!

"Get down!" Culver shouted from below, where a skirmish erupted.

Something impacted her, shifting her momentum. Slammed her into the concrete wall. Pain exploded across her face, jarring through her head, neck, and back. Her teeth clattered. Disoriented, she fell and twisted to Saito for help. Only . . . it wasn't Saito. The man standing over her had a weapon and black intent in his eyes.

She froze, afraid this was how she'd die. No more superheroes, no more saving the world one code at a time.

He pitched forward, head cracking against the wall, and collapsed, blood pooling like a twisted halo around his head. Behind him and up a few steps was Saito, who gave her a wag of his eyebrows as if to say that had been close.

Too close.

Mercy struggled to her feet and spied a blur above. Another man dropped from the upper floor, landing with a *thunk* near Mercy. He never hesitated as he pivoted to deal with Saito.

Impossible!

He sent Saito flying with a perfectly placed punch. A vicious hand-to-hand battle between skilled opponents ensued, but the attacker fought like he was on steroids with his rapid-fire strikes and relentless pursuit.

Thud!

Mercy felt the impact more than heard it, and turned to her left, where a third man lunged at her. She scrambled away but not fast enough.

As the third attacker's blow landed, her head snapped to the right, and her vision grayed out amid the violence.

Then a new whirl of movement—Baddar.

Echoing thuds and warbling grunts pulled Mercy back from the shadows. A heavy thud pounded against her. She blinked open her eyes and saw a dark shape. A body fell on her. But a flurry beyond distracted her.

On the landing above, Baddar fought like a fury with a man in a dark gray tactical uniform. It was terrifying, watching them brawl. Baddar so skilled and fierce. The other so . . . ambivalent, yet no less lethal.

With Baddar fighting for his life, Mercy shifted the body off her—cringing at the blood soaking her slacks. Through the steps below, she saw Saito and Culver fending off more gray soldiers. It felt like the Mad Titan swarming his army to slaughter their homeworld.

She had to do something. Mercy looked around, her head woozy from the blows. What could she do? She couldn't fight. Baddar was teaching her handgun proficiency, but she was still a beginner. As in, kindergarten. At this point, she was more likely to hurt herself or one of her team than an enemy. She cursed herself.

Then she saw it. The solution waited through the fireproof window of the door of the landing. She lurched upward and grabbed the door handle.

A weight plowed into her back. Her head bounced off the

door. Then she was drawn back. Tasting blood, she rammed her elbow up and back—straight into the guy's nose. Flicking the door handle, she expected her attacker to come again. But he didn't. She glanced back and saw the storm that was Baddar pummeling him.

Door open, Mercy flung herself into the hall. Surged at the small lever. Yanked it down.

Claxons screeched. Blinding warning lights whirled.

Almost at once, the gray assault stopped. They sped away with a shout to clear out. Civilians began to pour into the stairwell in response to the fire alarm. They stared at the bodies and Mercy, their faces ashen.

Sagged against the wall, she wiped the blood from her mouth as Baddar hurried toward her. His arm hung limp, and his leg had a vicious wound.

"You are good?" he asked.

Was she? Too many things. Too many pains. And her head ached like thunder. "Yes." Maybe. She didn't know. "Where's Karzai?"

"In a better place." Grief rippled through his Arab features. "Can you walk?"

Karzai was dead. Should she feel bad about that? She wasn't sure he'd been on the up-and-up, but his death had clearly affected Baddar. And he was beat up. "Can you?"

He nodded, then hooked her arm around his shoulder and led her out of the nightmare.

This mission had been a loss—unless Cell had managed to infiltrate via that USB. Which was somewhere upstairs. They'd have to remotely fry it, or it'd be a link straight back to Reaper.

SIX

Better judgment was for those who had options.

The crisp German air reminded Iskra of too many nights spent in this very attic, hiding from those who sought to use and abuse her. Hiding under the protection of a woman she neither trusted nor liked, but who provided an alternative. Now Iskra was doing the unfathomable. With Dani out of town for a couple of weeks and Leif MIA . . .

It is just for a short time.

"Mama, I don't like it here." Turning away from the dank room, Taissia wrapped her arms around Iskra's legs and pressed her face into them. "It's cold and smells funny."

"I know, my sweet." She squatted and manufactured a smile. "Did you know I lived here once myself?"

Taissia's gray-green eyes pooled with suspicion.

"It was many years ago, when I needed a place to stay." Iskra pointed to the bed beneath the dormer window. "I would lie there on a cot—there's a bed there now, so it's even better— and each night, I counted the ravens who roosted in the crow's nest. They can be seen if you look through the window just right." She angled them both to peer through the grimy panes.

Taissia pouted. "I don't like birds."

Frustration cinched this bad decision like a noose around Iskra's throat. "Neither did I," she confessed as she crouched. How could she convince Taissia it would be okay when she herself was not convinced? "It will just be for a short time."

"Please, don't leave me here," Taissia pleaded, burrowing into Iskra's shoulder and crying. "I'm scared."

"Only because it is new." Iskra wished she believed her own words. "And guess what? When I come back—we are going on a very long vacation. Just you and me."

Taissia lifted her head, quieting her sniffles. "And Leif?"

Aching at the hope in her daughter's words, Iskra pressed a finger to her small rosy lips. "Shh, remember? No names here."

"I want him. I miss him." Taissia gave a forlorn look at the bed and room. "He wouldn't make me stay here. It's ugly."

The tug on Iskra's conscience was powerful. Her daughter was right—Leif would not make her stay here, and he would probably be enraged that Iskra thought this was a good idea.

In fact, she did not think that. But it was the only option she had. If he knew what Iskra was doing right now . . .

Well, he does not. He was lost to his own fears and past. Which was why this was necessary. "We must be strong until he returns, yes? He needs us—"

"No, Mommy. Pleeease," Taissia whined, bouncing her legs in emphasis. "Don't make me."

"Taissia, please!" She cursed her short temper borne out of her own misgivings and desperation.

"This is where you were born, child," came a voice made husky by years of cigarettes.

Iskra shoved to her feet, glowering at the intruding woman. "I asked you to give me a moment."

"And you had one, *kotyonok*." Hands clasped over her stout frame, Bogdashka marched into the room, her low-heeled pumps thumping on wood floors. She rotated and stared at them. "You are a strong girl, are you not, Taissia?"

"*Do not*," Iskra growled, moving between her daughter and the older woman's glare, "work her. She is not one of your girls. She is not me." She advanced, narrowing her gaze with each step. "I swear on everything you hold sac—"

"I only try to help, *kotyonok*. You are making it hard on the girl—"

"*Taissia*," she snapped. "Her name is Taissia." She erased the last foot of distance, leaving no room for the older woman to gain control. "She will be safe here. Is that not right, Bogdashka?" It was not a question but a warning.

"If you have doubts, perhaps you should take her elsewhere." Cruelty hardened Bogdashka's face. "But"—her head wobbled as she gloated—"you do not have anyone else. Do you?"

Iskra lowered her chin and voice. "You know what I'm capable of—"

"Of course, I do," Bogdashka said with a dismissive wave as she sauntered around her. "I trained you."

"You *started* my training." Iskra moved to the window to regain her composure, hoping to draw Bogdashka's attention away from her daughter. She blew out a long, uneven breath, hating the truth, that she had no options. But it would be okay—for just a few days. All those years being kept by Hristoff had taught her that the only person she could trust was herself. And this was . . . wrong. "Listen." She turned.

Her heart skipped a beat, then two. Bogdashka's hands rested on Taissia's shoulders. The wide set of her daughter's eyes—terror—undid Iskra. That Taissia should know such fear at this young age dismantled every wavering conviction Iskra had that this would be okay. "Get your hands—"

"Where else will you go, Iskra? Who else will keep the child alive?"

Anger churned at this woman's exertion of power. "I will find something—anyone else."

"I thought this was urgent, dangerous, this mission of yours." A knowing gleam filled Bogdashka's eyes. And with it came a promise and a warning. She never killed children. She trained them, morphed them into weapons, each tailored to some purpose. "To find someone, yes?"

Iskra returned to the logic that had allowed her to come here: Bogdashka might not be the best thing for Taissia, but she wanted power over Iskra, so she'd keep Taissia alive. And her time with Taissia would not be long.

"Now, guess what I have downstairs," Bogdashka said to Taissia, physically urging her toward the steps. "Baklava!"

"With chocolate?" Taissia cast an uncertain glance back to Iskra, who stood trembling in fear—rage. "That's my favorite."

"I know, *kotyonok*. I know."

She always knows. That was her hidden message, and it recalled so many secrets tucked beneath that woman's graying plait. Those secrets were her power, her ability to destroy. . . .

Even me. Especially *me.*

No one in her right mind would willingly leave their child with this woman. *You are a terrible mother.*

But staring down the Armageddon Coalition and Ciro Veratti called for desperate measures. It was why Leif had gone rogue, why she was placing her daughter in the hands of the person who held the power to turn Taissia into everything Iskra had escaped. But the influence would be short-lived. Bogdashka would not have years or even weeks to ruin Taissia. A few days, and then she would never again see that woman.

Just a few days, Iskra vowed.

STUTTGART, GERMANY

Cracking his knuckles, Leif stared out the window of the Land Rover as Andreas drove into a city congested with traffic and pollution. He'd left the safe house a week ago. Enough time for the team to get stateside, rest up, and figure out how to hunt him down. Would they come?

Without a doubt.

What would he do when they did? Talking wouldn't do any good, because they'd have one goal—take him back. But he also had a goal: do whatever it took to get answers. He wasn't returning to Virginia for more of Dru's platitudes and excuses.

Iskra was his biggest concern. With her skills and the stake she'd claimed on his heart, she could do a lot of damage. The moment when she confronted him—and she would— her tenacity could be a problem. He'd seen what she'd done to find her brother, and it had been near-miraculous how she'd found Mitre, aka Andreas.

His gaze hit the guy driving the SUV. Light brown hair and trim beard. Intense eyes just like Iskra's. Both had an unparalleled mission focus, but unlike Andreas's methodical precision, Iskra was more . . . impassioned.

Which made her beautiful. And dangerous. Thus the dread about when she came for *him*. That couldn't happen until he had answers, because he didn't want to hurt her.

"Are you going to be my daddy now?"

Leif shifted. Taissia had whispered those words as he carried her half-asleep self to bed one night. It had stopped him in his tracks.

He pressed his knuckles to his lips, mind catching up as Andreas turned onto a *strasse* of row homes. Leif ducked to look out the window and take in the multistoried residences stacked on top of each other. Some shops on the lower level, apartments above. Rooftops perfect for snipers. Windows for shooters. This might not be A-stan or Iraq, but it still buzzed his nerves.

No good. No good. Too crowded, too easy to ambush. But Rutger wanted Leif to meet some people.

Andreas eased the vehicle to the curb and cut the engine.

Leif eyed the street, then used the side mirror to check their rear. To the right. And the left. Convinced he wasn't stepping into a shooter's alley, he opened the door. Brisk German air smacked him as he climbed out, ready to pull his weapon if a threat presented.

He stalked up the path with Andreas, around a corner, and then fifteen paces to the second red-brick house. Anemic and dilapidated, the building had an enclosed foyer with mailboxes. Andreas thumbed a code into a keypad whose numbers had long worn off. When a click sounded, he pushed open the door.

They stepped inside, and something raised the hairs on the back of Leif's neck. He unholstered his weapon as they climbed the stairs to a landing and entered the flat. It had a small front room with a fireplace and bookshelves. Just beyond, a small kitchenette and table. The setting reminded him of the haunting images from Chernobyl—dishes on the table, food half-eaten. TV playing in the front room. Playgrounds emptied. This was . . . wrong. Ominously, eerily *wrong*.

To his nine, a short hall offered three doors—likely two bedrooms and a bathroom. One of the doors creaked open and released a beam of light.

Leif snapped his weapon in that direction, as did Andreas. Advancing, they were ready to meet the threat.

A man turned the corner, zipping his pants. He looked up and, with a shout, pitched himself backward.

Holstering his weapon, Andreas stormed forward, barking in German at the man, who shouted back. A heated exchange ensued. The two were clearly familiar with one another.

"What's going on?" Leif lowered his weapon.

Andreas shook his head. "He says we are late."

"Did we need a reservation?"

"Do your job." Andreas glared at the guy, then at Leif. "Come." He stormed down the hall to the last room, which contained blacked-out windows, a rumpled bed, and well-read books cluttering a corner. He opened a smaller door. A closet?

Andreas leaned inside and reached up over the doorjamb. A distinctive *shunk* reverberated through the wall. He stepped in sideways, then moved forward—and vanished.

What on earth? Though Leif expected him to reappear, only the creak and groan of steps came. He peered in. Stairs too narrow to be called a stairwell sank into the darkness. The glare of Andreas' cheek was the only hint that he hadn't disappeared altogether.

Leif's old buddy Tox hadn't been fond of tunnels, and he could suddenly relate. He had to descend sideways to fit into the rail-thin passage. A dozen steps delivered him into pitch black. Had he missed a turn?

He hesitated, trying to hear which way Andreas had gone. Inching forward provided a smidgen more light. He paused to sort out his surroundings, which included black, dark gray, and oppressive gray, wood in various states of decay, and smells—musty, dank. Those odors surprisingly gave way to . . . yeast, bread. Laughter from above.

Disoriented, Leif recalled a bakery on the corner of the street. He should've hit bottom or a foundation by now. A dozen more steps had dirt crunching beneath his boots. He paused. Had he stepped into some time-dilation tunnel? Because this didn't make sense.

Where were they? *What* was this? Where had Andreas gone?

Dead ahead, darkness surrendered to a dull glow. Shapes shifted and rose. Through the sights of his weapon, Leif assessed the figures.

63

"Relax," Andreas said, pressing down Leif's gun. "You are among friends here."

Unease latched on as his eyes adjusted, transforming those before him from shadowy forms to . . .

Recognition punched the air from his chest. He stepped back, a chill cracking his bones. "No freakin' way."

SEVEN

Andreas shifted aside and swiped the wall. Light forced its way through the space, chasing away darkness and any doubt in Leif's mind that this was really happening. "There . . . this . . . It can't be . . ."

"Real?" Andreas arched an eyebrow. "It is, just as they are."

They. Men Leif knew, *had* known. But it wasn't possible. These men were dead. *Supposed* to be dead. "How . . . ?" This couldn't be. They had enhanced abilities, but they weren't immortal.

Andreas moved farther into the room, bypassing answers as smoothly as he did the sealed-off medical bay with hospital beds and IV drips. In what looked like a small cafeteria were three more men, their food ignored.

A sickening knot formed in Leif's gut as he met the gazes of men he'd trained with. Harcos, Muharib, Esger. The men from the Sahara Nine.

Neiothen. They were Neiothen. All of them.

All of us.

They were also the men he'd hunted with Reaper: Kampfer, Harbah, Dreng.

A sharp, daggerlike pain stabbed his skull with each heartbeat. It didn't make sense. Did he know these men from training with them or from hunting them? Both?

But . . . he didn't.

"Once we talk," Andreas called from the far side, "it will make sense."

"Really messes with the head, doesn't it?" said a dark-haired man.

"Esger." Who was supposed to be dead.

The very-much-alive man smirked at him. "Vidor, good to see you again."

Vidor. The sound of that name—his own call sign—hurt as much as the trigger call in the amusement park. Fear and adrenaline combusted, shoving Leif forward. "What is this? What's going on?"

Andreas stared him down with preternatural calm, as if waiting for him to step off. It was not until Leif eased back that Andreas motioned to the table and folded his six-three frame into a chair. "What do you recall of the accident that destroyed your career?"

Annoyed that Andreas had skipped past the whole dead-men-walking thing, Leif did not respond. He sensed a lot more behind the question than simple curiosity. And it irritated him. This whole thing irritated him. Told him to leave.

"Chopper crash." The chair next to him squawked as a scraggly man deposited himself there. "Wedged—"

"—on the cliff above," another said. His eyes were familiar. Very familiar.

He held his arm protectively to his side, hand fitted over the barrel of his M4. Glistening movement betrayed the blood gushing . . .

The assault of that memory made Leif's nerves jounce.

"You okay, Chief?"

Leif's brain sizzled with a deadly sense of déjà vu. Those words—that question. This guy had asked him that before. "Kampfer." But he'd been at The Hague. "Turi Vega."

"You knew me as Harcos." A half shrug. "Once. A while back."

"You died—I saw my guy trying to save you." Leif blinked, looked at Andreas. "You told my team Veratti had a sniper trained on him. Shot him."

Vega smirked.

Leif skipped his gaze to the guy in sweats and a T-shirt dragging an IV tower over the floor. When their eyes locked, Leif hopped to his feet, wanting to get away, feeling like he was trapped in a haunted house. "Huber." Bile rose in his throat.

"Easy," Andreas said, touching his arm. "Just breathe."

Hearing hollowing, Leif fought the order. Fought to understand. To make sense of this. "How . . . ?" He pressed his hand to his forehead. "You're all dead. I saw your bodies."

"You saw what we needed you to see." Andreas had a voice that could convince a rabid dog to lie down and show his belly.

Turi Vega, who used the call sign Harcos yet hunted as the Neiothen Kampfer.

Wafiyy Ibn Sarsour, call sign Muharib. Neiothen: Harbah.

Harald Elvestad, call sign Esger . . . Dreng.

Herrick Huber . . . Krieger . . . Bushi.

"What?" Leif scoffed. "You going to tell me that guy with his head bandaged is Guerrero?" He could still feel Dempsey's gray matter splatting his face.

"No," Andreas said quietly, his expression dark. "There was nothing we could do for Guerrero. I didn't reach him in time. Almost didn't make it in time for Kappi either."

Kappi. Leif recoiled, the face of Carsen Gilliam snapping to the fore. "He was . . ."

"Dead?" Andreas finished. "Thanks to your unwitting team and its actions in The Hague, we were able to intercept and save him."

"No way! He was dead."

"Yes, mostly." Andreas's lips quirked. "He will have visible, unsightly scars, but thanks to the enhancements, he is alive to fight another day."

Why did Leif feel like he'd stepped into some bad sci-fi movie?

"What?" Vega asked. "Did you think you were the only one who could run indefinitely and heal fast?"

What they were saying made sense in one respect and was absolute lunacy on the other. Light-headed, Leif tried to wrestle the situation into something manageable, something . . . fathomable.

"Kolya." A young woman entered a far door. "They're ready."

That was what Leif had called Andreas in the park—Kolya.

Though Andreas inclined his head at her, he didn't move. He sat quietly, as if thinking something over. Then his gaze met Leif's. "I'm not sure you're ready for this, but there is no more time."

"Ready for what?"

"You still cling to your idea of the truth, what you *want* to be the truth." Andreas shrugged. "I understand. What they did to us"—he shook his head—"should never have happened. But it did. And now we use it against them."

"Use what?"

A dark smile carved his face. "Everything."

Moving from the dank underground hideaway, up a flight of stairs, and into the open conference room felt more symbolic than Leif cared to admit. Behind him, the past, the once-thought-dead Neiothen. Before him, a half-dozen unknowns sat around two rickety six-foot tables pushed together. Two Asian males, another male and female, a disheveled guy who looked homeless, and finally, a woman, so pale she might not have any blood in her veins, whispered to Rutger Hermanns.

The thorn in Leif's side lifted his chin in acknowledgment. "Mr. Metcalfe." He motioned to a chair. "Please."

Resistance was pointless because he had nothing to prove, and he'd already learned more from Hermanns in two encounters than he had in four years with Dru. So he did as instructed, eyeing the able-bodied Neiothen who'd come with him.

"First," Hermanns said, "let me introduce my team."

"I really don't care about them," Leif countered. "I want to know about *them*." He indicated the Neiothen. "They're dead—multiple times over. Explain that."

"I will," Hermanns said with a smile. "But first, trust me in the order of things, *ja*?" He placed a hand on the pale woman's shoulder. "This is Dr. Hanna Sommer. I could give you her litany of accolades and degrees—and you would recall them all—but believe me when I simply say she is a brilliant geneticist." He then stood behind the homeless-looking man. "This is Alaric Stein, a biochemist with a number of specialties. And what he lacks in appearance, he more than makes up for in the lab. Beside him is Dr. Danek Pohl."

Leif recalled seeing Pohl on a magazine cover. "You wrote the article on war and the brain." The one that had really ticked off the guys at the FOB where Leif had been stationed.

Pohl held his gaze, unflinching. "I did."

"Danek is a retired brigadier general and neurosurgeon," Hermanns said. "He teaches at a couple of universities in the States."

"Head doctor," Leif taunted.

"In more ways than one," Pohl said with a grim smile. "However, not as a shrink. That falls to Selma, our resident psychiatrist." He nodded down the table. "She has a specialty in brain-injury medicine."

Leif glanced at a woman who seemed to have at least a little Latina blood, if her dark features were any indication.

"A shrink," Huber said with a sniff. "Never could get away from them."

Leif wasn't letting Pohl go—the redirection wouldn't work. "Are you responsible for the technology in our heads?"

A hesitation. "In part."

"Which part?"

"Before we get into that, let me finish," Hermanns said. "To Danek's left are Sora Tanaka and Asahi Kimura, extremely talented biochemists recruited from Japan."

The introductions were a waste of time and changed nothing. "Explain to me how these men were dead—multiple times—yet are sitting here living and breathing."

"You were dead, too," Vega asserted.

Leif jerked toward him. "Come again?"

"Wait," Hermanns said, inclining his head to the Neiothen. "Please, let me explain first."

"Why are you controlling the dialogue?" Leif asked, agitation rising. "You afraid they're going to say something that'll tick me off?"

"Yes," Bostwick asserted, her brown eyes fierce. "If Rutger is allowed to read you in, things will make sense. If the pieces come together in a random disorder that has no meaning, the reaction you're likely to experience may be significant and *significantly* different."

"Yeah, wouldn't want us mad, would you?" Huber had a bite to his words. He met Leif's gaze. "They're scared of us because they know what they did to us."

It was affirming in a strange, twisted way to have Huber and Vega—men he'd hunted down with Reaper—saying the very things that had been burning in his own head.

"My sister," Hermanns said, his voice pitched and commanding, insisting he be heard, "developed a serum about ten years ago that enabled soldiers to ignore their pain receptors and power through missions."

70

"Interferons in the parietal lobe," Leif muttered, connecting the dots.

"Yes," Hermanns said. "Her serum was so successful, it caught the eyes of the wrong person."

"Veratti," Leif suggested.

"No, not yet," Hermanns said with a raised finger, the weight of this story heavy on his shoulders. "Before Veratti there was someone else who encouraged Katrin, said she was onto something big—"

"Wilhelmina." Sneering made Hanna Sommer look all the more pale and deathlike.

After a slow nod, Hermanns continued. "She told Katrin that with this project, they could help soldiers around the world to return home to their families and loved ones. With her fiancé and some in this very room, she worked night and day on this project, unaware of what her sponsor intended to do with the work. When she learned the truth, Katrin decided to get out, take the research with her, and free the men she'd treated."

"Except Wilhelmina turned on her," Selma said with her lip curled. "She thought it poetic that Katrin be killed by the men she'd created."

"The *subjects*," Alaric Stein finally spoke up, his words intentional, "were dosed with a steroid cocktail that amped their responses and instincts. That, combined with the further-faster technology, turned them into . . . monsters. When Katrin fled, Wilhelmina sent them after her."

Face surprisingly devoid of emotion, Pohl seemed unaware of the tear sliding down his cheek as he stared into space.

"And the Neiothen?" Leif asked.

"The attack that night was brutal. Authorities had no choice—kill or be killed," Selma said, her expression dark. "The program had turned honorable men into tools of murder. That was never the intent for the Neiothen."

"A select few of us were chosen to remain and feign agreement with ArC's purpose. We were relocated after that," Stein said, "and discovered there were already more Neiothen in play—including all of you. Veratti started a new group, but they were impatient, unwilling to allow the body to assimilate to the changes. The Betas started failing. The technology wouldn't pair."

Bostwick nodded. "Behavioral enhancements weren't adhering, infections were rampant, resulting in disorientation and delirium. Before anything could become permanent, we attempted to deprogram them, so to speak. When that didn't work, we chose to block certain memories, a new and not wholly effective technology, which"—she shrugged sorrowfully—"did not work on all of them. Before Wilhelmina or ArC could learn of the failed attempts and order us to terminate them, we erased them from the program."

"Carsen." Leif recalled the story the guy had told him. "He was a Beta. But that doesn't explain us or our memory gaps."

"That's where I came into the program," Bostwick explained. "The serum had progressed to gene therapy, then technological enhancements, which all worked."

"Our original plan," Stein said, "was to return you to your respective units and governments."

"Veratti had another plan." Pohl had brushed away his tears. "So my task was to convince you of a certain order of events and program them into your mind, then release you back to your units with no memory of what happened, so that at a later time he could activate you."

"And you were okay with that?" Leif asked. "Wiping our minds—"

"Don't blame Danek," Bostwick said. "We thought we had created a workaround, a way to help you recall what happened. But we, too, were betrayed by Wilhelmina."

"The chips," Leif whispered, no idea if that was right.

"They were only supposed to monitor biorhythms and dose you with serotonin to reduce anxiety and fears. Keep you confident, calm." Kimura looked contrite, bothered. "Through threats against our families, they forced us to make them do . . . more."

"Like they forced us," Vega said.

Bostwick hesitated. "Actually, no. No participant was forced into the program. All of you came to us as volunteers."

"Bull." Leif searched for some semblance of recognition. "I don't remember you."

"Not remembering isn't tied to recruitment," Stein asserted. "Each man in this room was approached about the project through indirect channels."

"Meaning?"

"Because of your profile, you were invited to join the Netherwood project," Bostwick said. "As to who invited you—well, we contacted individuals in your spheres of influence to vet you, then once convinced of your compatibility, to pass along the information. We could not directly invite you because that would compromise our team. And if we were compromised, the project was compromised. Everything done to you was carried out with your clear understanding and consent . . . until Wilhelmina."

"Though you had a say, there are those who did not," Hermanns said, grieved. "ArC has what we've been calling second-generation models. The Gen2s are perfected, precise, and merciless. No longer can they be considered men. They are machines."

"What do you think?" Rutger stared out the window of the small conference room into the warehouse, where the Neiothen had equipment at their disposal to recover and improve.

"He wasn't ready." Andreas's reflection loomed in the glass, superimposing itself on Leif making his umpteenth attempt at the climbing wall, sans harness. Then he leapt from the midsection of the wall and caught a beam.

"I think you underestimate him," said Selma. "Leif Metcalfe has been waiting for this—in truth, he was programmed for it. Designed for it—all his life, if the Book of the Wars is to be believed."

"I agree." Rutger thought of the panels Leif had stolen, the ones that showed the great, bloody sacrifice that paired with the words from the book about blood and power in his hands. Leif was not the key, but he was integral to the success of any attempt against ArC. "And yes—it is undoubtedly to be believed."

"Then once Leif embraces the truth, he will be a force to reckon with."

"But against *them*?" Andreas argued. "None of us is prepared to face a Gen2. We've failed to stop Veratti, and that's *without* being confronted by super soldiers." He bobbed his head toward the gym. "Leif's team encountered Gen2s in London and would have been slaughtered had it not been for quick thinking on the part of one woman."

"Then you must get ready," Rutger said, conviction in his bones. "The final confrontation is upon us."

EIGHT

It wasn't the same. Never would be. Not until Leif was back, giving attitude and telling lame jokes. But Cell wasn't sure that day would come. Worse, he wasn't sure he wanted that day to come. Not after Taiwan. So many things had gone wrong: Peyton shot by an enemy sniper, they'd targeted the wrong Neiothen, and Leif had gone all Jason Bourne on them.

"Two weeks," Cell muttered to no one in particular as he glanced around the hub. Fourteen days since the fiasco at Durrani International in London when Reaper narrowly escaped, thanks to Mercy activating the fire alarm. With emergency personnel swarming, they had the ruse needed to slip into the chaos, which had also sent the super soldiers running back into whatever hole they'd scurried out from in the first place. "Are we seriously not going to talk about the Terminators that came after us?"

"They were some serious slag," Saito agreed from his station. "But so are we. Am I right?"

"Not so serious! Baddar and Culver are injured."

"Baddar held off multiple assailants while you sat in a bunker," Mercy bit out.

"I'm just saying those men"—Cell grimaced—"were *animals*. Like, no remorse. At all. Just slice and dice and move on. It was terrifying, watching the feed!"

75

"Imagine how we felt being in the actual fight," Culver growled, touching his shoulder were he'd been shot.

"Think they're more of the Neiothen? Is Leif with them?" Cell asked.

"Shut up, man," Culver barked, then answered his ringing phone.

Whatever. It'd been like this since they'd returned. The point was that they had exactly bubkes. Half the team wanted to race off to save Leif from himself, the other half felt betrayed and wanted to strangle him for abandoning them.

"Aw, man, that's great to hear about Peyton." Culver's Southern drawl twanged through the dimly lit bunker as he talked into a phone. He shifted in his chair, nodding. "Sure thing. I'll let them know. We're here for you when—yeah. I hear you."

Guessing Culver was talking to Adam Lawe, Cell was on his feet. Reaper seemed to be of the same mind. Baddar, Mercy, and Saito also huddled nearby, hoping for good news.

Culver finally hung up and swiveled to them with not-quite-a-smile. "Peyton's still in a coma, but she's finally stable enough to fly her home. They start back in the a.m."

"Is it smart to move her while she's still in a coma?" Cell asked.

Saito nodded. "If her vitals are stable, she's safe to fly. She could stay in a coma for an extended period, so what they're facing is long-term care. However, if she comes out—"

"*When* she comes out," Mercy corrected.

With a slower nod, Saito continued. "*When* she comes out of it, she's going to have a lot of rehab, and that's when they can determine the extent of the permanent damage, if any."

Though nobody would say it, the possibility existed that Peyton might not wake up. And if she did, whether she'd be able to walk and talk was another ball game.

"Lawe sounded good, relieved," Culver said.

"He had me worried," Cell admitted. "He's not usually a downer..."

"It's not every day you see a high-velocity round eat the chest of the woman you love," Culver growled.

"Fair enough. I didn't mean—"

"We're all on edge," Mercy said calmly. "And more than a little concerned about our situation and about our absent friends."

Baddar touched her shoulder, and surprisingly, she kind of leaned into it. Not much, but she definitely didn't shift away. Was something happening between those two? Why did that leave a bitter taste in Cell's mouth?

Because all the good ones choose the other guy.

"I take it you heard Devine is being prepped for transport back here," Iliescu said as he and Braun joined them in the hub. "She's not out of the woods, but Landstuhl can't do much else for her."

Had the director really come out here just to tell them that? His expression seemed to hint at more.

"Something going on?" Saito asked, glancing between the director and his DoD counterpart.

"Couple things," Iliescu said with a nod. "Charlie Harden's on his way down to talk about the third war mentioned in the Book of the Wars." He paused for only a fraction, then seemed to steel himself. "Analysts have been poring over SAT-INT, SIGINT—you name it—to locate Leif."

Cell straightened. "They found something?"

Dru pointed to the round table, then aimed a remote at the wall screen. "This was at a private airstrip about a hundred klicks from the Taiwan safe house. SATINT logs this as 23 June at 2359 hours."

On the footage, a silver SUV with blacked-out windows pulled up to a Learjet, which had its stairs extended and waiting. Two men exited the SUV and stalked into the jet, but their faces weren't visible.

"Height and gait comparisons give a ninety-percent likelihood that the second man to enter the jet was Leif," Braun said, as she acknowledged Harden, who entered the hub.

Heavy quiet draped the team as they studied the looping footage, hoping it would tell them more.

"With Andrew," Mercy sneered. "Right?"

"That's our belief," Dru agreed.

Cell wanted to provide plausible explanations for Leif being with ArC associates, but he didn't have it in him to reach that far. Not this time.

"So he . . ." Mercy's glossy gaze was locked on the screen.

"We stick with facts," Dru stated firmly. "Leif is with Andreas Krestyanov. That's all we've confirmed."

"Dude, if we acted only on *confirmed* intel, we'd be in pretty sorry shape," Cell argued.

"You never liked him," Culver said quietly.

"Reverse that," Cell countered. "*He* didn't like me."

"You called him Usurper," Saito challenged.

"Yeah," Cell sniffed, "and you all called me a coward for taking a promotion that put me here and has saved your sorry carcasses more than once."

"Why didn't you come clean with what you knew about him?" Culver's question crossed into accusation territory.

Cell balked. "What, so it's my fault Leif is now rogue and possibly colluding with the enemy? Which—in case anyone here forgot—is called treason." A thundering pulse wouldn't help him calm down. "And before you lay into me about that, let's remember we have a timetable. The U.S. is notoriously swift in dealing with traitors, because the longer they are alive to—"

A blurred fist came from his left.

An explosion of pain shot through Cell's jaw. Air swirled.

The room spun. Cell found himself on the ground, pinned by a two-twenty weight named Culver Brown.

It always happened. No superhero team was immune. They all fell.

Hand to her mouth, Mercy stepped back as Baddar and Saito drew a raging Culver off Cell, who now had a split cheek and lip. The injuries from their failed London mission must be aggravating their common sense. It had definitely grounded them for a while, and maybe that was part of what was eating at the fabric of this team.

Dru shoved Cell backward. One hand on Cell's chest, he pointed in his face. "Stand down. Hear me?"

"Me? Who's the one—"

"Enough! What's more important?" Dru shouted, looking between the men. "Being right or ending this?"

Like a dog licking his wounds, Cell shifted aside, head down.

A still-scowling Culver shrugged free of Saito.

The whole thing reminded Mercy of Tox and Ram and their falling out—not to mention how that ended. She was sick of this. Sick of superheroes falling. And she wouldn't believe that of Leif.

"Leif is our friend," she said, imploring them. "We have to put aside offenses and—"

"If the final prophecy is any indication," Harden spoke from the table, where he stood before his opened attaché case, "he may not be your friend."

Lips tight, she pivoted toward the analyst. "Tell you what—"

"I'm sure he didn't mean that the way it came out," Dru said.

"I meant it just like it sounds. Take a look." Harden pressed a button on the remote, and words splashed over the wall screen. "This is what the Book of the Wars states regarding the third and final war before the coalition completes their agenda, which"—he glanced at Dru and Braun—"experts agree is control of the economy in key countries."

As Harden started reading, Mercy allowed her gaze to wander the excerpt, the black words glowering at them from the wall.

A third angel appeared and took me into the bowels of the earth, where those from below writhe in the agony of their own doing while the great storms boast of his slaughter. Hatred pierces the heart of a warrior, then friend turns against friend, lost in their fears and anguish. So it was, the angel went out as a sacrifice. He went, to death, to victory, ready to confront the darkness that had rallied yet again to victory as those from below slumbered in ignorance. To rout their complacency, the final paladin seeks conquest. In his hands are blood and violence, dripping with vengeance and might; he cannot be stopped. None can stand against him, though to their death they try. Friends numbering zero and enemies in the thousands, he wars in the dark hour, his wrath relentless against those who oppose him. Man will know his fury but not his loyalty, which alone belongs to the one who built him. His hour has come. In this, he will not fail.

"That . . ." A wad of guilt and fear clogged Mercy's throat. "Is that 'final paladin' Leif?"

Harden gripped the back of a chair and bent forward. "That's my—our guess."

"To be clear," Dru spoke up, "we cannot know definitively that everything in the text refers to *this* paladin, to Leif."

"But Cell said Leif is the Ossi who got called out in the park," Saito said, "and that text says, 'those from below slumber in ignorance.' Does slumber mean dead? Because the Neiothen we went after are all dead, save Leif and Andrew. Tell me I'm right. I mean, they don't come back to life, right?"

"To the best of our very limited knowledge," Dru conceded. "We have to understand that interpreting prophecy is not our area of expertise. At best, these are educated guesses. Slumber could be sleeping, or it could be death. We can't know for sure what it means."

Mercy probed the text, desperate for some word or phrase to turn this away from Leif being evil incarnate, driven to brutality by a raging soul. What angered her was how easily she could believe it after what he'd done to Cell. How he'd abandoned them without a word. She recalled Iskra's chastisement over shifting loyalty.

"That's pretty muffed," Saito said, as the revelatory weight seemed to push him into his seat. "If that's Leif—if all this is him . . ."

"Then it means he's on a rampage, friendless, and"— Admiral Braun let out a heavy sigh—"unstoppable."

"No way!" Culver flung a hand at the wall. "You and that thing are wrong, because it says 'friends numbering zero,' and I count at least four right here. So either it's wrong or we are."

"Agreed. So what're we doing? Anything?" Cell asked, his expression contorted. "We just let him—"

"It says those who oppose him will know his wrath," Braun said. "I've seen Runt's wrath. Have you? It isn't pretty."

"True." Saito threaded his fingers together. "The more we go up against Leif, the uglier it's going to get. He ditched us to take care of this for a reason, so . . . we let him."

"Okay, so maybe three friends," Culver snarled at Saito. "I can't believe you, man. What about the rest of y'all? You with Saito, too?"

"No." Mercy felt sick. "I will not believe this! I will not *be* that to him, an enemy. Supers stick together—always. Leif will *always* have me as a friend."

81

"Easy words, like the wind," Dru challenged. "What Leif is doing?" He met each team member's gaze. "It can't happen. We have to stop him, and with everything we have."

"Dude." The laughter was missing from Cell's voice. "You saw the words—his fury—"

"It says we *meet* his fury. It doesn't say *lose* to his fury."

"Isn't that splitting hairs?" Saito ran a hand over his closely shorn scalp. "I'd like to keep the few I have."

"No, we help him. He needs us," Culver gritted out. "That is, those of us who are loyal."

"Maybe," Dru conceded, hesitating for a second that allowed Mercy to see something in his expression that unsettled her. "However, this could be the only chance we have to stop this, to stop Leif."

"We—*you* know him. You've worked with him." Determination cut a hard line through Braun's words. "That gives us a leg up."

Not liking the gleam in the rear admiral's eyes nor the direction of this conversation, Mercy clenched her jaw. Her stomach churned at the thought of hunting down Leif. Doing it as friends was one thing, but as his enemy . . .

"It gives us the chance to dance in his reticle," Saito countered, his brows drawn together. "We need to be on alert. Remember—he does not have a light trigger finger."

Braun lifted her chin. "Neither do we."

STUTTGART, GERMANY

Tic-tacking up the corner of the warehouse, Leif fought to harness his thoughts. The steel pipe was cold as he scaled higher. From there, he launched out to a low-hanging truss. He caught it and swung with nothing but thirty feet of unfriendly German air between him and the concrete floor. He arced his legs up and slipped onto the catwalk. Righted, feet dangling over the emptiness, he hooked his arms over a metal support. No panting. Barely a drip of sweat.

The belowground hideaway fed into this warehouse gymnasium, which was arranged into a dozen different training areas—obstacle course, weights, pool, firing range in the far right with ballistic barriers that kept the bullets and most of the sound inside. To the far right, a sealed medical bay was off limits for the protection of those in recovery. And to the left—that conference room where they'd given him the origin story of the Neiothen. Of Katrin and her team, of how it had grown from a well-intentioned program to a bad sci-fi novel under the direction of Veratti. And now? Now there was a worse breed. Yeah, cue the cheese and bad FX.

The only problem was the Gen2s were real, along with the technology. He'd seen articles and news pieces on bills going before Congress to get funding for enhancements for troops. But to find out he'd already been part of that? Whack.

He and the others had the ability to ignore pain and endure more for longer periods. Their bodies healed faster. It scared him to think about what the newer models could do. *Machines.*

And it worried him for Reaper. For Iskra.

What nagged his thoughts was the first scene in the two-paneled painting he had stolen from Rutger—six kings around one man. It hadn't made sense before, but now . . . with seven Neiothen left . . . He'd hidden the diptych painting, convinced it was a piece of him, an arrow to his past, and that he had to follow it. Why he thought that, what had convinced him—he couldn't say. Gut instinct. Like Fuji's bunk room in Djibouti City, with that Buddha tapestry—he had just known it was significant. Same with the panel. Saw it. Knew it. Stole it.

No doubt Reaper saw him as a traitor. Iskra had been furious when he'd gone on a fact-finding mission in Egypt last month and hadn't told her. So this? It'd be unforgiveable.

Just as well. It meant she was farther from him, farther from danger.

Was this worth it? He'd gotten answers but hadn't expected or anticipated what they'd mean. To learn he was one of the demons he'd been hunting. Which meant he had to be hunted, too. Right? It was a natural thought progression—if Reaper had hunted the other men in this warehouse, wouldn't they now hunt Leif?

And the book. The painting. Wouldn't it be better if he removed himself from the equation? He wasn't looking for the coward's way out—he just wanted closure. Reaper, under his direction, had failed miserably in the first and second wars the book mentioned. The third was about him, wasn't it? That wasn't good. In fact, it was pretty freakin' bad.

"In his hands are blood and violence." That was what the book said, blood and violence. He didn't want to be that. He was a fighter, a warrior, but not a . . . demon.

He stared at the concrete forty feet below him. Sudden impact—would it be enough to kill him? End it fast? Save everyone the pain he'd cause?

A whistle seared the air and snapped his attention to Andreas, who stood with the other guys. Their gazes swept suddenly up to Leif. A strange and startling revelation hit him—he was more like these guys than Reaper. The thought angered him. He hated that he was one of them. These men had acted as assassins for ArC, had been activated, then murdered people.

Andreas motioned for him to join them.

He hesitated, then figured why not. Using a steel pipe riveted to the crossbeams, he headed down. As he crossed the warehouse, he took his time, assessing the moods and postures of the men. Tense. Irritated.

Two more things they had in common.

"What do you remember?" Vega asked.

"About what?"

"The Sahara," Huber said.

Leif drew up at the memory. The danger of opening this vault when it had been hermetically sealed to prevent it from leaking into his life . . .

"Trust us," Andreas said. "There's a point."

Like it or not, he *was* one of them. Time to accept it.

"Fragments are all I remember." Leif met Krieger's— Huber's—gaze. "You, groaning as you lay beneath Zhanshi after the crash. And the drop-off that nearly took—"

"What crash?" Huber asked.

Leif frowned. "The *chopper* crash." Were they jerking his chain?

"The one that killed Zhanshi?" Huber asked. "The same Zhanshi who was resurrected to attempt an assassination of the Chinese prime minister?"

"Or Guerrero," Andreas added.

"Who died on the table," Leif muttered, catching their drift. The wild, panicked eyes he recalled switched from one location—that mountain—to another—the American Institute in Taiwan. His suicide.

Krieger's knees and panic buckled, sending him to the rocky path. He let out a string of curses and cradled his head. "Why do I feel so screwed up?"

Leif hadn't felt right either—nobody did after crashing on a mountain.

Another flashback hit—the embassy. *"My head," Dempsey murmured, frowning. "I keep having these thoughts. . . ." Fingertips to the side of his forehead, he flattened his lips. "The things I keep thinking about . . ." His face screwed tight. "It's not me. I was—Distinguished Service Medal. Service Medal. Up for Military Medal for Gallantry with Distinction." Confusion flayed his features. "This . . . what's in my head—it's not me!"*

A thump against his chest startled Leif back to the present. He caught the hand, twisted it—

But Andreas anticipated and thwarted the move. His gaze sharpened. "What're you remembering?"

Leif released him, stepping back. Wanting to step back from the mangled mess of memories. "A lot. Krieger. At the crash, he said his head felt weird—but we all felt that way." He shrugged. "I thought . . ."

"It was normal, after a crash."

"Yeah." Leif wet his lips. "But at the AIT, Dempsey said he was having thoughts that weren't his"—he squinted—"or something like that. Right before . . ."

"He killed himself." Andreas nodded. "He'd been initiated, but it went wrong. He was able to fight it. I couldn't get to him in time."

"Yeah, he kept talking about his commendations." Leif gritted his teeth. "I didn't care—just wanted him to put down the gun. Those memories . . . they kept blurring. Repeating. Different, though."

"We've all had that," Huber said. "Memory glitches. Tell us what you remember on Shaib al-Banat."

Leif swiped a hand over his mouth, a little freaked that he could talk about this in public when he'd been forced to bury it for years. And yet, suddenly not wanting to talk about it. "I came to on the mountain."

The other five nodded firmly.

"I was choking on the smoke but tried to assess the situation. You—" Leif frowned as he squinted at Huber. "You fell when the ground gave way." He angled his head as if he could get a better bead on what really happened. "You . . . were—"

"Dead?"

"Injured." He couldn't be dead if he was standing in front of Leif, but he also knew he'd come off that mountain believing his team dead, not injured. "They said everyone died. All of you."

Andreas folded his arms. "What were we doing there, our objective?"

"Extract a VIP asset."

"In the Sahara. Men from different countries."

"It's the military," Leif replied. "I've done stupider things."

"No doubt." Andreas jutted his jaw. "How'd the chopper crash?"

"RPG," Leif said. "Hit the rotors." As he said the last three words, the others said the exact same words. Haunting.

"What type of bird?" Vega asked.

"Huey," Leif said, expecting more unison speech, but he was wrong.

"HT-29 Caiman," Vega asserted. Spanish chopper. Not surprising, considering Vega's country, but . . .

"I recall a Mi-171Sh," Andreas said with a huff.

"Lynx Mk7," Elvestadt countered. "Which doesn't make sense, since they haven't deployed since 2015."

Leif laughed. "None of this makes sense."

"The Lynx was one of many mistakes," came the ever-intrusive voice of Rutger Hermanns. "And the point they would have you grasp? The crash never happened."

NINE

"What do you mean it didn't happen? I was there!"

"True. You were there, all of you," Selma Bostwick said with a grin and more than a little amusement. High off her own juice, it seemed. "But the crash itself never happened. It was staged." She and Rutger were joined by the retired brigadier general. "We had to find a way to reintegrate you into your lives, so we engineered the crash, being sure to give each of you—from your own perspective and respective countries— a narrative that was believable and cohesive."

"Which explains all the different choppers."

"But why fake the deaths?"

"Crucial," Selma said. "ArC did not want anyone to find you or for you to contact each other. That was the reason you were each assigned random code names that had nothing to do with personality quirks, appearance, or nationality. If the program collapsed or was discovered, they did not want you traceable, should someone come looking, so they buried you." She lifted a shoulder in a lazy shrug. "In more ways than one. The crash was the only way to make that happen. To convince you all that it happened, the last few weeks before releasing you entailed hours of training and enacting that scenario. You were drilled over and over."

"Brainwashed," Huber grunted. "No wonder we all had the exact same story."

"But the reports," Leif said. "The Pararescuemen who—"

"Our men. Reports fabricated with assistance from those within a military branch of each of your respective countries."

A trill of disbelief hit Leif. "The Sahara Nine . . . the men I thought were dead . . . the crash I blamed myself for . . ." The one that had driven him into deep depression, convinced him he wasn't fit for command. Anger rushed through his veins. It wasn't real. He looked at Hermanns. "None of it's real?"

"The Neiothen are very real." The German's vehemence seemed to carry a warning. "Never forget that. ArC took something that could have been good and perverted it. They intended to ruin your lives, but nobody can hide from God. He foresaw this and sent help."

The Book of the Wars. The paneled painting.

"And that's your justification?" Leif wanted to hurt someone. "Force-feeding us lies, sending us back to our homes with busted brains and backgrounds? Did you really think it'd work?"

"It did work!" Hermanns said with a laugh, but then he shook his head. "And this wasn't my idea. When I was able to decipher Katrin's works, when I found the first leaf, then the book, my next mission was to free those of you who'd innocently volunteered. Netherwood should *never* have looked like this!"

"But it does," Leif said, stepping back, a torrent tremoring beneath his skin. "You're good at keeping lies and being at peace with that. What else are you hiding? We can't finish this if we aren't playing with all the cards."

Hermanns gave him a long, appraising look. "'Learn from me, if not by my precepts, at least by my example, how dangerous is the acquirement of knowledge,'" he quoted, arching an eyebrow. "And we all know how well that turned out in Mary Shelley's story, *ja*?"

OUTSIDE STUTTGART, GERMANY

"Iliescu is blowing a major stack that you're MIA."

Phone to her ear, Iskra wiped her tears and squinted across the city from the top of the Frankfurt & Stuttgart Biologics office building. "Too bad." Her thoughts skipped back to Taissia. "She begged me not to leave her."

"Well, let's finish this so you can get her back."

"I am a terrible mother, leaving her there."

"No, don't go there," Mercy said, her voice clear despite the distance. "Sometimes the less-than-stellar option is all we have. She's out of mortal danger, and that's what matters."

"You do not understand."

"I get it. I do."

"No. I *lived* with Bogdashka. That woman seems sweet as sugar, but her sweet will rot your teeth and soul. She plays mind games, and I am afraid she will traumatize Taissia." The thought made her latte curdle in her stomach.

"Then we jump on this so she doesn't have time to do that. And trust me, I can relate."

Iskra hunched her shoulders, kicking the low brick wall that formed the terrace of the roof. "She was so upset."

"She'll be okay."

"You do not understand—"

"Stop saying that!" Mercy hissed. "I do. I *do* understand."

"How could you possibly? You had a good life—"

"Stop right there, Ororo Munroe. You have no idea what life I had before we met."

Startled by her friend's sharp tone, Iskra hesitated.

"My parents were married to their careers, so our home was literally at their lab. When they died, a partner took me in." Mercy scoffed. "No, she took *charge* of me and . . . well, she did more than care for me. She messed me up, nearly drove me to suicide. She's why I bailed. Went solo. So, trust me, I get it, and I'm going to do everything I can to bring you and your girl back together ASAP."

"I am sorry," Iskra said. "I did not know."

"No worries—nobody knows, and I wish I'd kept it that way."

Sensing her friend's regret, Iskra offered reassurance. "I am a vault."

Mercy sniffed a laugh. "Let's just do our best to keep a certain deputy director happy, because he's in a rage about you ruining his efforts to save you-know-who."

Eyeing the fountain in the square across from Frankfurt & Stuttgart, Iskra resented the director's insinuation. "Too bad. I have seen how he helps, and it is *not* helping *him*. I must do something."

"If he finds out I'm talking to you—"

"Then make sure he does not."

"Yeah, so not helping or happening. I've almost got—aha!" Mercy said. "And ping-o." She groaned loudly. "Do not tell Cell I said that, or I'll never live down using a Cell-ism. In fact, I might just dip into self-flagellation to punish myself for it." After clearing her throat, she exhaled. "Okay, yeah—looks like your patience is going to pay off."

Patience? This was determination.

"Hermanns' car is about two klicks out, seems to be headed in your general direction, so you might've been right about him going in to work."

Anticipation tightened Iskra's stomach. "Even if he is not, it is close enough for me to make a point."

"Uh, sans bullets, right?" Mercy said, her concern clear. "We agreed."

"You agreed." Iskra would do what she must to alter the course of this insanity. "Recall what I am."

"Leif's girlfriend? Super-hot Bulgarian with a twisted past?"

"You forgot the less positive aspects."

"And you can do the same. Because, hello? We need Hermanns alive."

"Why?"

"Be . . . cause . . ." Mercy drew out the last half of the word as if buying time. "He has the book, and if Leif really went off the rails and joined Andrew-who-is-Mitre, then Hermanns probably knows Leif's current location."

Point made.

"Things are messed up," Mercy said, "but we have our priorities: find Leif and get your daughter back. You can't do that if you let rage rule."

"Not rage, efficiency." Iskra stalked to the front of the rooftop and crouched, hoping to create less of an impression to passersby below. Between two structures on the other side of the road, she caught sight of Hermanns' black BMW SUV. A second later, it glided around the corner and aimed toward F&SB. "I see his vehicle."

Though Mercy's shout to wait sailed out of the speaker, Iskra ended the call, pocketed the phone, and made her way to the private stairwell. Down the steps, she hit the floor of his office and apartments. Why wasn't he staying at his estate after the fiasco in The Hague? It was more secure. More guaranteed he would stay alive. But perhaps he, too, had a lot to clean up after Veratti's bold moves.

In the main corridor, she mentally patted the knife strapped to her ankle and slipped her gun from its holster. Cradled it in a firm grip. She eased the door to a private passage open for a quick look.

Clear. Weapon at the ready, she crossed the marble, cringing at the way her shoe squeaked. She quieted her steps and slipped down the narrow corridor toward the suite.

Voices skated along the floor, distant and conversational.

Iskra strained to hear what was being said but couldn't make it out. She reached for the door handle.

"Drop it!" a voice commanded.

Iskra wheeled around, bringing her gun to bear.

Crack!

Concrete splintered, spitting shards into her face. Jerking away, she cringed and switched tactics. Hands up, she faced him. "Okay, okay."

"Drop it!" he barked again, advancing. His posture, his dark expression—and the bullet he'd already sent her way—warned he meant business.

So did she.

The door to her left opened. Iskra flinched.

Laughter bellowed into the corridor. "Iskra! Imagine my surprise."

A hand hooked her neck and drew her back against a strong chest. She hated herself for not hearing the second guard come up behind her. Sloppy. The first guard moved lightning-fast, disarming her. She possessed the training and skills to get out of this, but not without a lot of bloodshed that could injure her ultimate goal.

With a huff, she freed the tension from her limbs. "Apparently not too surprised," she said to Rutger.

"You always have to do things the hard way," he chuckled.

"You haven't seen *hard*," she growled. She may not have her gun anymore, but she still had her knife and her wits.

"If you wanted to talk, all you had to do was ask for an appointment."

"I've had enough talk."

Hands patted her ribs, waist, hips, and down her legs. Her pant leg lifted, and she was relieved of her knife. So just her wits.

"I want those back," she said.

Rutger shrugged. "What would we want with them?" He motioned her inside. "Now we can do business."

Iskra marched into the suite that was more penthouse than office. "Where is he?"

After a long, silent look, Rutger turned his attention to the room, then to the guards. "I thought you said you searched this place."

"Whole building, sir," the guard said. "It's clear."

Rutger laughed—and Iskra knew he was toying with her.

"We saw him with Mitre." She would never call her brother by the name he'd assumed. "Where are they?"

Rutger shrugged. "Not here." He pursed his lips. "Why would he be?"

"You know why!" She started forward, but a guard shifted. Awareness flared—he'd reacted very quickly. "You know what he is."

"A very skilled American operator." Rutger peered at her, his distinguished face needing some scrapes and bruises from her fists. "What else, Iskra?"

"The book—"

Another shrug. "He never returned it to me."

Frustration strangled her patience. "Enough of your games. I want to know where he is." This man was notorious for using nuance to deceive. He said Leif had never returned the book to him, but had Leif brought it back . . . and kept it? "Tell me or—"

"You are in no position to threaten me, Iskra."

Frustration depleted her energy. "Where is he, Rutger?"

"Leif is where he wants to be." He nodded to the guard. "I think Miss Todorova is done here. Kindly see her out of the building."

Iskra started. "Just tell me—is he in danger?"

"The only danger he faces is himself and the truth. And for both of those," Rutger said, "I think *you* should look closer to home—that is, if you want Leif to survive what's ticking inside him."

STUTTGART, GERMANY

Crisp and clean, the gallery smelled of light antiseptic. Dim lighting stirred tension at the base of Leif's neck as he spotted several black bulbs in the ceiling. Skirting the perimeter, he kept his head down and made his way to the back. At a desk tucked in a corner, a woman chatted on her phone, its glow illuminating her face.

Leif focused on a nearby painting, turning his back to the nearest camera.

"Hello," the woman said. "May I help you?" Now she stood in his periphery, but if he turned, he'd be recognizable through the black eye.

"Are you Anna Gottlieb?" he asked.

She blinked and smiled. "I—oh, are you Mr. Chase?"

It had seemed appropriate. "Yes."

Palms together, she pointed her hands at him. "Do you have—"

"Private, remember?" The topic of their conversation sat heavy in his messenger bag, and he'd made sure she couldn't detect it. He didn't want this exchange recorded. Most security cameras were video only, but he wasn't willing to risk it. Still, who would know he'd come here?

"This way," she said, leading him to a side office.

Head tucked, Leif followed.

"There's no camera in here, as requested," she said, opening the door to a room with black walls and furniture.

Leif closed the door, checking ceiling corners for bulbs and sprinkler heads for bugs.

"I take it this is a small piece." Ms. Gottlieb faced him with more than a little anticipation as she shoved her hands into gloves. "Where is it?"

Her near-reverent anticipation and respect for the artwork

chastised Leif for tossing it into his bag. But he'd had little time for long-term preservation—of the diptych or his life. He retrieved it from the interior pocket and handed it over.

Light bloomed in her eyes. She murmured something in German. "You were right," she said with awe, carefully turning the diptych over as if it were fragile.

Maybe it was. Leif hadn't really given it thought.

"Incredible," she whispered as she lowered herself to a chair and swiveled toward a lamp, its beam waiting in quiet repose to illuminate the past. "And he had it in a dirty, smelly bag."

Leif resisted the urge to sniff his messenger bag.

Her gloved hands rotated the diptych in several directions, allowing the lamp to trace every surface. "The wood—oak, perhaps teak—is in decent condition, considering its age. Marginal scuffing, despite rough handling." She unfolded it. "Exquisite."

Leif leaned in as if he hadn't already studied the piece for endless waking hours, not to mention the times it haunted his dreams.

"Paint is oil, and age is evident in minor cracks, which isn't surprising, considering the lack of care," she muttered.

He got it—she wanted him to feel guilty about his treatment of the artwork. But his concern lay more in its meaning and less in its age. Besides, the way she talked about the piece was like a coroner dictating the findings of an autopsy. "You aren't recording this, are you?"

Ms. Gottlieb started, then looked up as if she'd forgotten he was there. She blinked. "Oh. No." Pink stained her cheeks. "Sorry—it is just . . . do you realize—?"

"Can you tell me what the different scenes represent?"

Irritation pinched her eyes. "Well, the style is reminiscent of Hieronymus Bosch, but did he paint it?" She lifted a thin shoulder and pursed her lips. "That would be impossible to say definitively without lab testing."

"No. I just want to understand the—"

"What you don't get—"

"—meanings."

"—is that if . . . *if* this is a Bosch, then it's worth millions." Her face was flushed with excitement. "I mean, this *could* be his work. Bosch was known for working on oak, and this . . ." Again she turned it over, her gloved fingers lightly touching the surface. "He was also very well-known for his religious concepts and narratives, which were fantastic, if not macabre." A glare glanced off the left panel as she angled it steeply. "Like this scene on the lower right of what we'll call Panel A," she said, pointing to it. "It sort of mirrors his depictions of hell, except instead of hell, the key figure in this piece is at a lake with a friend. The clouds around them have macabre images, too—this one might be a demon sitting on the shoulder of this person. And here, the bloody image and the contorted face of the individual in this cloud."

"It's twisted, dark."

"That's because unlike many works related to hell and the underworld, Bosch's work made the souls in the paintings suffer psychological distress. They are driven mad by fear, chaos, anxiety. . . ."

Leif could relate.

"And in this painting, I think betrayal is also a key factor in the soul's demise."

"Betrayal?"

"Mm-hmm." She swung a magnifying glass over the panel. "Look at what's eating the dead man. Birds." She looked up over her shoulder at him. "Classic Dutch symbol of friendship."

An anchor dropped in Leif's gut, forbidding him from

moving on. Betrayal. Friend. He'd walked out on Reaper. And it was right here in the painting. "What else?" Desperation prompted him to ask, needing something other than his own prophetic betrayal.

"Well, I can give thoughts on the scenes, but interpretation is subjective, you understand." When he nodded, she refocused on the diptych. "The upper depiction on Panel B with the nine men—"

"Eight," Leif corrected. "This man and this one are the same."

"They aren't," she argued. "Look at the noses and hair—one is clearly longer than the other."

"His paintbrush slipped." *Weak*, he chided himself.

She huffed. "Scene one of Panel B"—she pointed to the uppermost section on the right side with a helmeted rider—"has three separate depictions within its sphere. The horseman goes from trampling a king to pointing to this long line of men, probably soldiers or warriors."

"Warriors?"

Ms. Gottlieb nodded. "Tall, muscled, carrying spears, following this man with a robe. Then the final scene shows this horseman walking among the clouds with a queen. Which means he probably died."

Leif's heart twitched. "Come again?"

"The columns, the clouds—classic utopian depictions of the afterlife."

He was beginning to wish he hadn't come. This final war didn't seem to have a happy ending. "And the last one, with the woman?"

"Yes, that's . . . interesting. The woman is the same in each scene, so I think this mirrors the horseman's timeline. Here, she's holding the man's hand, then another woman's, and finally, she's holding the man's body." Anna bounced her head from side to side. "*Ja*, that makes me more convinced that his final scene is the afterlife, where she is holding his dead body."

So, basically, he was screwed. No matter what he did, he would end up dead.

"But I'm not convinced this is Bosch."

"Yeah, same." He didn't care. And the less worth she assigned to the panels the better. It was time to bug out. He couldn't take any more bad news. Not today.

She let out a thick breath and sagged.

Fine. He'd bite. "Why?"

"Well," she said, her enthusiasm suddenly waning, "if you consider his most well-known work, *The Garden of Earthly Delights* . . ." She set down the diptych and tugged out her phone, pulling up the image of the painting. "You see that despite being broken into *three* panels—a triptych—the painting has many scenes. If you think of them in rows, they form a three-by-three grid, and overall, it creates one large picture. See?"

Leif nodded, having no idea what her point was. He glanced between the image on the phone and the diptych. "So this is a smaller, different variant."

Ms. Gottlieb huffed a laugh. "No. Look at it," she said, as if talking to a child.

Wasn't that what he'd been doing for the last hour?

"Your panels have no overall picture," she said, tapping the diptych, then snagging her phone. She motioned in a circle around the screen. "Each of the scenes of the *Garden* painting creates a big scene—a big picture, if you will." She tapped the diptych. "This . . . it's either not a Bosch, or it's—" She sat up, lifting the diptych and examining it. Suddenly, a vibrancy once more infused her eyes.

Which drew Leif in. "What?"

"This . . ." She laughed. "Look!" She angled it toward him.

"The left panel—you can just see the edges of a tree and a hand."

"Maybe he just didn't paint the whole tree."

She scoffed. "I am surprised you missed this. Look at the sides of the oak on Panel A—there are holes."

"I thought it was just old."

"No, they match the hinge marks between Panel A and B, which—if I am correct . . ." She grinned at him. "There's another panel. I am sure. What I have called Panel A is most likely Panel B, and Panel B is actually Panel C. The first one is missing." She promptly deflated. "Which means this is worthless."

No, it meant Rutger was holding out on him again.

"Well, thanks for your help." Leif took it back and pulled open his messenger bag.

"Wait!" she shrieked, holding out both hands to stop him. She gave him a shaky smile and rose. "Just wait right here. I want to get something for you to protect the panels."

"Oh, that's not—"

"It absolutely is. I insist." She left and returned a minute later with a black velvet pouch, which she tucked the panels into before placing them in a plastic protector with a zipper closure. "There."

"Thanks." Head down, he started for the front door, sliding the pouch into his bag.

"If you find that missing panel, let me know. I might be interested."

You and me both. He waved as he pushed open the door.

Mind leaden with her interpretations and the revelation of more, he crossed the street and aimed back toward the warehouse district. Should he be in awe or daunted that someone had prophesied—and painted!—his betrayal and death? A deep conviction, but it too closely paralleled his life right now not to be prophetic.

So . . . was this God warning him he was going to die?

What kind of revelation was that? Didn't everyone die?

"Leif!"

Jolted out of his thoughts, he glanced back as the voice struggled through his cluttered mind. Then he saw who it was and broke into a run.

TEN

Iskra groaned when he started running. "Leif!" With his advanced abilities, she was unlikely to catch him or maintain pursuit long enough to catch up. But she was not going to give up easily. He should know that.

Sprinting, she marveled at the timing—no sooner had she been kicked out of Frankfurt & Stuttgart Biologics than she had crossed the street and spotted Leif rounding the corner. She avoided a collision with a café chair tumbling at her— one of his diversions.

Curse him for being so athletic and so . . . Neiothen. She navigated a thick restaurant crowd, struggling not to lose sight of that blond head. A man stepped from the crowd— right into her path.

Cringing, Iskra shoved him away. Which diverted her. Allowed Leif to slip from view.

Where had he gone? She slowed, searching the area. Hating the cobbled road that threatened to wrench her ankle. Scanning faces left her with a sick feeling. She turned a circle. Where was he? Only strangers stared back.

No . . .

"Hey!" someone complained straight ahead.

Iskra's gaze homed in on the athletic form bobbing around a building.

Gotcha. Darting that way, she knew rounding a corner presented a perfect opportunity to be attacked. But she was counting on Leif being more desperate to evade rather than confront. She crossed the road.

A horn blared.

Too late, she saw the car but could not avoid the collision. The bumper thumped her hip and knocked her sideways. Pain rocked through her, and Iskra stumbled. Tripped but staggered up. Took a second to catch her breath, reassure herself she still had both legs. She offered apologies over the driver's curses and obscene gestures.

She moved out of the way, hobbling around the fountain, ignoring the people gaping as she hurried toward the corner—and stopped short. Pale eyes stared back. So did the muzzle of his weapon. Would he really shoot her? She lifted her hands slowly, this scenario reminding her of Greece. Of staring at the handsome stranger through the decontamination chamber door.

Iskra limped closer, slipping into the shadows of the buildings that formed the alley in which he stood.

"Far enough," he growled.

"Leif—"

"Pretty stupid, following me and nearly getting yourself killed. Who'd take care of Taissia?"

His words stopped her. He was . . . *concerned*? "I wasn't sure you cared."

His expression went hard as he adjusted the messenger bag slung across his chest. "Stop following me."

"I wish I could." Her heart raced, recalling what had been in that bag the last time she had seen it.

"You know what I am, what I can do. You can't keep up."

So why was he standing here talking? She took another step, knowing she needed to distract him. "I'll never stop trying." Mentally, she reached for the knife in her leg holster. Could she get it in time? The knife was necessary to take the satchel. "It's what we do for those we love."

"The man you loved is gone."

He would think she had betrayed him if she took the bag. And they would relive their standoff at the Pearl of the Antilles all over again. "He's standing right in front of me."

Leif's gaze skipped to something behind her.

She seized his distraction and lunged. But he did the same, his weapon still aimed in her direction. They collided and went to the ground amid the report of his gun.

Terrified that he had tried to shoot her, she bucked and kicked, using that to keep him busy while she extricated her knife.

"Keep still!" he hissed.

She brought up her blade.

Gunfire cracked close to her head and froze her for a second, stunned. Her heart pounded. Told her to get away before his bullet found its mark in her chest or head.

She gripped the canvas strap of the messenger bag in one hand and ripped the serrated edge through it. It freed, and she shoved him with all she was worth. Rolled to her right. Came up. Scrambled out of the alley. She took a breath, then shot across the square to the other side of the fountain. Brick and mortar spat at her. She cringed and pulled in tighter. Searched for an exit.

"Iskra! Stop!"

Ahead, she saw her course—a table, a car, an alley. In a zigzag, she could make it, even with an aching hip.

"I don't want you to get hurt," Leif barked from the far side.

Startled at the drastic change in him, she knew there could be no arguing it now. That he had shot at her . . .

She launched toward the table. Heard the crack of the gun—which had people screaming and running—almost simultaneous with the cobbled path spitting chunks up at her. In tears, she dove behind a stand and scooted, breathing quick and panicked. Yet focused. She couldn't stay here for long. Bullets could go right through this cover. Breathing around the ache in her hip, she pitched herself at the small blue Fiat and tumbled around the grill, feeling the thump of the book in the bag as she hugged it close.

Gunfire echoed in the square.

It was then she heard it—not just one shooter, but two.

Which meant he was distracted again. Bolting for the alley, she prayed she didn't feel fire shoot down her back—or worse, face-plant because of a mortal wound. The shadows yanked her into their cool embrace. Stumbling backward and hugging his satchel, she peered back toward the fountain. Toward the continuing report of gunfire.

Leif crouched behind a vehicle, firing around the front. What was he . . . oh no. Her pulse spasmed when she spotted not one, but two men targeting Leif. He was in a fight for his life. Alone.

Her stomach plummeted as she recognized one of the men—he had been with Veratti. Was he an ArC operative?

A terrible epiphany struck—Leif had not been shooting at *her*. He had been protecting her. And she had betrayed him.

TYSON'S CORNER, VIRGINIA

If Jessica Cruz, a Green Lantern, could confront her anxiety and leave her apartment . . . then Mercy Maddox could face this. Even Cruz-conquer it. Granted, Jessica's anxiety didn't vanish in one fell swoop. But at least she'd faced it.

Let's do this.

Mercy squared her shoulders and left the bathroom stall. As she passed the sinks, she caught her reflection in the mirrors. It slowed her. Beach waves framed her face—not too sexy, but gone were the everyday ponytail and snark.

Well, maybe not the snark. That couldn't be extracted, even

with gene splicing. She'd chosen the navy blouse for modesty and touch of feminine flounce along the neckline. Her slacks cast a more casual and conservative tone than flirty flare. She was sure her nerves were as evident as . . . as . . .

Gripping the door handle, Mercy froze, a strange trill running down her spine. What kind of omen was it that she couldn't even come up with a Marvel analogy for this moment?

A bad one. A very bad one.

Maybe she should leave. Go to the bunker. Because . . . Iskra. It had been ten minutes, and she hadn't messaged back. What if something had gone wrong? After all, someone had blocked Mercy from piggybacking satellite feeds to help her friend.

Yes. Go back to the bunker.

Ugh! To do that, she'd have to leave the restroom. Which would mean walking right past . . . him. Those puppy-dog-brown eyes would go on full assault against her weak self, flaying her with his hurt. Disappointment.

"You're being stupid," she hissed to herself, yanked open the door, and stalked to the table. Planted herself in the chair.

That ever-assessing gaze slid over her. "You are okay?"

"Yes, I'm fine." It was her own personal reminder. Because this was a good thing. Being here. On a date. With a handsome former Afghan commando who had a ready smile and stalwart attraction.

She liked Baddar. A lot. But in so many ways, he was just too . . . perfect. And she was too flawed.

His smile wavered, and Mercy hated herself for it. Because it was her fault.

"It's hard to relax," she said, then chastised herself for going there, for opening up to a man who would probably think she was a head case. "Ya know, when we should be looking for Leif." That sounded legit, right?

His smile slipped. "He would not want us to starve, yes?"

Mercy lowered her head. Nodded. She was terrible at this. She'd never gone through the hoops, so to speak. Her romances had always been with guys she'd worked with, and things had just . . . happened. There wasn't any of this introvert-annihilating small talk.

"You are quiet."

Mercy glanced up, only then realizing she'd been staring at her plate since she sat down . . . however long ago that had been. "Sorry."

"If you did not want to come, you could say no."

Heart in her throat, she reached across the table and placed her hand on his where it rested beside his utensils. "I'm sorry. It's not you—and I *did* want to come."

"Did."

Mercy swallowed. Drew back. Fisted both hands in her lap. "Look, Baddar." She met his gaze and saw what she'd dreaded—hurt in those dark beautiful eyes. "I'm not good at this . . . dating. It's awkward, like some cruel ritual people force themselves to go through as they chase happily-ever-after dreams. Me? I just want to skip to the end." And that would be marriage. "I mean—not the end-end, but . . ." Huffing, she blew out a breath. "I only mean, I know you like me. And you know I like you."

"You do?"

"Of course I do. We're friends." The dreams she had just shattered by using the "F word" on their first official date.

The thing was, Baddar Amir Nawabi was a lot of man, a powerful man with a powerful presence. The idea of him swallowed her up. And she had no idea what to do with that. When he found out who she was, who she really was . . .

She lifted her fork, telling herself to just chill and eat. But her fork froze over the mashed potatoes.

What if she lost Baddar the way she had lost Ram?

Lost, because she had him. Didn't she? If she wanted

him. And she did—well, not like that, not now, because . . .
morals and all.

But this gorgeous man was every bit the warrior like Ram.
And that was terrifying—seeing the way he'd fought in that
stairwell. The fury and violence of him drew such a dichotomy
to the quiet, mild-mannered commando sitting so awkwardly
in this high-end restaurant. They should be back at her place
eating pizza.

His large, callused hand closed over hers. Warm, comfort-
ing, strong.

Mercy swallowed and met his gaze, hating that she'd put
the wounded-dog look into his expression.

"Friend." His word was quiet but true. "I am glad for that.
For now."

As he said the words, Mercy realized how wrong she'd
been. He wasn't just a friend to her. And she didn't want things
to stop there.

"For now," she agreed, then added, "but not forever."

Holy Human Torch, his face lit up with hope and unreal-
ized dreams.

ELEVEN

"This is all we have after three weeks of looking for him." Alene Braun sighed, glancing at the stills of Leif at the airstrip with Andreas Krestyanov.

"He is the best," Dru said, "which is why we recruited him to the team."

"He got recruited because you knew he was connected to the Neiothen." Her accusation was a shot across the bow and a warning to be straightforward.

"No." How had she figured out that he'd known?

Braun barked a laugh. "Please. I've known you too long and seen you in situations most of these newbs couldn't imagine."

He had to give some truth to get her to back off. "Okay, yes—I knew something happened to Leif when he came off that mountain. But I also felt the puzzle pieces he laid out were too neat and too . . ." How could he phrase this? "Like I was assembling a thousand-piece puzzle, and in my hand I had the right shape for the final piece that would pull it all together—answer all the questions—and it fit, yet it didn't. The image on it didn't match the rest. Right size and shape, but wrong picture. What he told me? It fits, makes the time-line work, yet . . . it doesn't."

"So you knew something was up." Braun sniffed, more than a little offense in her tone. "How? How did you know he was—"

"I didn't know," he said, too aware this could bite him in

109

the rear. "But there were facts that I tried to chase, and every time I did, I got warned off or shut down. It was getting obvious and obviously dangerous."

"The intel you *do* have?" She pointed toward the hub, where Reaper sat, heads and spirits down. "You need to read them—and me—in on it."

"No way. Too dangerous."

"For whom?" Alene said with a hefty dose of venom. "Their team leader is MIA, gone rogue by all accounts. Yet you sit there spitting out a narrative contrary to what we're seeing and experiencing. How do you reconcile that?"

"Because I'm *protecting* Leif." He stood, unwilling to be questioned by someone who didn't have all the facts.

"Read them in. I mean it—or I will."

"You don't even know—"

"Exactly. Bad intel or accurate intel—your choice." She glowered at him for several long moments as the silence thickened between them. "It's clear you know why he went to ground. They need to know, too." Her lips thinned. "*I* need to know."

This was a ticking bomb. No, it was worse—it had a megaton blast yield once opened. He'd avoided that for the last four years. Haphazardly opening it now would guarantee death.

"I'll give you twenty-four hours to inform them and figure something out," Alene warned. "Because in forty-eight, I'm going up the chain with it."

"Do that, and Leif has zero chance of staying alive."

"How am I to know you're not the one behind him going MIA? What if he's been under ArC's control this whole time, and you—"

"That's not true."

"How am I to know that? How do *you* know? Look at Ibn Sarsour and Kurofuji! They had no idea they were sleepers

110

until they were putting holes in heads. You cannot guarantee Leif isn't the same, that the young man who led Reaper, who had access to our systems, people, and weapons, won't come in here and decimate everything."

"He wouldn't do that."

"You can't know that!" she roared. With a fat exhale, she shook her head, nostrils flaring, before coming to her feet and tapping his desk. "Forty-eight and it goes topside."

"You'll regret this. I promise you."

At his office door, she stared over her shoulder. "Careful, Dru. That sounds like a threat."

He watched her leave, cross the hub, and enter her office. A couple of heads swiveled his way, including Cell's. Dru had no time or patience to expend on them. Not right now. He packed his attaché case and strode out of the bunker, ignoring the call of his name.

Leif had really messed this up by going to ground. Running.

Yeah, he was running all right—but not *from* trouble. He was sprinting headlong *into* it. Eyes wide open. Stubborn, defiant spirit embracing whatever danger presented itself. Was that one of the Netherwood alterations to his psyche, or did he come by it naturally? His brother Canyon hadn't been much different.

Up the concrete tunnel and into the parking garage, he wondered how to nail this down. Get Leif to come back. If that...

Too late. Alene had called him out and wouldn't back down until she was satisfied. He yanked open his car door and stuffed himself inside. Hit the steering wheel. After a huff, he raked a hand over his face and hair. After placing an online order for sweet and sour chicken and chow mein to arrive shortly after he did, Dru started the car and headed out. Chinese food didn't fit with his health regimen, but neither did this stress-inducing fiasco.

At home, he let himself in, punched in his security alarm code, then headed into the kitchen. He retrieved the mail from the counter where his housekeeper had left it. Rifling through the envelopes, he heard a car rattle up the drive. The fifteen-year-old Camry belonged to Dustin, a college student trying to make ends meet while he earned his degree.

Dru's stomach growled as he dumped the junk mail in the recycle bin and glanced out the window. The delivery guy climbed out of the car.

Dru lifted a hand to wave . . . then saw his face. Before he was seen, he jerked out of view and palmed his weapon. That wasn't Dustin, but he had the kid's car. It could've been borrowed. Was Dustin busy at the restaurant?

On his phone, Dru dialed, telling himself he was overreacting. But after that conversation with Braun, talking openly about Leif and the Neiothen . . .

No, it couldn't be.

When the line picked up, he lowered his voice. "Hey, is Dustin in today?"

"Dustin no here—do delivery. Be back soon."

Well, crap. "Thanks." If Dustin was doing delivery—then he'd have his car. And this guy buzzing the doorbell must've intercepted him between here and Ming Wok.

Likely, Dustin was dead. If Dru wasn't careful, he would be, too.

The bell rang again.

He angled his head so his voice sounded more distant. "Who is it?"

"Delivery from Ming Wok," the man announced through the opaque door. He could have a gun under the carton he held.

An assassin would need to make sure his mark was dead, which meant coming inside, one way or another. Dru could just shoot him through the door. But what if Dustin had switched routes or cars with another driver for some reason? He could see the headlines: *Deputy Director of Operations Kills Chinese Takeout Delivery Guy.*

Better to get him on his own turf, familiar ground.

Weapon tucked at the small of his back, Dru opened the door. "Hey."

Midthirties, clean cut. Though the guy tried to act all chill, Dru was trained to see things others missed—like the tension roiling through his shoulders. The way his gray eyes reconned the living and dining rooms in the space of two seconds, likely to verify Dru was alone.

This guy was here to deliver—but not chow mein.

Dru reached toward his back pocket. "Oh shoot. Left my wallet in the kitchen." Deliberately, he stepped back, holding the door as a barrier. "C'mon in. I'll grab the money." He kept his hands loose and his stance ready.

"Yeah." The guy shrugged. "Sure." He stepped inside with the takeout boxes and a drink Dru hadn't ordered. The lid of it wasn't on correctly.

No sooner had Dru detected that than the drink sluiced out—right into his face. Eyes clenched, he dove at the man's gut. They collided against the wall, sweet and sour chicken splattering across the room and floor, making traction impossible.

The assassin twisted and hooked Dru's neck.

Realizing the inherent danger, Dru dropped to his knees with a yank, swiping the guy's legs out from under him at the same time. He felt the assassin's momentum flip backward.

They went down. Laid out, his own arm now around his assailant's neck, Dru held him in a scissor hold. The attacker thrashed, noodles working against the restraint. Letting this man up meant death. And that wasn't going to work.

A foot snapped upward, nailing Dru in the face. His teeth clacked and pain reverberated down his spine. He had enough training not to release the assassin, who was throwing punches, doing all he could to free himself. Dru just had to hold on, keep him deprived of oxygen until he was unconscious. Temptation screamed to make that permanent, but he needed to know who had sent him. And most importantly—was this connected to Leif?

TWELVE

REAPER HEADQUARTERS, MARYLAND

The spit was hitting the fan and a little too close to home. Cell folded his arms, noting the ominous cloud hanging over the hub as four Marines in tac gear escorted a chained, hooded prisoner down the access corridor to the brig. Director Iliescu brought up the rear, his cheek swollen and split. Blood and something else stained his shirt.

It bothered Cell in strange ways to see the director, who was fastidious about his appearance, unkempt. Or maybe it was his haunted look.

Reaper grouped up as he came toward them.

"Are you okay?" Mercy moved closer with a limping Baddar.

Iliescu nodded, slowing, though his gaze tracked the security detail.

"Braun said you were attacked in your home," Culver prompted.

"Posed as a delivery guy, but he was driving the car of the college kid who normally delivers. Had I not recognized the car, he might've gotten the drop on me."

"By your face," Culver noted, "he dropped *something* on you."

"My skull is thick."

"I'm surprised he didn't use a suppressed weapon through the door," Culver said, processing the incident.

"He likely had to confirm the kill. After I secured him, he

wouldn't talk and had no ID or phone to identify him with."
Dru huffed. "He's a professional. I want to know who sent him."

"Maybe they can get it out of him." Saito had a lot of insinuation in those words.

"Bringing him down here . . ." Culver said, squinting. "That
means you're keeping this off the books."

Iliescu bobbed his head. "For now."

There was something a little off about that. And by a little, Cell meant colossally. Holding a man who'd attacked the
deputy director of operations of the CIA in a belowground
bunker that technically didn't exist . . .

"Couldn't you get more intel with prints and blood?" Mercy
asked.

"Already on it," Iliescu said, a distance in his gaze. "But if
he's who I think he is, then that won't get us anywhere."

One thing Cell always admired about the director was that
he had it together. Even after being roughed up by an assassin, he still held that confidence, the air of a man in charge.

Except . . . something was . . . missing. Off.

The director patted Culver's shoulder as he looked at the
team. "Dig hard and fast. We need to find Leif before they do."

Culver crossed his arms. "You think this is connected to
Runt? How?"

"The noose is tightening—they came after me, I guess,
because I'm getting too close. Or, like us, they can't find him
and thought tossing my place and me would net intel. And
I'm getting pressure from all sides." The director's gaze hit
Braun, who was emerging from her office with an ashen expression. "Let's find him—and that book. Maybe it'll tell us
how to write a happy ending."

Cell watched Iliescu leave. Why hadn't he told the others
what he knew about Leif? Why not come clean? Because Cell
knew what little he'd unearthed was the sun-glistening tip
of the proverbial iceberg.

"Cell." Culver planted his backside on the hub table. "What can we find out about Veratti?"

"Besides the fact he is controlling the Neiothen, and therefore a very real threat to my ability to breathe and exist?" Cell's mind ricocheted off the video of Leif buddying up with that long-legged psycho Andrew.

"What if we've been going about this wrong?"

"Well, obviously we have, because we have exactly zilch." Cell pointed to his office. "I'm digging into Hermanns, trying to find something that leads to Leif."

"Right, but why Hermanns?" Culver prodded. "He's not the head of the serpent—that's Veratti."

"Which means if we go after *him*, we end up dead or dispatched to some black hole in Area 51 by whomever in the American government he's bought."

"You don't seem interested in finding answers."

"I'm *interested* in not ending up six feet under. I'm *interested* in figuring out what Hermanns had that made Leif go all Anakin Skywalker on us."

"Why are you so petrified of Veratti?" Saito asked. "He's not the first in the Most Wanted deck we've gone after."

"But he *is* the first one incredibly adept at making enemies"— Cell patted his chest in frantic emphasis—"disappear or turn up dead. I do not want my face on *his* deck of cards." Shrugging didn't dislodge the ten-ton boulder attached to his shoulders. "And he turned a new Leif, if you get my badly placed pun. Now . . . I have things to do."

He paused. Considered the team and the expressions that read like coding right off his own motherboard. With a sigh, he returned to his desk. Shoved both hands up over his head and tried to bury the guilt that seemed hot-wired into this entire Book of the Wars mission.

Getting over Leif choke-holding him was harder than he'd imagined. It was a technique they'd all been taught and had used in combat. But to have the arm of a friend slip around his neck . . . to know what was happening . . . nothing compared to stepping from suspicion into confirmation that Leif had turned against them.

Cell drew in a long breath, taking in his workstation. The trails that led nowhere. He clicked the tab on the biologics company Hermanns owned, the one whose system Iskra and Mercy had broken into. Headquartered in Germany, Frankfurt & Stuttgart Biologics had a subsidiary office in New York and other offices in France and London. Doing well, turning a profit, nothing mind-blowing or nefarious. He'd already gone through its records and reviewed analysts' reports from within the CIA as well as the CDC, since F&SB dealt in the biological. He'd even re-reviewed the files from that gallery in France where Iskra had the run-in with Andrew. He double-checked those files, but this time the second listing on page fourteen—Alisz Vogt—nagged at him.

A German. Hermanns was German. But so were a lot of people working for him in his *German* company.

Yeah, so move on, numbskull.

But he couldn't. Especially with the way his luck ran these days. Listed as a consultant, Alisz Vogt received regular payments from the gallery in France. A German in France. Not terribly unusual. But when he saw the amount deposited each month, Cell started considering a change of profession.

There was something about her. What? What what what?

Gritting his teeth, he searched backward through the company's locations, thinking maybe some nugget would stand out that previously hadn't. It was a desperate thought, but sometimes desperate worked. Two hours on London and still nothing. He hit France—he'd love to be there. Anywhere away from this place and this nightmare.

Hours later, his phone rang, and he let out a low moan

118

of frustration. Why wouldn't they just leave him alone? He grabbed his phone. "What?"

"Um," came a soft, sweet voice, "I think you were looking for me."

Cell frowned, glancing at the caller ID too late. "Who is this?" He softened his tone, because hers had been more matter-of-fact than threatening.

"Why are you looking into me?"

"If you want me to answer that, you have to tell me who you are." But his hand had already moved the mouse over the tab, and his gaze rested on a name. No way.

"Alisz."

His heart tripped. Trusting his self-installed program would track her call, he swallowed. Tried not to freak. *Sound calm. Natural. Like you know what you're doing. And how she freaking found you.* "This is a surprise." Considering he hadn't told anyone he was looking for Alisz Vogt nor tried to contact her. "How can I help you?"

"What makes you think I need your help?"

"Well, since you knew I was searching for you, I don't think you do," he said with a nervous laugh. "But you haven't threatened me yet, so that leaves a guy wondering."

"I think we can help each other, Mr. Purcell."

Cold splashed through his stomach. How had she gotten his name? His gaze sprinted over the open tabs, wondering which one had given her—"The gallery."

Her laughter was light, infectious. "See? I knew we would make a great team. Can we meet?"

Not if he wanted to live. "Yeah, I don't think that's smart."

Another twitter carried through the connection—a breathed laugh. As if she knew who had the winning hand. "Like you said, I haven't threatened you, so there's nothing to fear from me."

"I would have to disagree."

"But *you* found me, and I don't assume you're out to kill me."

"Maybe you should." He cringed at his asinine comment. What was wrong with him? *Hang up, you idiot!* "I mean, we have no trust—we don't know each other." *Right. Trust—she backtraced your search somehow, and you want to talk* trust?

"Oh, but I do trust you, Barclay."

Hearing his first name was a mallet upside his stupid head—sounding a dozen different alarms. "Why?" Why had she initiated contact? Why hadn't he hung up yet? His gaze struck the narrow window in his office door, and he made sure nobody was watching or listening.

"Meet me. We'll talk."

His stomach seized. Meeting was a majorly bad idea. "Okay." He smacked his forehead.

"Wonderful. I'll text you the location and time," Alisz said, sounding pleased. "Good-bye, Barclay."

"Yeah. See you . . . Alisz." He lowered the phone and pressed the red icon to end the call. Stared at it, disbelieving. *What* had he just done?

"Alisz?"

Cell jerked toward the door—which now stood open. "What?" How much had Mercy heard?

Her brown eyes were rich with suspicion. "Alisz who?"

"Just this person . . . a woman"—*no duh, Sherlock*—"I had been . . ." Why did he feel the need to hide? No, he wouldn't start doing that, not like Leif. "She's a consultant who works for Hermanns."

Mercy's gaze narrowed. "Consultant." Thick tension pinged between them like a tennis match, and he didn't know what it was about.

"Art consultant." He didn't know that for sure. But it was a decent guess, considering she worked at a gallery. Why was Mercy so . . . uptight?

She smirked. "Didn't think you'd replace me so quickly, Barc."

"Never." Though he grinned, he was irritated, because it was Mercy who had said it wouldn't work between them. Not to mention the whole thing with her and Baddar. "You replaced me," he said with a shrug. "Several times."

She scoff-laughed, leaving the office and calling over her shoulder, "Oh, Barc. You could never be replaced."

He let out the breath trapped in his throat. Irritation rolled across his shoulders, and he wondered why he felt like he'd done something wrong. Not with Mercy. With Alisz. Was he walking into the den of a Black Widow?

STUTTGART, GERMANY

Leif sat on the edge of the bed, cradling the Ruger between his palms. Eyes closed, he relived that confrontation with Iskra over and over. Seeing her had sent him into a mental tailspin. Like a chopper that lost rotor control, he was about to crash and burn. Having to run from her, yell at her to leave him alone, get away. Then her getting caught in the crossfire with the Gen2s. A bus had rumbled past the fountain, allowing Leif to drop down a manhole and avoid being turned into roadkill.

He glanced at the still-healing wound in his bicep where he'd taken a bullet before escaping those demons.

Why? Why had Iskra come? Of all people, he'd expected her to understand. But she hadn't. Instead, she'd stolen his satchel, absconding with the book and panels.

He pressed the top of the slide against his forehead, the steel cold against his skin. He'd known walking away in Taipei could irreparably damage their relationship, but after their encounter in the square, they probably didn't have one. He'd wanted a life with her. That was the whole point of what he'd done—to end this nightmare so they could have a peaceful

Soul Raging

existence. But the look in her eyes said she didn't understand. She wanted him to come back, to be who he was before.

Like he told her—that man was done. And he wasn't going to let people feed him lies for breakfast, lunch, and dinner. While he wasn't sure who he was right now, he knew one thing: he didn't want to be a pawn—not for anyone. Not Dru. Not Veratti, ArC, or its henchmen. Yet he felt like he'd walked right into that exact situation with Hermanns. No, he'd charged headlong. Right into a den of vipers. This nightmare was his own doing.

Iskra's look . . . she really thought he'd shoot her. That wrecked him.

Maybe there was an easy solution to . . . everything. He slid his finger into the trigger well. Firmed his grip. Lifted the gun, aiming the muzzle into his mouth.

His phone buzzed.

He ignored it, not wanting to end it all, but feeling no other option existed. This ... this would be best. For all.

The phone buzzed again with another call.

He just wanted to be left alone. End the tether ArC had on him.

A series of beeps—a text this time.

Then another buzz. If he hadn't put scrambling software on his phone, he'd have ditched it long ago. He suddenly wished he'd tossed it in Taipei.

Groaning, he lowered the Ruger. Puffed out a breath. Glanced at the screen.

I know you're there. Pick up. Metcalfe up, pup.

At his brother's taunt, he nearly smiled. Canyon always had to be the one to butt in, tell him what to do. His brother's life hadn't been pristine, but he'd always been direct. But he couldn't fix Leif's problem. Not this time.

You know what you're doing is wrong.

Classic Canyon bait. Antagonize to force the person to engage.

Tell me how to explain this to Mom.

Low blow, using their mother. But this was no different than any other op their mother wouldn't be told about, so again—not working.

You're an operator, so you know I'm blowing smoke.

Leif sniffed a laugh.

Give me something, man, or I'm coming after you.

That wasn't smoke. That . . . that was a promise.

THIRTEEN

STUTTGART, GERMANY

Heavy guilt had driven Iskra away from the square that day when Leif vanished, apparently—hopefully—still alive after facing those shooters. Why had she been so quick to think poorly of him? Maybe because of Mitre and how ArC had broken him. Her brother had been her friend and hero, yet so callously turned from her. Why would she expect any less of Leif?

But she should have known Leif had stronger mettle. She was no better than the others, than Reaper, who surrendered their belief in him, trading it for doubt and accusation. They all thought his actions were a clear demonstration of his intent. Yet they had been wrong. So very wrong.

This reminded her of when she was a little girl and asked why God allowed bad things. Her mother had always said, "God's character does not change because we are hurt by a situation that does change."

The same was true of Leif. His character spoke of a higher road. And in the heat of the moment, in a split second of panic, she had let fear override and assume the worst.

Face in her hands, she fought tears over not giving him the benefit of the doubt. He was hurting and wanted answers. And she had stolen the one thing that held answers. Her gaze strayed to the satchel.

Her phone vibrated, startling her. She glanced at it, and her heart tripped at the text.

Give it back.

She picked up her phone and dragged the satchel across the hotel bed. Held it tight against her chest. It was her only way back to him.

> Only when you return what I want.

I told you, he's gone.

> Then you have a problem.

No reply came, and Iskra's heart treaded the chasm she had created. She couldn't leave it there.

> You trusted me, and I failed you. Let me fix that.

Minutes ticked by with only remorse for company.

> Please. Talk to me.

No more texts came, and Iskra knew she had failed Leif again. What if this was the key? By taking the book, she prevented him from getting answers. But if she handed it back, he would leave her again.

REAPER HEADQUARTERS, MARYLAND

She would not be Sharon Carter and kill the beloved Captain America at point-blank range. But maybe she could do it from across the world. And not really kill him, but maybe lojack him via the system.

But first . . . first Mercy had to resolve a nagging suspicion about Barc's newfound Alisz. Who could very well be a mega-ton pile of trouble. She didn't want to be right. Yet Barc was way too good at ignoring painful events and missing the entire lesson that should come from them. She'd been right about Mei but had only scolded him. If she was right about this one . . . well, she'd have to intervene.

Fingers dancing on the keyboard, she dug into the system. Bypassing security measures and ethical measures—moral ones, if someone wanted to be technical about it—to find the logs from Barc's phones.

The timing of this encounter couldn't be coincidental. No way Alisz had shown up on her own merit, just out of curiosity, with the entirely too gullible Barclay Purcell. And someone Mercy knew years ago had been masterful at posing as a demure Little Bo-Peep who'd lost her sheep and needed someone to help her find them. Then she'd turn into the vicious wolf that devoured everyone. This Alisz had the same bad wolf breath.

Mercy used the phone records the Agency kept to find the number Cell had been talking to. That'd been easy, but it didn't give her vital records. Thus, she kept digging. Barc found Alisz via Hermann's gallery in France . . . but that was just a name. So for Barc to find Alisz's number meant it'd been listed somewhere in a casual, I'm-not-a-serial-killer kind of way. Like maybe a student record—that had been a favorite tactic back then. Of course, at their current ages, pretending to be a student grew more difficult to substantiate. So what had Alisz—

Ah. A flat lease.

Made sense. Mercy scanned it, checked out the email address tied to the lease. The cosigner . . . she stared in disbelief at the name. Her stomach churned. No no no. This could not be happ—

A rabbit hopped across the screen.

Mercy shot backward in her chair, her heart thundering.

The rabbit went up on its hind legs and turned to face her. With a sickening laugh, it jumped toward a hole in the ground. "Off with her head!" a shrewlike voice shrieked as the rabbit slid down the bottom of the screen and disappeared.

Mashing the power button, pulse pounding, Mercy searched for her phone. She had to talk to Iskra. She spied it and—after a glance to be sure the system had powered off—she lunged for the device. Snatched it up. Dialed. It rang with lethargy. "C'mon, c'mo—"

"He's here!"

Mercy froze, her own panic temporarily stymied. "Who?"

"Leif! I tried to stop him. He was livid, shooting, and I thought he was going to kill me."

Mercy couldn't process the words. "*What?*"

"It was a mistake," Iskra breathed. "After I escaped, I glanced back. There was someone shooting at him. He"—a sob wracked the line—"he wasn't attacking me. He was *protecting* me. I thought he was trying to kill me, and I—oh, Mercy. I betrayed him. He'll hate me."

"Betrayed?" She scrambled for understanding. "You're not making sense, Iskra. How did you betray him? He left *us*, remember?"

"I stole his bag."

"What bag?" Silence struggled through the line, disconcerting Mercy. "Iskra? You there? Where's Leif now? What's going on? You need to come back."

"No," Iskra growled. "I'm not leaving until I find him and get Taissia back."

Right. Of course. "But what if he leaves Germany?"

"He won't," Iskra said, thick conviction in her voice.

"How do you know? I think we have to reconsider everything we thought about Leif after all this." Mercy could not see Leif as anyone's lapdog, nor as someone who was going to sit idly by. "I guess it makes sense that he'd stay in Germany, since Hermanns is there—"

"Rutger knew giving Leif the book would buy his soul."

Realization hit. "That's what's in the bag?" Mercy gasped, standing. "And you have it now?"

Silence gaped for several long seconds. "Is there a reason you called?" Iskra asked coolly.

"You have it," Mercy muttered. "Oh my gosh. Dru—"

"If I leave Germany, I leave him—lose him. I will not do that. Not after all he has done for me."

"But we need that book." Mercy shoved her bangs off her face. "I get it. I'm pretty tightly wound right now, too. Things here are so messed up, with Dru, the attack, and—"

"What attack?"

Mercy widened her eyes. "That's right—you weren't here. I thought they would've briefed you. Dru was attacked in his home. He brought the guy in, and they're trying to extract information from him."

"An assassin?"

"If he is, he's not very effective. I mean, Dru was busted up but alive."

"How did they find him? And why Dru, if Leif is here with Rutger?"

Right. Because if ArC's guy had Leif in his clutches, why go after Dru? "Good question, especially since Leif has the book—or had it—and Rutger has Leif. Annnd, now we have a bigger witch to fry."

"Witch? I do not understand."

"It's the reason I called you. Barc has stepped in it again, this time with someone he found through that art gallery where your brother nearly ran you down on his motor-cycle." *Slow down, Merc.* "Okay, let me back up. So I know this girl, and I'm telling you, she's a very big problem. In fact,

I wouldn't be surprised if she's got ArC on speed dial, if not hot-wired right into her skull."

"How do you know her?"

She drew in a breath. "I shared a room with her when we were with that woman I told you about who took me in after my parents' death—Mina. The things she did to us girls belong in some twisted science-fiction movie. She should be locked—no, she should be shot!" Surprise coiled through Mercy at how much venom still bubbled in her veins toward that cruel woman. "Alisz and I were her favorites. Alisz was essentially my dark side. She's . . . bad, Iskra. And I'm scared. Scared for Leif. Scared for us."

"How do you know it's the same Alisz?"

"At first, it was just a really strong hunch, but I found her coding—she always used a white rabbit. It's her. No doubt."

"Talk to Cell. He likes you. Tell him he must cut this person off."

"He won't listen."

"Give him the chance to make this right, then, regardless of what Barclay says, you need to inform the director. Everything must be done to protect Reaper and Leif right now."

Nodding, Mercy sighed. "I know you're right, but this is all so wrong. We're all betraying each other or stabbing each other in the back in one way or another. I have a bad feeling about where this will lead." She cringed, realizing how many times that had been said in Marvel comics as a harbinger. Trying to stay positive, she looked across the hub to Barc's office. And failed at the positivity. "I'll call when he's cut me out of his life."

Iskra laughed. "Give him more credit."

"You haven't dated this guy or hacked his computer. I know what his villainous side looks like."

"But *he* is good—and he trusts you."

129

"Only when I agree with him." She shrugged. "Okay, bye."

Ending the call, she drew in a long breath and exhaled slowly. There was nothing to do but *do it*. But what would she say to him? *"Don't trust Alisz, she's evil personified—she's really Mary Alice Walker, aka Typhoid Mary."*

The parallels were startlingly terrifying. Mina had often pitted Alisz against Mercy. Forced them to vie for food and clothing. Compete until they were both so desperate to eat they didn't care who they hurt. They could both fight. Both hack. That last confrontation . . . Mercy couldn't take it anymore, and Alisz had seized on her weakness. Mercy went a week without food for that mistake.

Sick to her stomach, she made her way to Barc's office and rapped on the doorjamb. Only the ticking of his keyboard responded. "Barc?"

He shifted. "Hey." His gaze swiveled between monitors.

"I need to talk to you."

"Sure." He pecked away, his gaze never lifting. "What's up?"

"Alisz."

Fingers freezing, he looked at her. "What?" The question had an edge to it, like a guillotine blade ready to chop off the objection she posed. "Don't."

"She's not—"

"It's all over your face—whatever you're about to say to warn me off." He nodded at her. "Just don't. I know what I'm doing."

"I doubt that," she said softly, easing into his office. "At least, not with regard to her. She won't help you." When he kept working, she moved closer, hating to see his trust sorely misplaced. "Alisz is a *lure*. She's trained to do this. To bait you—"

"She's got full scans of the Book of the Wars that we weren't able to secure. Also, she found video of Leif with Rutger Hermanns, one we couldn't find. A feed that gives us a starting point on locating him." He leaned back and considered her. "That's a lot more than anyone else has given us lately."

"It's all bait, Barc. Where do you think she got that intel? How did she know you'd want it?" She tapped his temple. "*Think!* Isn't it convenient that she just happened to have it?"

"Someone had to have it."

"You are not this stupid! She's a plant," Mercy growled, his calmness infuriating. "Alisz wanted you to find her because she has intel that only ArC could've provided, and they want an operative in our organization. This is what she's trained to do. To lure you in—"

"Good-bye, Mercy!" He returned to his keyboard. "It's not the first time you've called me stupid."

The truth cut deep, making her ache for her careless words. "I—"

"Why can't you believe that I might be smart enough to have actually earned this job? That I'm good at it? That I know what I'm doing?" He stood and motioned toward the hub. "I was Special Forces, too, ya know. I worked with the best of the best. I've been on two teams that saw the most evil of creatures and events. So don't tell me I'm stupid or not thinking it through. I have." He pitched his pen down on the desk. "But she's the only one giving me actionable intel, and I need it. We need it."

Mercy swallowed, feeling terrible. "You're very good . . . but you see a pretty face and lose your mind!"

"She *told* me," he said with a huff of disbelief. "She told me you'd do this."

Mercy drew back, surprised at the shadows crowding his normally lighthearted features. "What?"

"That's right. You're not the only one with knowledge about those you think are dangerous. Alisz said she knew you, that you grew up together in Germany."

Bile rose in her throat.

"Funny—that's not something *you* ever told me." He cocked his head and narrowed his eyes. "And she said you'd think she was a plant, that she was just doing this to get into my system or something."

The blood drained from her face. Alisz had told him. She'd *told* him. "Barclay . . ." Realization washed over her, as cold as the dread draping her shoulders and spilling down her back. "She's just like Typhoid Mary—"

"C'mon!" he roared, rage exploding through his features. His right arm swung and nailed the coffee mug on his desk. It flung across the room. Splashed her face with cold coffee before shattering against the wall. A shard flicked her face.

With a gasp, she jerked away.

Barc's eyes went wide. "Mercy!" He started forward.

She scrambled back—right into a solid mass that swept around her. Barricaded her. Tall, with broad shoulders. Dark wavy hair. Eyes black as night and lit with fury, Baddar held a hand toward Cell. "No. Stay there." His other arm reached toward her.

Instinctively, Mercy caught his hand and felt him nudging her backward.

She moved out of the office, rattled. Shaken. Angry. Hearing sounds, knowing Baddar spoke low and evenly to Cell before turning toward her.

His thick arm curled around her as he guided her down the corridor toward the elevator. He punched the button, and though she had no messenger bag or keys to drive herself home, she entered the steel trap. The doors slid closed.

Baddar pulled her into his arms. And she went. Willingly. Sobbing. Unable to understand what made her cry. What made her accept Baddar's comfort. But she needed both of them, desperately.

STUTTGART, GERMANY

"Guardians! It is a good name, yes? Better than this blood-lust name Neiothen," Rutger said, addressing the men gathered in the warehouse. For this talk, he'd opted for their training area, which had a more rudimentary, rigorous feel than the sanitized conference table that seemed to make them feel like cornered lab rats. "You have been through much and endured more than any person should have to. They stole from you not only your identity, but your will. Both of which you have regained. And now . . . now I return to you what you are—warriors, soldiers. The finest. The best."

The men glanced at one another in question. Leif stood to the side, arms folded over his chest. Beside him, standing in similar fashion, Andreas.

"Do you not think it time to give back what they have wreaked?" Rutger continued. These were dangerous words that could get him killed, but enough was enough.

Interest lit their expressions. All, that is, except one.

"So," Leif said, roughing a hand over his mouth and neck, "you're telling us that someone stole our identities and will from us—made us slaves to their whims. And now . . . are you having a *whim*, Hermanns?"

"I'm having *relief*, Mr. Metcalfe, because I am finally able to hand you the opportunity to strike a blow against ArC," Rutger said with a sardonic smile. "We are working to confirm the location where we believe they are genetically engineering the newer models of your kind. This is a much more advanced technology than what my Katrin designed. In this program, they care not for the protection of the soldier, only the result. Therefore, these soldiers are less human and more program."

The men shifted, agitated and anxious.

"You want us to stop these new Gen2s—the very ones we've already been told we *can't* stop?" Elvestad asked in his grating voice.

"*Nein*, this is not about me or the Gen2s. It is about you! About a chance to destroy a lab like the one that altered you. That violated your sacred trust in them to *help* you, not turn you into soulless, will-less soldiers." Indignation wove through Rutger. "Netherwood must be stopped. We have people working to tear down the infrastructure, corrupt the technology and coding, but we must also destroy the labs themselves. No stone is being left unturned against this insidious work." He had expected the men to be ready for this opportunity, but their blank expressions made him wonder if he had pushed too soon.

"What you're suggesting is lethally dangerous," Leif said. "I've seen Veratti's handiwork. I know his vengeance."

"If you did not come to stop this, then why did you come?"

"Answers. I want to know—"

"You *do* know—these are the men you trained with. The program that robbed you of six months so they could reintegrate you as sleepers."

"But how did they get that past SOCOM? Or JSOC?"

"You must ask this?" Rutger laughed. "Do you really think only foreign armies are infected with ArC agents? Do you think only"—he motioned to Ibn Sarsour—"London was infiltrated? Or perhaps only Sweden? No! They are everywhere. Just as demons can enter churches through corrupted vessels, so have these agents entered the American military and government. They hold the highest positions, and that is how ArC has managed to remain hidden and unhindered."

A vibration rumbled in his chest pocket, and Rutger drew out his phone and saw the ID. "Please," he said, glancing at the men again, particularly Leif. "I will let you talk to decide if this is what you want, *ja*? But time is precious. The longer we wait, the more Gen2 operatives you will have to go up against." He met Andreas's gaze, hoping to relay the imperative nature of convincing the others to join them. They were not trying to make them soldiers for a cause, but to end the nightmare once and for all.

He answered the call as he started toward the secure wing. "Hello, *mein alter Freund.*"

"The facility's in Durban, South Africa."

Conviction firmed in Rutger. "I am surprised you are giving me this intel."

"As am I, but hear me—I have no time to vet this, so it may not be legit. However, I'm told this camp will be gone by the end of the week."

Rutger rubbed his brow. If it was a ruse . . . "We'll see to it."

"You're hesitating."

"I am not, *nein*, but they—the men are afraid my intention is to use them as Veratti has."

"Tricky waters."

Rutger heaved a sigh. "*Ja.*" A knock on the door drew him around. "*Ein* moment," he said to his friend, then met the pale gaze of his visitor. "How can I help you?"

Leif Metcalfe glanced at the phone, hesitating. "Going up against Veratti is too dangerous. Half the men here aren't strong enough to confront anyone, let alone Gen2s. This'll get them killed. And sorry, but if I'm dead, I can't get the answers I need."

"*Ja*, it is dangerous. And those not ready are not going," Rutger agreed. "But you . . . not going against him *will* get you killed, because he will hunt you down, just as assuredly he is already hunting me." He drew himself up straight. "I have done what I can, though my actions are late in coming. No more vacillation. My affairs are in order. Should Death come for me, then I meet it with a clear conscience, knowing I have done what is in my power to stop Netherwood."

Rutger motioned to the window overlooking the gym. "See them, Mr. Metcalfe? See them training and toiling so hard to beat their situation? The Jews were taken into captivity in Babylon and toiled for hundreds of years, but there came a Babylonian king named Cyrus. He is mentioned over thirty times in the Bible."

Leif gave him a confused look, no doubt wondering where Rutger was going with this.

"In Isaiah 45, God says:

> "'Cyrus is my anointed king.
>> I take hold of his right hand.
> I give him the power
>> to bring nations under his control.
> I help him strip kings of their power
>> to go to war against him.
> I break city gates open so he can go through them.'"

Rutger smiled at the young man with such a great burden on his shoulders, a burden he never asked for. "God did not do that to elevate Cyrus, but to free His people so mankind would know He was Lord." He drew in a long breath and exhaled slowly. "Think of these men as the Jews. And you are their Cyrus."

Leif's jaw tensed, considering him. "I have no idea what that means, but I'm ready to do violence against Veratti."

"I am relieved to hear it," Rutger said earnestly. "They will need you and your leadership."

He gave a grim nod. "I'm in." After one more glance at the phone, Leif asked, "Who's that?"

Rutger flattened his expression. "No concern of yours."

Lips taut, gaze sharp, Leif left.

Rutger returned to his call. "Now . . ."

"Bet he didn't like that last line."

"It made him angry, made him more invested in what he's doing, more determined to carry it out."

"You are a cold son-of-a-gun."

"I learned from the best." Despite the other man's laugh, Rutger felt no humor. He had learned much from his friend, who had not always been friendly. "You should know that I believe he is on to me."

"Leif?"

"*Nein.*"

"Veratti."

"He was aggressive this last time we met. If I am killed, be sure you finish this. For Katrin. For Leif."

"You're overreacting."

"That is the only way I am still alive," Rutger said. "Promise me you will do it. Promise you will give him the answers."

"He'll be ticked—"

"Promise!" The chill of death raised the small hairs on the back of his neck and trekked across his shoulders.

"Fine. But I cannot promise to be as effective as you, since you're already plugged into that blasted coalition."

"There are assets around you, Dru. Find them before they destroy everything."

FOURTEEN

Buttoning the jacket of his Zegna bespoke suit, Ciro Veratti emerged from the armored SUV into the belly of the concrete facility that shielded the inhabitants and personnel from the unrelenting fury of the South African sun. Several industrial fans groaned in their struggle against the inhumane temperatures.

A sniveling man rushed toward him, his sweat-thickened mop clumping into his eyes as he inclined his head and stretched out his hand. "Mr. Ver—"

Ivo and Ettore swept in front of the man, cutting him off.

Ciro had seen this face numerous times—Cecil Bordeur, the director of scientific operations at the southern facility. And he liked him no more now than he did with thousands of miles and technology separating them. So he focused on the other person here to receive them. Janina Bisset had never given him a warm reception, but she certainly gave plenty in her ability to fine-tune their technological efforts with the Neiothen.

"Ms. Bisset."

"Mr. Veratti." Her fine square jaw and mauve lips perfectly accented her brown hair, which was queued back. Ah, the fire in her eyes! "To what do we owe this unexpected visit?" Annoyance tinged her question.

"Are you bothered by my presence, Ms. Bisset?"

"On the contrary," she said, motioning toward the large steel doors the guards opened, "we are honored. But every interruption and distraction could set our progress back by weeks. I understood we were short on time, so this . . . visit is unexpected."

"You suggest I might sabotage your work." He nodded her ahead of him through the doors.

With elegance and authority, she moved into the corridor, which boasted bright lighting and much cooler temperatures. "I would never say that, sir."

"But you feel it. You are frustrated with me for coming." He entered a small room with an expansive bank of blackened windows whose uppermost sections leaned out of the room over something not visible.

Ms. Bisset considered him, more than a little fear in her eyes. No doubt wondering which would get her killed faster—a placating lie or bald truth.

Bordeur slithered in and coiled around her. He looked at his counterpart, then to Ciro. "I—"

"Yes," she asserted, speaking over the snake. "I know you see everything that goes on here, with all the surveillance equipment and nightly reports from Haverstock. Risking a slowdown in production—"

"Would be infuriating," he agreed, ambling toward the windows. "So let us get on with this demonstration. I do not want a report or a video to tell me what you are doing." He slid his gaze to hers with an appreciative smile. "Nothing but good has been said of what you've accomplished, so I would see it for myself, experience it."

Reticence held her fast, but she finally skirted a look to Bordeur and nodded. He rushed to the side of the room and palmed a panel. Lights in the control room dimmed, and the blackened windows cleared, revealing a series of walled-off areas set up in a two-by-six grid.

"As you know," she said with a nod, "each room has a different challenge, and they are incremental, with the easiest being the lower left, then up the left side until they end on the right."

Peering down into the giant box created a sort of elabo-
rate and expensive dollhouse effect. Ciro's gaze rested on the
center, where two walls that looked like a jagged rock with
multicolored, randomly placed divots devoured the floor-
to-ceiling space, interrupting the view. A man was nearly at
the ceiling, pausing and two-handing one of the grips as he
assessed a parallel wall.

"These have graduated and are merely keeping on top of
their training," she said.

"So," Ciro said, his own palms sweating when he realized
the man hadn't anchored himself to a safety line. It was easily
a thirty-foot drop. "They're"—he hauled in a breath as the
man shoved with his legs and launched out at the other wall,
seemingly suspended midair before he caught a blue grip—
"ready." A smile split his uncertainty, dividing him from any
doubt. "*Incredibile!*"

"Ready?" Janina Bisset repeated with a furrowed brow.
"There are still irregularities in their biorhythms, among
other concerns. It would be better if we had more time."

"Mm, indeed it would be, but I'm afraid we have no more."
He eyed a man on a treadmill, head high and his pace a steady
clip—not quite sprinting, but not far from it. He couldn't last
much longer at that speed.

"I respect that you have a timetable, but you brought me
on—"

"I brought you on because of your brain, not your mouth
or arguments," Ciro barked. He clicked his tongue. "You are
much like Katrin."

A grievous realization. Hopefully Dr. Bisset would understand her place and responsibilities before she ended her
time, too.

The man was still running. "How long has he been on the
treadmill?" Ciro asked.

Bordeur nodded eagerly. "Five—"

"Minutes?"

"—hours."

Ciro glanced at the director, incredulous. "He is not even sweating." Concern replaced his surprise. "You run them too hard. Keep this up—"

"It is not us," Janina Bisset asserted. "He is on his rest period, but he is trying to break his last record for the run."

"And what was that?" Ciro asked, disbelief choking him.

"Eight hours."

"It cannot be. That is—"

"Impossible?" she mused. "That's what we specialize in, Mr. Veratti, as you've insisted." She looked down into the training center. "As you know, the men are given supplements and other medicinal cocktails that increase stamina and inhibit pain and fear, so they can act decisively and effectively. Of course, that is after they have been enhanced with our innovative procedures."

Disbelief gave way to thrill. They had a chance. They truly had a chance. "I would see more!"

She indicated a door. "We can walk the entire facility without intruding on their training or distracting them."

"No, I will go down."

"I—"

He faced her, hoping he did not have to *encourage* her to oblige him.

She tucked her chin. "Of course. This way."

Through the door, she led him around the side of the training center and into a stairwell as she typed into a phone. They stepped into a narrow passage, open above just like the rest of the boxed-off spaces that bisected the length of the building. As their entourage approached the center, he heard the clink of weights and the grunts of athletic effort fall silent.

A man appeared from the right—he had a presence about

him that commanded respect and attention. He could clearly handle himself.

"Colonel," Ms. Bisset said, easing forward, "Mr. Veratti wanted to . . ." Her hesitation bespoke her confusion. Perhaps her concern as well.

"Meet our prodigies," Ciro said with a rueful smile. "See what they are about, what they can do."

The colonel snapped a nod, then pivoted and shouted something that sounded more like a primal call of the wild than intelligible words. In seconds, the men formed up, feet shoulder width apart, hands behind their backs. Relaxed. Confident.

"Raoul," the colonel said.

A man jerked straight. "Sir." His black hair was shorn close.

"A demonstration of your abilities for our benefactor."

Dark eyes shadowed by an intensity that left little doubt as to what he could do flashed to his colonel. "ROE, sir?"

"Rules of engagement," Ms. Bisset whispered in explanation.

Ignoring Bisset, Ciro gave a sharp nod to the hesitating colonel. "Impress me."

The colonel turned to Raoul. "Whatever it takes, soldier."

Raoul's eyes hit Ciro—and he would not admit to the sick feeling of dread that tumbled through his stomach. But when the man's gaze surfed the others around him, Ciro felt relief at not *experiencing* whatever this man would do to impress.

Raoul moved like lightning, gliding forward with stealth and ease. Straight between Ciro and Ms. Bisset. So quick, so focused, that Ciro only saw Raoul's eyes locked on him. Barely caught a crisp, clean scent before the soldier—still not breaking eye contact—returned to his place in formation.

Ciro frowned. Was that supposed to impress? That he could move fast? "I am not—"

A strangled yelp came from behind.

Someone bumped into his back. He shifted and scowled at Bordeur, who slumped against him. Ciro pushed him off with a muttered oath at being interrupted. "Get yourself to—"

Gurgling, Bordeur twisted. Staggered. And collapsed. Only then did blood spread over his light blue shirt.

Shock riddled Ciro. He stepped back. Glanced from the dying—dead?—man to the Gen2, who stared straight ahead. No remorse. No hint he had just delivered a lethal blow. "What—? How?"

Raoul didn't respond.

"He is trained to answer only to his colonel," Ms. Bisset said.

Adrenaline bottoming out, Ciro felt the telltale tremor in his arms. "Why him?" he asked, stepping forward. "Why did you kill Bordeur when you could have killed me?"

"Speak up, soldier," the colonel ordered.

"Tactical advantage, sir," Raoul said. "He's enough to make a point, but not high enough up to disrupt our program."

"He was second in charge!" Ms. Bisset objected.

Raoul gave her an apathetic shrug. "Replaceable. You weren't, and the commander could have the entire program terminated." Another lazy shrug. "Besides, Bordeur refused me second helpings on the meatloaf last night."

Nervous chuckles trickled through those still standing.

"What did you use to kill him?" someone asked. "You don't have a weapon."

"With respect, sir, anything can be a weapon," Raoul said. "Ms. Bisset had a pen in her clipboard."

She glanced down at the brown fiberboard in hand and gaped at the apparently missing pen.

Greco leaned in. "A call, sir."

Irritated at the interruption, Ciro glared at the proffered phone, then snatched it. "Hello?"

"Sir, your asset in Germany reports Rutger's Neiothen have

learned the location of the facility you're in. They're coming to intercept."

"Understood." He ended the call and nodded to the soldiers. "Gentlemen, you are about to have an opportunity to test your skills like never before." He started for the door, then hesitated and spoke over his shoulder. "None should be left alive."

FIFTEEN

DURBAN, SOUTH AFRICA

Gliding through the warm waters of the Indian Ocean, Leif guided his dive prop to the surface and glimpsed the Golden Mile, a sandy stretch of beach that ended on one side at the uShaka Marine World. Hours after close, the amusement park lights were lessened but were made up for by the superb—or as their native consultant called it, *lekker*—nightlife throbbing through the city.

Abandoning their props, the others bobbed to the surface and treaded water as they waited.

Leif scanned the dark waters that seemed to play catch with the lights of KwaZulu-Natal's biggest metropolis. Though Durban was South Africa's second-most populous city, the people were being exploited and therefore were poverty-stricken. In a city that could easily hold its own against Cape Town or Johannesburg, police struggled to combat the high crime rate, and this coastline had become a thriving den of criminal activity.

The Neiothen had considered hiking in from north of the city, but that would've had them trudging through slums and encountering a desperate population—drawing attention and trouble. The images of the thriving city set against the poverty of slums and miles of garbage disturbed him. South Africa had its troubles, but they seemed increased since ArC had made its moves across Africa.

To his right, a black shape swallowed the lights of the city. Leif sank lower and eased his weapon from its holster as a boat approached. The others were already slipping beneath the surface, and Andreas gave him a nod before vanishing, too.

Nose and eyes above the water, Leif kicked to keep himself afloat as the boat swung astern, the engine churning a foamy wake. Someone moved from the wheelhouse to the stern foremost.

With criminal activity rampant in this port, Leif wasn't taking risks or prisoners. He aimed at the person and registered the four Neiothen approaching from both starboard and port. Light came in a series of flashes from the pilot, unaware anyone was so close.

Using the SureFire mounted to his gun, Leif sent his reply.

"Hurry," the man said in heavily accented English. "Coast Guard not far."

Holding point, Leif waited as his team stealthily eased onto the craft.

The pilot finally caught sight of Andreas and let out a yelp. Clearly rattled to find them already aboard, he gave a nervous laugh. "Yes, good." He gave a frantic wave to Leif, who caught the edge of the rig. "We hurry."

Leif climbed up and noticed the fishy scent. Several bins of fish sat along the hull.

Lights whirled, and deep voices hollered Afrikaans over the bow. A *Namacurra*-class harbor patrol boat loomed toward them, swinging a spotlight across the deck. Even as Leif dove for cover, the other Neiothen slipped over the port side and back into the water, narrowly avoiding the beam. Leif slithered up behind the baskets of fish, tugging a net over him as he struggled not to recoil at the accosting stench.

Within minutes, two Coast Guard patrolmen thumped on board, rattling off something in their native tongue. They thudded closer, flashlights sweeping the deck, the fish. Leif forbade himself from moving as the beam glared in his eyes.

One patrolman stormed belowdecks as the other got into a shouting match with the boat's driver, who waved wildly. The coastie shifted toward the fish baskets. Kicked one. These weren't well-meaning patrolmen. They were men looking for bribes.

With options this limited, shoot-to-kill was his only choice. Weapon trained on the coastie, Leif was not about to lose to corruption and willed him to go the other way. This mission depended on getting to shore. No way was he getting stalled in the ocean before he ever set foot on land.

Go back, he willed again.

The man kicked the basket of fish crammed against Leif's leg, then held out a hand to the driver. The second coastie returned, and both stood, shaking their heads. One produced handcuffs.

No freakin' way. This could not happen.

The first kicked the basket again, then shifted and kicked harder—and this time, he made contact with Leif's boot.

The coastie jerked at the hard impact, and his gaze swung downward.

Leif steadied his breathing, ready to fire. Planned how to shoot one, then extricate himself and hit the other. First part of that plan was an ace. Second part . . .

With an exclamation, the boat's pilot hurried to the other coastie with a placating tone. Rattled something off. Then produced a wad of paper.

Bright whites shone beneath the glower of the searchlight as the two coasties slapped the driver's shoulder, gave Leif's position one more confused glance, then shook a warning finger at the driver and disembarked.

Bribes were a common currency in South Africa. Leif hated it, but suddenly found himself grateful for it. Grateful it was enough to get the coastie to look the other way.

Hearing the *thump* on the side of the boat, he knew the

Neiothen were there. "Go," he growled, still concealed. "Get us out of here." He slid from behind the baskets as the others slipped back onto the deck.

The rumble of the engine vibrated against his backside as he stayed low and shed his dive suit. Andreas knelt and tugged the ruck closer, then distributed their gear. Five minutes delivered them to a less-populated and dimly lit section of beachhead. They scrambled up the sand, divided into two groups, and hustled across the street, guided by the GPS. With Hermanns' technological experts, they'd plotted a path of well-timed surveillance blackouts. By sticking to the shadows and the plan, they should go unnoticed.

In a light jog, they wove around and behind the Southern Sun Elangeni and Maharani resort hotel and headed southwest, ducking around the Grey Street Complex and across a half-dozen train tracks. The route took them east again and past—unbelievably—a KFC, of all restaurants.

The medical facility loomed just off Dr. Yusuf Dadoo Street. It was a center for the deaf and blind—a sick cover for what happened below it.

Never slowing, they traveled the five klicks in record time. Leif had to admit, it was really nice not having to conceal his abilities or worry someone would notice he wasn't out of breath or exhausted. Not having to hold back or feel bad about the enhancements. All Neiothen were enhanced, and that made the operation go faster and smoother.

Crouched in an alcove around the corner of Charlotte Maxeke Street, Leif used his thermal nocs to scan the street and the twenty yards to the facility. He eyed the purported entry point. Getting here and getting in, however, were two entirely different things. Intel knew this was the location—most likely. They weren't a hundred percent on that. Through a process of elimination, they had determined it must be belowground. HUMINT proved all six aboveground floors were in use for medical research, but they'd been assured there were no actual patients.

Hermanns' tech team had warned it was likely the facility's security protocols were off the normal grid, that even when it went dark for a couple of minutes, there'd probably be additional surveillance measures in place.

In other words: be prepared for contact.

Still, they were ordered not to engage. Only to reconnoiter. Find out what or who was down there and report back so a detailed mission plan could be assembled to ensure efficacy.

Sticking to the shadows, Leif and Vega hurried along Charlotte Maxeke toward their entry point. Andreas, Elvestad, and Ibn Sarsour were scouting from the north. Since the building was sandwiched between others, they only had to worry about two sides.

Vega surged ahead and used his skills to bypass a keypad. A soft click granted them access to the doctors' entrance. Leif slipped inside.

"November Five and Four are in," he subvocalized in their short-range comms. He slid left, his back to the wall as he cleared that side, hearing Vega do the same to the right. Their lines of sight crossed, and they both faced forward, reading for any engagement.

Leif took point, and Vega swung around, walking backward to protect their six. As they moved through the semidarkened hall, the GPS devices strapped to their wrists also mapped the interior of the facility. Leif glanced at his and saw the grid filling in doors and rooms in response to Andreas's team working their way through halls on the other side of the building. This would make it easier to execute their actual raid later.

That bugged Leif. If they were here . . . why not execute? But he was the new guy, still learning, so he'd play by the rules.

Has that ever worked for you?

149

Shouldering aside the thought, he slowed as he noticed a juncture ahead. A mirror mounted on the opposing wall threw a swell of light into the hallway. He felt the gentle press of Vega's back against his own and crouched, eyeing the corridor in each direction. To his three was a heavy door with a stairs sign. To their nine, another corridor.

Over his shoulder, he signaled to Vega, who nodded. Leif checked the mirror again, then did a quick look-see to verify the hall was empty. Something tugged at his awareness. He glanced again to his three. They'd been told six floors—aboveground. What if the stairs also went down?

He had Vega hold point on the passage as he slipped to the heavy door, eased it open, and nosed his muzzle into the stairwell, scanning left and right, up and—sure enough—down. With a jerk of his head, he redirected Vega.

"November Five and Four in"—he glanced at his GPS—"east side stairwell. Heading down."

Realizing too well the fish-in-a-barrel risk, they hugged the concrete wall as they descended. With each step, Leif anticipated trouble. Down two flights to a landing. Then three more flights until they came out in a narrow, dark corridor with a lone door at the far end.

Death trap, anyone?

Something vibrated in his brain as he stared at the gray door thirty feet away and the halo of blue light around a biosensor pad. *This has to be the Gen2 lab.* What would they face? Would opening that door get them killed? Bigger problem—how would they get past the biosensors? His gaze popped to the ceiling, where two black bulbs peered ominously down at them.

Using the laser weapon Hermanns' team had provided, Leif aimed at the first camera and pressed the button, sending a short burst that disabled it, then hit the second one.

"Contact!" Vega hissed through the comms, his weapon thwapping three times. "Target down."

150

Leif pivoted, went to a knee, sighting their six where a guard crumpled to the concrete. There was a hidden checkpoint under the stairs that they had missed. *So much for* only *reconning.*

Vega was dragging the body out of sight.

"Wait." Leif pointed to the biosensor pad—the only way to get access. Together, they carried the body to the far end of the hall. They used his hand and badge to clear the sensor. It beeped, and then Leif noticed the eye-level camera. He nearly cursed. They hoisted the guard upright and wrestled the body into place so Leif could lift the eyelid. "Three . . . two . . . go."

Vega swiped again and held the man's palm to the pad as Leif angled the head and eye at the camera. The light blinked green.

Whoosh! Sanitized air rushed at them.

Leif snapped his weapon toward the opening.

Vega whirled, pinning the body to the wall and monitoring their six.

"Clear," Leif said. "Hide the body inside."

They moved the dead guard into the small vestibule of the new area and tucked it behind a corner bin. On a knee, Leif glanced at the map on his wrist and frowned. It wasn't logging their movements anymore. He checked the upper right of the screen and gritted his teeth. No signal. In fact, the map had logged them going down only two levels. They must be too deep underground for a signal, but this equipment should've still worked.

"November Three, come in," he subvocalized, eyeing Vega, who looked concerned. He skipped a glance around their new position. No doors. The wall curved out, away from them with no access points. No entry or exit. No cameras. Nothing.

What the . . . ?

Vega moved into the open, his steps cautious, expectant.

The lone light dimmed, and a section of wall slid away, revealing a small hub that held counters, systems, and . . . thick, darkened glass.

"Whoa," Vega murmured.

Leif trailed him, reticent. Instinct screaming that they were walking into a trap. But how was that possible? Nobody knew they were coming.

Be prepared. Hermanns' warning echoed in his head.

"Check this out, man," Vega whispered as a system came to life, its display muted.

The dark glass slowly cleared, providing a view into a brightly lit lab. A large, hairy shape loomed on the other side.

Vega pitched backward, right into Leif.

"Easy," Leif muttered, flicking up his nocs and nudging past Vega. "It's one-way." He scanned the small area that seemed to be an observation deck overlooking six bays and, on the far side, an unlit lab.

Brown and broad, the hairy back in the nearest bay fogged the glass, forming a strange halo that emphasized powerful shoulders.

"Hey." Vega nodded at the console.

Leif eyed a joystick flanked by arrows. He leaned it to the right.

The door behind them whooshed shut. The octagonal observation hub rotated to the left with a hard *shunk*. Another room slid into view on the other side of the glass. This one contained sectioned-off rooms of cots. The observation hub's one-way glass met another window that was part of the lab on the other side. Enough barrier to protect observers.

A warbling sound seemed to bounce off the walls. Leif searched for an audio switch and flipped it. Shrieking pierced his ears as he noted something in the corner of a room—a man slumped against the glass, gripping his head, his face contorted.

Stricken, Vega reached over and slapped off the sound, accidentally hitting the directional switch. The hub rotated again, this time opening to a room of complete chaos. While the previous lab they'd looked into had a clear window, this one had a steel-reinforced window in a steel cage. Hairy orange shapes trounced and jumped. One leapt toward the glass, thudding against it hard.

"Orangutans," Leif said with a breathless laugh he didn't feel.

He and Vega drew back as the nearest creature fell to the floor. Flung itself away, then, focused on the glass, took a running start and hurled itself at it again.

Horror struck Leif. The primate's features . . . It was definitely an orangutan, but there was a . . . humanness about it somehow.

"*Dios mío,*" Vega hissed.

There were four of the beasts, all in a wild, frantic rage. The orangutan repeated the move, as if it somehow knew this was the way out. As if it knew someone who didn't belong was on the other side. Despite the impacts, the glass held strong. This time, however, something fluttered on a nearby wall.

Leif flinched, half expecting something to attack him. Instead, a piece of paper floated to the floor. He retrieved and read it. "'Japan approved experiments that would allow for animal-human hybrids to be born for the first time ever.'"

"No way. That's fake." Vega stared in disbelief at the primates, the one with the nearly human face.

"It's an article from *Business Insider* dated 31 April 2019."

"No way," repeated Vega, but his words held no conviction now. "This . . . no way." He looked ready to blow chunks. "They did this? They really did this—crossed an ape with a human?"

"Why are we surprised by human-animal hybrids? Look what they did to us." Leif grieved for the poor, crazed creature as the sickening truth registered. "They're playing God."

"Not playing God," a male voice echoed through the hub, sending Leif and Vega back to reality with a dose of alarm. "Helping Him."

Leif scanned the hub, the ceiling, searching for a camera and suddenly realizing he and Vega had no escape. No way to contact Andreas or call for help. Crap. He finally spotted a small circular nub on a monitor.

"Ah, see? You're one of the finer specimens we've created," the disembodied voice said—but something in Leif's mind snagged on an inflection. Did he know this person? "It's sad that we must terminate you, because really, if you were the success we'd hoped, you wouldn't have trapped yourself here."

I know that voice. A face drifted in the fog of the past. Leif angled his head, as if that'd help him pull it up from the dregs of the past.

"We're not alone," Vega said to the camera.

"Ah, do you mean Mr. Krestyanov, Mr. Ibn Sarsour, and Mr. Elvestad? They are being dealt with as we speak."

It wasn't a surprise that this person knew their names. The Neiothen and whatever was going on here were undoubtedly connected. ArC knew about the Neiothen, since they'd originally created them. But something else disturbed Leif. Something he couldn't put his finger on.

And then it came to him. "Veratti!" Leif growled.

"Good-bye, Mr. Metcalfe, Mr. Vega. This time? Do us a favor and stay dead. It would make things so much easier."

Hissing filled the hub, snapping Leif's gaze upward. To a vent.

"Gas!" Vega covered his mouth and nose, jerking to the main door. He jiggled the handle. Eyes watering, he shook his head saying it was a no-go.

Leif banged on a section of wall with a door-shaped depression, but it wasn't an exit. His chest tightened as the odorless gas seeped around his nose. Just like China. They had to get out, but there was no—

Wait! Leif threw himself at the joystick and clicked back, left. Then one more. The hub whirred, and he nearly smiled. The door-shaped depression now lined up with a half-glass, half-steel barrier. He toed the half-steel wall, and it popped free, providing an opening between the hub and lab.

SIXTEEN

DURBAN, SOUTH AFRICA

They broke out of the observation room into a very cramped security hub. "Close it," Leif muttered over his shoulder.

Vega shifted, bumping him as he squirmed to give room so he could swing the door shut. A heavy click thunked through the confined space. It reminded Leif of the first time he'd encountered Iskra in the lab in Greece, when she'd beaten him and escaped with the Book of the Wars, which she'd stolen from him again in the square.

A barrier jutted out from the security hub, dividing the space into six cages, three on each side.

Even as he searched for an exit, Leif had the chilling realization that the creatures had stopped shrieking. Warm threat spilled over his shoulders, raising his hackles, and somehow he knew. Knew they were watching. With extreme stealth, he slid his gaze to the side.

Almost immediately to his right, a large, hairy spine rippled as the creature unfolded and came to its full height.

Holy crap.

It was easily seven feet tall, and though he half expected red, crazed eyes, Leif found normal brown eyes flecked with a raw, determined awareness.

"Um, Chief . . ." Vega whispered, his words worried.

"Yeah," Leif breathed, still staring at the gorilla.

"Plan?"

Running wasn't an option. Behind them—a gas-filled cham-

156

ber. Ahead—beyond the security vestibule, six creatures seemed to grow in size, reacting to Leif's and Vega's presence.

Not good.

Why have a vestibule here if there wasn't an exfil? *What am I missing?*

"Chie—"

Thud!

The vestibule wall bucked beneath the impact of a gorilla's punch. Though this primate was normal, Leif couldn't help but recall the other one. The one that seemed eerily human. The gorilla lifted both arms and banged again, the steel cage rattling beneath the blow.

Vega grabbed his tac vest and jerked him back.

Then Leif saw it—the thin plastic barrier jutting out from the vestibule divided each side from the other, forming a very narrow corridor. He hesitated into it. Wondering if the cages would hold the primates.

Their exit enraged the gorilla. With a chortling roar, he lifted both fists over his head. Shrieking and squawking vibrated as the other primates, smaller but still fierce, copied their alpha. The wall again bucked and wavered.

Just a few more fe—

Leif cringed as the hairy shoulder of a gorilla barreled toward him. It slammed into the thin barrier that bowed out. Pressed against Leif, pinning him. He gritted his teeth, looking away from the gorilla that roared in his face.

Uttering a curse, Vega dug in and pushed to help Leif get free. "Company," Vega growled.

At the other end, a lab came alive with lights and moving shapes.

Banging erupted behind them—the other primates alive with fury at the human invasion into their territory. With a grunt, the largest gorilla shifted, which allowed Leif to scramble free.

Vega hauled him to his feet. "Go go go!" he hissed as they tripped over each other to get clear.

Shot by security or pummeled by primates—there weren't a lot of options. More than a little unnerved, Leif rushed down the expanding corridor.

Vega corkscrewed out of the passage, landing on the floor. Stalking around the perimeter with his weapon up, Leif went wide, sweeping the lab.

A guard leapt at him. Slammed him against the concrete wall of the bunker. His head bounced back. Leif stabbed a knife-hand into the guy's side.

The man groaned but didn't relent in his punches.

Leif didn't either. He had to change this. With his boot, he swept the guy's leg—but the man hopped away, thwarting the maneuver. Blocking one strike after another, Leif noticed Vega locked in a similar battle. Only as he switched tactics did it dawn that not only did his attacker have the same skills, he also had a vicious determination—not to immobilize but to kill.

This had to be a Gen2.

Dread spiraling at the revelation, Leif threw himself forward, sliding his forearm along the guy's neck while simultaneously hooking a leg.

Again, his opponent anticipated the attack.

Desperation whispered in Leif's ear. Fear, something he hadn't felt in a long time, spilled through his veins, a quiet whisper that caused hesitation and mistakes. His next blow missed. The Gen2's didn't.

A tremor of alarm made Leif stagger. If he went down, he probably wouldn't get up again. The realization threw him into fight-or-die mode, jacking his system with adrenaline. Which then bottomed out at the cold, painful truth that he couldn't win this one.

The Gen2 launched. Shouldered Leif's gut, knocking the air from him. He blinked and did his best to drop, but he was pinned between the concrete and the Gen2, who pummeled him. Agony radiated through his torso.

With a growl, Leif slipped his arm over the man's head and hooked his neck. Squeezed for all he was worth. Pulled up, applying more pressure against the throat.

The Gen2 didn't slow.

So help him—Leif knew he'd vomit or pass out if the guy threw another punch. His legs trembled.

An enormous shape loomed behind the Gen2.

Breath backed into his throat, Leif froze as the gorilla roared and threw a large, meaty fist. Despite the waffling barrier, he struck true and hard against the Gen2's head. Dropped the man to the ground, unmoving. This seemed to satisfy the enraged beast, which gave a grunt and then turned away.

Leif pivoted. Saw Vega in a worse situation—on the ground in a choke hold. But this guy wasn't just trying to put Vega to sleep. Dark intent gleamed. There was little chance of stopping him, so Leif scrambled across the floor for his weapon, came to a knee, and turned. Aimed and fired. The Gen2 toppled.

Vega flipped onto all fours, coughing, rubbing his throat. He shook his head as he met Leif's gaze with a look that mirrored his own terror.

Cradling his aching ribs, Leif indicated the exit. They hurried out of the lab, spotted an elevator and a second set of stairs. They chose the stairs for options and the ability to defend themselves. Though neither had much fight left in them, Leif knew they had just escaped Death's knell by nothing more than dumb luck and a gorilla's rage.

ROCKVILLE, MARYLAND

He was going to jinx this and end up arrested or sacrificed on some weird altar.

Cell didn't have good luck when it came to women—they were either too good for him or too dangerous. For once, he just wanted to meet a woman who was somewhere between lovely and lethal. Mercy would ask where the fun was in that, but the fun was in actually *keeping* a girlfriend . . . and his head.

The smarter side of his brain said that Alisz Vogt was more trouble than she was worth. It still bothered him that she'd backtraced him. That alone said the head he wanted to keep was likely to come off.

He glanced at his phone, once more taking in the reddish-brown hair and blue eyes in the photograph. She *was* pretty. And smart. Wicked smart.

Which totally confirmed Mercy's point that he lost his mind—she had no idea—when a pretty girl was involved. She'd tried to talk him out of this, and he should've listened. After all, she had a point—but this wasn't about him. It was about Leif. If Alisz knew something, and she claimed she did, he'd be remiss not to follow this lead.

He peered out the coffee shop window, looking for Alisz. So what if she was pretty? He needed to connect with the intel she had, not her blue eyes.

He groaned, rubbing a hand over his face. *Head in the game, Barc.*

What if he screwed this up? Or said something stupid that made her leave?

"You really are adorable, aren't you?"

Startled, Cell glanced over his shoulder. "Alisz?" He came to his feet, his foot catching the leg of the table. He tripped into her worse than a cheesy romance movie.

"And graceful," she said with a laugh.

He shrugged, straightening as heat climbed into his face. "Thanks for meeting me." Though according to intel he should stand two inches taller than her, he noted they were eye to eye. That forced him to check her shoes.

160

Black combat boots gave her the extra height. Shredded jeans, tank top, and a flannel shirt tied around her waist beautifully complemented her personality.

"I'm sorry," she said with a lilting German accent, her brow rippling in apparent confusion. "Anything else you'd like to inspect?"

More heat crowded his cheeks. "Sorry. I just—you're taller than expected."

"Yeah, and you're not."

Wow, rude much? "Is that a bad thing?" He sounded defensive.

She lifted a rueful eyebrow. "We will see."

Feeling awkward, he stuffed a hand at her. "Barc—"

She rolled her eyes and shifted around him. "I thought we were past all that. I mean, I wouldn't have come if I didn't know who you were." She moved to the chair facing his laptop, which she tapped. "Are you ever without that thing?"

Surprised by her casual demeanor, Cell returned to his seat. "Rarely." He frowned, realizing he never went anywhere without it. Was that a sad commentary on his life?

With a mischievous grin, she reached into her messenger bag and produced her own laptop.

So maybe not sad. At least, she couldn't think so, especially considering her system, which wasn't an off-the-shelf variety. "Custom?"

"Is there any other way?"

Man, she got it. Understood. He found himself grinning. "I'm glad you came." *Remember, possible ArC agent.* "I appreciate the risk you're taking."

A braid dangled over each shoulder, and a small tattoo peeked out from her tank strap. It looked like a twenty-sided die. No way.

"TAZ?" If there were a litmus test for the perfect woman,

she was rapidly ticking off the boxes—especially if she honestly knew about *The Adventure Zone* podcast.

"Barclay," she said coyly. Swiveling into a better position, she leaned across the table and folded her arms. "Are you flirting with me?"

"Definitely not." But he was. Because he hadn't learned with the other perfect women.

WASHINGTON, DC

Having survived the nightmare that was the Beltway, Dru cleared the security checkpoints and made his way down the old halls of the Eisenhower Executive Office Building for a meeting he'd known would come but had hoped wouldn't. Answering for what happened in The Hague was taking longer than expected, only because the incidents were large-scale and the investigations in-depth.

"You ready for this?" Admiral Alene Braun asked as he approached the meeting room.

"They know I don't have additional intel for them," he grumbled. "They just want to bludgeon me with their disapproval."

"They're going to ask about Leif."

"Of course they are. But I've given them everything I can, so this is a waste of time."

"So you *do* know about the attack last night."

Why had she brought that up? "Our people on the ground reported in about it." He wouldn't say more.

At any given time, operations were happening around the globe that few knew about and even fewer would acknowledge. After hearing from their asset and station chief, Dru had phoned Hermanns—four times—with no response. Whatever happened in South Africa, it had gone bad. All he cared about was making sure Leif was alive.

Alene met his gaze. "HUMINT and SATINT show Leif onsite."

Her words made his heart skip a beat—as if she were reading his thoughts. "Then show me, because I have no intel that says he was there." Lying came easy in the protection of those under his charge.

"You're too close to this." Challenge glinted in her gray eyes. "You've made some questionable calls related to him in the—"

"We made calls, Alene. *We.*" He wagged a finger between them. "You and me. It's our task force, our guys."

"When he went rogue, I gave you a warning." Her lips were taut. "Clearly you didn't take that seriously."

It finally connected. This meeting, him being called to answer for Metcalfe. "You did this? This is because of you?" He cursed. "You have no idea what you're doing, and with only half the intel—"

"Plan to hold us up all day?" growled the voice of Secretary of Defense Tucker Vanhorn behind him.

Dru muttered to Alene, "This isn't over," and turned to the stout SECDEF, who glowered openly. "Morning, Tucker. Sorry for the delay."

He followed the SECDEF into the room and tried to remind himself that he was the deputy director of operations of the CIA. Not some punk kid facing detention. Secretary of State Hugh Luther and two other uniforms—General Bradley Wheeler and Sergeant Major Rick Wayne—sat, their expressions strained with annoyance.

"I take it you're aware of the situation in South Africa?" Vanhorn took his seat at the table.

Eyeing Wheeler, Dru situated himself next to Braun. Though he resented the way the SECDEF said that, Dru focused on one key fact: his chain of command did not include the SECDEF or the secretary of state. He answered to his boss, Collin Powers, who reported directly to the POTUS. "I'm aware of an incident there."

"*Incident*? A hospital for disabled persons was attacked and heavily damaged! Years of research lost and innocents injured," Vanhorn said, his voice growing louder.

"What're you talking about?" According to Dru's asset, none of that had happened.

"Last night," Wheeler said, "five men broke into the belowground laboratory of a hospital that treats and cares for disabled persons."

"That's news to me." Dru tugged out his phone and looked for communication from the station chief in South Africa. Nothing. Had it happened afterward? Was the SECDEF's intel fabricated? "I have no knowledge of an insertion into a facility like that. You have people on the ground, verifying this information?"

What if it was the same facility? What if the narrative was wrong? Or what if . . . had he been given bad intel?

SECDEF wiped a finger under his nose. "They're en route as we speak. Are you telling me you sent this guy down—"

"As stated, I had no knowledge of this." There were times in his career when he knew he'd been set up. When he saw the light in the dark and knew it was a missile heading right at him. "Even if I had assets down there, you would not expect me to compromise them."

"Let's cut the bull." Vanhorn drew off his glasses and tossed them on the table. "Your man was seen exiting that building. *Your* man. You told me—"

"I'd like to see that intelligence." Dru glanced at Braun. Then to the others. "Where are the images? Where are these accusations coming from?"

Wheeler nodded to the sergeant major, who opened a leather folio and slid two glossies across the table.

"Our asset will not be named at this time," Vanhorn said.

Hovering over the photos, Dru thought through what he was seeing. Interior images. From within the facility.

Armed men moving through semidarkened halls. "Images are grainy."

"Are you seriously denying that's Metcalfe?" Vanhorn demanded.

Dru shrugged. "The photos are grainy. Leaves room for doubt. But as said, I didn't have a man down there. And if I did, why would I hide that?"

"Maybe because disabled persons were injured in this incursion."

Dru hesitated, as would be expected. "Like I said—I have no knowledge of that. How many ways or times do you want me to say it? Where did you get these stills? They're from within, so I'm guessing you got access to the facility."

"I'm disappointed," the SECDEF said. "We want to know why Metcalfe—"

"A hospital for the disabled—you seriously think he'd do that? And why does a facility like that have high-end security feeds? In South Africa?"

There could only be two reasons for disparate reports—someone was trying to cover up something, or he was being kept in the dark. Maybe both. He'd been in the espionage racket long enough never to think himself immune to betrayal.

Wheeler threaded his fingers and rested his hands on the table. "On 23 June, your operator, Leif Metcalfe, while on mission in Taipei, Taiwan, exited the assigned safe house and did not return. Is that correct?"

Dru glanced at Braun, knowing she had informed them of that event, then met Wheeler's steel gaze again. "General, you know I am under no obligation to answer your questions about operations or persons under my purview."

"So he *is* still under your control?" Wheeler pushed.

"Good day, gentlemen." Dru stood. "If you have any concerns, direct them to Powers."

"That's a mistake, Iliescu." Vanhorn rapped his fingers on

the file. "I'm meeting with the POTUS in twenty, and nothing—*nothing* tells me I shouldn't recommend direct and immediate action against Leif Metcalfe."

"You can try," Dru said with a grim smile. "But they'd have to find him first." He strode out and headed down the hall, ignoring the feet giving chase.

"Dru."

He'd expected Alene, but the voice was Wheeler's, which spun him around. "Don't play games with American lives."

Wheeler scowled, drawing back. "What d'you mean?"

"The intel you sent down!"

Confusion rolled through the man's weathered face. "What intel?"

Dru hesitated, wondering if this was more maneuvering to get out of trouble for the snafu in Durban. "Your assistant called me—"

"When?" Wheeler's head cocked, then shook. "I haven't asked her to contact you in . . ." He shrugged. "A week. Maybe more." Concern filled the gaps between wrinkles. "I'll start digging."

Dru was coming to understand that same *something*—someone had set them up, tried to get Leif killed and Dru blamed. It likely meant there was a mole. Perhaps even Wheeler's assistant. "Just make sure it's not my grave you're digging."

SEVENTEEN

STUTTGART, GERMANY

"It was like a ghost came out of the shadows," Andreas said gravely.

Elvestad grunted, wincing over his swollen-shut eye. "Sarsour didn't have a chance."

"How'd you get free?" Leif asked, still furious about the op. He shared an angry glance with Vega, who had his own wounds to nurse.

"The alarms . . ." Andreas pinched the bridge of his nose. "They created confusion. The sound . . . I think for some reason it affected the Gen2s, so we seized the chance to get out." He lifted his arm, revealing bruises and cuts, and shook his head. "They're vicious."

"Hermanns knew what he was sending us into and didn't warn us. I'm going to kill him." Leif stalked into the training facility and headed up the stairs.

"Wait!" Andreas hurried behind him.

Leif checked the conference room. Moved into the gymnasium—and bumped right into Hermanns. A blind rage drove him to make this man hurt for what he'd done. Instinct threw a hard right hook, nailing the older man in the jaw.

Teeth clacking, Hermanns stumbled back. Blood trickled down his split lip.

"You set us up!" Leif gripped Hermanns' lapels and hauled him off his feet. Slammed him against the concrete wall. "You want us dead? Is that it?" He shouldered in. "Didn't think we'd figure it out?"

"*Nein*! I would never." Hermanns struggled, choking from the twisting of his dress shirt that was squeezing off his air.

"Hey!" Andreas wedged between them, forcing Leif back, pushing against his chest. He thrust all his meaning into his dark eyes. "Stand down."

"No way," Leif growled. "He set us up. Because of him, we're down one man—how can you be okay with that? Wafiyy died! Hermanns needs to answer with a little blood of his own."

"*Nein*," Hermanns insisted. "Never! It does not make sense that I would do all this"—he motioned to the facility—"to assist your recovery, to help you be Cyrus to the Neiothen, only to try to kill you."

Man, Leif hated that analogy. "You didn't think we'd figure it out, but there is no way—*no way*—that was accidental. The lab was empty. Personnel gone, save Gen2s and animals."

"It was a night op to ensure such a situation."

"No!" Leif barked. "What was happening in those labs requires round-the-clock monitoring and research." He pointed at Hermanns. "Because of you, they *knew* we were coming. Knew we'd be there." His next breath staggered through his lungs. "It was an ambush."

"It wasn't empty upstairs," Andreas countered gravely. "There were people in wheelchairs and with walking canes. We avoided them, but things got bad very fast when the shadows came alive."

Hermanns gaped at them. "I had nothing to do with that—"

"Bull!" Leif charged forward. "*You* gave us that intel. *You* sent us there." He paced, feeling like the gorillas in that place.

"But you made it out—"

"Ibn Sarsour didn't! Vega and I got out on dumb luck," Leif shouted. "If that gorilla hadn't taken out the Gen2, I would've been dead. And Vega—maybe all of us. It was muffed from start to finish."

Andreas shifted, his expression contemplative, concerned, as he eyed Hermanns. "Where did the intelligence come from, Rutger?"

The man hesitated, touching his split lip with a handkerchief. "It was . . . a trusted source."

Too vague. "Who?" Leif demanded. "Who told you to send us there?" He narrowed his eyes. "Who are you protecting?"

"You must not get distracted," Hermanns said. "Do you understand what the economic structure will look like if Veratti succeeds? All trading, all purchases—from your toilet paper to your homes—will be done through his program. His authorization. Nobody will be able to trade or invest without this program. He will control *everything*."

"It sounds a lot like the mark of the beast."

"It is so much more than a mark," Rutger said. "And this power does not belong in the hands of one man. It will crush free trade, and countries will collapse. Poverty will skyrocket."

"We're getting off topic," Leif said with a growl. "That op was compromised before we left here."

"Not possible!"

"He's right," Vega said with a shrug. "Our comms went down when they should've worked."

"It was too coordinated," Andreas added. "Someone told them we were coming."

Hermanns shook his head, then suddenly his eyes widened and bounced to Leif. "This." His voice and body shook as he moved toward Leif. "This is what the painting predicted!" He scanned Leif's body. "Where is it?"

Leif drew back, still itching to inflict pain on him. Still convinced he'd betrayed them. "Where is what?"

"The triptych!" Rutger's eyes were alive, his excitement so profound that he didn't realize his mistake.

But Leif did. Anger charged through his veins at yet another deception. "So there *is* a third panel."

Hermanns faltered. "I . . ."

"You said *triptych*, but there's only two panels. An expert I talked with said the alignment was off—that there was a missing panel." He wanted to strangle this man. "Is that true?"

Defeat seemed to press Hermanns down. "*Ja*, there is another panel."

"You hid it from me." Like everything else.

"You stole that painting from my own home!" Hermanns laughed. "But no, I did not hide it from you. I simply . . . did not bring it up."

"Why—" Leif lifted a hand, then pinched the bridge of his nose. "I don't care about the whys anymore. I'm done. I just . . ." Annoyance cloyed at him, tugging free his last ounce of self-control. Would he ever turn a corner that wasn't rank with lies or betrayal?

"Do not give up. I beg you. Listen—the triptych," Hermanns said, "is what helped me find the first pages of the Book of the Wars. Whoever painted it had the book as inspiration. The scenes are both prophetic and allegorical."

A gut instinct had told Leif that.

"The scene by the lake, do you recall it?"

How could Leif forget? The twisted depiction of two men sitting by a lake, around them several clouds on which played out violent, macabre scenes.

"Two men," Hermanns said. "The murders in the clouds. A betrayal of friends."

A chill ran down Leif's spine. The expert had suggested that as well. "What're you saying? That you set me and the others up at that facility?" He might kill Hermanns if he said yes. The rage was hot enough that he wasn't sure he could stop it.

"No, but a friend did." Sadness gripped Hermanns' features. "The same mutual friend who has the third panel."

He had not expected his part in this journey to end so soon. But the facts being what they were, Rutger knew the time was upon him. And now he would take to his grave the aggrieved expression of young Leif, upon whom the sun rose, illuminating his anger and the betrayal behind it. He had so hoped to bring peace to the young men who had endured so much, to give them the hope Katrin had begged him to pour into their tormented lives.

It would not be.

Because if Andreas and Leif were correct about being set up —and he did not doubt their veracity—there could only be one answer.

With an aggrieved sigh, he signed the last of the many pages and set down his fountain pen before looking at his solicitor. "That is it, *ja*?"

"*Ja*, Herr Hermanns. Your will is complete."

After a few stamps of an official seal and signatures by the solicitor and his security chief, Arno, as witnesses, it was done.

As Arno walked the solicitor out, Rutger eased into the leather chair in his library, leaned back, and closed his eyes. "Ah, forgive me, Katrin," he murmured into the musty quiet. "I did so try to change things."

"Excuse me, sir."

Eyes still closed, he grunted. "Mm?"

"On the phone, a Frau Wilhelm—"

"*Ja*." Rutger opened his eyes as Arno crossed the room and handed him the phone. "Wilhelmina."

"You old fool," she all but crooned. "I warned you—"

"And *I* warned you," he said, his tone brooking no argument. "I will not have to speak to you again."

"I have no doubt of that, because you are as good as dead, Rutger! He knows—"

"Of course he knows." Rutger laughed. "That has been half the fun, outfoxing the fox. And what do you call for, but to crow over my demise?"

"I have only been trying to help. You know how I loved Katrin."

"You did no such thing, you witch!" It angered him how she managed to get a rise out of him so easily. "Your interest has been and always will be for yourself. No one else." He was so very tired of the game. "I have never been fooled by your pandering. Entertained? Yes, but never fooled."

"Let us set aside this idiocy and talk about what really matters—those men. You have failed them!"

The connection went dead.

Ah, with that, she did wound him. For her words were true and sharp.

"It is not yet over." He had hope for the Neiothen because of Leif. But the angry, vengeful young man had a lot of hills to climb before he reached the summit.

Leif would be Cyrus to the Neiothen. One hundred and fifty years before Cyrus was born, God had named the future king to subdue nations, disarm kings. He'd said He would equip and arm Cyrus for battle. It was now upon Leif to be that to the Neiothen—to lead them out, to strip the corrupt from the governments, and level ArC.

So Rutger lifted his phone, opened the camera. "Ah, Leif. You have been betrayed and the truth hidden. If you are getting this video, I am gone, but the truth is not. Recall what I said of Cyrus. Isaiah 45 also says, 'This is what the Lord says—the Holy One of Israel, and its Maker: Concerning things to come, do you question me about my children, or give me orders about the work of my hands? It is I who made the earth and created mankind upon it. My own hands stretched out the heavens;'"—his fingertips reached toward the tomes lining the wall, and he saw not books but the future—"'I marshaled their starry hosts. I will raise up Cyrus in my righteousness: I will make all his ways straight. He will rebuild my city and set my exiles free.'"

Rutger sighed, then turned his mind to the Book of the Wars and the seeming sister passage that read so eerily similar to Isaiah 45. The writing he had deliberately concealed from the scans given to the Americans and Leif.

He continued. "What I failed to share with you was a page of the Book of the Wars of the Lord that I feared would deter you from pursuing your destiny, what you are so clearly to accomplish. The page from the book reads, 'The Lord, the Holy One of Israel, and its Maker, says concerning things to come, you have questioned those from below and given them condemnation about their work. It is I who ordained that what was intended for evil should be turned, thwarted, and worked for good. Al'el will stretch out his own hand against those who rise against the Lord to thwart His Word. Now I raise up Al'el and will make all his paths straight. He will rebuild the army to demolish the strongholds and set them free.'"

Rutger took a staggering breath. "And the most beautiful of all? The truth that forced me to hide this and separate the third panel from the triptych? Al'el that is raised up? Al'el is beautifully transliterated . . . *leaf.*"

MILAN, ITALY

"Damage to the facility was significant, but the fallout has really shaken the brass and Hermanns."

At his penthouse, Ciro stood on the terrace overlooking the city with a near-strategic view of Piazza del Duomo. It always seemed fitting that from here he could see the Gothic cathedral, Duomo di Milano. "It is about time we deliver some of their own medicine to them. That fool." He shook his head. "Rutger always thinks he is one step ahead."

"I was more than ready after they killed two of our new gens. It's a significant setback, but nothing we can't recover from."

"Quickly, I hope," Ciro said with no small amount of warning.

"Already in play. Thanks to the footage and the political fallout, I'm being reassigned. My new position will be of notable use to ArC."

This secret asset was too high on himself. Still, the empire was growing and taking the economy with it—and annihilating any chance for a comeback. "I am surprised you would so fully and eagerly turn against your own, Colonel." It reminded Ciro of another who had spent a decade in alignment with the right principles and motives. "And you are sure the facility intel went through him?"

"Only way they could've known. We knew there was a leak," the colonel said, his tone vehement. "Now we found it."

"No." Ciro watched the glittering spires of the cathedral as clouds drifted overhead, altering the light that struck the gleaming structure. "No, now we plug it."

He ended the call and smoothed a hand over his mouth, releasing a long, contemplative exhale. Why must he always teach them? Why could they not simply follow the path? What was so difficult about it?

Rutger was out of touch in that villa of his in the hills. *Far too lofty, old friend. Far too lofty.* This was why Ciro preferred the thriving metropolis of Milan with its history and beauty. Fashion and business. One was not left to contemplate futile doctrines, and no doubt that was what Rutger was once again caught up in.

Ciro selected a contact on his phone and set it to his ear as it rang.

"I expected your call."

He nodded, squinting as a shard of sunlight stabbed through those clouds. "You betrayed me. Again."

"You go too far, Ciro. Your evil knows no bounds—that you would endanger not just innocent children, but the disabled! After what you did to Katrin, I should not be surprised, yet I hoped you would see the light. But no. No, you thirst for power, and Risen . . . it must stop."

"Agreed!" Finality vibrated through him. "It is time to say good-bye, Rutger."

EIGHTEEN

Having tucked away the stolen satchel, Iskra walked the cobbled street toward the four-story building where she had once lived and that now harbored her daughter. After hearing from Mercy about the events with Leif and his new friends in South Africa, she felt an urgent need to retrieve Taissia and return to America. Somehow, their apartment overlooking the hazy city had become home. Gone were the mansions and lavish lifestyle with Hristoff. Now she had a budget and bills. And she was glad for it.

Iskra hooked into the empty car-park courtyard and strode over the gravel path, rocks crunching beneath her shoes. At the door, she keyed in the code that had worked all these years. When no click sounded, she glanced at the door and saw it slightly ajar. Bogdashka would throttle the person responsible.

Not her problem. Iskra nudged it open and stepped inside, securing the door behind her. "Hello?" When no one answered, she started up the stairs to the main level, anxious to see her daughter. Taissia would be thrilled to go home. The thought made Iskra take the steps two at a time. As she cleared the landing and hurried up the last four steps, something registered.

The quiet.

She slowed, glancing around. Where was everyone? The hairs on the back of her neck prickled. Now she hurried for a different reason. On the second level, she rushed to the library, where Bogdashka officed. Two steps away, she noticed that door was also ajar. Hesitating, she peered down through the stairway rails to the foyer. She normally would have encountered someone by now.

Her gaze rose again to the attic apartments where she had last seen Taissia. It had always been gloomy up there, but now it seemed . . . haunted. Her breath caught, and her nerves vibrated in the eerie silence billowing through the house. This wasn't right. . . .

Wood creaked to her left—the library.

Iskra eased the weapon from the small of her back. She strained to listen, to catch a voice or even the skittering of rodents in the walls. Nothing. Terrible foreboding rushed over her as she advanced, her mind accepting what her heart denied.

Hand on the large, heavy door, she hesitated, afraid of what she'd find on the other side. Courage mustered, she shoved open the door and sucked in a hard breath. "No."

Where she expected confrontation, attackers, she found none. Where she expected walls lined with books and musty old furniture, she found none. Where she expected Bogdashka or her bodyguard, she found none. No one. Not a single soul.

"Taissia!" Iskra bolted out of the empty room, grabbed the handrail, and threw herself up the stairs three at a time. "Taissia!" Though she scoured the bedrooms, she found only desolation. Up the next flight to the attic, her pulse exploding adrenaline and panic through her.

"Taissia! Taissia, please!" Tears choked her as she scaled the last steps. Pitched herself toward the room tucked in the corner under the eaves. Momentum carried her into the wall, the paneling cracking as she rebounded. She vaulted at the door, which surrendered to her force.

Empty.

"No!" Iskra turned a circle, not wanting to believe it. "No, please!" She would not accept this. Grasping, straining, she begged for this not to be happening. Maybe she was in the wrong house. Wrong day. Wrong life. Anything!

She snatched her phone and dialed Bogdashka. An automated message played, informing her the number was no longer in service. "Augh!" She gripped her hair. "Think!"

Options running low, she tried a few contacts, digging way back into her past, but it was as if Bogdashka, the entire school, and her daughter had vanished into thin air.

Like a ghost, her daughter's scream howled through her mind, begging not to be left here. Wailing that she didn't like it. And even Iskra's own better judgment warned her. Yet she ignored them all. Now her daughter would pay.

Iskra skipped a step and threw a punch into the wall. The plaster chomped into her knuckles. Pain told her this wasn't a nightmare. It was real. Very real. She pivoted and this time kicked the wall with a feral scream. She punched it again. And again. Emptying her rage at her own stupidity, at the woman she trusted against her own intuition. Her fury that Taissia was no doubt experiencing the horrific brainwashing Iskra had endured. That so many had endured at the tutelage of a woman who was no woman.

Hair in her face, damp from her raging and tears, Iskra dropped back against the wall, pounding the support it provided. Her breaths came in heaving gulps as she slid to the floor, furious—at herself, at Bogdashka. But mostly at herself for handing over her daughter. It was her fault Taissia would be broken.

Sobbing, she grieved that she had lost the one part of her life that was innocent, perfect, beautiful. The one tether she might have had to Leif—

Leif.

Hope struggled past her grief. Shattered, she called his

number. Knew he wouldn't answer. But she must try. "They took her," she sniffled. "Leif, they took Taissia. Please . . . I need you."

The shards of her life shredded her—she had never needed anyone. To be in this place, to want the help of one person and not have it . . .

STUTTGART, GERMANY

Death had an odor and visage that looked and smelled a lot like Rutger Hermanns' home, where Leif had been crashing since leaving Reaper. It seemed smart at the time—away from the city and prying eyes. But now . . .

As he approached the door, Leif felt his hackles rise—it wasn't closed or locked. A shoe just in view—Arno. Flanking the entry with Andreas, who entered first, Leif snaked in behind him, scanning for intruders.

"He's dead," Andreas said of the security guard, who lay in a bloody halo. "Rutger." He looked at Leif. "I'll check the office—you, the library."

Where were the guards? Why was the place abandoned?

With his Ruger at the ready, Leif traced every door as he made his way to the library, anticipating contact. More of those Gen2s that made him think of razor blades, the way they sliced through lives. He advanced toward the library, nerves buzzing.

Hermanns was sitting in his favorite leather chair, head lolled to one side, mouth agape. His hand rested over his bloodied chest.

Leif darted to him and shoved a palm against the wound.

The pressure—and no doubt pain—made Hermanns' eyes snap open. He drew in a wet, ragged breath. Stared at Leif, eyes unfocused yet searching for understanding.

Cursing, Andreas joined them. Dropped to a knee to assist, a phone in hand, likely to contact emergency services. "Rutger, who did this?"

"We need to lay him down," Leif said. "Staunch the bleeding."

"Do it!" Andreas said, leaning in and lifting his mentor.

Hermanns gurgled as they situated him on the floor. He coughed. His head shifted as if he were trying to shake it. "Too late. Go. Hurry."

"Who did this?" Leif repeated. "Why?"

Eyes drifting closed, Hermanns parted his lips, then seemed to breathe his last with his entire body.

"Rutger!" Andreas shouted.

Hermanns startled again, twisting in pain. "Leif," he croaked.

"I'm here." Leif hovered over him. "Tell us who shot you. We'll take care of it."

"N . . ." Rutger wheezed. His fingers moved to Leif's, his gaze distant and yet fighting for control. "Dr . . . Dru . . ."

Leif choked, disbelieving what that name on Hermanns' lips meant. "Dru did this to—"

Hermanns angled aside. His face screwed tight. His chest lifted, then wheezed out in one final exhalation of life. Only as he lay dead did the value, the immense character of the man too readily believed a villain make itself known to Leif. And with it—the daunting last word—a name.

Dru. Why? Why would Dru do this?

"*Polizei*," Andreas muttered as the sirens screamed distantly. "We must go."

As he stood, Leif glanced at Hermanns, wishing they could've saved him. With that sucking chest wound and their limited supplies, there was nothing they could do. Forlorn, Leif moved to the library door, snagging a tea towel to wipe his hands. As he did, he glanced back into the darkened interior. Not long ago, this was where his life had taken a new course.

Andreas clapped his shoulder. "Come on."

They sprinted out of the house and climbed into the car. In the passenger seat, Leif sagged, trying to think. To figure out why Dru had Hermanns killed.

"It was ArC," Andreas said.

Leif looked at Andreas, who held a gold coin. "What's that?"

"The coin of the founders—there were five of them in the beginning." Andreas rotated the piece of gold between his fingers. "They each had to pay a gold coin to Veratti, vowing their wealth, their loyalty, and their lives."

"Why would they take him out? He was helping them!"

"No," Andreas hissed as they passed the first emergency vehicle. "He was not. Only ever did he stand against them. Rutger was an expert at making sure they did not know what his other hand was doing while he served their whims. But since his sister died, he has worked to destroy what Veratti built. It was slow, and it angered me to see the snail's pace, but he never wavered at making Veratti pay for what they did to Katrin."

"But the facility—they knew we were coming."

"They did," Andreas agreed, "but why would they kill him if he told them where we were?"

Leif had to nod. It made sense. He'd let his anger and thirst for vengeance blind him to the common-sense truth. "He said Dru did this." Buoyed with a new determination, he straightened in his seat. "I need to get back to the States."

"Think they can help?"

"I'm not going back for help. I'm going to repay a favor."

NINETEEN

It had been a week since Leif and the Neiothen hit the facility in South Africa and the SECDEF had all but threatened his career. Since then, Dru had activated assets on the ground in Durban and tapped analysts stateside to pore over the cyber-trail of that facility. He couldn't explain how intel had gotten some wires crossed. And now Hermanns wasn't responding. Then there was the whole nightmare called Leif Metcalfe.

Everything was falling off the rails.

"Please," Dru begged, knuckling his desk as he considered the latest report from the asset. "Just give me something to work with." He wasn't sure who he was talking to—he hadn't prayed in years. It didn't seem to do much good these days, especially in this political climate.

That his asset hadn't been able to gain access to the facility gave him not only pause for concern, but also another layer of conviction that the building wasn't just a center for the deaf and blind. It had to be a cover.

Dru grabbed his phone and dialed his assistant. "Hey, do we have the intel from the attack—pictures or the report—"

"Not yet, sir. I followed up this morning, and they said it's almost ready."

Slamming down the phone did nothing for his frustration. He planted both palms on the desk, unable to sit. Unable to figure *anything* out.

A soft rap on the door drew his gaze up as Alene entered.

He wanted to groan. "How will you betray me today?"

Her expression was grieved. "We just got word that Rutger Hermanns was found dead in his home—shot in the chest."

Unbelievable. Dru dropped into his chair and huffed out a breath. "When?"

"Yesterday morning. Security footage caught the killers leaving the premises."

He had a really bad feeling about where this was going.

"It was Leif."

Dru cursed. He leaned forward and rubbed his hands over his face, then looked at her. "I want that footage. We need to have our analysts go over it."

"They're already on it," Alene said.

Unexpectedly fast. "How'd that happen?"

"When Vanhorn notified me, I asked for a copy, and it was in my inbox by the time we hung up. Before coming over, I sent it to our analysts."

With Vanhorn already believing Leif's involvement, there'd be more pressure to move against him. And by the look on Alene's face, that had already happened. Dru was starting to feel like he wasn't the deputy director of operations anymore—she was.

Was that in the works? Were they looking to replace him? He honestly didn't care—as long as he got Leif back alive.

"They aren't happy," Alene said.

"Who is?" Dru bit out, then snorted. "Maybe Veratti." He gave a cockeyed nod. "I imagine he's probably hosting a rave about now."

"We need to do something," Alene implored. "Send the team—"

"Where?" Dru jerked forward in his chair and narrowed his eyes. "Tell me, Alene. Tell me where to send them. Because you seem to have intel I don't. And you're real buddy-buddy with Vanhorn and his minions."

"I am a joint chief and must conduct myself—"

"Of course." He flopped back against his chair and lifted his arms. "We're just your team, part of your infrastructure."

"Don't get petty. This is a serious problem."

"What was your first clue?" he snapped. "You may have forgotten, but I'm not one of your lackeys. I'm under CIA purview, and our rectangles on the org chart? They're on the same line—equal!"

She shook her head. "I'd like to see you funnel that anger into stopping Leif, not dividing your team."

"Divi—" Dru bit his tongue on an epithet. "Tell me how I'm doing that. Am I the one going to the SECDEF and the secretary of state with—"

"Enough!" Alene stood and walked out of his office.

Dru had an urge to throw something at her retreating form. But as she rounded the corner, another person appeared. He jerked straight at the sight of the attractive brunette, stunned to see her back in the bunker. "Iskra." He'd all but given up on her returning without Leif. In fact, hadn't she told Mercy she wouldn't?

"Problems?" she asked with a rueful arch of her brows.

"Too many. How can I help you?"

She slipped in and closed the door. Locked it.

Hesitation trickled through him. "Do I need a tactical vest?"

Demure and tentative, she held a leather satchel and considered him for a moment. Her expression was taut and inscrutable. Then her eyes glossed.

Concern tugged at Dru. "What happened?"

She swallowed and crossed to his desk, where she set down the satchel. Resting her hand on the bag, she stared at it. As if she wanted to say something. She wet her lips and stepped back. Lifted her dark eyes to him, a tear slipping free. "They have my daughter."

Dru jolted. "Who? How?"

"That satchel"—she nodded to the bag on his desk—"may be the only way I can get Leif to help me find her. Please—"

He flagged under the hope in her expression. "Iskra. I . . ." He sighed and tapped his desk. "Leif is on the verge of being declared an enemy combatant, maybe a traitor. He allegedly killed Rutger Hermanns and attacked a facility full of disabled persons."

"He would never do that!" Iskra's gaze was hard, decisive.

He stared at her, a painful cocktail of frustration and failure writhing through his chest.

"You *know* he wouldn't."

"Leif might not, but I'm not so sure he's . . . *Leif* anymore." Curiosity got the better of him, and he peeked into the satchel. "Holy—" Awe struck him as he pulled out the Book of the Wars. He gaped at her. "How'd you get this?"

"I encountered Leif in Germany and thought he was trying to attack me, so I stole it from him during a fight." Another hard swallow. "Afterward, I realized he had not been shooting at me, but protecting me from two men pursuing him." She tucked her hair behind her ear. "Perhaps what you think he did to Rutger . . . maybe that is not as it seems either."

"I want to believe that—I really do—but we have him leaving the scene—"

In the bag, his hand hit something else, and he drew it out. He schooled his features and slowed his heart. Prayed she hadn't noticed.

There was something inscrutable about Iliescu and . . . startled when he drew out the plastic bag containing the velvet pouch, which concealed the bi-paneled painting. Worried. But when his expression went hard, Iskra knew he was going to lie. "That was in the bag when I took it," she said, hating that she felt the need to test him. "Any idea what it is?"

"I . . ." He seemed to wrestle with his conscience as he drew out the panels. "A painting of some kind, obviously." He shrugged. Tucked it back in as if to hide it. "We can give it to Artifacts and have them—"

"No." Iskra retrieved the palm-sized paintings and turned the hinged set over in her hand. This was important enough for Leif to be carting around and important enough for the director to lie. Which meant she had to be careful. "The book—we should keep it close until we can study it and learn all we can. Do you not agree?"

The words were her thrown gauntlet. A challenge to see where Iliescu stood. She hated the uncertainty whispering through her, echoing the betrayal Leif felt over the deputy director's inaction. But she had to know the meaning of the look that had rippled across him regarding the strange bi-fold paintings, which *did* mean something. Yet he'd lied. Here was his chance to fix that. Convince her he wasn't betraying them.

His gaze ricocheted from hers to the satchel. His hesitation had her reaching for the bag again. She'd been so convinced she should return—now she knew why.

"I need you to realize something," Iskra said, her voice leaden. "I came here with this, believing in you. Believing in the relationship you had with Leif, *Dru*." She had never used his first name before. "They have taken my daughter. Because I thought Leif trusted you and Reaper, and that his anger was more about his fears than betrayal, I decided to trust you as well, so I returned." She held his gaze without faltering. "Now I see in your eyes something that concerns me. Makes me wonder if Leif was not wrong after all."

He seemed to search for answers around his desk, his attention landing on a framed print—a photo of him and Leif on a boat. Did Dru see Leif as more than an asset? Maybe as a protégé? Friend?

Anger wrestled past her composure, her usual ability to keep her focus sans emotion. But then, she'd done that most of her life. "I am not liking your hesitation."

Dru let out a long exhale. "Iskra—" He saw something over her shoulder and visibly flinched, uttering an oath. Swiftly, he swept around her, motioning her back. "Hide that," he ordered.

Confused, she looked into the hub foyer, saw two men in uniform, and jerked back to the desk. She snatched up the satchel and slipped the strap over her shoulder—who noticed a woman carrying her purse?—and emerged from his office. In the hub, she skirted the newcomers and the growing argument.

Watching the uniforms head into Braun's office with the director, she joined Canyon. "What's going on?"

"That's the SECDEF. So we either just got shut down or taken over." Canyon pivoted to her, then narrowed his gaze. Those blue eyes came into sharp focus. "What's wrong?"

Iskra drew up, surprised at the definitive way he asked and that he knew something was amiss. "What do you mean?"

"What's wrong?" he repeated with an edge.

It unnerved her how much he was like Leif. "Noth—"

"That doesn't work with me," he said, his tone firm but not gruff. "Iskra, with the way things are going, let's skip protective measures. I see the grief in your eyes. And you're not at the top of your game."

She understood Leif came by his intensity honestly. Trust in Dru broken, she needed a new ally. "Bogdashka vanished with my daughter."

Canyon came alive, reflecting a fierce protector. "*Taissia*?"

The way he said that brought her anger bubbling back to the surface. "I went to pick her up, and they had cleared out.

She is gone, and I have no idea where to start looking." She shoved her hair aside. "I checked with some contacts in the area, but nobody has seen them."

"Does Leif know?"

Relief washed over her again, because with that question came the same hope she held—that if Leif knew, he would be here. "I tried to call him." Why were her fears so loud and her confidence silent? "I did not want to come back without either of them, but I had no answers and no help."

"You do now," Canyon reassured her. "Think this is ArC-related?"

"It would not surprise me." She hated to think about the possibilities. What that meant for Taissia.

He hugged her, and it broke loose her tears. "We'll find her—and Leif. Both of them." He released her and stepped back.

"What's going on?" Culver asked as he came over.

"Someone took her daughter."

"Whatever you need," Culver asserted with the same ferocity.

"Thank you," Iskra said.

Canyon nodded toward Braun's office. "Any news?"

"Nesto is stepping in as consultant," Culver said as the team grouped around them.

"Which has Braun and Iliescu livid," Saito chimed in.

"Correction." Mercy eyed the officers. "Braun isn't upset. At all."

"You saying she's in on it?" Cell approached with a female guest Iskra didn't know.

Mercy stiffened, turning away from them. "I'm saying, Braun isn't upset." She gestured toward Cell's guest. "And *she* shouldn't be here."

"*She*," the newcomer said, "has a name and was invited here by Director Iliescu."

"Allowed," Cell corrected. "He *allowed* you to come." His guilt hung heavily on his young face.

Iskra didn't know her but already didn't like her, especially with the stiff tension roiling between her and Iskra's friend. "Who are you?"

"This is Alisz," Mercy said, with a ticked cock of her head.

Alisz. The one who had been trained and reared by the same toxic influence who raised Mercy. The same woman Mercy had tried to get Cell not to communicate with.

"Alisz Vogt." For a newcomer in a place where many already appeared not to like her, she had a lot of dark satisfaction in her face. "And you are?"

Iskra definitely did not like her. "Not interested." She started away from the central hub, determined to find a place to stash the book and panels until Alisz and the new invaders were gone. Why had she thought this was a good idea, to return and talk to the director? Had she just jeopardized everything, especially her daughter and Leif?

STERLING, VIRGINIA

The home was a mix of colonial and Southern plantation styles, with its white façade and navy blue shutters. Situated pleasantly on an acre atop a knoll, it had a nice view of the Northern Virginia horizon—and in the distance, between branches shedding their leaves, a glittering hint of the Potomac. The rising sun seemed symbolic in many ways. The sun had set on his hope for a quiet, peaceful life. Now it rose on a new direction, an outlet.

Leif returned the framed print to the mantel, noting there was not a mote of dust in this place. Glancing around, he took in the oil paintings, the furnishings, the tasteful decoration, but his gaze swung back to the picture. He traced its edge. He'd never been much for sentimentality—his younger sister and mom had controlling shares in that—but the picture recalled days when he still believed that those who said they'd take care of things actually would. Trusting a man who invited him out on a boat for a lazy, relaxing weekend had built some of that belief. The same friend who hand-fed him delicacies and lies as the yacht ambled down the river, flanked by majestic hills littered with the splendor of fall. In a few more months, the leaves would be turning again soon, years later.

Rutger Hermanns had named Dru with his dying breath and previously told Leif that a friend had the other panel. A "mutual friend." Then there was the painting itself, and its symbolic depiction of the betrayal by a friend.

Hands on his belt, Leif turned and considered the ambiance of the home that so clearly reflected the man he'd trusted.

How much had Dru known?

All of it.

There was no way he couldn't have. And for that, he had to answer.

But first . . . Leif searched the rooms, closets, drawers. It had to be here. Hermanns named him as his murderer.

Dru had set him up. Lied to him. Tried to get him killed. What else?

There was a kind of rage that made Leif break things and limbs. Another rage, a quieter, more dangerous one that forced him to conserve energy, to think, plan, and retaliate.

He stalked into the bedroom. Crisp and clean. Nothing out of place. Except the pants and shirt laid out on the bed. The sound of water running in the shower. Sliding his Ruger from its holster, Leif waited in the bedroom that had a pristine view of the backyard with no neighbors to obstruct the view. Quiet, undisturbed. That was how Dru liked life, no matter how false that solitude.

Well, Leif was here to disrupt the status quo.

He peered at the shirt and tie on the bed. Touched them with the muzzle of the gun. Shifted them slightly. The same way he'd mess with Dru's life—altering things just enough to get the desired result. He had to, since nobody else would. But . . . doing this, being this person—it wasn't what Leif wanted. He'd expected to have the wife, one-point-two-five kids, nice car, home, family pet, and maddening normalcy.

But others had chosen for him, altered that course. Altered his head, his life.

He strode toward the bathroom.

It was time to return the favor.

Dru dried off, wrapped the towel around his waist, and stepped out of the shower. Yesterday's bombshell invasion of the joint chiefs and SECDEF, who decided Reaper needed overwatch in the form of Colonel Nesto, had been enough to make Dru leave the bunker before he resigned in anger and frustration. Alene had known they were coming, and that was the bugger of it all. He'd been betrayed by his own. Back home, he'd had too much bourbon as he sat, thinking. Trying to figure out how to get Leif back and not get anyone killed.

He shook his head as he stepped into a pair of boxers and strode into the bedroom. His phone lit with a new call. He glanced at the screen, shock trickling through his system at the notification.

Voicemail from RH.

The sense of being haunted rushed through him. "How . . . ?" Rutger Hermanns had died two days ago! He coded in and retrieved the message.

"I must warn you, old friend," came Hermanns' heavy,

weighted voice. "I trusted the intel you provided for the facility in South Africa. I trusted that you wanted answers as much as we did and to make those responsible pay, so I gave it to them. I sent them down there. We trusted you, and you ambushed them. Perhaps I should not be surprised—it was a long game, and these days, can we truly know friend from foe?"

Dru lowered his head and covered his eyes. He had received and passed on bad intel. Intel that cost lives. He balled his fist. Hermanns was right—who was friend and who was foe? Apparently Wheeler wasn't the friend he'd thought.

"But that is neither here nor there. I call because my time is up. I will soon be dead. Veratti is aware of my betrayal, just as Leif is now aware of yours. He knows, Dru. He knows the intel came from you."

Dru stared up at the ceiling, as if he could escape.

"I should not tell you this, but in the chance that the intel was a mistake, that you yourself were fooled, I warn you. He will come for you, my friend. They will come, demanding answers and much more. Though I have sent him a video detailing everything I know and encouraging him to look past his own wounds, I cannot stop what he intends, and I am not sure that I would want to." A pause gaped through the line, then the sound of sniffling. "We trusted you. And that was met with betrayal."

Dru expelled what felt like a toxic breath as the call ended. "It wasn't me," he muttered. But it was. Just not on purpose. Running a hand down the back of his neck, he reached for his slacks—and froze.

His gut cinched. He shot a glance around the room.

You're overreacting.

But he wasn't. He'd laid the tie straight. Now its end was flipped up, pointing toward the door. Swallowing the acrid taste in his mouth, he checked his phone. No notices from his security alarm.

Rutger's warning screamed in his head, and Dru reached behind the nightstand for his gun. And cursed—it wasn't there. Dread coiled in the pit of his stomach. He pivoted toward the closet and snagged the 1911 from the top shelf. Verified a round in the chamber as he coded in on his phone.

"Good morning, Deputy Director," said the officer on watch.

"Have there been any interruptions?" He grabbed his slacks and stuffed them on.

"Uh . . . no, sir." The tech sounded confused, concerned. "Is there a problem, sir?"

Dru turned toward the bedroom door.

"Sir? Do you need me to send a QRF?"

"No. Patch me through to Braun." Dru peered down the hall to the living room. He hurried forward, clearing rooms as he advanced to the kitchen.

Light erupted.

Weapon up, Dru jerked, searching for a target. Then he remembered the motion sensor lights. The open-concept floor plan had been intentional and served him well, giving him a clear line of sight on the dining room, the kitchen with its large marble island, and the living room with its fire—

He stilled, his gaze on the mantel.

Pulse rattling like a Gatling gun, Dru took a step back and cursed. Darted a look around his home again. Checked windows, the yard, and the street. Nothing. He didn't have an expansive view, but it was enough to know if there was trouble. Of course, a sniper was unlikely to be seen from here, and if there was one out there, it would be too late.

Again his gaze trailed the wall to the fireplace that bisected the bookshelves. To the mantel and the lone picture sitting atop it. It showed the yacht the day he'd made a commitment to himself and to Leif. Beside that picture lay the

Glock removed from the bedroom. It faced the picture that now had a target drawn over Dru's face.

"Dru," a voice said through the phone, "what—"

"Lock down the bunker." He rushed back to the bedroom.

"Why?"

"Do it! Lock it down!"

TWENTY

Killing Dru in cold blood in his own home wouldn't help. Wouldn't make the point that needed to be made. Leif hoped to find the third panel, his coup d'état against this insidious game that had devoured his life. He'd been struck by a bad case of a good conscience. Yet he didn't have the panel.

It didn't make sense. None of it—why would Dru kill Hermanns? Was he a witness to the Durban facility? Was that it?

Nah, too simple. Then again . . . maybe not. Another reason that drove Leif from the director's home. If Leif connected Dru to what ArC was doing and Dru was responsible for Hermanns' death, he had to answer for it.

Now, perched on the sofa in Iskra's apartment, Leif held the picture Taissia had drawn of them and recalled the night in his condo when he'd been standing on the balcony and Taissia had asked for a sibling.

He pitched the drawing onto the table and rubbed his knuckles. Dreams long gone.

Rotating his head, he wondered when Iskra had last been here. By the dust and stale smell, the apartment hadn't been lived in for a while, yet there were fresh vegetables in the fridge. So she was back, but maybe not long enough to clean. Then where was she? What had she done with the book and panels?

Unlike the last time he'd left, this time he sought her out as soon as he'd returned. But not to talk. Just to see her. No, more than that. He wanted her in his arms. Wanted the reassurance she somehow always gave. He missed the sound of her voice. He itched to talk to her, but he'd destroyed his personal phone before Durban and hadn't accessed his messages online. No way he'd give them a bead on his location.

The sat phone he'd used with the Neiothen vibrated. He tugged it out and frowned at the message. From Rutger? Not possible. He was dead. Was the number and name ghosted? But nobody had this number. . . .

Going against his better judgment, he accessed the message. A video of Rutger.

"Ah, Leif. You have been betrayed and the truth hidden. If you are getting this video, I am gone, but the truth is not. Recall what I said of Cyrus . . ."

Leif pinched the bridge of his nose as he listened to the message. Man, he did not need these thoughts in his head right now. He wanted to see Iskra. Make sure she was okay after the encounter in the square. Find out what she'd done with the book and panels. His gaze hit the hall, and for a split-second, he saw Taissia racing down the foyer and leaping into his arms. Strange how much he wanted that.

He'd come here, not to his brother, because he didn't need complications. He needed answers. And for those responsible to pay.

Voices in the hall pushed him off the couch, and he tucked the small comms piece into his ear and tapped it. "Six en route."

He climbed out the window and used his parkour skills to scale the building to the roof. From there, he made his way across the rooftops to the parking structure. He strode down the ramps until he found the black SUV idling just as planned. He climbed in and shut the door.

Andreas considered him. "Is he dead?"

"Not yet."

"You lose your nerve?"

"No, I figured out how to make the payout bigger."

"And her—was she there?"

Leif stared out the window as they waited for the others to show. "No."

"It is better." Andreas considered a small gray sedan gliding past. "We do this—you do not want her there."

Was that the assassin in Andreas talking or the big brother? Iskra was his sister, and he rarely mentioned that, yet there always seemed to be a deferential tone when he talked about her. Was the "can't feel" thing real? Or was it an angle Andreas worked so he didn't have to explain himself? None of the other Neiothen had that issue, though with their effectiveness, many wondered.

"Three and Four on approach," the comm crackled as headlamps popped around a corner. The second black SUV backed in next to theirs. There were no cameras in here, and with the concrete walls, it was almost as impenetrable as a belowground bunker as far as radio interception was concerned. Two minutes later, the third SUV appeared.

Andreas glanced at him. "You sure you can do this?"

"It was my idea."

"They're your friends."

"*Were* my friends." He gritted his teeth against the simmering rage. "Dru set us up. Killed Hermanns. He's been lying to me for years. He knows more than he's letting on, and I'm going to find out what he's hiding."

"That sounds like you trying to convince yourself."

Leif tugged the balaclava over his face. "Let's do this."

PART TWO

TWENTY-ONE

"Look, I get it—you don't trust her. I'm not sure I do either, but she's been cleared by Iliescu. Let's get over this, Mercy," Cell said, pushing as much annoyance into his words as he could.

Mercy lifted her eyebrows. "Oh, you are definitely Barc'ing up the wrong tree."

Despite his own waffling doubts, he had gone through protocols. Her presence here was legit. "Alisz is *cleared* by—"

"Actually," a deep, gravelly voice intruded, yanking his attention to the new colonel who threw his rank around, "effective immediately, that access is rescinded." He nodded to the Marines with him. "Take her into custody."

Cell came to his feet. "Sir, that is completely—"

"Within my right. Sit down, Purcell."

"Wait a minute!" He tensed as the Marines pressed in behind Alisz, but Canyon put a hand on his shoulder, staying him. "That's not necessary," he called out, lacking conviction.

"You're convinced she's innocent?" Canyon asked, weight in his tone, which made Cell hesitate—and angry.

He should have a more definitive gauge on her, since he'd gotten her into the bunker. He was more sure than not that she was a friendly.

"I know you'll get me out," Alisz said to Cell. "Or . . . I will have to rely on my own ingenuity."

"Meaning she'll bust herself out," Mercy warned.

"Not going to happen," Nesto bit out. "She will not have access to any computer systems. We are well aware of Miss Vogt's *specialties*."

That drew Cell around. "What does that mean?"

With a curl of his lip, Nesto ignored the question and moved to the conference table in the main hub. "Okay, people, gather up. We're going to establish some ground rules."

"This is bunk." Cell watched as Alisz was led through the doors to the holding tank.

Culver, Saito, Baddar, and Mercy shared looks as Canyon and Iskra stood from desks at the rear of the hub.

"You're Viorica." Nesto sneered at her.

Iskra said nothing. Most in this hub knew she hated that name now that she was on this side of the assassin life.

Nesto's gaze hit Leif's brother. "Who are you?"

Canyon folded his arms. "I thought you knew everything."

"You will answer—"

"No," Canyon stated flatly. "I won't. I'm not tasked to you, nor do I answer to you."

"Then I'll have the Marines escort you out."

"Do that, and you'll answer to my boss."

"And who is that?"

Canyon lifted a phone and dialed, then held it out with the speaker on.

"Office of the chairman of the joint chiefs," came a polite but clipped voice.

Nesto glowered. "You've made your point." He frowned as Canyon hung up. "So who are you?"

"The guy you don't know."

And they thought Leif was alpha? But there had to be a reason he was refusing to give his name to this colonel.

"You son of—"

Claxons screamed through the building, shrieks throwing themselves against the wall and rebounding. The team twitched, unholstering weapons and turning as they assessed the bunker now bathed in red, swirling lights.

"This is not a drill," a mechanical voice announced. "Active Threat Warning."

Massive iron grates and steel doors thudded into place, sealing the bunker tight.

Cell shared uncertain glances with Culver and Saito, then Mercy. The walls and floor vibrated, just like his nerves.

"What's going on?" Nesto started toward Braun's office, but the formidable admiral headed him off.

"The deputy director called me, and I activated it," Braun said.

"Shut it off," Nesto ordered.

Frustration seemed to tighten the admiral's eyes. "I can't," she shouted over the claxons. "There is an active threat against the bunker. It won't shut down until security clears the entire bunker and verifies there is no threat in the building or our systems."

"Where is Iliescu?" Nesto growled.

"Coming down the access corridor even now," she said, glancing at the steel door adjacent to his office.

"What's the threat?" Culver hollered over the alarms.

Braun's shoulders lifted and fell in something that looked a lot like defeat. She said something, but the claxon drowned out her words. "Leif," she shouted, her expression saying everything.

"Why would the threat be Leif?" Canyon demanded, his expression fierce.

"Leif believes Dru betrayed him," Braun explained, "so he's coming to settle the score."

Mercy flew past them to her laptop and started typing.

Wait, no, not her laptop—the main system.

Cell went to her. "What're you doing?"

Hair dangling over her shoulders, she leaned closer to the monitor, her fingers zipping over the keys with precision and determination.

"Don't let her," Alisz cried from her cell. She had a thin line of sight on the hub.

Irritated that Alisz barked orders at Reaper, Cell focused on Mercy working away. Feverishly. Frenetically. What was going on? "Hey, what're you doing?" When she didn't answer, he leaned in. "Mercy."

Something in her eyes wasn't right.

"Mercy!" he snapped, touching her shoulder.

She slapped his hand and went right back to work.

Admiral Braun ordered a Marine to silence the claxons, then glanced at Mercy. "What's going on?"

"Our training is going on," Alisz asserted loudly from the back. "She's accessing facility security protocols."

Cell glanced at the monitor and felt a twinge of angst. Alisz might be telling the truth. But he couldn't imagine Mercy putting them in danger. His gaze followed her coding. She *was* accessing security measures. "Merc."

"No time, Barc," she bit out.

"Tell us what you're doing—is Alisz right?"

"She's an ArC operative, and you're questioning *me*?"

He reached around the back of the terminal and yanked the cords. The monitor went blank.

Mercy gaped and froze. Blinked. "What'd you do?"

"That's what I want to know. What were *you* doing?"

Her brows furrowed as a dark shape formed up behind her—Baddar. "I was *saving* him."

"Him?" Cell leaned in. "Leif? Why would you be saving anyone?"

"She feels there's a threat," Alisz said.

"Stay out of my business," Mercy growled over her shoulder to Alisz. "You shouldn't even be here. You're a menace!"

204

"There are a lot of places I'm not supposed to be, but right here is where I want to be."

"Why? To corrupt the process?"

"Do you hear her?" Alisz asked with a wry smile, shaking her head. "Does that sound like your friend?"

"Shut up!" Mercy snapped, then settled her frustration and hazel eyes on Braun. "Admiral, this woman is an asset owned and trained by those loyal to ArC. If you don't let me finish—"

"You were trained at the same place." Braun's words were almost a question.

"I escaped years ago," Mercy said evenly, "with Dru's help. I've been on my own for a decade. Ask him."

"Unfortunately," Braun said, "he's not here yet, so I can't."

"Yes," Mercy hissed, "because those security walls locked him out. He is who I was trying to save."

"What do you mean *save*? He's stuck in the tube."

"No," Mercy huffed. "When the Active Threat Scenario goes live, any of the tunnels that detect unauthorized movement release a nerve agent."

Alene started. "H-how do you know that?"

"It's my business to know." She nodded to her disabled system. "I *think* I managed to shut down those measures on the access Dru uses, but I couldn't confirm that because *Cell* killed my system." She lasered him with a glower. "If Dru was in that tunnel when the agent released? You killed him, Barclay."

Cell had to admit he was starting to feel a little sick.

Mercy's lips went taut. "Alisz Vogt is a danger to this hub and to those in it, Admiral."

"A danger to you, Ariadne," Alisz taunted.

Ariadne?

Mercy's cheek twitched. "How did you find me? Is that why you went for Cell? Because you were trying to get to me and couldn't? So you used him, manipulated him into believing you liked him, and bam! You're in the one place you couldn't breach and talking to the one person who vowed never to speak to you again."

Cell swallowed hard. He'd known he was getting in over his head, but this . . . he couldn't have messed up this badly. They'd . . . connected.

"Convenient, don't you think, Barc?" Mercy's eyes brightened with anger. "You just happened to find a link to the intel nobody had been able to find. And all through a professional systems saboteur."

This could not be real. But the truth resonated in Alisz's expression that the scenario Mercy laid out was true. Anger charged past his idiocy. "Are you *serious*? You used me?"

Alisz's confidence faltered. "It . . . not in the way you think."

Cell barked a laugh. "How you think that makes sense is beyond me."

"What's our status?" Dru's commanding voice demanded as he entered the facility and closed the access hatch.

"Chaos," Canyon groused from the side. "Glad you made it, sir. You can thank Mercy for that."

"Not surprised." After a nod of thanks, Dru waved them over. "Group up. We don't have much time."

"For Leif?" Canyon asked.

Dru gave him a pained expression then swiped a hand over his mouth. "A facility in South Africa was hit last week. SATINT and HUMINT indicate Leif was a part of it. I believe he was acting with Rutger Hermanns."

"Who's now dead," Braun added.

"I saw the news on that attack—it was a hospital for the disabled." Culver's blue eyes darkened. "You seriously think Leif was involved?"

Dru hesitated. "I do, but I believe he was acting on bad intel."

"What proof do you have of bad intel?" Nesto demanded.

"We can play armchair politics, or we can get ready for what's coming," Dru growled at the colonel.

"You mean Leif is coming," Canyon said.

"He was in my home and left a message—a target drawn over a picture of me," Dru said.

"That's not just a message—it's a threat," Nesto corrected.

"Why would he do that?" Culver asked.

"If Runt wanted to hurt you," Saito said, "you wouldn't be here talking. I'll point out that he got into your home and *didn't* act against you."

"Agreed. I think he's coming here for the book. I think he wants to make a point." Dru's gaze hit Iskra's. "Do you have the book?"

"No, I stashed it for safekeeping," she said, drawing in a shaky breath.

Cell balked. "Are we talking about the Book of the Wars? You have it and didn't tell us? If Leif shows up and it isn't here—I don't want to see that." His hand reflexively went to his throat.

"Leif *is* coming and he's not . . . himself," Dru said. "Let's prepare, but be clear—we do not act against him. No matter what."

"If he attacks," the colonel said, "you can bet your beret I'm going to shoot."

"You'll go through me, first," Canyon warned with a sinister calm.

"Whatever it takes." Nesto wasn't backing down.

"You haven't gone up against these Neiothen," Saito argued, "so I'd go easy on that trigger, Colonel."

"That's exactly why we need swift, decisive action against them," Nesto retorted.

"You have no idea what you're saying," Dru countered. "And I will not let this bunker become a slaughterhouse because of your trigger itch. Get it under control. If forced to engage, it will all be non-lethal."

"Agreed. Pretty sure every member of Reaper will take it personally if you go after one of our own, Colonel." Culver folded his arms.

"Sir?" came Mercy's tentative, worried voice. "You really think he's gone to the dark side?"

"Dark side? No. However, I think he's letting his anger control him. After the facility, Hermanns' death—"

"Also," Braun spoke up, "Wheeler's aide was found dead this morning."

Dru started. "*What*?" He paled.

And that nearly made Cell soil his pants—the director was rarely ever caught off guard, and the aide's death *scared* him.

Crack! Pop!

The unmistakable report of a weapon rocketed down the corridor, followed by a scream. Weapons snapped out with a fluid grace only found in the experience of skilled operators. They aimed in the direction of the confrontation. Amid the still-whirling emergency lights, Culver, Saito, Canyon, and Baddar stalked purposefully toward the threat.

Cell cursed himself for hesitating, unwilling to be in Leif's crosshairs or hands again.

A tinkling noise carried heavily, closer with each *tink*.

"Flashbang!" Canyon bellowed.

Pop! Hiss!

Culver swung away as a crack rent the air. He went to a knee, and the red splotch spreading over his chest—he was shot!—warned of the threat descending upon them.

Cell shifted, weapon in hand, panic in his chest as six armed men in black lightweight body armor stormed the hub.

TWENTY-TWO

REAPER HEADQUARTERS, MARYLAND

Light exploded, searing her eyes. A deafening boom punched Iskra. Smoke billowed into the bunker, squeezing the air from her lungs. Ringing shrilled through her ears, driving her to the ground as she gripped her head and squeezed her eyes shut. Coughing and on all fours, she waded through the disorientation and pain, aiming for the conference table. Shots persisted amid hand-to-hand combat.

Iskra blinked hard against the burning gas, drew her knife, and scrambled to the other side of the table. Through the chair legs, she watched men in black tactical gear seizing the chaos caused by their flashbangs and moving through the hub with intent. Three quick shots seared the air.

Canyon gripped his leg, then Saito and Baddar. Those few, precise shots effectively crippled what the flashbangs had not—Reaper. None of the wounds were life-threatening, just enough to slow the men and make them rethink trying to take control.

"Please, no—wa—" Cell strangled a scream as he stumbled back.

She had to find cover. Buy time to figure out a strategy. Iskra peered under the table toward the bathroom door. Could she make it without being seen? She glanced back at the chaos to be sure the attackers were distracted, then slid forward—straight into the muzzle of a weapon.

Iskra froze, hands up, not wanting the immobilizing shot to

be a permanent one. She could not die here, not with Taissia still in Bogdashka's clutches. The man freed her of the dagger and thumped her over the head.

Pain wracked her temple. She fought the instinct to fight back.

Another Neiothen—that was what Dru said they were, right?—hauled her up and pitched her toward the team gathered in the center of the hub, gripping their wounds. Even injured, Reaper kept their focus and formed a protective perimeter around the women. They stared out at the balaclava-clad men who pointed automatic rifles at them. Hazy smoke hung in the air, giving the ordeal a terrifying aura.

These insurgents had seized control in under thirty seconds, leaving no doubt that they were, in fact, Neiothen. There was really only one way for them to be so efficient—they knew the enemy. *Knew* Reaper, this bunker. And that meant Leif was here. The thought was repugnant—he was better than that. Yet . . . he had broken into the director's home.

"Your injuries are non-life-threatening unless you decide otherwise," said a Neiothen via voice changer.

"What do you want?" Colonel Nesto demanded.

"You're not in charge." Another Neiothen aimed his weapon at the colonel's left leg—the one without a wound. "Need more incentive?"

Fists balled, Nesto vibrated with anger that seemed to make even his white-blond hair redden.

"Everyone on the ground," yet another Neiothen ordered, his voice masked as well. "Hands where we can see them."

Stunned as the Neiothen stalked through the bunker, Iskra eyed Dru, who was holding his bloodied thigh. She grabbed a scarf draped over a chair and shifted toward him.

"He's here," Dru whispered to her.

"I can't believe he'd do this." She did not want this to be

true. She wanted to say this wasn't Leif—but it was. Anger did strange things to people, changed them.

"He would—he believes I betrayed him."

"Did you?"

"Not in the way he thinks," Dru conceded grimly.

"That's what Alisz said to Cell. It didn't help him feel less betrayed." Iskra frowned, her gaze surfing to the Neiothen as she tightened the scarf around Dru's leg. "What did you do?"

"Later," Dru said with more than a little irritation. "Right now we need to figure out which one is Leif and get him isolated."

"In case you hadn't noticed, they all look alike," Cell muttered, intruding on their conversation.

"It's a race between us and them." Dru eyed the Neiothen. "They only have ten minutes before quick-response units and the National Guard swarm this place. It's automatic when the Active Threat Scenario is triggered. It takes them that long to assemble, brief, and get onsite."

"We cannot let this get out of hand," Canyon gritted out as he bound his own wound with a torn sleeve. "You and I know why he's here—and it's legit. You can't let this destroy him. Call off the cavalry."

"I can't," Dru countered. "They're required to clear the building before an ATS downgrade."

Iskra worried how this would end. Who would still be alive. She again studied the half dozen balaclavas. The mouth portion was firm, molded, and the eyes shields made it impossible to find Leif's pale blues. "How do we get him alone? Talk to him if he's angry—"

"Quiet." A shove against her back pitched Iskra forward.

She caught herself, cheek colliding with a table. Wincing, she palmed the concrete floor and steeled her anger.

Once the Neiothen moved away, Saito inched closer. "It

doesn't make sense. The book had nine names. Most of those died." He nodded to the insurgents. "There's too many here. They can't all be Neiothen."

"We need a plan. Fast," Culver growled, holding his chest. He was the only one who'd taken a bullet in the torso.

"And you need a hospital." Saito shed his shirt, leaving him in an OD-green T-shirt, and pressed the button-down to Culver's wound. "Hey," he said to the insurgents, "my friend here needs a doctor, but you just shut us off from help."

Black heads swiveled around to each other, but no words were spoken or action taken.

Iskra wondered what that was about. Maybe they just didn't care if someone died.

"Dru Iliescu," a mechanized voice called out.

Iskra glanced at Iliescu as a Neiothen caught the director by his collar and hauled him toward the front of the facility.

Another trained his M4 on Dru as he was led aside. "Are you related to Ion Iliescu, the former Romanian prime minister charged with crimes against humanity? Records indicate you are just as guilty of crimes against humanity—against those under your command and your friends."

"Romanian?" Iskra whispered, stunned. "What does that matter?"

Dru's gaze remained straight ahead, aimed over the heads of Reaper and other bunker personnel.

"Do these people know what you've done? How you killed a man who called you friend? Who trusted you?" The Neiothen pointed his weapon at Dru's temple. "You need to pay—"

Iskra drew in a breath.

"Wait!" Canyon hobbled forward. "What's going—" When a Neiothen surged at him, he grabbed the weapon and yanked it toward himself. But with blood-slicked hands, the weapon slipped, and the insurgent struck hard and fast, coldcocking him in the face.

Canyon staggered back, pinching the bridge of his gushing nose. He dropped hard next to her and shook his head as their eyes met.

The Neiothen glanced at Reaper. "Anyone else feeling like a hero?"

"We have one task here," another intoned. "So if you stay calm, you stay alive."

Baddar lifted his hands as he knelt. "Tell us what you want. We can help."

Beside him, Mercy grabbed his arm and hissed a no.

A Neiothen brought Alisz out of the tank and thrust her at the feet of the leader near Dru.

"Who are you?" He planted a foot on Alisz's neck. "You don't belong here."

"You're right. Does that mean I get to leave?" she said demurely, though fear glimmered in her eyes.

The Neiothen drove his boot into her side.

With a strangled grunt, Alisz curled up, gripping her ribs. "Name!"

"Alisz Vogt," she grunted. "Prisoner or friend, depending on who you ask."

"Please." Braun came to her feet. "Just tell us what you want—"

"On the ground, Admiral. Don't make us say it again." The leader nodded to Alisz. "Get with the others."

As Alisz settled near Cell, Iskra assessed the Neiothen. Which one was Leif? "Do you see him?" she whispered to Leif's brother.

"Your left, farthest back," Canyon whispered, looking forward instead of the direction he suggested as he wiped away the blood on his face.

Not wanting to betray their conversation and get kicked or punched, Iskra took her time glancing over her shoulder. The table blocked her view. "I cannot see him." But another thought struck her—the man who had pulled Dru from their group had the same height and lanky build of her brother. Was that Mitre? If these were the Neiothen, then he would be here, right? She tried to gauge his actions and movements, compare them with Mitre's.

And if Mitre *and* Leif were here . . . then *was* this about the Book of the Wars and the painting she'd stolen? Iskra again checked behind her but still couldn't see the one Canyon suggested. She shifted and pushed up on an elbow. If she could—

Pain exploded through the back of her head, and her arm snapped out from under her. She fell to the side just in time to see Canyon move like lightning.

He caught the weapon and jerked it forward, flipping his legs and—because Iskra was in the way so the Neiothen couldn't retaliate—managed to sweep the guy's feet out from under him.

She scrambled aside and came up. An arm hooked her neck and hauled her back against his chest. She stilled, too aware that these Neiothen moved like cold, methodical machines.

Canyon faltered when he saw her predicament. Eyes ablaze, he lifted his hands. "Easy," he breathed.

"Two," a voice called from the back.

With a shove, the Neiothen released her.

Iskra strained and finally spotted the man Canyon had referenced. He seemed right, but he wasn't looking at her. He was looking forward. All attention had focused on something at the front of the bunker.

Near Braun's office, a short, stout man dragged the admiral to her feet. "Let's go."

One of the Marines instinctively lunged.

"No!" Braun's cry mingled with the shot that cracked the air.

214

The Marine toppled back to the ground, clutching his chest.

"Stay down, stay alive," one of the mechanized voices repeated.

Canyon stared at the Marine, who was grimacing and pale. He lifted a hand. "I'm a combat medic. Can I tend the wound?"

"Negative," the Neiothen intoned.

"Shooting and murder are very different charges," Canyon challenged.

Iskra doubted these men cared about being brought up on charges if they were willing to besiege a black ops command center on U.S. soil. And if they were Neiothen, then most of them were not even American.

"Ossi." One of them nodded to another.

Ossi. Iskra's heart skipped a beat at Leif's Neiothen call sign, but she couldn't figure out who had spoken or who they spoke to. But it confirmed Leif was here.

Three Neiothen—including the man at the back who wouldn't let Canyon assist—stalked past them into the area of the joint offices of Braun and the director. She watched the one she thought was Leif for proof of identity. His helmeted head turned toward another, and the two stared at each other. Were they hesitating? Waiting for someone to speak? Or did they have a way to speak without being heard?

Either way, the Neiothen's stance erased any doubt that he was Leif. He pivoted in front of Braun and Dru, who had their backs to the team. His posture radiated the anger and fury she had seen in the German square.

Two Neiothen snaked in and out of cubicles, cutting cables. They bagged laptops and devices.

A soft scraping came from her left. Iskra spied Cell inching his laptop off his desk until he lowered it to the floor. What did he intend to do? Her stomach tightened, knowing that if he was discovered, they'd likely kill him.

Covering her mouth, Alisz was whispering to him, though she pretended simply to be staring straight ahead.

O Holy Mother . . . Iskra prayed they would not tempt the anger of these men anymore. No wonder Mercy said not to trust Alisz—she put others in danger.

Cell worked one-handed, his other still gripping his wounded leg, so he was slow. Mercy shifted, shielding him from the view of the leader.

Crack!

Smoke puffed over the keyboard. Somehow there was a spray behind Cell, too. He let out a strangled cry. It wasn't smoke that had erupted from his back.

"Cell!" Iskra shouted, realizing what had happened.

With a groan, he crumpled and landed on his side. Blood spilled over his back and the floor.

Canyon lunged to help Cell, but a Neiothen shouted for him to stay.

Leif—at least she thought it was him—slapped his hand at the other Neiothen, his stance confrontational. Angry. The one who had shot Cell cowered.

"Ricochet—off the laptop and into his gut, out his back." Canyon nodded to Saito, who checked the Neiothen, then moved regardless of the stay command. Canyon shifted in front of them. "Stomach wounds are tricky. He's treating him, or he'll die."

"No," came a firm voice from the far side.

"We're not stopping," Canyon said. "You'll shoot us all before we'll just watch one of our own die. My brother knows that. I think you all do."

The Neiothen turned, their postures strangely stiff. They were looking at each other but, again, nothing was being said or done. She grew convinced they were talking—Reaper just couldn't hear it.

"What's going on?" Mercy whispered.

"Helmets are masking their words," Canyon said, mirroring Iskra's thoughts as he glanced back to check Saito, who was hauling a med kit closer and digging out an IV. "That's top-level gear." Jaw set, shoulders squared, he met Dru's gaze and stared for an eternity.

"What's the director doing?" Mercy muttered.

"Cell," Saito growled. "Stay with us!"

"Don't do this," a nearby voice pleaded.

Leif didn't acknowledge Dru. Didn't give away his identity or position.

"You know this is wrong."

Jaw clenched, he clicked off his internal mic. "I warned you," he hissed. "Trusted you."

"Hey!" Andreas barked, storming over to Canyon. His brother had countermanded the order to save Cell's life and, with Saito, was running IVs and oxygen. Cell looked bad.

Leif keyed his mic to the team. "Leave them." He then hit the external. "Only the medics with him. Everyone else back to the center."

"Don't get distracted," Vega warned him. "They're playing on your sympathies."

"We can fix this," Dru intruded again. "Trust me—we can get it sorted. I know I—"

Fed up with the poison coming out of this man's mouth, Leif lifted his weapon as he rotated and aimed at Dru. "The devil was once an angel."

"External's on," Andreas alerted through closed comms.

Leif didn't care. He wanted Dru to get the meaning—he was going to be more careful about who he trusted from now on.

M4A1 tucked firmly into his shoulder, he kept his stance

relaxed. He'd never felt so in control as he did now—despite the river of rage rushing through his veins.

Hands up, Dru stared at him, unwavering. "Hear me out."

"No!" Leif growled. "No more." Never again. He plowed forward. "Down!" He motioned to the floor. Breathing felt like lifting hundred-pound weights. "On your knees, or they'll be mopping your gray matter off the concrete!"

"Better," Andreas muttered, his mic still internal. "It's the end he deserves after killing Rutger."

"The end?" Leif hesitated, scowling at Andreas. "That's not the plan."

"Plans change."

He thought of how plans *had* to change in the Durban facility because they'd been set up, lost a man, and nearly died facing the Gen2s. Did Dru know about the orangutans? He'd certainly known more about Leif than he'd ever let on. Had spewed years of lies.

"Let's go, Ossi," Vega said. "Time's up. We got what we need to end this."

It was bad enough, breaching this bunker. Leif had to turn away before he did something he couldn't take back.

Dru shifted forward. "Please—"

Placing his finger on the trigger had the desired effect. Dru stopped short. Eased back. It surprised Leif how much he wanted to pull the trigger. How much he wanted Dru to understand the futility that had been his life. The gouging effect of betrayal. If only—

White-hot fire speared Leif's head. With a growl, he slammed the heel of his hand against his temple. His knees buckled. He fought for mental purchase around what felt like a steel pike driving through his skull. He saw Dru rush him.

Andreas manifested between them, slamming his M4 into Dru's head. He caught Leif's arm. "You okay?" he asked privately.

Leif shook his head, swallowing as the pain abated. "Yeah." He glanced at the director.

"He's alive, but I can change that," Vega promised.

He recalled the Taipei children's park—the sound that went through his head. That meant . . . "I think there's an ArC operative here."

TWENTY-THREE

A sharp whistle sailed through Leif's comms, as if confirming his words.

He grunted. "What is that?" he asked, keeping his movements small. He did his best not to react. It was part of the method to this insertion: everyone moved with precision and nobody took the lead, so Reaper couldn't identify Leif. But Dru had. He'd guessed.

"What are you hearing?" Andreas asked.

"A . . . whistle." Man, the shrieking made it hard to think. He shook it off. "It's the same as what hit me in the park, only . . . quieter. Less painful."

"I don't hear it," Vega said, "and that's not something I'll forget anytime soon."

Glad for their internal mics so Reaper didn't know what was happening, Leif focused on the task. On this . . . ordeal. He eyed Cell curled up with lead in his gut from an apparent ricochet after Vega had shot the laptop. Cell had likely been trying to communicate with someone on the other side of the emergency doors. The punk always had to find those soft spots to poke.

But Leif hadn't wanted this. Yes, he needed answers. Yes, he still intended to get them, but *this*? The worst of it was, he wasn't sure he trusted anyone in this room right now because, to them, *he* was a traitor. That meant they would treat him as such.

"Six minutes," Vega subvocalized.

Four to finish up here, two for exfil. It'd be tight.

That whistle resurfaced, and Leif steeled himself with a hissed oath. Was his ear bleeding? It felt like it.

Dru groaned and came to, shifting a hand to the back of his head. His gaze rose to Leif. Sharpened. Full of hurt.

Good. Now he knew what betrayal felt like. Leif had laid trust at this man's feet like a loyal dog, and the director trampled it without remorse.

Just over Dru's shoulder stood a woman he didn't recognize. The others seemed to distance themselves from her. Who was she?

Didn't matter. Because it was Canyon and Iskra who hammered his conscience, what with her sad eyes and the *I'm going to bust you upside your head* look from his brother.

"Let's do it," Andreas ordered.

Surprise smacked Leif. "What?"

Vega and Andreas cuffed the director's arms and hauled him to the conference room.

"What're you doing?" Conflict twisted Leif's gut, guessing what they intended. "This wasn't part of the plan." Making them pay had been the point, but . . . this looked like punishment.

"You're too soft," Vega said. "They need to answer for what they've done."

Dru wrestled against them. "Hear me out! I can explain."

"No!" Leif growled, spinning on him. He was sick to death of explanations, but he also knew that if he didn't intervene, there was no telling what the others would do to Dru. "No more!"

"Your destiny," Dru said. "What you're doing—what you're seeking? It's your destiny. I could give you thirty reasons why."

"Destiny?" Blind rage threw Leif forward. He punched Dru,

sending him sprawling. "Is that destiny?" His pulse thundered. "You're going—"

"Hey!" Carsen shouted, leveling his weapon at the unknown woman, who had tripped into Colonel Nesto.

The brawny officer stumbled and cursed, rounding on the girl. "What're you doing?"

"I wasn't *doing* anything." She looked terrified. Then again, she didn't.

"Easy!" Canyon called as he rose from his haunches, hands bloodied.

"Time's up!" Vega surged forward. "End Iliescu and get out of here."

Destiny . . . "No! Nobody kills him," Leif subvocalized, suddenly recalling something he'd seen in Dru's office when he'd pulled the laptop. He hurried back, snatched the photo from the desk, and stuffed it in his go-bag. "Leave him," he ordered.

"He needs to go down. He killed Rutger."

A shriek screamed through the facility.

Vega turned his gun on Dru, and Leif pivoted just in time to sweep the muzzle up. "I said *no!*"

"Incoming!" Andreas warned the team. "Time to bug out!"

"Flashbang!"

Canyon grabbed Iskra and spun away, tucking her head and protecting her.

Iskra closed her eyes and opened her mouth as the concussive burst slammed into them. After counting to five, she pivoted with Canyon. Coughing, she hurried through the haze and slowed, not able to see well.

Ahead, a dark circle seemed to move through the smoke. A hatch. It swung closed. A false wall panel slid into place, concealing the access point.

She raced toward it, too late, and slapped the wall. Banged, trying to find a way to release the mechanism.

"Where'd they go?" Canyon asked.

Iskra motioned toward the wall. "Back there, somewhere. The whole wall moved."

Frustration crowded his blue eyes, but he nodded. "Let's help the others." He limped back to the hub with her.

Iskra took in the scene. Chaos was the order of the day, with Nesto on a secure phone trying to release the bunker from lockdown and Braun tending a groaning Iliescu. Saito and Baddar lifted Cell from the floor and hurried him to the small surgical bay. Canyon knelt beside Culver, who was alive but pale and clammy from blood loss.

Groaning reverberated through the hub and lights stopped swirling. The heavy steel barriers retracted into the walls, allowing in more soldiers and Marines, along with a dozen or so other armed personnel. SWAT still milled about, ensuring there were no further active threats.

Iskra felt useless—but also glad that professionals were taking care of the wounded. She watched as an EMT delivered Iliescu to a chair and then placed an ice pack on the back of his head.

"What's the status here, Director?"

Iliescu winced—whether from the man or the pain couldn't be discerned. "Unknown, Mr. Secretary. Insurgents are gone, one man is in surgery with life-threatening wounds, another"—he nodded to Culver—"shot in the chest."

"And you?" The concern in the secretary of defense's eyes surprised even Iskra.

"I don't have a wound I didn't deserve," Dru said.

The SECDEF nodded as he took in the bunker. "What happened? How in Sam Hill did they get in here?"

Heat darted through Iskra, recalling the hatch the Neiothen had disappeared through. Mentioning it now meant they would have a lead on finding Leif. And she was not sure that was the right thing. Not yet.

Then again, Leif was part of a team that had shot nearly every member of Reaper and nearly killed the director. But . . . it had been him, had it not, who intervened when the Neiothen aimed at Dru's head? But still, he participated, attacked his own people.

Guilt over the secret she harbored pushed her away from the conversation, not sure where to go, whom to talk to. She found herself wandering toward Mercy. Hand to her forehead, she struggled to sort out the insanity that had devoured their lives, unable to process her thoughts. It was like her brain and heart were shutting down.

"You okay?"

She flinched at the soft voice of Admiral Braun at her side. "Yes. No."

The admiral gave a soft laugh. "I can very much relate to that." She shook her head. "It's not every day you watch a Marine give his life for you." The security services were bagging the young Marine's body. "I'm not even sure I knew his name."

"Jim Lake," Iskra said quietly. When she first joined the team, she had made it her business to know all the names of those working in the bunker, because she had deemed every one of them a threat. Hristoff and Veratti had their hands in some deep pockets, and she did not doubt someone was spying on her for them.

"Do you think Leif was here?" the admiral asked quietly, her head tucked.

"Yes." Admitting it was not a betrayal, yet somehow it felt like one.

"They did a fine job, not really rallying behind one person until the end. It became clear then. Think that was Leif leading?"

Yes. "I do not know." Iskra deliberately kept her hands at her sides, avoiding the tell of folding her arms, which would suggest she was trying to hide something. "How could he be in charge of another team when he has only been gone a few weeks?"

"You're having a hard time believing it was him."

"This was not Leif," Iskra said. "Not the Leif we know."

"It's hard to fathom him working with ArC."

"He is not."

"You sound convinced."

"ArC took my daughter," Iskra said in a dull voice. "They would not do that if they already had Leif in their corner. They needed a hostage to leverage against him." Speaking those words helped her cement her own convictions. Her belief in Leif.

"I didn't know." Admiral Braun almost sounded sincere. "I'm sorry. Do you know where they're holding her?"

"No."

"We'll find her."

Iskra gave a curt nod but said no more. Nobody understood the things she'd done over the years to save her daughter . . . except Leif. She didn't know what the Neiothen were after, but she would find him. Give him a chance to answer. She owed it to him, after all he had done for her.

"Do you think your brother was among them, too?"

The admiral was asking a lot of questions. Was she blaming Iskra? She considered the stout woman for a long moment. "Mitre is coldhearted, so it is not difficult to accept that he was here."

The colonel stormed across the hub to Iliescu. Though his words weren't detectable, his gruff tone was clear. Iskra did fold her arms then, not caring if she telegraphed a message. Her instincts told her that officer was trouble.

"He means well," Admiral Braun said, "but he's the proverbial bull in the china shop. He's going to bring this thing down if we aren't careful."

"What thing?" Iskra asked. "Reaper? Leif?"

"All of it." Braun sighed and shook her head. "If you'll excuse me, I should insert myself before the testosterone war detonates."

Dru sat behind his desk, mostly because the blow on the head was still blurring his vision and turning his stomach. The EMT said he likely had a concussion. Seated across from him were the SECDEF and Nesto, who had somehow elevated himself above Braun.

"You failed this bunker," Nesto said through gritted teeth. "They relied on you, and you brought the serpent right into it."

"Don't we have better fish to fry?" Dru asked. "Or do you seriously think blaming me is the right way to spend our time here?"

"What else would you suggest?" Nesto barked.

"How about the systems the insurgents took? The phones, laptops, tablets? What about the men they shot and wounded? I didn't see you trying to stop or thwart them."

"What? You think I was in on it?"

"No, I think you're a coward who hid when the trouble started."

"Listen, I want to hear it all," the SECDEF said. "Start from the top. When you first noticed them coming—"

"Right." Nesto shifted to the edge of his seat and nodded. "Of course, sir. I had been here—"

"I wasn't speaking to you, Colonel." The SECDEF gestured to Dru. "If you don't mind, Director."

Braun opened the door and stepped inside. "Sorry I'm late. Following up on some things."

"Good timing," Dru said. "SECDEF wants to hear what happened. We'll need to notify Lake's family."

"Already working on that."

Dru launched into a detailed explanation of how he'd detected an intrusion at home, the weapon pointing to the picture. Something registered at that moment, and he flicked his gaze to the side of his desk. The picture was gone. Hand over his mouth, he felt the blood drain from his face.

"One heck of a shock, wasn't it, to find someone had been in your home without alerting your security or surveillance." SECDEF nodded grimly. "He didn't steal anything?"

Dru had to play it cool. Not overreact to the missing picture. "No, not even the weapon he could've easily made off with." Instead he'd used it to make a point. And it still surprised Dru that Leif knew so much about his personal life, right down to where he'd hidden the gun.

After thirty minutes of grilling by the SECDEF and patronization by Nesto, Dru sat alone with Braun. She mentioned something about debriefing Reaper individually, and then they chatted about the useless intel they'd extracted from the operative who'd posed as the Chinese delivery guy. The Agency had taken possession of him, and if they didn't get anything out of him, he'd be stuck in some nameless, windowless prison for the rest of his life for trying to kill their deputy director.

Dru's thoughts kept coming back to the missing frame. At some point, Alene left him alone with his doubts and fears. Leif. The picture.

"Director." Saito rapped on the open door. "They're taking Cell up to the hospital to do a CAT scan, make sure the ricochet didn't do any internal damage, but he's stable."

"Thank you—for stabilizing him and for updating me."

"No problem, but Canyon deserves thanks. He stood down the Neiothen so I could get to work. Oh, and Culver is stitched up and heading home to rest."

So that left Mercy, Iskra, and—

"Saito."

"*Hai.*"

"Where's Cell's friend, Alisz?" Dru was on his feet

"Went with him in the ambulance." Saito sniffed. "Kind of glad to get her out of here. Didn't trust her."

That shouldn't have been allowed. She was free after having access to the bunker. Was her presence and the subsequent insertion coincidence? He needed to find out. "Find her, bring her back."

Saito hesitated. "I thought you cleared her."

No time to explain. "Just get her back here."

"Okay, but isn't searching for the Neiothen top priority? With Cell down, we need more hands—"

"Find her. We'll handle tracking the Neiothen."

Leg pinching with pain, Dru reached for the phone but once again thought of the picture and dropped back against his chair. He knew. Leif *knew*. The picture at his house that Leif had pointed the gun at? It hadn't just been Dru in that picture. He'd been standing in front of the yacht he'd named *Your Destiny*. Leif had put it together and knew the picture on his desk wasn't just about friendship. It was about protection.

"Director?"

He glanced up as Iskra entered his office. "Hey. You okay?"

"No," she said quietly as she moved farther in. "What did he want?"

He sagged, shoving his mind away from the picture. Away from what it meant. "I don't know. He never asked for the book or the painting—which, where are they?"

"Safe." Her eyes were hard, uncooperative. "But I didn't mean what he wanted from the bunker. I meant—what did he want from *you*? From this office? He risked the last few seconds to come back in here. Why?"

Dru couldn't answer. Didn't want to. That would open a can of worms he couldn't come back from. A confession he wasn't ready to make. "I couldn't tell you," he lied. "Obviously they were looking for something."

Her lips thinned. "He found whatever he was looking for," she said with an edge to her words. "He came in and exited fast. I am pretty sure you know what he took, because you are way too calm and collected."

Iskra might've been an operative, a trained killer for Hristoff Peychinovich. She might have gained a reputation for being painfully persuasive, but there was a reason Dru Iliescu was the Deputy Director of Operations with the CIA.

"I am calm," he said, deliberately focusing inward and slowing his heart rate, his racing thoughts, "because I've had an attempt on my life, a threat to my career, and Leif broke into my home. My task force"—he indicated the hub, where a sense of order was slowly returning—"was attacked, several shot, and one member is en route to the hospital." He drew in a long breath and slowly exhaled. "If I was panicked, I'd make mistakes and invite more trouble." He held her gaze for several long seconds. "I cannot afford more mistakes."

Iskra had an iron will and a steel spine. Arms folded, she returned his stare and unnatural calm. "What mistakes, Director?" That she stood at the corner of his desk and didn't take a seat told him she was positioning to dominate this conversation. "I'm really struggling to believe Leif did this in the first place, so whatever brought him here . . ." She nodded, the weight of her thoughts visible in her stooping shoulders. "It was big. And I'm going to find out."

"Focus on finding Leif," Dru said. "Because after what happened here, if they can definitively prove he was involved, Braun and those with oversight will pull the plug, strip me of authority, and deal with him in their own way."

"Deal with him?"

"You're a smart woman, Miss Todorova. You know what it means."

"Your acerbic responses tell me I'm hitting a nerve."

"My last one, apparently." He stood. "Time to get back to work. We need to determine which direction the Neiothen went." Hands on his belt, he inclined his head. "Unless you feel the need to question me more?"

Irritation rippled through her features as she turned and walked to the door. Touching the handle, she looked back. "I only came in here because Leif considers you a friend. I thought that would matter to you."

No, Leif considers me a traitor.

TWENTY-FOUR

When Iskra walked out of the director's office, she was more convinced than ever that Leif had found what he'd been looking for. Back in the slowly quieting hub, she spent the next hour writing what she remembered, hoping something would reveal itself. The last of the SWAT members left, taking with them the dozen military police. Lingering behind were a handful of uniforms.

Canyon joined her. "What'd he say?"

She eyed Mercy, who was working at a station. "That he did not know what the men wanted."

"And you don't believe him," he said, angling his head, his all-too-perceptive gaze seeming to catalog her facial responses.

"Leif hurried into the director's office before leaving. He wasn't in there more than a minute before returning to vanish with the others." She nodded in that direction. "He went in with intent and exited quickly."

Canyon bobbed his head, looking toward the main foyer, thinking things through. "Maybe he wanted to verify the Neiothen had pulled all the director's devices. That'd be the right amount of time to get in and out."

Iskra bristled. "He could've seen that from the door."

"Maybe he was being thorough," Saito added, joining the conversation. "I can see Leif doing that, double-checking."

"Since when?" Mercy scoffed, sauntering over with a grim

231

expression. "Leif never babysat anyone. He trusted them to do their jobs so he could do his."

Iskra agreed. "No, he didn't go in there to be thorough. Think about it—they came in here and did what, steal computers?"

"Computers," Mercy said, "that will be shut down and remotely wiped as soon as they're powered up. The Agency won't allow anyone to get a lick of information off them, if those guys have any say." She nodded to the suits still working on the main systems at the central hub.

"Leif had to have known that," Iskra muttered. "They knew how to get in here. Surely they would know there were protocols for the computers."

"Maybe the systems were a ruse," Canyon offered, scratching his jaw. "They come in, the guys run through snatching computers and phones."

Saito palmed his bandaged leg. "And we watch them, concerned."

"So," Baddar said, taking up a stance behind Mercy, "what did we miss?"

"I am not sure we missed anything," Iskra said quietly. "I believe they came here because of what I stole from Leif in Germany."

Canyon scowled. "You stole from him?"

Guilt tugged at her conscience. "Not my best moment, but in my defense, I thought he was attacking me in an attempt to get away. He drew a gun. I saw he had a satchel and took it—only realizing afterward that he was protecting me from other gunmen. I do not know who they were."

"That satchel contained the Book of the Wars," Mercy said.

"And a small bifold painting."

"Why'd you take them?" Canyon asked.

"Because I thought if Leif had gone to the dark side, which seemed to be the case when he pulled a gun on me—"

"Which you just admitted was a misread of the situation."

She nodded. "I thought he had been activated like the other Neiothen, so I could not trust him with the Book of the Wars. And Reaper needed it to learn about and stop the last war. And I hoped taking it would . . . force him to come back to me."

"Which it did," Canyon said with an appreciative look. "Perfectly."

Her heart stuttered at the truth of that.

"But we have the scans of the book, don't we?" Mercy asked. "Sorry, I'm just trying to understand why we even care about the actual book anymore."

"We all are," Saito said. "This is really confusing and messed up. Including that Vogt chick. Is anyone besides me concerned?"

"Any time a new element is introduced, skepticism is natural," Canyon said. "Including the addition of me."

"Taking the satchel seemed right at the time," Iskra said, "but you have a point. I do not know why we need the book when we have the scans."

"Scans aren't good enough," Harden said, appearing from the side-access tunnel with a slow grin. "Sorry. I wanted to come when I heard about the incident, and Dru informed me earlier that you had the book hidden somewhere." He stared at them and seemed to understand they all saw him as an outsider. "Listen, the scans were great, but with the actual book, we can do testing. We can use special equipment to see if more text is hidden in the leaves. Nuances show up with the right tools."

"But it doesn't change the prophecy, right?" Mercy asked. "So why would Leif come back for that?"

"I think it was the painting he wanted," Iskra said. "He stole it from Hermanns' estate before the Taipei mission, but I did not think it important—odd, yes, but I was distracted by my brother." She shoved her hair from her face with a sigh.

"Regardless, I shouldn't have taken the satchel, and now I have irrevocably damaged my relationship with Leif." Her throat felt raw. "He was my only hope to get Taissia back."

Canyon touched her shoulder. "Don't give up on Leif so easily. He's a Metcalfe. We know the right road, even if it takes us a while to travel it. And we'll find your daughter, one way or another."

The desperation of that thought, of knowing another day had gone by with her daughter in dangerous hands, made her stomach roil. "But I do not think that will happen without Leif. They must have taken her to draw him out."

"Can we back this landslide nightmare up to Vogt again?" Saito said, narrowing his eyes at Mercy. "She seemed to know a lot about what you were doing. And called you by a different name."

Mercy tightened her lips.

"No response?" Saito challenged.

"No," Mercy said, then sighed. "Not until I speak with Dru."

"I hear the Neiothen say 'Ossi,'" Baddar said. "That is the name for Runt in Taipei, yes?"

"It was," Iskra said. "And I believe it was Leif who went into the director's office just before they left." She felt like she was beating a dead horse. Maybe she should just let it go.

"Did Iliescu say anything was missing?" Saito asked.

"He said he couldn't tell."

Saito sniffed. "Have you ever known the director to miss a detail?"

This almost sounded like they believed her. Iskra peered over Canyon's shoulder at the director's office. "There are too many things happening lately that are not adding up."

"There was that attempt on his life," Mercy commented. "That Chinese food delivery gone wrong."

"Right," Saito said, "and they locked that guy in the tank."

His brow knotted in confusion. "I don't think I ever heard what happened to him."

"CIA took him," Mercy said.

"So y'all think that's connected to this?" Canyon asked. "To the Neiothen?"

"We never got read in," Saito said. "Maybe we should ask."

"Excuse me!" Nesto's voice boomed through the bunker. "Anyone here actually doing any work? Anyone know where these guys went when they left the bunker?"

Mercy whirled around. "Sorry, but that's Cell's specialty, and since he's in the hospital, we just—"

"I don't care what you were *just* doing," Nesto barked, crowding into their space. "You've got hacking skills, Miss Maddox, so stop pussyfooting around." His gaze blazed, red rising through his complexion. "You've all had enough time to sit around and whine about what happened. Now find out where those men went. Run surveillance. Hop security feeds. Find them! I want IDs on each and every one."

"IDs?" Canyon straightened and unfolded his arms. Challenge in his posture and tone. "You recall they wore balaclavas and voice-masking devices?"

Nesto shouldered into Canyon, who held his own. They were two very evenly matched men, except one had control of his temper. "Are those excuses you're sending my way, soldier?"

"Just facts. Facts that make it pretty impossible, unless you have software that can see through tac gear, to do what you're asking. But if you have that tech, it'd be helpful to these operators, who would very much like to find and retrieve one of their own."

"That your way of saying Metcalfe was involved?"

"That's my way of saying we want him back. Wherever he is."

Nesto's fury colored his cheeks again. "Then—"

"Colonel," Admiral Braun called from outside her office. "Let's talk."

Iskra tried to hide the smile that crept onto her face, watching Nesto do his best to save face and extract himself from the confrontation he'd started. The irony was that he'd tried to ply information from Canyon, but the former Green Beret had a defiant streak like his brother's and hadn't given an inch.

"Was that necessary?" Nesto's growl snuck past Braun's office walls. "I was—"

"I know very well what you were doing, and while I may have agreed to your temporary assignment here, I will not allow you to tear down a team that is doing their darndest to disrupt ArC's influence and efforts."

Canyon rolled around with a grin.

Saito sniggered. "You love ticking him off."

"One of life's finer pleasures." Canyon nodded to Iskra. "So the book and painting?"

Iliescu stepped from his office, glanced their way, and hesitated. The elevator door dinged, a strangely regular sound that felt out of place now. However, when the doors opened, Cell emerged, holding his side and walking slow and stiff under the aid of Alisz Vogt.

"What in blazes are you doing?" Iliescu growled. "You should be recuperating!"

"I agreed to go to the hospital for a CAT scan to make sure I wasn't going to die in my sleep tonight or something," Cell muttered. "But I'm not staying there. You have *no idea* where they put things when you're unconscious."

Baddar touched his shoulder. "It is good to have you back."

"I'm only back because we need to find out where those guys went." Something had shifted between Cell and Alisz, considering the way he didn't mind her assistance or hovering.

"Here." Alisz rolled the chair over to him. "Sit, and I'll wheel you around."

"I don't need a wheelchair."

"Sit," Saito said, "or I'm going to recommend restricted bedrest for a month."

"Restricted my big hairy—"

"Purcell!" Iliescu barked. "Sit down or leave. I won't have you dying on us because you pushed it too hard, too fast."

Alisz pushed him to a station. "Can I get you anything?"

"Yeah, some space," Cell bit out, then winced. "Sorry. Can I blame that on the pain and meds?"

Though Alisz cringed, she plastered on a smile.

"We'll see how long she can keep up that charm," Mercy said with a smirk. "Barc is testy even when he's not acting like a baby."

Fire shot through his side as Cell turned to the analyst bent over a dolly stacked with new computers. Tensing to ward off the pain, he gritted his teeth. "Derrick, how long till we're up and running?"

"Ten, twenty minutes." When Cell groaned, Derrick shrugged. "There are six guys working on it."

"Anybody got anything on the Neiothen's exfil or tracking them outside the building?"

The lanky analyst walked over and offered a tablet. "DIA sent surveillance pulled from a bank two klicks away. We haven't been able to check it out because of the situation."

Leaning on the desk, Cell glanced at the others. "They crippled us—it was intentional, to slow us down."

"That and the security protocol," Saito said from the main conference table.

"So we have no idea why they came, how they got away, or where they went." Iliescu shook his head. "They made no demands."

"No, but they sure left a lot of reminders," Saito said, touching his leg.

"Okay, here we go," Derrick announced. "This system's up."

Cell lunged forward. All kinds of fire and pain roared from his gut. He grunted, tightening in on himself, which seemed to make it worse.

"You should go home," Mercy said. "You need—"

"I *need* to find him." Cell knew this was *his* problem. His fault. It was messed-up psychology, but what could he say? Everything about him was messed up these days.

"Where do you want to go?" Alisz's voice was soft as she leaned over his shoulder.

Ashamed to need this much help and feeling even more awkward toward Alisz, he pointed to Derrick. "That system. I need to—"

Without waiting for him to finish, she nudged the chair in that direction. Once he was in place, she sat next to the station. "What can I do?"

"Nothing," he muttered as he tried logging in and was rejected. He hadn't wanted to trust her. She knew too much about Mercy, but she'd legit been there, caring for him at the hospital. And now. Her kindness was wearing him down— but was it an act? Did he care? With this much pain, he didn't.

"Oh," Derrick said, indicating the computer. "All logins have been changed because of the breach. You'll have to code in for a new login."

Cell grabbed his phone but hesitated. The woman at his right was supposedly very gifted with systems. If she saw his login . . .

Her hand rested on his shoulder, drawing his gaze up. She smiled, squeezed his arm, then walked away. A gracious exit so he could secure what he needed. Another way she was whittling down his misgivings. She was beautiful and smart.

Which meant she wasn't going to stick around. Not for him, anyway.

He coded in, provided his bona fides, and got set up. In minutes he was surfing his way through the surveillance cameras.

"I need to make some calls," Iliescu said, returning to his office.

Iskra shifted, her lips thinning as she watched the director. She started after him, then slowed to a stop. Hung her head and turned back to the hub.

Cell frowned. "Did I miss something?"

The concern that had been evident on her face pulled in close. She looked at his computer. "Think you can find the Neiothen?"

"That doesn't work," he said wearily, his gaze back on the feeds. "Y'all keep doing that thing where you don't answer my questions but instead divert to some other topic. It doesn't work. I still want to know what I missed."

Mercy popped his head.

"Hey," he balked, "wounded soldier here."

"That's what you get for worrying us. And . . . you missed a lot."

"Wait, you were worried?" He wanted to milk this, but he really had no energy. "Well, you're too late. My heart already belongs to someone else."

"Would that be me?" Alisz parked herself back in the chair.

"No." Cell flinched—his quick retort had hurt her, but he didn't have anyone in mind. "I mean . . ." She was attractive, but . . . "It was just a joke. To make her jealous."

"Jealous?" Alisz smiled around him. "But Mercy already has a special someone in her life. The Arab, right?"

"Baddar," Cell corrected. He cleared his throat but felt even that pull on the muscles in his stomach. "Anyway . . ." He scanned the footage at a fast clip, then rewound it. Repeated

239

the viewing. Next he watched the various feeds from the access passages.

"What's going on?" Saito muttered as he took the chair on Cell's other side.

"That's what I want to know," Cell said slowly as he worked. In one feed he found Iliescu waiting at a locked hatch, then he was joined by a Marine . . . then two, three . . . until there were more than a dozen standing there while two men worked to hack the locking mechanism.

"What am I missing?" Canyon asked.

Cell switched to an exterior feed and ran it forward fast enough that he wouldn't be sitting here all day but not so fast he'd miss something important. "Well . . ." He loaded the final angle. "There are only four access points to this hub, and I've viewed all footage and found exactly zero unfriendlies. And I am calling them unfriendlies, because hello? Bullet in the gut, thank you very much."

"It was a ricochet."

"I don't care what kind of *chet* it was," Cell said. "It hit me and hurts like crazy."

"Which is why you should be resting," Mercy chastised.

"I'm sorry," he said, looking at her, which made him cringe in pain. "But you have no say in my life. Remember, you have a man now." He nodded to Baddar.

"Jealous much?" Mercy smiled.

"Wait. You didn't argue. Seriously? You're a thing, the two of you?"

Canyon tapped Cell's arm and pointed to the monitor. "Can we pay attention here?"

"I am paying attention," Cell grunted with a glare. "Are you?"

Canyon frowned.

"What did you see? On those feeds. Tell me."

"Nothing. The access tunnels are empty."

"Exactly." Cell pulled up the parking garage and let it run for a few minutes. "And here?"

"Nothing," Saito muttered.

"Exactamundo." Cell lifted his hands in question. "So where, ladies and gentlemen, did our psychotic Neiothen go?" He sent the various feeds to the large screens around the hub, then let Alisz roll him around to face them. "That's every possible way they could've entered or left, yet . . ."

"They're still here?" Saito wondered.

"No," Canyon said. "Iskra saw a hidden hatch close here." He tapped the screen. "But like you said—the feeds don't show them exiting."

"Wait, you have intel and didn't share?" Cell meant to tease, but by the look on her face, he'd failed. And yet . . . he hadn't. "Isn't it time we moved past hiding things from each other?"

Iskra swallowed but couldn't hide her guilt-ridden expression.

"You mean, like you hiding that Leif was a Neiothen?" Saito challenged.

"That's my point exactly. I screwed up. If I'd come clean, maybe he wouldn't have choked the breath out of me. Maybe if Iskra had mentioned that she had the Book of the Wars and this whatever painting—"

"Okay, hold up," Canyon said, lifting his hand. "Let's just—"

"You seriously saw them leave?" Mercy asked, frowning at Iskra.

"Not directly," Iskra said. "I saw a hatch close. It's hidden behind a panel on the other side of the elevator."

Cell gaped, trying to figure out why she hadn't told them sooner, but more importantly—was there a camera on that tunnel? If so, why hadn't Command sent that their way? "But you did know that much, and we could've had analysts all over it for the last hour."

He lifted his phone and dialed Braun's extension, knowing he did not have the strength or willingness to walk the twenty paces to her office.

"This is Braun."

"We need to talk about the secret passage by the elevator." He waited for her response but didn't hear anything. "Admiral?" He glanced at the phone and frowned.

"How did you know about that?" Her stern voice closed in from behind him.

Cell swiveled and peered through Reaper, who were clustered around him. "I didn't."

"After the flashbang," Iskra said, "I saw the hatch close and the panel slide into place over it when the Neiothen left."

Braun's face went ruddy. "Why didn't you say something?" she nearly screamed. "Did you tell Iliescu?"

"No," Iskra said.

"Admiral, are there cameras on that passage?" Cell asked.

Braun threw a sharp look at Iskra. After a huff, she shook her head. "No cameras. That tunnel isn't in use—it flooded two years ago during a hurricane. But it feeds into a parking structure, where there *are* cameras." She gave him the location of the garage.

Cell went to work and pulled the recorded footage. "And on the monitors . . . now." He peered at the one dangling over his terminal. They watched and were met with the same frustrating result.

"Nothing," Saito muttered.

"Wait," Canyon said. "Back up."

Cell scowled but did as requested, then let it play.

"Here." Canyon pointed to the big screen on the wall. "Put it up here."

"What're you seeing?" Iskra turned as the video sprang onto it and started playing.

"Okay . . . there! Stop."

Cell clicked, his heart thumping a little wildly. Though he was staring at the same thing on his monitor, he saw nothing. "Dude, what—"

"Tighten in on this vehicle."

"*Vehicle?*" But Cell complied, zooming and cleaning up the image.

"Bingo." Canyon thumped the screen, where the reflection of a man in black tactical gear was removing a balaclava.

"I don't understand," Mercy whispered. "How is his reflection in that car but he's not showing up on the video?"

"They knew where the cameras were," Canyon said, "and stayed out of view but didn't think about their reflections."

"Good work," Braun said, nodding as she considered the images. She patted Cell's shoulder. "Can—"

"Sharpen that up, son, and get me an ID on that face," Nesto intruded into the conversation.

"That's as good as it gets," Cell said, taking entirely too much pleasure in letting down the colonel. "It's a reflection, so the facial quality is already hindered."

"Send it to me," Nesto barked.

Almost curling his lip, Cell rolled his eyes.

"You rolling your eyes at me?" Nesto demanded.

"No, sir," Cell coughed, then grabbed his side. "Just this wound . . ." He saw the way Saito and Canyon smirked. "Corrupted image coming your way." He did not like the way Nesto had barged in, and he found himself wondering if this guy was connected to ArC. Man, he did not like having a hunch about this guy. Because his hunches, more often than not, were right.

"So you can't find them?" Braun growled.

"If we had more analysts and several very long days . . ." Cell said, trying to sound contrite but knowing it came out sarcastic. "Not with them knowing where the cameras are."

Nesto growled—literally—and stormed back to his tiny office, which had been a closet before his intrusion into the bunker.

Braun massaged her shoulder. "Keep trying to find more, Purcell."

"Will do, ma'am."

Alisz shifted, her eyes a little brighter as she watched the admiral leave. Her gaze hit Nesto's office, then Braun's. She was on to something. He didn't know how he knew, just did. It was still hard to trust her, to open up to her, but she'd stayed at the hospital. Helped him make his break and get back to the hub.

"Alisz?"

She started, jolting in her chair.

"You got something?"

She swallowed but then gave a clipped nod. "I . . . I think—no," she corrected, looking down. "There is a way to track the Neiothen."

He wanted to laugh, but that was the last thing he'd do—it hurt his wound. Besides, he had this strange compunction not to alienate her. "What do you mean?"

"They have these chips in their heads—RFID."

"What?" Canyon asked, scowling.

"RFID," Alisz repeated. "Resonant frequency identifier."

"He knows what it means." Cell felt like a fool at her sudden interest in tracking the Neiothen—tracking Leif. It struck him that coming to the bunker had been her idea. Not that she'd said it directly, but . . . "I thought you were an art analyst. How do you even know about them?"

"I am an art analyst," Alisz laughed. "By day. But I'm—well . . ." Her gaze hit Mercy. "She and I aren't too different."

"Don't start that trouble here," Mercy bit back. "Not now."

"What trouble?" Alisz's innocence was a tad on the fake side.

"Wrong tac," he warned, shaking his head. He wanted this to be a bad dream. Couldn't he just once meet a smart, sexy hacker who was really what she claimed to be?

"Look, we may be similar"—she flinched when Mercy twitched toward her—"except *I* can't track that RFID." She nodded, her gaze too eager. "But Ariadne knows how."

"What? No!" Mercy surged toward Alisz and growled, "What're you doing?"

"Oh. That's right—"

"Airy-who?" It still galled him that he hadn't known Mercy's real name.

"Stop." Mercy seemed ready to kill. "Alisz, I swear—"

"She hasn't told you. After what just happened here, I'd think you'd want to know."

"You have no right," Mercy hissed, her face coloring with anger.

"Mercy, Miss Vogt?" Braun said with a curt nod from her office door. "With me."

"Wait," Cell said, frowning. "What's going on?"

His stomach hurt, and it had little to do with his wound.

Anger trembled through Mercy's limbs, making them heavy, and her head thickened with an explosion of adrenaline. When she entered Braun's office, she couldn't bring herself to sit. It felt like surrender. So she crossed her arms and moved to the far side of the admiral's desk.

After all these years . . . She'd broken away from her nightmare past and had magnificently managed to evade its toxic tendrils. With Dru's help.

The click of the door shutting resonated like a hammer coming down. Or maybe a guillotine, severing her career.

"I guess she wants us to talk it out," Alisz said.

Sure enough, she and Alisz were alone. At the door, the admiral stood with her back to the glass.

"I'm not doing thi—"

"Why?" Alisz shrugged. "I'm the same as you, Ari."

"Do *not* call me that," Mercy growled, rolling her shoulders as if she could get away from that name and what it meant, where it came from.

"Ariadne is your name."

"My name"—she drew in a leaden breath—"is Mercy Maddox."

"Is that how you deal with all the lies you've told over the last ten years?"

"It is who I am, who I choose to be." She glowered at Alisz. "Why?" She snapped her hands out for emphasis. "Why did you do this? You deliberately baited Cell, wormed your way into his search so that he'd ask for your help. You knew— *knew* he'd bring you here." She was so angry, she couldn't even find a Marvel parallel for Alisz. She didn't want to. She'd wanted to erase this woman from her life. "This could not have happened at a worse—"

"No," Alisz said, her tone ardent as she swept forward, "it's the *perfect* time." Her braids shifted with her emphasis. "Don't you see? That's why I came now. This is—"

"Have you been tracking me?"

Alisz straightened. Then cocked her head. "*She* has been tracking you."

"Mina," Mercy breathed. The name alone was acid on her tongue. She turned, rubbing her forehead as she fought burgeoning tears. "I left her and the school because I am not that person. I never was. I don't want—"

"How can you be so selfish?"

Mercy scowled. "Selfish? I'm not being selfish—it's for those people out there that I'm—"

"*Those* people need the skills Ariadne has. Those people need you to act, to use your training."

Wait. Something . . . Why was Alisz telling her to help Reaper? Alisz was as much ArC's pawn as Mina was, so why was she advocating for Mercy to help Reaper? "Mina's with ArC."

Alisz shrugged and rolled her eyes. "Yeah?"

Mercy studied her, the girl who had not gotten away from Mina and the school. What was going on? "With what's happening out there, revealing my . . . past"—she tried to breathe normally—"doesn't *help* anyone."

"Are you insane? Of course it does! Why are you hiding what you can do, anyway?"

"I've never hidden what I can do," Mercy snapped. "I just don't flaunt it. And if you had kept quiet, I would've been working on it without unnecessarily complicating things."

"Complicating?" Alisz frowned. "Unnecessarily?"

"Please, Alisz," Mercy hissed. "Just back off. In fact—when are you leaving?"

Alisz's freckled face darkened. "I have no plans to leave any time soon," she said defiantly. "Why do you think this is just about you? I've made a connection with Barclay."

"No no no." Mercy swung around the desk and moved toward her. "You are not—just stay away from him! Barc's a good man, and I will not stand around while you mess with his head, then rip out his heart."

"Wait, you mean the way you did?" She cocked her head. "He told me at the hospital. Do you have any idea how much you hurt him?"

"You don't know anything about my relationship with him. I've known him a lot longer and—"

"What? Are you angry because he likes me now?"

Mercy was going to stab her. With a pen. In the carotid. "You are sick," she snarled. "That was your problem—you always managed to reduce things to teenage drama. Who liked whom. Who hated whom. There's a massive war brewing,

and men are being killed, including someone I call a friend."
She sniffed. "So stay out of my business. And if you ever mention my past again—"

"What will you tell them?" Alisz challenged. "I mean, you have to explain this, right? Or are you going to lie to them more?"

"I've never lied to them," Mercy countered.

"So they know your name is Ariadne Wolff? They know that?"

"Many people use a pseudonym to protect their identity."

"Does that work for you, Ari? Did it work when you were with Ram?"

Mercy threw a punch. "Do not *ever* speak his name again."

Hand over the cheek that was swelling, Alisz didn't yell or grow angry. Instead, there were tears. Drawing up a breath seemed to bolster her. "You can't keep it, Mercy."

At the door, Mercy hesitated, confused.

"You can't keep this life. Mina won't let you."

"So you *are* spying for her." Mercy turned, ready to confront that challenge. "That was your first and last mistake. Because I promise—"

"You're right." Alisz's expression went strange, vulnerable—and she swallowed. "You're right. Mina told me to contact Cell. Ingratiate myself. Find you. And I jumped at the chance," she gritted out. "I hated you for leaving us. I wanted to make you hurt the way we—" She hung her head, sagging. "But as I headed over, I thought . . . maybe I could get away, too. Like you—start a new life." Her chin dimpled with choked-back tears. "I haven't tried in a very long time. I'm tired of it. I want a life, I want what you have." Her eyes glossed. "*That* is why I came here."

Overwhelmed by dueling emotions—angry that Alisz was here at Mina's behest, but also moved that she seemed so sincere, so desperate, and she could so perfectly recall her own desperation to flee—Mercy struggled for a clean breath. Yet . . . at the school, Alisz had been magnificent at turning the training scenarios in her favor. Was this another of her quick-witted twists?

"I have traced you for a long time, and when I saw that you were safe here, that they protected you—"

"No." Mercy stabbed a finger at her. "No, you're not doing that. *I* kept myself safe by being smart, by not playing the cards you're playing. This is not a game, Alisz. ArC nearly killed the very man who bought your pile of crap and brought you—"

"Into the sanctum?" Her tone went petulant, hurt. "That's what this place is to you—something you value, a safe place."

Mercy drew back, realizing exactly what she'd done— revealed the value she placed on Reaper, on Cell—and cursed herself.

"You better hide that Arab, Ari, because if Mina finds out you're in love—"

"I am not in love!" Her heart thundered.

"—you know what they will do. She has never forgotten you. Every other girl at the school endured her rage when you escaped. We got punished because of you. If you thought she was cruel before—"

"So what? You want to punish me?"

"Yes!" Alisz snapped, the first hint of real anger since she had entered the bunker. She drew back with a sardonic smile. "Very good." She lifted her chin. "I haven't been drawn out like that in . . . well, since you left." She smirked. "Very good, Ariadne."

In the school, there had been countless exercises in which they had to extract information, lure a person into a compromising situation that could be exploited. Her more advanced studies were then active scenarios where Mercy—who failed at the social-skill set—had to hack systems.

Part of her said the desperation roiling off Alisz was too genuine to be faked. But was it? Did Alisz truly plan to escape from Mina and the school? Mercy had been through the fire and came out on the other side. What if she could help someone else do the same?

"Why do you want to leave?"

Alisz snorted. "You have to ask?"

"I mean after all this time. Why now?"

She blinked rapidly, as if fighting off tears.

"You do recall I taught you that," Mercy said.

The tears fell away, replaced by a smile. "So you did."

"Just more of the game, I see."

"No!" Alisz lurched forward. "No, it's not a game."

"I'm losing patience, Alisz. Tell me why now. Why here? What did Mina want you to accomplish?" Mercy scowled. "I will make sure Dru buries you if you don't come clean."

Alisz looked down. "To get in here, make contact with you." Her eyes met Mercy's and shifted quickly. "Because I'd been there so long, because I'd kept to myself and obeyed like a *good* girl, she got careless about talking near me. I overheard things. Learned things." She nodded to the door. "Do you remember Nonna Kat?"

Something detonated in Mercy at the mention of that name, the woman who had cared for her, loved her. She recalled hours with Dietrich and programming races. At the tender age of five, she could do more with a computer than most adults. He'd taught her to disassemble one, build one. Then Nonna Kat died and left Mercy to the cruelty and brutality of Mina.

"I learned Nonna Kat didn't die of cancer. Mina killed her."

Mercy started. Tears and anger sprang through her system. "No, that—"

"She found out what Nonna Kat was doing, how she planned to escape, how she'd been training you on the side. Mina made a decision that cemented her relationship with Ciro Veratti. She had Nonna Kat killed and took you under her wing. To reprogram you."

Reprogram. Mercy felt a hot, leaden weight in her chest. Long ago she had shut out the cruelty of Mina's ministrations. Her endless hours of drills. The horrible things she'd made her do. Mercy had failed in acting, making her a wash as a spy, but her other skills . . . "I am not a computer to be—"

"No, but you do have what it takes to alter this final war, Ariadne."

"What're you talking about?"

Alisz snorted. Then frowned. "You really don't know?"

Mercy's stomach squeezed.

"To prove my sincerity, I'll tell you the truth, all of it, and I will not use any of my skills against you. You were pro— trained . . ." Alisz paused and seemed to consider her words. "Mina said Nonna Kat trained you to destroy the Neiothen if she could not undo the training. That's why Mina wanted me to come." She nodded. "To force you to find and stop them. They want those men dead and you can do it by tracking them through the RFID. Now, the real question is, what will you do?"

TWENTY-FIVE

Head in his hands, Leif crouched on the edge of a parking structure overlooking the Potomac. To the southeast lay the small inlet where he and the others had exfil'd from the bunker. Through the haze of the stun grenade, he'd seen Iskra standing on the other side of the hatch. Saw the hurt in her eyes, but also . . . understanding.

He didn't know if that made it worse or better. He certainly didn't feel better. This wasn't a course he should be on. It angered him that he'd been pushed to this point. Forced to take the situation into his own hands.

Don't blame anyone but yourself.

It was true. No matter what he faced, the choice was always in his hands. He chose this path. He hurt Iskra. He balled his fists, thinking how close the others had come to plugging Dru for good. How close control had been to escaping his grasp. Andreas had surprised him in the bunker. Had seemed so resolved to do violence. Then again, Andreas was like Carsen—both had suffered badly from what happened under Netherwood's scalpel.

But it wasn't just Netherwood—Ciro and the scientists—that was responsible. Dru . . .

Leif gritted his teeth and slumped onto the ledge, dangling his feet over the sixty-foot drop, cool air swirling around his legs.

". . . I don't have definitive proof. You know me. I've put my

own assets on the line for you." Had he? Had Dru really put assets on the line to help Leif? Or was it just a lot of talk?

"If you do this, if you succeed, I vow to help you get those answers . . . I'm not hiding anything about that black hole. About what happened to the Sahara Nine . . .when I have something I can bring into the open, I will."

Leif tugged the framed photo from his vest. Glanced at the image, then out at the darkening skyline. He didn't want to prove himself right, but . . . it was right here. Wasn't it?

He slammed the picture against the concrete, taking perverse pleasure in the sound of shattering glass. Holding the frame, he couldn't bring himself to remove the photo. But he had to. The resistance was just him not wanting to face a friend's betrayal.

Jaw clenched, he recalled Hermanns talking about the painting. The betrayal of a friend. Anna Gottlieb, the art expert, had mentioned the lake scene was symbolic of betrayal. Of a friend.

But maybe he was overthinking this. After all these years . . . the way Dru had gotten Leif back on track with a career and being productive . . . didn't Dru Iliescu deserve the benefit of the doubt?

Leif glanced down, grateful the irritating glow of a nearby billboard kept him from cutting his hand on the shards. He plucked the picture from the wooden frame and stared at it. It was a copy of the one he'd marked on the mantel in Dru's home. That was what had keyed Leif onto it. Why Dru had the photo in both places. It was too symbolic. The picture of him and the director aboard Dru's yacht. The boat Dru had named in the bunker. *Your Destiny.*

He wanted me to find this. Maybe not today, but the setup was clear. But why would he do that if he'd been hiding the truth from Leif? Hiding it in plain sight, which meant he wasn't really trying to hide it.

Still . . . he'd hidden it.

Was Dru on the up-and-up? There was no way to know right now. Leif folded the picture and tucked it into the pocket of his tac pants. Angling the frame down, he traced the side of the wood. Fingered the edge. Glanced at the back.

Was he wrong? The width seemed too thick. Or was it? Maybe it was just a solid frame. Leif dug his thumbnail along the corner but found nothing out of the ordinary. It had to be . . .

He huffed, lowering the frame. He was too desperate to prove Dru wasn't the betrayer in the painting. That, despite his gut instincts, the painting *wasn't* prophetic. That it wasn't tied to the Book of the Wars.

His phone buzzed in his pocket, unsettling him because only the Neiothen had this number, and they weren't supposed to make contact. Just rendezvous at the appointed time.

He tugged it out, recognized Andreas's code, and answered. "What's wrong?"

"That's what I want to know."

Leif frowned into the night.

"What happened at the facility?"

"What d'you mean?"

"I expected you to neutralize Iliescu. He killed Rutger. Betrayed you—us."

"If I killed everyone who betrayed me . . ." Leif shook his head and sighed. "I need Dru alive." He turned the picture frame over. "I need to talk to him about the painting."

"What's he got to do with that?"

"Something Rutger said," Leif admitted, hoping that divulging this now would be enough to fend off more questions over why he hadn't killed Dru. He rested the frame on his leg and pushed his gaze across the city again. "I'm not real excited about becoming what they programmed me to be—a sleeper assassin, a killer."

"It would be justified."

"See, that's the problem," Leif muttered. "Justified comes from the Latin *justificare*, which means to do justice to." He grunted. "I can't say killing a man is doing justice."

"They do not hesitate when it is us," Andreas said.

Leif grunted, rubbing his thumb along the corner of the frame as he thought about that. "We've already lost some, and if we stay on this path"—his thumb hooked a small ridge, and he worked at it—"more of us will die."

"ArC is not going to *do justice*, they are going to do violence. In the bunker," Andreas said, "you said you heard whistling."

"Yeah."

"Did you notice the woman bump the colonel?"

Leif thought back to that curious incident. "Yeah."

"I think he had an activation wand."

That made him hesitate. "So I was right. He's ArC."

"Our chips have unique RFIDs. You're the only one who heard the sound."

Gut twisting, Leif swallowed. Stared at the groove he'd worked his thumbnail into. "He was targeting me."

"That, or it was a good way to figure out which of us was you."

"To kill me."

"As I said, they are not seeking justice. They are seeking success."

Leif propped the picture against his leg and dug his thumbnail downward.

"I'll meet you at the rendezvous."

"Yep."

The frame backing split apart. Fell. He jerked to catch it. Felt himself swaying out into open air. He cursed and yanked back, his hand snatching a piece of the backing. He fell backward off the ledge. Landed hard on the garage rooftop and uttered an oath. Then laughed off the adrenaline buzzing his brain, glad he was alive. He'd nearly taken a leap of faith that would have proven deadly.

Leif lifted the piece he'd caught. His heart spasmed. It wasn't a photo—it was a painting. Half thrilled, he stared at it, realizing the horrible truth: it was the third panel.

He recalled Hermanns' words about the betrayal. And it had been Dru. His friend *had* betrayed him—this was the fullest betrayal. He'd had this panel the whole time, which meant Dru *knew* what the prophecy said. He'd known about Al'el—leaf. Leif.

Me.

REAPER HEADQUARTERS, MARYLAND

There were times Iskra did not know what to think or feel. Like when Mercy stormed out of Admiral Braun's office looking completely wrecked. She strode through the hub, straight past Saito and Cell, and rounded the corner leading to the medbay and bathrooms.

Baddar went after her.

Canyon turned to Iskra. "Any idea what that's about?"

"No." They all knew Mercy's past had caught up with her, but nobody wanted to believe she could be anything other than their ally. Yet questions remained. Mercy was the closest thing to a friend that Iskra had, but somehow Alisz—still in the office with Braun—unleashed doubt on that relationship. And she did not like to suspect her friends, so maybe she should talk to her. Iskra walked slowly after Mercy, not wanting her perception of the determined young woman to be altered.

In the hall outside the restrooms, Baddar stood in the corner, holding a crying Mercy.

Feeling like an intruder, Iskra backed off. Her friend would talk when she was ready, and whatever was going on with this Alisz had apparently rocked Mercy's world.

Iskra's entire life was trembling. Taissia was missing, her friend hurting, and Leif . . . She had no idea where Leif was.

When she returned to the hub, she spotted Director Iliescu heading out of the bunker in a hurry. When he gave a quick glance back, their gazes connected, and she not only saw his hesitation but felt it. He was leaving? After what just happened? With Cell trying to find the Neiothen?

Something told Iskra to follow him. Which made no sense. Who was she to follow up on the deputy director of the CIA?

Yet instinct forced her to obey. Problem number one was that the director exited via private access. She had no idea where that fed out to.

"Cell?"

"Yeah," he said, looking up—then grabbing his side with a grunt. He gave her a half smile. "What's up?"

Iskra leaned in conspiratorially. "Could you do something that may or may not be . . . approved?"

"You mean legal."

"If you want to be technical."

He considered her for several long seconds. "What?"

Her conscience pricked that she was more concerned about Iliescu than Taissia. "Two things. Can you look for my daughter? She was taken in Germany." She wrote down the address. "Maybe you can find something that will help me rescue her faster."

"I'm on it." He glanced at the scrawled address. "And the other thing?"

She tucked her hair back. "Follow the director."

His eyebrows flung upward, and he skated a glance around. "Whaddya mean, *follow*?"

"Can you get me a track on his phone so I can follow him?"

"Are you *insane*?"

"Usually." She shrugged, but there had been enough lies and nuances. "Something about what happened here felt off."

He frowned. "You think he was in on it?"

"No," she said quickly. "Nothing like that. I just—I think to find Leif, I need to follow the director. Whatever Leif took from his office at the end . . . it's important. When I asked the director about it, he blew me off."

"So that's what the weird vibe was earlier."

"I know he is concealing something, and I hope it is related to Leif."

"You're asking me to do something very illegal that could cost me my job."

"It could also save lives. Is your job more important?" It was an unfair challenge but one she needed to use to coerce him.

"No," he said grimly, "but the paycheck helps a lot." He roughed a hand over his face. "I find myself wishing I was still facing timeless heroes and supernatural artifacts."

"I . . . do not know what that means."

He sighed and shook his head. "I can't believe I'm going to do this, but I'll give you twenty-four hours." He nodded to her phone. "I'll send the link, but you have to promise none of your Viorica talents come out to play."

"Thank you."

"Nope, you did that thing—evaded the promise." He wagged his hand at her. "Cough it up."

Iskra kissed his temple and hurried away. She could not make that promise, because those skills were exactly what she needed to shadow the deputy director of the Agency. She headed over to her station and grabbed her things. Her phone pinged with the link from Cell, along with a text:

He likely has software that alerts him to tracers.
Be ready.

Ten minutes later, she was in her car heading east. Thankfully, it was dark enough not to worry about Iliescu spotting her when she caught up.

Using the GPS tracker link, she finally spotted him after nearly thirty minutes, coming out of a grocery store with a bag of food. He climbed into his SUV and pulled away. Next stop was a liquor store, where he purchased some spirits. Back in his car, he headed out toward Annapolis. Iskra allowed more distance, relying on the GPS and grateful it allowed her to lag and still know his location.

Her phone rang. There was no name on the screen.

Iskra faltered. When Veratti called, his information did not show up. There were few people who had her number, so the chances that it was him were high. She accepted the call and waited for him to speak first.

"Too busy to talk to me, Iskra?" Veratti chided.

"I am driving," she said. "It is illegal in Maryland to use your phone while driving, and I must avoid drawing the attention of the authorities."

"I thought you would take this more seriously."

"I take being arrested very seriously." She squinted against the headlamps of a vehicle in the oncoming lane. "But let us skip formalities. You took my daughter."

"No. That was not me, though I found the move brilliant." He clicked his tongue. "I wish I had thought of it. What better way to tie up your loyalties, yes?"

"A dangerous way," Iskra warned. "You know where Bogdashka took her."

"Of course."

And yet he withheld that information. "Do you expect me to find that book for you when you threaten my daughter?"

"You already found the book," he said, making her heart hiccup.

How could he know that? Only Reaper knew. . . .

"If you want little Taissia to remain alive and untainted, I would move quickly to get me that book. You'll be contacted. Don't let me down again, Iskra. It will be a costly, *childish* mistake."

When the call ended, Iskra banged the steering wheel. Resisted the urge to do something violent. Her anger crested then collapsed, leaving her in tears and challenging her ability to see the dark road clearly.

Oh, Taissia. My sweet, innocent girl. I am so sorry . . . so sorry I handed you into this nightmare. God, protect her. Please.

How? How did Veratti know what Reaper knew?

Alisz. Iskra hated the thought, but it made sense, since the young woman was new. Suspicious.

Glancing at the signal tracker, Iskra realized Iliescu's vehicle was no longer moving. After verifying the map, she turned onto Chesapeake Avenue, then slowed, gliding past Second Street. Driving down that road could reveal her.

Taillights vanished around a corner that dead-ended in a building. Iskra parked on Chesapeake. Using her phone, she walked First Street and was halfway down the block when Iliescu's tracker showed him in the water.

What? Iskra craned her neck and spotted the yacht club signs. Skipping a step, she wondered if he was already on a boat. He had to go through several steps to get a boat powered up before he set out, right? Still, she hurried and banked left at the large building marked *Bavaria*. His SUV occupied a slot perpendicular to a dock with a dozen boats and yachts moored.

Iskra made it to a white SUV and peered along its length, watching as the director stepped onto a very nice yacht with black windows running its length. The design was sleek and impressive—expensive. She drew in a breath as light caressed the name of the yacht scrolled across its transom. *Your Destiny.*

Somehow, Iskra connected the final dots. Dru had said something to Leif in the bunker about destiny. The photo on Dru's desk of the two men on this same yacht—that was what Leif had taken in the raid. And Dru had been trying to draw him here. Leif was coming *here*!

Should she just wait? Follow Iliescu onto the yacht? And then do what?

"Yeah." The director's voice boomed amid the clanging masts and lapping water, the dock eerily quiet at this late hour. "Heading out now. Yeah, okay—no. Look, I told you I'd take care of this." He grunted. "He'll come to me." He snorted. "Don't worry how I know. He will."

"He'll come to me."

When he climbed the stairs to the top canopied section of the yacht, Iskra seized the chance and scurried aboard, moving as light on her feet as she could along the Portuguese bridge. Afraid of being seen, she hurried to the foredeck, where she found an open lounging area.

Oh no. Where would she hide? A table was straddled by two long cushioned benches. Panic drummed—there was nowhere to conceal herself.

The director's form, silhouetted by soft lights, appeared almost directly above her and moved to her right. With a gulp, Iskra flattened herself against the bottom wall, peering straight up past the blackened windows to the bridge above, and prayed like never before that she wouldn't be discovered.

TWENTY-SIX

Cool night air tore at his windbreaker as Dru guided his Monte Carlo 86 yacht down the Chesapeake Bay. Dropping the hint to Leif in the bunker, in front of everyone, about *Your Destiny* had been a risk for many reasons. One, anyone there might've recalled the name of his yacht. Two, Leif might not remember. He had perfect recall, yes, but he was also greatly affected by that chip in his head and the months-long programming. Third, Leif was ticked, so inviting him out to a secluded area . . . But he believed in Leif more than he was afraid of him.

Seated on the flying bridge, Dru reveled in the beating wind. The yacht had been an extravagance, one of a very few he allowed himself. It was perfect for an escape from technology, agents, and stress when he needed to think and breathe. But with its top speed at twenty-nine knots, he wasn't going to outrace anything. On the other hand, with four cabins, a galley, two wet bars, a hot tub, and a salon, he was set up for a nice weekend getaway with friends . . . or alone.

This trip, however, wasn't about relaxation.

He glided beneath the Chesapeake Bay Bridge and headed to open water, trying not to think too hard about the danger he was walking into. At the bunker, he'd been certain one of the Neiothen was going to shoot him and that the one who'd stopped him was Leif. Anger, though controlled, had radiated off him like steam.

Forty nautical miles out, Dru let the engines idle and sat back, thinking. Praying his clues about *Your Destiny* had been enough, and yet afraid they were. It meant—

Something creaked behind him, a noise inconsistent with the yacht.

He whipped out from the upper helm and turned to the salon. "Le—" The name died on his tongue as he stared past the upper galley into the salon, where a person emerged from the shadows. "Iskra," he breathed. Then he cursed the implications of her presence onboard. "No, you can't be here." He rushed up into the salon.

She leveled a weapon at him. "Stand down, Director."

He drew up short, flashing his palms. "Iskra, this is a bad idea."

"There's been a lot of those, apparently." She wagged her eyebrows. "Nice boat."

He hesitated.

"The name—you used it in the bunker during the attack." She tilted her head. "Why are you luring Leif here?"

"I understand that you want to find—"

"I do not know what you are doing," she snapped, "why you are ambushing him, but—"

"*Ambushing*? No!" Dru inched forward.

"Unless you want holes in this luxurious yacht or your chest, stop moving," she said, her eyes unusually dark in the low night lighting he'd set on the flying bridge. "Just tell me why you did it."

The throaty twang of a high-speed boat snatched Dru's attention. He glanced starboard. "Pray that's not what I think it is." He hurried back to the upper helm and nodded at her weapon. "Aim that out there, not at me."

Moonlight ran its bright fingers over the hull of a fast-moving craft.

"Who is it?" Iskra asked.

"Either Leif or ArC. And at this stage of the game, I'm not sure which is worse." He motioned aft. "Go belowdecks."

"No, I am better in view. If it's ArC, Veratti would not want me killed."

"Why?" Dru said. "Do you really think you have value to him?"

"He wants the book, and he knows I have it."

"Where did you hide it?" Did it matter anymore? He wasn't sure.

She huffed. "Where he'd never think to look—his own loft."

Dru paused and smirked. "Smart." He activated the touch-screen control panel. "I think the book is a moot objective at this point in the game. And Leif will kill me if anything happens to you."

"I do not know that he cares," Iskra said.

"You know better than that." He opened a panel and drew out his own weapon.

"I'm not sure I do," she said quietly, her gaze on the approaching boat. "They're not slowing."

"Yeah, I noticed." He focused on the custom touch screen of the yacht's helm, directing power to the engines and activating them.

"They're coming straight at us," Iskra noted, her voice pitching.

The speedboat roared nearer.

Dru watched, somehow trusting—stupidly?—that the boat wasn't going to broadside them. Iskra shied away, as if that would protect her. In truth, if she wasn't killed on impact, she could be ejected through the glass canopy.

The speedboat swung hard to the foredeck, sending a wave of water across their bow as it shot away.

"What are they doing?" Iskra whispered, her voice breathless, mirthless. "Are they just playing with us?"

Dru stood, glancing at the speedboat as it circled around. "The next pass won't be a scare tactic."

"Or a distraction."

At the new voice, Iskra spun aft at the same time as Dru. Her weapon came up instinctively at the dark shape there. "Leif."

Amazed Leif wasn't wielding his Ruger, Dru flung a hand to the side, catching her arm so she wouldn't shoot. "No." He wished he could explain without stirring the boiling pot. He had no idea how many Neiothen Leif had brought aboard, and he wasn't going to take his eyes off him to find out.

Leif hadn't moved or spoken.

Tension radiated through the salon, and Dru shifted. "I'm glad you understood my message."

"What do you want?" Leif asked, his voice terse. "Did you bring her to soften me up?"

"No. You know Iskra has her own mind. She snuck aboard at the dock." He shrugged. "As to what I want—isn't this more about what you want?"

"What is going on?" Iskra started toward Leif. "What are you doing? Why—"

"Stay there!" Leif ordered.

Iskra drew up short. "Leif . . ."

"I'm not here for a social visit. Let's get on with it."

"Can we go belowdecks?" Dru asked, wanting a semblance of privacy and reassurance there wasn't a crosshairs painted on his head.

"Negative," Leif said. "We stay here where my team has a bead on you. If anything goes wrong or I give the signal . . ."

Exactly what he'd hoped to avoid. "STK." Shooting to kill felt overzealous but helped Dru gauge Leif's frame of mind. The threat was clear. "I was surprised at the disabling tactic you and the other Neiothen used in the strike on the bunker."

"No small talk," Leif said, resolute.

Rubbing his jaw, Dru lowered himself to the long couch that spanned the upper salon. Ironically, he realized his head was probably the only visible part of his body to the Neiothen. Like one of those shooting gallery ducks at a carnival.

"Why did you want me here?" Leif asked.

"To offer my defense." Dru squinted at the young man packed with resentment and anger.

"Not interested."

"Then are you interested in knowing that Mr. Purcell is fine? He had surgery, and by some miracle, the ricocheted bullet one of your men fired missed vital organs. Braun's Marine wasn't as lucky—dead. Culver is stitched up and more than a little ticked, but—"

"Not my concern."

Iskra huffed, apparently disliking the coldhearted answers as much as Dru did. She seemed to want to say something but didn't.

Had Dru miscalculated? Had something been done to Leif since he left? Had that implant triggered something . . . else? What if Dru's earlier misgivings were right—that this man wasn't the Leif he knew, the one he wanted to protect?

"Do you mind if I pour myself a drink?" he asked, pointing to the wet bar.

"They're watching," Leif warned.

"Right. Your team." Dru used the time and distraction of getting a drink to figure out what to say, how not to end up as shark bait in the Atlantic. He pulled the whiskey from the cabinet and poured a drink.

Leif stood silently.

"I'm sorry," Iskra said with more than a little irritation in her voice, "*what* are we doing here?" She moved toward Leif. "What is this? Why are you treating us—"

"One more move, and they'll tag you," Leif warned. "Viorica is a trained assassin, and they won't let you any closer."

The words seemed to strike Iskra hard. Her eyes glossed. "*Who* are you?"

Oh, that wasn't good. Her question would only drive Leif toward more frustration and distance.

Dru needed to draw the attention back to himself. "Leif, I did not kill Rutger." He lifted his snifter and moved closer again.

Fists balled, Leif stared back—hard. The recessed lights seemed to pulse along the bulging veins in his neck. "With his dying breath, he named you his killer."

Rutger had said Dru killed him? "No—"

"I *asked*," Leif growled, his lip curling, the words churning and mirroring his roiling anger. "I asked who killed him, who broke into his home and shot him point blank." His blue eyes sparked with the pain of that memory. "He named *you*." His nostrils flared. "Tell me you haven't been working all these years to hide the truth from me."

Dru pulled his gaze away, disheartened. Grieved. He looked at his drink. Tossed it back, willing it to numb him. "I don't know why Rutger said I killed him. It wasn't me. I was here—and I didn't hire anyone to do it."

"Then why did he name you?"

Dru moved back to the wet bar and poured more drink. "Rutger has been in contact with me for a while. Years. We are—were—friends. Maybe he was going to tell you—"

"About this?" Leif held up the painting.

Guilt made Dru swallow hard. He set down the liquor. Braced himself against the alabaster wet bar, drowning in self-hatred.

Leif stormed over and slapped the painting down on the bar. "You had this. The entire time. You knew *everything*."

The painting sat in Dru's periphery, next to his hand. But he wouldn't look at it or acknowledge his guilt.

"How long have you known about this painting, that it's

about me?" Leif breathed down his neck. "That this whole thing is about me?"

The truth hurt. "It does involve you, but not only you."

"You didn't answer my question." Anger was a poison, hot and virulent. Streaking through Leif's veins, demanding vengeance that would not be sated. At the back of his mind, he knew that. Knew that this was a dangerous, empty path.

Dru considered him for several long seconds. "Do you really want to know?"

The question nearly pushed Leif over the edge.

"Because the answer isn't nearly as simple as you think."

"Try me."

Dru turned his glass on the counter. "Before I do, promise you will hear me out. *All* of it."

"No. No promises. Not anymore. Not to people who can't keep them."

"Fair enough." Dru sighed. "What I know, I've known for a long time." He swallowed, guilt trudging through his olive skin. His shoulders lifted. "Since the Sahara."

The whole time. The whole. Freaking. Time.

Battling for restraint, Leif fisted his hands. Bit his tongue to keep from lashing out. "You've been lying to me all these years. Telling me you were looking for answers."

Dru watched him, his expression . . . broken. "Did Rutger tell you about his sister?"

What did Rutger's sister have to do with this? "Yes."

"Katrin was brilliant," Dru said. "She started an experiment to help soldiers fight unwinnable battles after her nephew— Rutger's son—was killed in combat." He motioned with his hand. "There were other generational motivations, but that was her catalyst."

"He didn't mention a son."

"I am not surprised," Dru said wearily. "It is not a pleasant story. His unit tired out and ultimately lost their lives in an incident. Katrin vowed to make sure soldiers could hold out, those who had the will to do so." He sniffed. "She had an amazing mind and a naïve heart. Her work was stolen from her. When she tried to stop those with malicious intent, they killed her."

"I know all this," Leif growled, patience thin.

"Right." Dru looked chagrined. "The point is Rutger. He buried himself in ArC's network, pretended to be an obedient lackey to Veratti. All in an effort to use back channels to find the Neiothen Katrin had been working with—they'd been stolen from her as well—and fulfill his last promise to her. To save them.

"When you came back from the Sahara, I knew something wasn't right. The story coming down the pike about what happened to you was too perfect, too familiar. I started asking questions, inquiring about certain elements. Every story I heard, even yours, was the same. The *exact* same story." Dru dumped the whiskey down his throat and winced as he swallowed, then poured another glass. "Rutger picked up on my inquiries and contacted me privately. We met, agreed to stay in touch. It wasn't right away, but once I gained his trust, he gave me that panel for safekeeping."

Iskra shifted on the couch. "But you sent us after Rutger. How could you do that when—"

"Rutger and I understood each other, but we also understood the entity we were fighting. If we ever seemed to be pulling punches, it'd be a red flag to ArC. Neither of us could afford that. We had too much to lose."

"You're saying that by sending Reaper after him, you were *protecting* him?" Leif said with a snort.

"In a convoluted way, yes. It kept him alive."

"Until now," Leif bit out. "All this time, and you knew—*knew* what really happened to me." He banged the hull. "You kept it to yourself, hid it. Lied to me."

"I knew *what* had happened, but I didn't know *who* did it!" Dru barked. "Though we could point to Veratti as the head of the serpent, we could not identify links in the chain. And they were there, because your records were too tight. Those missing months accounted for too well. And every blasted time I pushed, assets got killed."

Leif stilled, surprised.

"That's right," Dru snapped. "It wasn't just about you. I wasn't just protecting you, but every person I knew, even my own life. This thing was an incessant ticking bomb with trip wires, motion sensors, and multiple redundancies. I've had counterparts around the world secretly, silently digging. I had to be surreptitious, especially when I realized how close the traitors were—right in my own bunker!"

It was a real tale of woe. And granted, much bigger than Leif had realized. His gaze hit the portrait panel. Something nagged at his brain about it. Like a tapping on the shoulder that wouldn't stop saying, *"Pay attention to me. I'm important."*

But why was it important? That was why he'd come. He'd found the third panel and couldn't interpret its meaning. People dancing around a leaf—a victory around a leaf. Around Leif. "I don't get why he hid this. Why didn't you tell me? It's obvious that it's connected to me, considering the leaf. And the Book of the Wars page that mentions Al-el, a leaf. But it shows victory—what's so bad about that?"

Something passed through Dru's eyes, some grief, some . . . anchor that pulled the rest of his confidence and courage into the depths below them.

"What're you holding back? Did you know about the Book of the Wars? Was sending us after that—"

"That was a private war between me and Rutger," Dru admitted. "I realized he knew too much, and he confessed he had it. I insisted he turn it over so I could help you and figure out what to do about the Neiothen. He refused."

There was still something . . . "You're leaving something out. Tell me," Leif insisted, pleading more than he'd intended. Which churned the demon within. "Answer me!"

Dru lifted his snifter like he was going to take a sip—then pitched the entire contents of it on the panel. Amber liquor rushed over the scene, covering the celebration, blurring the celebration.

"What're you doing?" Leif roared, snatching the painting away. But it was slick—thicker than alcohol. He glanced at his hand. Saw a smudge of color. "You ruined it!"

Unrepentant, Dru set down the glass.

Leif swiped at the painting, watching the depiction blur away. "What'd you do?"

"Look at it, Leif."

"I am. It's ruined!"

"Rutger had the real painting covered up."

Leif shook his head. "What?" He glanced at the panel again, saw tinges of another color peeking out. "Why?"

"Because . . . he was afraid you would lose heart."

Somehow, he felt the truth was finally glowering back at him. He used his sleeve to dry the painting . . . and saw a new one revealed beneath the running colors. On a grassy field, a giant leaf had been painted—brittle, cracking, and yet somehow . . . *bleeding*, its blood flowing and mingling with the life force of a dozen other mutilated bodies.

Swallowing the bile rising in his throat, Leif couldn't move or process. "What . . . what does this mean?" Cold dread choked him.

"Rutger and I . . . we believed . . ." Dru heaved a sigh. "He had an analyst look at it. The symbolism is clear—the lives of the Neiothen are dependent on you. Life for a life."

"You mean, I'll die."

TWENTY-SEVEN

"No!" Iskra refused to believe it. Refused to listen, thinking about how much had come true with the Book of the Wars. "Maybe . . . our lives are what we make them." The words sounded hollow in her own ears.

"Every depiction has a leaf or a man—me," Leif muttered.

"Rutger believed in the prophetic nature of these artifacts without reservation," Dru said somberly. "I never understood how he could then have it painted over. He did not tell me he covered it, but I was determined to find out if the painting was really as old as he believed, so I had it tested. When I did, that's when I found out about the painting beneath it. The analyst suggested the recurring man is integral to the overall success of the paintings, the effort—as we know—against ArC."

Leif looked forlorn. "My mom always said no man knew the hour or day of his death," he said quietly. "But I guess now I know the manner. What am I supposed to do?"

"No!" Iskra gripped his arm, barely realizing what she was doing—clinging to him, not wanting to lose him. "I will not accept that."

He glanced at her, a turbulence in his pale irises, a desperation. Like he was searching for something. "The Book of the Wars is God-ordained, Iskra. His prophets recorded wars in it all through the ages. I can't discard it simply because I don't like a passage."

272

"Leif." She pressed her face to his shoulder. "I will not accept that you are going to die."

"We all die sometime," he said.

"We will find a way to stop this."

"Stop it?" Leif snorted. "Haven't you read the third war? I don't stop it—I *start* it. *Have* started it—what do you think the bunker was?" He touched his ear, and only then did she see the comms piece. On his feet, attention clearly diverted, he rushed to the bow. "Where?"

"What's wrong?" Dru asked.

"Two high-powered speedboats coming."

"Yours?"

"No."

"How'd they find us out here?" Dru asked, powering up *Your Destiny*. "We can't outrun speedboats, but we can make hitting us a little harder."

"Andreas is coming up. We need to ditch this boat."

"Do you have any idea how much this cost me?"

"A lot of good sense, apparently." Leif smirked, but he wasn't going to leave Dru behind. Not an option. "Either the boat dies, or you do."

Dru turned back and brought a screen to life. "I'll be a distraction."

"No way. Come with us. Forget the yacht!"

"Get off my boat!"

Leif hesitated, knowing time and options were limited. "Forget the boat!" But he saw the resolve in the director's face. He pivoted to Iskra. "Go!"

After a brief hesitation, she finally rushed toward the stern, then hustled down to the lower deck.

On the port side, Andreas brought the powerboat up. But

Your Destiny pulled ahead, the speed increasing with each second. While Andreas worked to stay with the yacht, the challenge and danger would only grow with the speed.

"Come on!" Vega reached out to help them get aboard.

Leif snatched a life jacket from the rail and thrust it at Iskra. "Put it on!" When she obeyed, he threaded his arms through one as well.

Dru watched from the wheel, trying to keep aligned with the powerboat.

"Easy!" Leif shouted, then nodded to Iskra. "Now!"

She clambered onto the flattened couch, arms stretched out for balance. He caught one hand to steady her as she shifted into position.

Your Destiny veered to port, pitching Iskra forward. She stumbled, nearly vaulting overboard. He caught her by the waist. She straightened, hand on his, and glanced at him, face white.

He remembered her nearly drowning near the facility in Cuba. Was she remembering that, too? He helped her gain her feet. "You got this."

She nodded. This time, she moved faster and with more determination. With a lunge, she vaulted across the water.

His heart went with her as she flew at Vega, who stumbled but caught her. He shifted her to the deck, then gave Leif a thumbs-up.

Your Destiny went hard to starboard. And kept turning, exerting tremendous force against Leif and the powerboat, which veered off to avoid a collision. The yacht jounced over the waves, salty spray soaking his clothes as he struggled to stay on his feet. Dru was glancing to his three as he drove.

Sparks flew off the instrumentation.

"They're shooting!" came Dru's distant shout.

Weapon drawn, Leif took aim at the nearest attacking boat. A few well-placed shots forced it to pull away.

Dru glanced back, nodded. "Go, get off!"

He couldn't leave Dru to fight this out on his own. Tapping his comms, Leif said, "Take out the speedboats!"

"Negative," Andreas shouted back. "We need to bail."

"*Attack the boat!*" Leif sighted down his barrel and squeezed off more rounds as another boat came up from his seven.

Pillows on the stern exploded with fluff, indications of the return fire aiming at Leif. To make himself a harder target, he went to a knee and fired again. But even as he eased back the trigger, Leif saw something from the other boat that froze the blood in his veins.

Smoke and fire puffed. A gray plume streaked toward them.

"RPG!" he roared as he pivoted, dug his foot in, and shoved off the deck, his legs feeling every bit of weight and resistance the water exerted against the yacht. Like one of those dreams where he couldn't run faster than slo-mo. His limbs seemed heavier than a tank. Planting one leg. Pushing forward. Landing. Pushing another. It took forever.

Strangely, through the chaos—the howl of the wind in his ears, the growl of the yacht's engines, the shouts of the Neiothen, Iskra's screams, Dru's muffled words—he heard the shriek of the rocket-propelled grenade.

With a clap, the high-adrenaline moment punctured.

Fire exploded.

Leif was lifted from his feet. Suspended in the air. Catapulted off the yacht.

TWENTY-EIGHT

SOMEWHERE IN THE CHESAPEAKE BAY

A fireball erupted, the glow so achingly bright that it blinded Iskra. In a blink, the thump of a heartbeat, came the gust of air that punched her backward. Rammed her into something. She struck her head, breath knocked from her lungs. Vision robbed.

Iskra dropped into cold, wet blackness.

Warbling came painfully to her ears. Something pressed her shoulder.

She blinked and turned—groaned when pain exploded through her head and shoulder. Wincing, she looked up at . . . "Mitre." Her heart stuttered at the concern in her brother's eyes. But that wasn't possible for him anymore.

"Easy. You took a hard blow." Behind him, flames danced. The yacht was on fire!

"Leif!" She leapt up.

"No." Mitre pushed her back. "Stay. He's in the water. I saw him jump."

"We have to help him," she argued, staring dumbly at the flames eating through the yacht. It was so surreal. So . . . distant. Too distant! She could not stop remembering the way Leif had been there one second, gone the next. Ripped away by some vengeful sea god.

"We're looking," Mitre said as the boat turned a slow circle, the engine low.

"The propellers could kill him!" She clambered to the side, searching for Leif and the director. Where were they?

A spark caught her attention—made Mitre jerk. A shot? He whipped around, barking commands, and tucked his weapon against his shoulder. Another spark hit something and splintered the fiberglass. A small fire erupted and sizzled out just as quick.

Shots streaked across the boat. Chewed wood and carbon fiber. Immersed in panic, she traced the choppy, churning waters for Leif. Her mind ricocheted. The boat that had attacked *Your Destiny* was now focused on this one.

Across the darkened waters, the other speedboat jounced along, racing them. Fire seared her thigh—a bullet had sliced across her leg. She cried out, but it was lost to the elements as Mitre veered away from the burning yacht.

Holding her leg, she scooted to the side, searching. "Leif," she shouted over the turbulent ocean.

Their wake bubbled, foaming and thrashing the water. A shape bobbed in the waves.

"Leif!" Without warning, she was thrust against the side as the boat jerked to her right and lurched away from the attackers at high speed. Away from *Your Destiny*. "No!" she screamed. "No! Go back!"

The powerboat tore away.

Throat raw, she watched, powerless, as the distance between her and Leif grew. "Go back!"

The shorter Neiothen who'd held her was braced against the hull, returning fire.

Tears streaming down her face, Iskra stared helplessly across the gnawing distance. She sank onto the deck and clung to a cleat, sick at the motion, sick that they had left Leif. What about Dru? She had seen a body in the water—but was he alive?

Without warning, Mitre brought the boat around and

headed straight for the enemy boat. Breath trapped in her throat, she glanced between the grim determination in her brother's eyes and the black waters bisected by the lone light of the oncoming boat.

Was he going to ram them? A head-on collision? Mitre said he did not have compassion. Did he have common sense? Their speed erased the distance too fast. As she glanced at the other boat, it registered that one of the Neiothen was crouched on the bow, holding the rail that ran its length.

By the saints. Were they all mad? She moved back, panicked. They were going to collide, be killed. There was no way she would survive. Iskra only then noted the two Neiothen staring at the other boat as warriors on a battlefield. Poised to embrace the inevitable.

Stomach churning, adrenaline spiraling, she held on. Swallowed the dread that filled her mouth with an acrid taste.

The remaining distance vanished. The boat was on them.

Iskra tensed, waiting for the crack, the explosion. To be catapulted from the deck.

Instead, she felt the slightest change of direction. The man on the bow launched into the air. Sailed out and onto the other boat. He landed in a roll and snapped up his weapon at several dark shapes there waiting. They descended on him.

Even as that registered, their boat chugged to a stop. She glanced at Mitre as he leapt onto the other boat, too. Shouts and shots strafed the air. Light exploded across the waters, shattering the darkness and blinding her.

Iskra jerked away, wincing at the stress on the back of her cornea. Was it an explosion? She peered around, and realized it was a beam of light. Stadium bright. She traced it back to its source—a large white boat that looked padded all around its hull. A small slash of orange, white, and blue painted its side. Friend or foe? She reached for her dagger.

A horn squawked, and a voice ejected itself into the air. "U.S. Coast Guard. Stand down. Stay where you are."

Unsure whether to be relieved or more stressed, Iskra rose to her feet. The search beam stayed on the other boat as the Coast Guard cutter closed in. A smaller beam probed the powerboat Iskra was on.

"Set down your weapons and put your hands in the air. Prepare to be boarded," the Coast Guard ordered.

She lifted her hands, but her gaze slid over the waters, trying to find *Your Destiny.* In the far distance, fire danced and rippled across the waves.

A sideboard craft swung up alongside. "We're looking for Dru Iliescu."

Iskra started, giving them a quick once-over before being convinced they were legitimate. "He isn't here. He was on the yacht," she said, pointing toward the burning wreckage. "He and my friend were there when they"—she indicated the other boats—"hit them with an RPG."

A Coast Guard officer came aboard, ball cap tugged low on his brow. "What's your friend's name?"

"Leif," she answered, her heart aching. "Leif Metcalfe. Please hurry. He was blown into the water. We have to find him."

The officer considered her, then angled his head. "Come with me, ma'am."

"I need to find my friends."

He motioned her forward. "Yes, ma'am. That's what we intend."

She climbed onto the smaller craft. Once she was seated, they pulled away, and the officer's gaze strayed to something behind her. As the craft bounced over the choppy waters, she saw two other officers forcing Mitre to his knees. The Neiothen who'd been at the rail lay unmoving on the deck. Another was on his knees, hands on his head and surrounded by armed patrolmen.

"Director Iliescu sent out a distress signal," he shouted over the twang of the engine and wind in her ears. "Said to find you and Metcalfe."

She checked on her brother again, aching to see him being handcuffed.

"That one took at least three bullets, killed at least two, and lost one of his men," one of the other officers shouted to another.

Iskra stared at the fading form of her brother, saddened by what he had become—a trained killer. They had both dealt in the business of death. She had gotten free. Would he?

MILAN, ITALY

Watching the children laughing on the lawn of his home gave Ciro immense pleasure. His son had invited his entire class to his party, and Ciro approved. What better way to show they were normal and like every other family than to celebrate his son's birthday?

"You should come down," Benedetta said from the door of his library.

"I told you," he said, tucking away his irritation.

"Yes, yes, but you always have appointments and meetings." Only his wife would speak to him so boldly.

"I am prime minister, my dear. Would you have me tell all of Italia to wait?"

"For one hour? For Jacopo? Yes."

Perhaps he should. It would be a good reminder to those under him that they should be dependable enough that he could extricate himself long enough to enjoy cake and presents.

His phone vibrated on the table. He turned from the windows and retrieved the buzzing device.

Benedetta huffed and crossed her arms, daring him to answer it.

But one look at the screen told him he had no choice.

"You need to be there for him."

"And you need to learn your place, Benedetta." He turned his back and accepted the call as his wife left the room. "Colonel."

"The men are dead," he said.

Irritation scraped Ciro. He stretched his neck. "Unfortunate. I thought you had that secured."

"The Neiothen may not have technology as advanced as the Gen2s, but they've had it longer and have adapted. They're . . . swift. Strategic. The only comfort is that they also suffered high casualties."

"I hear excuses, Colonel." But that they had eliminated some of those accursed Neiothen . . . good.

"The Coast Guard intervened when the Gen2s tried to go after Leif and the director, taking the matter out of my hands."

"No, Colonel. You surrendered control."

"He's in the prophecy, the Book of the Wars. We can't expect to undo that."

"*Why?*" Ciro shouted. "Why can we not? Those are made-up fables, you fool! We prove that with our efforts. Risen will go online, and we will have control of the world's economy. Armageddon is a fiction—a myth! Why can we not disprove some brittle old book? It was lost to humanity once, and it will be so again." Anger surged through his chest and drew him straight. "You have surrendered your life. Good-bye, Colonel."

"Sir, give me another chance. You don't have anyone else—"

"Wrong, Colonel. There is always someone else."

Amid the colonel's objections, he ended the call and made another.

"I'm afraid the colonel has outlived his usefulness."

"Understood."

"Do you?" He wandered to the windows. "Because I have had to remove several who did not, and Risen is far too close to going online to let anyone with anything less than resolute determination stay with me. We cleared your path to that bunker for a reason. Do not fail me."

"Of course not. I've been working on an idea."

"If Mr. Metcalfe and Miss Todorova are still alive by the end of the week, you will not be."

He ended the call, hating that he had resorted to threats— no, these were not threats. Threats by their very nature were violence unfulfilled. His were warnings of what was to come unless their obedience could dissuade him. Gen2s would enforce it. Enforce his will across the globe.

He rubbed his chin, shifting his focus to Jacopo, who stood at the head of the picnic table with his friends gathered around him. As it should be.

He made another call. "I want Risen to be ready to launch Friday."

"Not a problem. We're conducting test runs right now. Things are smooth."

Pride swelled. "I knew I could count on you." It had been such a massive risk. "Do they suspect your protégé?"

"They suspect everyone, but no—they're not really looking at her right now. There was some initial concern, but no longer."

"It amazes me," Ciro said, leaning against the glass, "how readily they step into our traps."

"You read them well, and it paid off."

"And had it not been for your foresight from the beginning, had you not realized what Katrin developed . . ."

"Then you would have nothing."

He resented the truth of that, but he could not argue it. "And you are certain they do not suspect her . . . or you?"

"Me?" She laughed. "Iskra already knows I am the devil personified for taking her daughter, but I do not believe she understands, not fully. But she will. And I cannot wait to see the terror in her eyes when she realizes it. I owe her this."

SOMEWHERE IN THE CHESAPEAKE BAY

Limbs aching from the cold, choppy waters, Leif kept his distance from the yacht, waiting for it to blow any second. Expecting to tread water for a long time, he'd ditched his shoes and pants, the heaviest of his clothing. The average water temperature of the Atlantic in July hung in the sixties, but it seemed especially cold tonight. That might not sound too bad until it was all that stood between you and living.

He still hadn't found Dru. Though he swam around the yacht, the only thing he could see on the upper deck where the grenade had hit was the carbon fiber canopy that had lost its portside supports.

Fire licked starboard but didn't seem to be progressing or worsening. He thanked God the Gen2s hadn't hit the engines or gas tanks. It seemed their intention had been to kill Leif and the director, not sink a boat, so they'd turned their fire-power against Andreas's powerboat, which had raced away. He'd heard Iskra yelling but was glad they'd kept going so she could escape.

Between him and *Your Destiny*, he didn't see any oil slicks or gas halos on the water, so he treaded closer. The yacht was surprisingly intact after that RPG. He grabbed the aft deck and hauled himself up. Water trickled off his bare, shaking legs.

"Dru?" Leif called, moving around the table and reaching for the rail to the upper deck and the open salon. He climbed, finding the stairs strangely warm on his cold feet. As the deck came into view, he hesitated. The canopy lay across the deck, half melted by the fire that was working its way into the belly of the yacht, having already eaten through the upper deck. The once built-in hot tub was slanting downward into the cabins of the main deck. He considered the Portuguese bridge as a means to get to the bow.

"Dru!" Leif shouted. "Dru, you up there?" Though he listened, the crackling and popping fire made it hard to hear anything.

He spotted an extinguisher and grabbed it, then sprayed the upper deck, spotting a slow burn happening in the VIP suite below. There wasn't enough in this extinguisher to snuff out all the flames. He swung back down to the main deck and took the Portuguese bridge to the bow but stopped when he saw the windows to a guest room were blown. A body, arm trapped under it, sprawled across the daggers of glass on the padded bench beneath the windows.

"Dru!" Leif shoved forward, cursing that he'd had to ditch his shoes. Glass sliced his feet, but it was the least of his worries. He reached for the director, who lifted his head and grimaced before collapsing back on the cushion. Leif realized his arm wasn't trapped—it was *gone*. Missing from the elbow down.

Tourniquet!

"Hold on. I'm going to remove your belt." Leif undid the buckle, then tugged the black leather belt free.

Dru grunted and shook his head, muttering incoherently.

"Quiet. I'll get this on, and we'll get you to the raft." Blood slicking his hands, Leif worked fast, knowing every second counted. But even as he tightened the strap around the stump, he realized it wasn't bleeding as badly as it should be.

An odor hit him. Recognition hit—*fuel*. There was a fuel leak somewhere.

With the tourniquet secured on Dru, Leif shifted. "Hold on. I'm going to lift you."

"Leave . . . me," Dru huffed.

Leif ignored him, grabbed a life vest from the nearby couch where they had been stored, and hooked it over Dru's head. He latched it and then slid his hands under Dru, glass slicing his arms, and scooped him up. Hearing the director groan and expel a wet-sounding breath disconcerted Leif. He'd seen enough combat injuries to know things didn't look good for the director. But he had to try to save him.

A high-pitched whistle streaked his ears. Oh no. That fuel had caught a flame.

Leif pulled Dru against him and scrambled for the bow. He planted a foot on the sofa and climbed atop it. "Deep breath!" he ordered as he vaulted over the rail.

Bright light rent the power of darkness. Heat scalded his back, trickling goosebumps down his spine as another explosion lit up the night.

A powerful hand punched them into the cold water and plunged them down . . . down, pulling Dru from Leif's grip. The director slipped away, but Leif snagged fabric. A leg. He latched on and kicked hard, forcing them back to the surface, where night had turned to day.

He hauled in a breath, yanking Dru with him. The director popped up, the buoyancy of the life vest keeping him on the surface, but he was limp, his head listing. Face still in the water.

Leif hooked an arm around Dru's neck and pulled him against his chest. Felt for breath. Nothing. He shook the director. "Dru!" Treading water, he did his best to pump his hand against Dru's chest, knowing the life preserver was limiting his effectiveness. "C'mon!" he growled. "Dru! Dru, c'mon. Wake up!" He kicked hard and did his best modified chest compressions, holding the director with one hand and pounding with the other.

Dru coughed. Gagged. Vomited water and gagged again.

Relieved, Leif again hooked his neck and held him close. "Just hang in there," he said, glancing around the expanse of water. Hoping, praying someone would come back.

"Leif," Dru said, the exertion making him cough again. "Listen. Rutger—"

"Shut up," Leif hissed against his ear. "Just work on staying alive. Okay?"

"Listen," Dru rasped. "Please . . ."

"I got all night." It wasn't funny and probably his worst-timed joke ever.

"The Book . . . missing part . . ."

A leaf was missing from the book that was more like a scroll, but they'd known that since the beginning.

"Rutger . . . destroyed . . . made me . . . memorize it," Dru said, his voice growing faint amid the fire simmering and the yacht sinking. "'Al'el must go to the deep and there yield a mighty blow . . .'" A shudder stole his breath, and he fell back against Leif's shoulder, then went still.

"Hey." Leif bounced his shoulder. "Dru."

"So . . . sorry . . . tired."

"Yeah, well, die later."

Dru heaved a breath, then rolled his head. "'At last the final war comes. Al'el must . . . move fast . . .'" He struggled against chattering teeth, his blood pressure no doubt dropping. "'. . . and use his mind . . . to wit and war. Blood . . . spilled . . . then so much more . . . raging soul delivers . . . lethal blow . . . back where it started . . . stands against those who reap. Facing . . . betrayal and danger, his blade has come, sealing . . . fate.'"

Leif felt the icy tendrils of fear snake around his heart. That . . . that didn't sound good at all. "Very encouraging."

Dru coughed a laugh and took in a mouthful of water.

Irritated with himself, Leif pulled him up and back, making sure his face was out of the water. "Sorry."

Shaking his head, Dru groan-coughed. "Fate," he breathed.

286

"Book doesn't . . . it doesn't say . . ." He went still, then jerked. "Leif."

"Relax. Save your breath."

"Won't . . . make it."

"Not if you keep talking." Leif searched again for a boat or ship. Something. Why hadn't anyone seen the explosion? Where was help?

"Sorry."

"No," Leif growled, chest tightening with the words, knowing where the director was going with this line of dialogue. "Don't do that. Save it."

"Braun—" Dru went tense. "Look out for"—he wheezed— "her."

"Don't worry. We'll make it back, and you can—"

The rumble of a motor caught his attention.

Leif swung around, probing the waters.

A beam of light stroked the surface.

"Here!" He waved, kicking to keep them afloat. "Here!"

The beam caught them.

He let out a shout, then a laugh. "Help's here." He waved again, feeling the ridiculous need to make sure they didn't lose sight of him. "Right here."

The boat surged, water lifting and tossing them back a few more feet as the hull breezed up alongside. Hands dangled over the side.

"He's in shock. Lost a limb. Take him," Leif said, catching the hull and nudging Dru toward them.

The director was drawn out of the water, and then others assisted Leif onto the deck. His legs wouldn't hold him up. He stumbled and tripped.

"Whoa, Chief. Here you go." A coastie directed him to a bench—but what he saw was Iskra. Relief choked him. Instinct pushed him to her, but his legs missed the memo and buckled.

Iskra caught him, hooked his arm over her shoulder, and guided him to a bench. Shivers wracked his body, but a thermal blanket dropped over his shoulders. He caught the edge and pulled Iskra tight into his hold.

"He's gone," someone said.

Leif peered over Iskra—and saw the coastie sitting back and not working on Dru. "No!" He surged from the bench. Crashed to his knees. "No, he's alive." He scrambled on all fours to the director. "He's alive." He stared down at the unblinking eyes of his friend.

Ashen, mouth agape, Dru lay unmoving.

Leif started compressions. "Count for me!"

"Chief, he's gone. Not breathing, no pulse. Significant trauma and blood loss—not only from his arm, but the glass in his back likely bled him out."

"Count!" Then the coastie's words registered, and Leif paused, staring down at his lifeless friend. "Glass?"

"It was pushed pretty far in—the life preserver hid it," the coastie said, nodding to the flotation device they'd cut away to work on Dru.

Leif crumpled. "How did I miss that? I shouldn't have missed that!"

"Even if you hadn't, there was nothing you could've done."

"He was just talking to me," Leif said, placing a hand on Dru's chest. He gripped Dru's shirt, wishing he could bring him back. His eyes burned. His heart burned. Dru couldn't be dead.

Gentle hands pulled him away, and Leif turned, wrecked. Not wanting to talk. Not wanting to look at Iskra's face. They fumbled their way to the bench, and he dropped down hard.

"I'm sorry," she said, tears in her eyes.

Leif tugged her against his chest, cupping her head. Staring at Dru. Fighting the tears. Realizing that the man who'd mentored him, saved him, protected him . . . was dead. A sob wracked his chest. Tears blurred his vision. He'd gone out on a limb to get Leif answers. And he'd died for it. He'd apologized.

But, really, it was Leif who owed the apology.

Now he also owed a debt.

TWENTY-NINE

"How ya doin', Cell?"

Cell glanced at the red-bearded cowboy. "You know, it's really amazing how my wound hasn't miraculously healed in twenty-four hours like yours."

"What're you grouchy about?" Saito frowned at him across the hub.

"Oh, I don't know. It's not like a half dozen men broke in here, shot most of us, then left. Or that Veratti is trying to effect a world takeover, or that our team leader has gone rogue and his assassin girlfriend is MIA, as well as the deputy director." Cell lifted a hand, immediately regretting the move as it twinged his wound. "And let's not forget the new evil overlord who's as friendly as a rabid javelina."

"A what?" Saito asked.

"It's a pig thing," Culver said. "Looks like Pumbaa from *The Lion King*."

"Only uglier," Cell added. "And meaner."

"Can we *not* get off topic here?" Saito slapped down a folder. He glanced at Alisz sitting in a nearby chair. "Which one of you is going to explain what was said earlier about Mercy being able to find them?"

"She can," Alisz said. "The Neiothen are activated and initiated using RFID. It was cutting-edge tech back when it was implanted. And each one has a unique RFID with which to locate them. If you know how." She cocked her head. "And Mercy knows how."

"How do you know what Mercy can do?" Baddar challenged.

This time Alisz didn't answer, locked in a visual duel with Mercy, whose face was crimson, despite what Cell imagined was a reassuring touch from Baddar. It was surprising how much Alisz riled Mercy.

"Let's have it," came the very grating, commanding voice of Colonel Nesto. "Cough up why you know this. Maddox— you too."

Man, Cell wanted to take that guy down a few notches.

Mercy's glower shifted to the colonel. "You will have to talk with Director Iliescu about that."

Alisz stood. "I don't understand. You can help your friend. Why won't—"

"No matter my past or what I can or can't do—you are not trusted here, Alisz. You told me in there that you were sent by ArC!"

"Hold the fluff up," Cell said, his heart racing. "ArC?"

"No! That's not . . . wholly true," Alisz admitted. "I was trained by the same woman who trained Mercy."

"No, Nonna Kat trained me. Mina *destroyed* me. It's why I left more than ten years ago. You?" Mercy's chest rose and fell raggedly. "You stayed. You continued to work for them and can't be trusted."

"Who's Nonna Kat?" Cell hated that he was learning so much about Mercy—who he'd thought he knew pretty well— from a girl he'd met online. A girl who'd apparently used him to get here.

Mercy touched her forehead. "She was a woman who worked with my parents."

"Doing what?" Canyon tucked his hands under his armpits.

Mercy shrank, then lifted her shoulders. "I . . . I can't

discuss that." She glanced around, then quickly added, "It was a condition of my Agency contract never to speak of it."

"I think key intel is missing and may be mitigating factors in what's happening here, with Dru, with my brother." Canyon roughed a hand over his mouth, but his gaze remained locked on her.

Some sixth sense told Cell that if anyone could sort this out, it'd be Leif's brother.

"Mercy," Canyon said slowly, "are you aware of some way this secret connects to what's going on?"

She swallowed.

Canyon straightened, his eyes lasering her. "Because Dru is MIA. Nobody can find him. My brother—your team member—is in trouble. And if I'm hearing this correctly, you might be able to help them. Am I tracking right?"

"It's not that simple," Mercy said quietly. "What Alisz is talking about—I don't recall that. But . . ." She glanced at the floor, forlorn. Then drew up. "Most of what I do feels like instinct because of Kat and Dietrich."

"Who are they?" Saito asked.

"Kat was Rutger Hermanns' sister," Alisz asserted.

Mercy scowled. "No, she wasn't. She—"

"Katrin Hermanns?" Braun asked, easing into the conversation.

"Nonna Kat used a different last name," Alisz said. "But she was definitely Rutger's sister."

"No, I . . ." Mercy said, frowning and now uncertain. "She was just Nonna Kat to me, then she died, and Mina took over."

"You know this Katrin?" Nesto asked, glancing at Braun.

The admiral didn't answer right away. "There was a Katrin Schreiber connected to a very early program." She studied Mercy for a long time. "Is there any chance—*any*—that Alisz is right and you can find them?"

"I will, of course, do anything to help Leif and Dru, but I'm not aware of anything special I can do," Mercy said. "Alisz was never trustworthy. She always got in trouble. I didn't trust her then, and I don't trust her now."

"It was an act," Alisz said with emphasis. "I was to drive Mina crazy to draw attention away from you. It was all part of the plan."

"Mina's plan? What, to punish me?"

"No, Rutger's! It wasn't about you. At least, not all of it. Acting out and getting under Mina's skin was a *pleasure*. That woman didn't have a nice bone in her body, and what she did to all us girls?" Alisz shuddered. "When Rutger asked me to do this with the promise of keeping her off my back, it was more than I could refuse."

Mercy rubbed her temple. "Your lies are as bad as your snooping. I didn't even know Rutger existed until I got this job."

"Exactly as he wanted it. It wasn't just the Neiothen Rutger was trying to save—he was going after the girls, too. Trying to dismantle Mina's influence as much as he could."

Admiral Braun bent over Cell's system and pulled up a picture. "Put that on the wall." As he complied, she addressed them. "Is this the woman you two are talking about?" She pointed to the wall.

Mercy seemed to visibly rattle. "Yes, that's Mina. How—"

"She's been on our radar for several years, but recently a lot more. Though she has been very careful not to be directly connected with Veratti, we have reasonable cause to believe she is at the very top of ArC's org chart." Braun narrowed her gaze at Mercy. "I know what she's doing in that school of hers—but you don't fit the mold, Mercy. You are terrible at subterfuge and not operative material."

"You're right. I hate subterfuge—it's too much like lying, and I had a lifetime of that once Nonna Kat died. I hate fake. I can't do it." She pulled in a long breath, then let it out.

"Mina forced me into scenarios where I had to save lives by hacking, transfer money from banking institutions into her accounts, steal state secrets, ruin politicians or whomever she wanted destroyed—all with a few keystrokes and false cyber histories. If I failed the assignment, I didn't get hurt—someone else did. She was heartless but effective. Coding was my gift. The only thing my young mind could cope with, since I didn't have to see the people I hurt. At the school, however, I did see the girls who received my punishments."

The ominous groan of freight elevator doors opening in the side hall severed their conversations. Amped tension. Hand on his weapon, Culver rose, and Saito joined him. A curse hit the air as they both stepped back with grim expressions.

Mercy stilled, her face blanched.

What was going on? Cell wheeled into view and froze. No . . .

Two Marines entered with a body bag on a gurney. Behind them, looking like a drowned rat, Leif limped into the hub, head down, wearing gray sweats and a Navy T-shirt. Scrapes and cuts marred his hands and arms. When Iskra hovered and offered help, he rejected it with a minuscule shake of his head. His cheek twitched with something Cell couldn't identify.

Iskra wasn't much better. Her tied-back hair looked damp. Walking stiffly, she wore a Navy hoodie and sweats as well.

Leif's gaze almost met the team, but it veered off as he kept moving, locked on the gurney's quietly squeaking wheels. Admiral Braun fell in step with them as they made their way back to the medical bay.

A chill slipped down Cell's spine, and he couldn't look away.

Canyon strode to his brother, gripped the back of his neck, and pulled him into a hug. Patted his shoulder. "Glad you're alive."

Leif tensed but didn't pull away. Closed his eyes. Seemed to take a breath, then stepped out of his brother's hold. Nodded.

"Who's in that . . . bag?" Mercy sounded panicked, raw.

Leif peered over his shoulder at the team. "Dru."

No. Unable to move, Cell noticed the name sent a shockwave through the bunker that made Culver and Saito stagger. Gasps and curses hissed into the air. Mercy's choked cry was the loudest. Face in her hands, she shook beneath sobs as Baddar drew her into his arms, his head bowing to hers. As if bowing in honor . . . of . . .

No. This wasn't right.

Cell's mind refused to process that the Marines had wheeled Iliescu . . . "He's dead," he muttered. It felt like trying to plug in a lamp, but the adapter was wrong. *This* was wrong. Iliescu couldn't be . . .

He looked at the director's office, a cold vacancy washing through him. Even now, Iliescu's bark—scolding, hard—howled through the concrete. He stared at his hands, feeling the need to return to his computer and . . . what? He couldn't extract the director's life from some hidden data byte controlled by Death. But he sure wanted to try.

"What do you think happened?" Culver asked. "Runt looked pretty wrecked."

"You think he killed him?" Saito asked quietly.

Canyon lunged but stopped himself. "You know better than that about my brother." He glowered around the bunker. "Tell me you know that."

"We do." It rankled Cell that they would even think that. But . . . where had Leif come from? How had he hooked up with the director and Iskra? "If he was responsible, they'd have brought him in cuffs and dragged him to the tank. Braun would've informed us of the director's death."

"I think we need to pull together," Mercy said around a

sniffle. "Rather than accuse and blame each other. There's been too much of that."

"Agreed," Canyon said. "The best thing we can do for Dru and Leif is to stop this train wreck before more people we care about get hurt."

Silent nods sent them all to their corners. At least, that was how it felt as Cell rolled back to his station, skating one last glance at the others, who were at their desks, heads down. Hearts down.

THIRTY

REAPER HEADQUARTERS, MARYLAND

When the doctor finished stitching his leg and applying burn salve—with a hefty warning that he really needed to go to a burn center—Leif sat up and pulled on the Navy sweatshirt again.

"What I didn't know," he said to Braun, "was that glass had punctured his lung. That, combined with the blood loss from the missing limb . . . nothing could save him." Something in him broke off and set adrift.

"So you *were* here. Part of the Neiothen insertion," the admiral said.

Leif clenched his jaw. "I was."

"Did you shoot anyone?"

"Negative."

Silence hung in the medical bay as Braun seemed to struggle over whether to believe him or not. "I'm sorry," she said, her features lined with grief and concern. "Sorry you went through another attack. Sorry Dru had to die like that." Her mouth twitched with restrained emotion. "Thank you for trying to save him." Her eyes reddened. "He thought of you like a brother."

The gravitas of those words pushed Leif's gaze down. He rubbed his knuckles hard and tightened his trembling lips. The wave of memories drenched him again. Dru's words. His apology.

"What I don't understand," Colonel Nesto said, unfolding his arms as he leaned against the wall, brooding, "is how—"

"Colonel." Admiral Braun's face shone with disapproval. "Later." She nodded to Leif. "Despite those heroic efforts, there remains the matter of your . . . actions."

"Understood."

"I don't think you do, Chief," she countered. "We're talking dereliction of duty, assault with a deadly weapon, grand theft of government property, trespassing into a secure area, conduct unbecoming . . ." She huffed and shook her head. "There are so many more."

Head down, Leif had no defense.

"But since there's a nightmare brewing, I'm putting that on hold—"

"You can't!" Nesto came off the wall.

"In light of Iliescu's death, I am acting director"—she glowered at the colonel—"of this team until such time as a replacement is named." She held up her phone. "You *will* face formal discipline for your actions, Mr. Metcalfe."

Leif knew he deserved every book they threw at him. Serving a life sentence in Leavenworth could never compensate for losing Dru. But . . . they had to finish this. He held his tongue, hoping that was where Braun was going.

Iskra appeared from behind a curtain, a butterfly stitch on her cheek and the same weight in her expression that sat on his shoulders.

"Right now, we have a mission—and that's to end ArC." Braun expelled a thick breath. "I think we can both agree on that."

"You seriously trust him?" Nesto growled. "He went *rogue!*"

Braun examined Leif, weighing, measuring. Then her gaze drifted back to the colonel. "And he nearly got himself killed trying to save Dru. What did you do?"

Nesto gaped at her.

Braun shifted her attention back to Leif, then sighed. "You are not to leave this bunker without my express authorization."

"Understood."

"I have an op to get underway." She nodded to the doctor on her way out. "Send his clearance ASAP."

"I want a copy, too," Nesto barked. He sent Leif a heated look before following Braun back to the hub.

Dr. Dodson worked quietly on his handheld for a few minutes, leaving Iskra and Leif to stand in awkward silence. Ten minutes later, he gave Leif antibiotics and painkillers.

"No," Leif said. "Ibuprofen is fine. Nothing to interfere with my ability to perform."

"That scald on your back has to be painful—to the point of interfer—"

"Pain reminds me I'm alive." Unlike Dru. "Am I cleared?"

Dr. Dodson sighed. "I need to review your bloodwork."

Leif hopped off the table to make his point clear. "Time's ticking, Doc. Like a bomb. Which is set to go off and destroy the world as we know it. They already killed the director. I don't want them to kill anyone else."

Irritation scratched at the doctor's eyes, but he gave a nod and strode into an adjoining office.

Alone with Iskra, Leif couldn't bring himself to look at her, even when she crossed the room and propped her hip against the examination table. She bumped his shoulder with hers. "How are you?"

He swiped his thumb over the scratches on his hand, the ones he'd gotten lifting Dru. "He died thinking I hated him." Bobbing his head, he tried to stem the squall of grief. "I was so convinced he was holding out on me that I never thought for a second he was really, honest-to-God trying to protect me." The squall was overtaking him, the grief stronger than his will. "I didn't want to see it. I was so angry at him, at the world."

She threaded their arms and leaned into his side. "Dru knew that. But he *was* holding out on you." Her smile was still small. "Just not for the reason you thought."

"He kept saying we had to be careful, that those behind what happened to me would act if they thought I was digging." He cocked his head. "He was right. They acted—decisively. And took his life."

She faced him. "You do know Dru *was* looking for answers, right?"

"He said that, but I didn't believe it when I bailed in Taipei. I was fed up, ticked. Then, having that asinine code fry my brain . . ." He slid his hand down her arm and laced their fingers. "I'd had enough inaction and needed to know. I was afraid I'd be the next Neiothen killing friends and family— you." He shook his head. "I couldn't let that happen. And yet, I did."

Iskra reached for him, and he took her into his arms. Buried his face in her neck, crushing her against his chest. "I'm so sorry," he breathed. "I thought I could fix this. But I snatched it out of capable hands and ran straight into the trouble I was trying to avoid." Tremors of grief washed over him, demanding tears, but he defied them. Then understood that defiance was as much a part of the trouble as walking away. "I failed, Iskra. I failed, and because of it he died."

She bounced her shoulder, forcing him to lift his head. She cupped his face. "Dru died because of ArC. Because of Ciro. Not you."

Shouts echoed through the hub.

Still holding Iskra, the only right thing in his world, Leif looked toward the disruption and saw the team coming out of their seats. A deep voice boomed across the concrete bunker.

"Nesto." He broke away from Iskra and stalked out to the main area.

"Mr. Metcalfe," Dr. Dodson called, bringing Leif around. The

300

doc held up a tablet. "Just sent your clearance through. Same for you, Miss Todorova."

Leif nodded as another shout rang out. He stalked toward the action, assessing the tension. A comical standoff was going down—Reaper on one side, Nesto and Braun on the other. "What's going on?"

Silence was the only response. He looked at Culver and Saito, then Cell. Baddar, Mercy, and the new girl. So, the silent treatment. He guessed he deserved that, too. Where was Canyon?

"It seems," Nesto growled into the thick air, "that this team is untrained and undisciplined, refusing a direct order."

"Not sure which team you're referring to, but mine is the best." Leif planted himself in the middle of the confrontation.

"Yours?" Nesto scoffed. "You walked out and abandoned them. What makes you think you have any say here?"

Leif had to take that punch, no matter how much it hurt. "Because I am the only one who was in the water when the director was killed. I was in the basement of the South African facility where ArC is experimenting with human-animal hybrids. I know more about this than anyone." He folded his arms and felt the protective salve and bandage along his spine tug against his shirt. "Admiral Braun, what order is the team taking exception to?"

"It was not my order," Braun said quietly, scowling at Nesto.

"It's my order," Nesto growled. "I was given oversight—"

"You were given an advisory position," Braun corrected with more than a little annoyance as she cringed away from him.

Interesting. Braun countered Nesto, whom she clearly detested, yet also feared doing so. What had them ready to throw down?

"He told us to spy on you." Saito fell in line next to Leif. "Interact, take notes, and report back to him."

"We told him it wasn't going to happen," Culver chimed in, forming up on the right.

Leif understood why the colonel would ask that of Reaper. After all, he'd betrayed everyone here, gone on his own. But . . . His mind started shuffling the deck of cards this man dealt. The amusement park . . . Nesto had been with Sienna, hadn't he? That was what General Elbert had said, that Sienna had been attached to Nesto. And . . . Egypt . . . Chibale.

"We are cursed because we let Colonel Nesto do this," Chibale had said.

Nausea churned through Leif. His friend Ausar had died because of this man. Why, with his perfect recall, hadn't he made the connection before now? How had he missed it?

Leif locked on the colonel. "What did you do to the village?"

Nesto frowned. "What village? What're you talking about?"

"The village in Egypt, the one decimated by the Meteoroi." The tremor in Leif shifted from anger to a focused, decisive compulsion to act. It was coming together. Finally. After all this time. All this time he'd been looking outward when the demon had come to roost in their own bunker. Because if Nesto had been connected to Sienna, who was a Neiothen, if Nesto had been involved in the Meteoroi activity in Egypt, and now had advisory oversight of Reaper . . . "Who sent you here? Assigned you as advisor?"

"General Elbert," Nesto stated. "Why?"

Elbert. Who'd been poisoned in The Hague, saved when Saito trach'ed him. The same general who'd told Peyton that Sienna had been assigned to Nesto. Why would Elbert know about that?

Unless they were all connected. Egypt. The Meteoroi. Sienna. Nesto. General Elbert. All interlocked into one gigantic entity.

ArC.

Holy prince of Egypt! How had they missed that?

The tide had turned. In fact, it'd turned so many times, Cell had no idea if he was about to hit shore or drown. He was pretty sure he knew what Leif had figured out, and to anyone who knew Reaper's prodigal leader, it was written all over his posture. His tone.

"You're associated with a man who altered the environment of an Egyptian village, killing dozens," Leif bit out.

"You have no proof—even if you did, what's your point? The Neiothen are *associated* with you, who went rogue and committed numerous crimes. You should be locked up!"

The tension simmering in the hub was developing into a full boil with a back-and-forth between Leif and Nesto.

Wounds aching, Cell noted the zero distance between Saito's fingertips and his thigh-holstered weapon. Same with Culver, only the big guy had no problem resting his palm on the grip.

"Cell," came Mercy's hushed whisper.

He angled toward her, but something about the standoff caught his attention. What was it? What had changed? Cell peered from behind the oval conference table and past Leif's shoulder.

Braun.

His heart thumped. When this mess started, Braun had been at Nesto's side. Now she'd moved a couple of feet. Her features tightened, and she drew up her shoulders so much her neck disappeared. Though good with politics and diplomacy, she didn't have a poker face. The nearest Marine eyed her, then homed in on the ensuing argument between Nesto and Leif. As he should—Leif was volatile. In most situations. But not this.

303

It was his spidey sense, Mercy would tell him. But something was definitely tingling—no, crackling like a live wire, bouncing and jumping all over the place—at the back of his mind.

"Cell," Mercy hissed.

Enough to pull his gaze. He diverted but not all the way.

"Look." She surreptitiously scooted a tablet across the table.

Eyes on the showdown, he slid his fingers over and caught the edge of the tablet. Pulled it to himself. Braved a glance down at the split map. Half the screen showed Cuba with numerous dots. The other half . . . Maryland—here. Two red dots glared like the eyes of a serpent ready to strike.

No, not a serpent. Neiothen. His blood ran cold. Mercy had been working to isolate the Neiothen RFID signals.

She shifted to him, then turned her back to the others and whispered, "Once Leif showed up, I started searching for an RFID signal here so I could figure out how to isolate the others."

Cell leaned closer, watching the team, but especially Nesto and Braun. He didn't miss the way Baddar positioned himself behind Leif and the others—yet directly in front of Mercy, blocking Nesto's view of her.

"There's *two*," she hissed, her hazel eyes wide. "Here."

His heart beat a little faster. Not just Leif's. Who else? "Can you pinpoint who it's coming from?"

She gave a quick shake of her head.

"It was you!" Leif's voice cut through their conversation. "When I was here with the Neiothen—"

"You mean when you attacked a U.S. military installation?"

"—the sonic resonance in my head—it was you. *You* had the device. That's why she"—he indicated to Alisz—"knocked into you."

"I don't know what you're talking about."

304

Alisz jutted her jaw. "It was in your hand."

Nesto stabbed a finger at her. "I don't know why you're here—"

But Cell saw the trouble—his gut clenched with shards of agony, paralyzing him. Preventing him from warning the others. No!

Braun snatched the Marine's weapon, pivoted, and fired.

THIRTY-ONE

REAPER HEADQUARTERS, MARYLAND

Leif rushed Braun, who seemed stunned by her own actions. He placed a hand on the back of her neck, and with the other, he held her hand that had the weapon. Firmed his grip. "Give me the gun, Admiral," he insisted, relieved when she released it.

Culver and Saito hurried to render aid to Nesto, who was bleeding out. Mercy ran for the doctor.

Leif was relieved when his brother slid up and secured the admiral—with a firm but gentle hold on her arm and the back of her neck—as Leif handed the weapon to Cell, who walked away with it, ejecting the cartridge and clearing the round in the chamber as he headed to the weapons locker. Rescue breaths and chest compressions were performed by Saito on the dying colonel.

Braun stared at Nesto, gaping and face flushed.

Needing to secure her, Leif guided her away from the scene. "This way, Admiral." He led her to the back of the hub as the doctor rushed past them.

"You have to detain me." Her words were quiet and . . . empty as she moved under his direction without resistance or, it seemed, will.

"Yes, ma'am."

She'd shot a man in cold blood. Committed murder. Of course he had to secure her to ensure she didn't harm anyone else or herself.

He gently directed her to the holding cell.

"I had to. I'm sorry," she breathed. "I knew when we were in the medical bay." Her eyes came to his. "You know, don't you?"

What was he supposed to know? Had she put together the same pieces he had about Nesto? But shooting the colonel point-blank without warning or provocation . . .

He gestured to the MP at the holding cell, who hesitated with a frown, then hurried to open the cell.

Resigned, Admiral Braun stepped inside. In the middle of the cell, she stopped and turned. Her short hair seemed unusually dark against her stunned pallor. Her gaze met Leif's, and she lifted her chin. "Someday I hope you'll understand and not think the worst of me."

"I don't think the worst of you." He'd had his own misgivings about Nesto, but she must've had more than misgivings to shoot him. He eased away as the MP started closing the barred door.

"Leif."

He held out a hand to the MP.

"Bring in Admiral Manche. Don't trust Elbert."

Interesting. He'd met Manche on the *Mount Whitney*. He'd handled Andreas. If Braun was saying that, should he listen or ignore her?

"I know you don't understand," she said softly, "but . . . for Dru's sake, trust me."

"He said to watch out for you, so I will."

Her expression seemed to crumble, and Leif could relate—he knew what it was like to fail Dru. He nodded, then stepped back as the door groaned shut.

What in the insane world was going on? Alene Braun was the epitome of self-control and wisdom, so trying to align that with the woman who had coldheartedly killed a colonel . . .

"Could you send word up the chain about this?" Leif asked the MP. "See if you can get hold of Admiral Manche."

"Yes, sir." The MP strode to the small office connected to the holding area.

After one final glance at Braun seated on the bench, Leif turned and saw Iskra lingering near the juncture of the hub and the rear passage. She was propped against the wall, hugging herself. When she noticed him, she sagged a little deeper.

"You okay?" he asked.

Her dark eyes were glossed with unshed tears. "It is just so much. Director Iliescu, Braun and Nesto, when you left, Taissia . . ."

"Taissia?" Something in him tightened.

Squeaking wheels rolled past—the Marines and Saito rushing Nesto into the medical bay, Dr. Dodson riding the gurney and continuing compressions.

Leif urged her around the corner and back to the hub. "What about Taissia?"

She wilted. "I took her to Bogdashka because Dani was gone and I had to find you. It went against everything I believed, but I knew Bogdashka would at least keep her alive. When I went back to get her, they were gone. All of them. The entire building was empty."

Shock and rage jolted through him, thinking of that little, beautiful imp caught up in their nightmare. "Why didn't you tell me?" Why couldn't he breathe?

"I did!" Iskra railed. "I left messages on your phone, begging you to help."

Leif hung his head. Hated himself. "I ditched that phone." He pulled her into his arms. Held her close. The only thing he could do. "I'm sorry, Iskra. We'll find her. I swear."

Every corner he turned in this maze of death delivered another blow, another way he'd *hurt* the ones he'd meant to protect. "I'm so sorry, Iskra."

He wasn't sure how long they stood in the corridor like

that, but his mind never slowed, exploring scenarios and tactics to find Taissia.

He shifted in front of her, his instinct to get a plan together to retrieve her daughter. "What do you know about Bogdashka?" They started back toward the hub.

"Besides the fact that is not her name? That she went by the code name Bodhan when I was still with Hristoff?" She wrapped her arms around herself as they walked up the ramp. "She is terrifically cruel in a very subtle way. For a long time, I thought she was a saint, my savior. But I quickly grew suspicious that she was the cause of . . . many situations. I believe she is how I ended up with Hristoff."

"Why do you think that?" Leif walked around the wrought-iron rail that cordoned off the conference area.

"Everything Hristoff knew, she knew. Or vice versa." Iskra nodded to him. "When we were in Istanbul, she knew many things she should not have, including my location. Then Hristoff showed up. She called me while I was on the run—just before I saw you. It was a huge mistake on my part."

"Maybe," he said with a teasing grin, "but it gave me a chance to get to know a beautiful Bulgarian brunette."

She slid him a coy smile, but her gaze hit something to the side. She sucked in a breath. A storm burst across her features. "What are you doing?"

Confused, Leif followed her.

She stomped forward. "Are you *trying* to get my daughter killed?"

His heart skipped a beat at those words, his mechanisms erupting and demanding he protect the little girl. But what stalled him was the person she aimed her words at. The only person Iskra called *friend*.

"What?" Mercy's expression held shock, hurt, and defensiveness. "What're *you* talking about? I'm sitting here, minding my own business with Barc—"

"This!" Iskra snapped her hand to the monitors, where the face of a woman in her midsixties stared out with no little amount of condescension. She looked like someone used to being in control. "Why are you looking into Bogdashka? I told you she would hurt Taissia!"

"Hold up," Cell said. "Mercy didn't put that up there. I did—for Admiral Braun. Right before everything went to crap."

"And second," Mercy said in a tight, controlled voice, her eyes flashing as she shrugged off Baddar's placating touch, "*never* in my life would I do anything to hurt your daughter—she's like a niece to me. That you think I would cuts at the very fabric of our friendship. Ororo Munroe knew the difference between friends and enemies, and I thought you did, too." She drew in a long breath. "Finally, I have no idea who Bogdashka is, but *that*"—she nodded to the wrinkled, tired, shockingly pale face framed by hair too dark for her age—"is Mina Schultz. The woman who turned me into a machine and ruined my life. The woman I got away from over ten years ago and vowed never to cross paths with again."

Wide-eyed, Alisz slid into the confrontation. "You know her?"

Iskra shifted, swallowing as her gaze hit Leif's, like she was looking for backup or assurance. When he moved closer, she peered up at the screen. "*That* is Bogdashka."

Leif stilled, glancing at the screen. "You sure?"

A mocking laugh trickled out of her. "I know the woman who feigned being my advocate only to exert control." She nodded, her nostrils flaring. "That's who I left Taissia with two weeks ago."

"Her full legal name," Cell said, his voice heavy with the news he was about to deliver as he retrieved his laptop, "is Wilhelmina Maria Schultz."

"Wilhelmina," Leif repeated, recalling the phone call. "Rut-

310

ger said she was in charge of the project that created the Neiothen. She killed his sister."

"Katrin," Alisz supplied, looking at Mercy. "Like I told you."

"Bogdashka?" Iskra squeaked, her features a tangle of confusion. "Bogdashka is Wilhelmina?"

"I wouldn't be surprised." Cell pulled something up on his system. "Check it out—she sits on the board of Hermanns' company, Frankfurt & Stuttgart Biologics." He waved at the laptop. "As well as over twenty other businesses and organizations. Look at the list. You'll recognize a few. Like Aperióristos Labs."

Leif eyed Iskra. The place they'd first met. Which might sound romantic had they not been trying to kill each other.

"Yep, same lab that had the book," Cell said. "Also of note, how about the Quantum Technology Conference?"

The Hague incident.

"It's a Who's Who of ArC operatives," Mercy mumbled, shaking her head, then exchanging a haunted look with Iskra.

Leif checked Iskra. Her expression was blank, stricken. Hand to her stomach, she shook her head. He could only imagine what she felt, realizing the woman who had Taissia was directly connected to ArC, possibly a key figure. It sickened him. Worried him for Taissia. The spry little five-year-old had stolen his heart. Anger vibrated through his system.

"I knew," she said. "I *knew* I shouldn't leave her there, but I was too busy trying to find you."

The stab of that expertly placed truth struck Leif center mass.

"I stood in that attic room and felt it—the chill, the warning." Iskra shoved her hair off her forehead, her palm resting there. "I knew it was wrong, and what did I do? I walked out and left my daughter with that monster! Willingly!" Her shout echoed across the bunker, stilling the team.

Because of him. Because Leif had left to find his own way,

his own answers. And now a five-year-old child was paying for that.

Her gaze was skewering. "You had better be worth it, because if she—" A sob choked her words. He started for her, but she stopped him. "No."

Harangued by guilt, Leif stared at the floor. He looked at her, hating himself. *This* was the very reason he'd tried to separate himself from them. To save them. Protect them. And what a sick, twisted, ironic fate that his attempt to protect them had put them in grave danger.

"I will never forgive you—"

"Hey," Mercy said quietly.

Though she meant well, Leif held up a hand. "She's right. I'm to blame. I deserve her hatred and anything else she wants to throw at me." He glanced around at the others. Landed on Cell. "All of you have a right to hate me."

"It occurred to us," Cell conceded.

"I screwed up. Thought I knew what I was doing, so freakin' determined to get answers, I didn't care what it took or who it hurt." He lowered his head and steadied his breathing. "I was wrong. And I regret it." He considered the friends he'd let down and knew it was time to make amends. "Ask what you will of me, and I'll answer as honestly as I can."

"Not sure we have that much time," Culver snarked, his movements stiff. "And I don't appreciate getting shot."

"You ditched us, went against us, attacked us," Saito said slowly, methodically as he gave a grave shake of his head, then pursed his lips. "That's not easy to come back from."

Leif hated how true those words were. "Understood. I own that blame. I'm sorry." His own words sounded cheap, despite being sincerely spoken.

Culver nodded.

"What's to keep you from ditching us again to do what you think is right?" Saito's candor was appreciated.

"Fair question," Leif conceded. "I'd like to say I won't, but I don't know what's coming. What will hit us. But after losing Dru, I can say I'll do whatever it takes to protect each of you. This isn't about me, though I thought it was." He sniffed. "It's about all of us."

"Yes," said a gravelly, unfamiliar voice. "Agreed."

Leif turned in that direction and found a brawny blond admiral. "Manche."

Behind him trailed a half-dozen operatives dressed in black tac. Easy to recognize his own kind—special operators, likely Navy. Maybe black ops. They'd sure gotten here fast.

"Am I supposed to like your presence here?" Mercy asked petulantly, scanning the newcomers.

"Nobody has to like anything as long as orders are followed." Manche strode to the hub and pointed to the table. "Have a sit. Let's talk."

The team filled in the seats, though it was clear Iskra wasn't entirely pleased about having to do this with the face of her daughter's kidnapper hanging over them.

"Mr. Purcell, take that down, please." Manche indicated the screens as he lowered himself into a chair. Without the glare of the monitors, the room darkened ominously. He sat straight, arms on the slick surface and fingers threaded. "I'll be directing operations for Reaper until such time as the DIA and CIA can choose appropriate replacements for Iliescu and Braun. Any objections?"

Mercy folded her arms, eying the ops team that arced in and leaned against the walls. "Does it matter?"

"Not in the least, young lady," Manche said curtly. "But I like to know what I'm dealing with coming into an active team."

Leif wondered how the admiral's abrasive nature would integrate with Reaper's unique, dynamic personalities.

"We don't have a lot of time for meet and greets, to stroke

egos and wag tongues about who we like and who we don't." Manche's expression was taut, focused. "Reaper—heck, the whole world—is faced with an enemy that isn't slowing. Who has once again one-upped you. Anyone have a problem if we skip platitudes and get to work?"

"Prefer it, sir," Leif said.

"That's what I wanted to hear." Manche cocked his head toward the rear of the bunker. "Admiral Braun will remain in custody for now, but she does have credible intel regarding the Armageddon Coalition that I think we need to act on."

"Any idea why she killed Nesto?"

"A few," Manche said. "You're all intelligent individuals, or you wouldn't have been assigned to this team. Therefore, I'm sure you've considered that Colonel Nesto was likely compromised, and—as has been evidenced today—Braun probably was, too. So we move forward with intel carrying the direct expectation that it's a risk, a potentially lethal one. And while I am confident in your abilities, in light of Braun's actions, contingencies are vital to protect the mission and our personnel." He nodded to the operators. "Meet my contingency."

Leif appreciated the planning but . . . "Contingency how?"

"We'll get to that in a minute."

"And the intel?"

"Glad you asked." Manche smirked. "It seems ArC has been ramping up a program they intend to switch on within the next twenty-four hours. We believe it's why things have escalated so fast in the last week."

Mercy leaned in. "A program?"

"Yes, Miss Maddox, one that is most likely right up your hacking-loving alley, and we intend for you to be heavily involved in the disruption of this program."

"This is why Dru had us in London?"

Manche seemed impressed. "Indeed."

She sat a little straighter, her attitude toward the admiral shifting. "What does the program do?"

"It's the proverbial switch they're throwing on restructuring economic delivery across Africa, Southeast Asia, the Balkans, and parts of Europe. Without this program, nobody will be able to purchase so much as a stick of gum."

"That's the reason for all the ancillary skirmishes," Culver suggested.

"That is correct."

"How am I supposed to disrupt this?" Mercy asked, curious, intrigued.

"That's the trick of the thing," Manche admitted. "Since we're just now getting this intel from Braun and comparing it against our own efforts in Naval intelligence, we can't answer that yet, but as of five minutes ago, you were given access to secure files about the program, which we're told has been dubbed Risen."

I will rise.

I will rise.

I will rise.

The trigger phrase for the Neiothen. It couldn't be a coincidence.

"Sir." Leif ran a hand over his mouth. "What about the Neiothen and the newer super soldiers?"

"Gen2s," Manche said with a nod, then looked to Iskra. "They're part of the army ArC is building to protect and enforce this economic system. Your brother did us a favor on that boat. His team killed several in an all-out brawl. There is no avoiding the new models when we go up against ArC, so knowing your enemy is your best defense. Since we have limited intel on them, we'll be dissecting them, too. Veratti can pull the trigger on the program, but the soldiers take time. And thank the Lord he isn't some white-haired wizard with a legion of orcs at his whim." His gaze hit Mercy's. "See? You're not the only one who can make superhero analogies."

With a smirk of her own, Mercy winged up an eyebrow. "You're referencing Tolkien. That's not superheroes."

"My ten-year-old son would beg to differ," Manche said.

"Sir," Leif said, "I want to be sure you're aware that Iskra's daughter has been taken captive by a woman likely connected to ArC."

"Wilhelmina Schultz," the admiral announced, then lifted a shoulder almost in a shrug, "according to Braun."

Leif started. "She knew about that?"

"Alene didn't have proof, but since Schultz was involved, that was her guess." Manche nodded. "Alene Braun is under suspicion for treason, but she will not speak to her loyalty or justifications for the murder of Nesto. At this point in the game, however, we cannot afford to just disregard her credible intel."

"Credible intel—it's been vetted, then?" Leif asked.

"As best as possible. Everything she says is going through multiple layers of fact-checking." Manche returned to his seat. "Most of the intel, though, is lining up with HUMINT, SATINT, and SIGINT. It's why I'm here and why a plan is being put in place to hit ArC and take down that program." His gaze landed on Iskra. "And save an innocent child."

"Hit ArC," Leif repeated. "We have a location or person in mind?"

"COMINT has revealed a significant attention around 26 July for Risen to rise, if you'll pardon the bad pun." Manche gave a grim smile. "For those at this table, the location is rather poetic."

That was ominous. Poetry and combat didn't mix well.

"The Pearl of the Antilles."

"Guantanamo." Leif side-eyed Iskra, recalling their stand-off at the secret facility, her diving into the choppy sea. "Since Braun was a joint chief, how deep is the contamination among the military?"

"No telling."

"Contingencies," Leif muttered.

"You read my mind, Chief." Manche placed his hands on the table. "There's a facility a short distance from the Pearl." He nodded around the table. "You've been there. That's where we need to go. We have an insertion plan for Reaper. However, if Reaper fails, these operators"—he nodded to the newcomers—"will be in place to blow the facility."

"With or without us in it?" Culver asked.

"Whatever needs to happen in order to prevent Risen from going online," Manche said, narrowing his eyes. "Get this straight, Reaper—you have your chance for vengeance and redemption, but the bigger priority is stopping the coalition. If they succeed, our planet will be plunged into a terrific economic crisis that we're not sure we can come back from."

Mutterings skittered around the room, uncomfortable with the plan and the contingency, but also understanding it.

"Are you referring to the facility beneath that installation?" Iskra asked quietly.

Manche gave her a long, hard look. "How do you know about that?"

Iskra glanced at Leif, who nodded for her to explain. "When looking for the Book of the Wars recently, I believed the person who took it from the lab did not leave the facility. So I returned and dived, convinced the book had not left the facility either."

Jaw muscle bouncing, Manche stared at her. If he meant to intimidate Iskra, it wasn't working. Maybe he didn't understand her background. She'd faced down worse.

The admiral punched to his feet. "Chief, a word?"

Feeling the need to reassure Iskra, Leif touched her shoulder as he slid around the chair. The waters they were navigating were tricky and dangerous, with way too many questions regarding who was friend and who was foe. He had to admit he hated the idea of returning to the Pearl. The sea had almost taken his life and Iskra's. What if this time it succeeded?

The new operators seemed to enhance that danger, promising that failure meant death.

THIRTY-TWO

REAPER HEADQUARTERS, MARYLAND

It had been an hour since Leif and Manche had gone into Iliescu's office and shut the door. Though Mercy and Cell discussed ArC's economic program and how to best disrupt it, Iskra felt useless. So she pulled up a map of the naval base in Cuba.

"You okay?" Culver asked from across the table.

Her gaze automatically hit the door where the admiral was talking with Leif. "My daughter is missing, and he's concerned about *my* loyalty."

Culver frowned. "Didn't hear him say that."

"We both know that conversation is about me."

"Not sure it is," Culver said. "Think about what Leif's done and what's been done to him—he's a Neiothen. If anyone's suspect, it's him. How do we know that chip in his head hasn't been reactivated? Where are the other Neiothen who hit this bunker with him?"

"You mean my brother?" Iskra swiveled to face him, forcing herself to remain calm. "He and the ones who saved me from the Gen2s are in custody. We do not know that any others are still alive. Or are you doubting Leif's loyalty?"

"You're not hearing me."

"I'm hearing quite well," she countered. "You just questioned whether he has been reactivated." She rested her arms on the table. "You called him a Neiothen. Do you think his being here is a ploy, a tactic of ArC?"

319

"No, ma'am, I don't." He squinted. "Do you?"

"Of course not."

"Then why'd you say it?" He cocked his head like someone racking the slide of a gun. "Let's not put words in each other's mouths. I'm not an enemy. I was just trying to get you to see that, if you look around, we can have doubts about a lot of the members here. But it's not worth it. You want your girl back."

Iskra drew up a little at the reminder.

"We want her back, too." Culver held her gaze firmly. "Because she's the kid of one of our own."

Did he really see her like that, one of their own?

A loud bang cracked through the bunker.

Reaper responded, reaching for weapons as they turned toward the noise.

Eyes full of fire and fury, Leif stalked toward them, the door behind him rebounding off his attempt to slam it. "Cell, put it up there." He pointed to the wall monitors, and his gaze met Iskra's. "We'll get her back."

What? His dark tone scared her. Made her stand, her pulse ratchet. At his side, she looked up as the little arrow icon on the screen hit PLAY.

Iskra was not prepared for what she saw. She recoiled, hand going to her mouth. Tears stinging her eyes. The video showed Taissia sitting in an empty room, hugging her knees and wailing.

"Hello, *kotyonok*." Bogdashka slid in front of the camera, the one-way glass behind her all that separated the witch from Taissia. "It was very kind of you to bring me your little girl. You could not have timed it more perfectly."

"It's her," Mercy whispered. "It's Mina."

"Where did this come from?" Culver asked, frowning. "It's to Iskra, but you got it?"

"She sent it to me," Alisz quietly admitted, "and I gave it to the admiral, so everyone here would know I'm not working for them."

"Aren't you, if they're communicating with you?" Culver challenged.

"Focus, people," Leif said.

"You will not come after her," Bogdashka continued. "Taissia will stay safe if you do as I say. If you do not . . . well, you know how I handle disappointments."

Swallowing a sob, Iskra shook her head, wanting to find comfort in Leif's arms. Trying to listen past her drumming heart.

"Do not attempt to stop Risen or the Gen2s. What I ask is a small thing, a pittance compared to the life of your precious daughter, your love child with Valery, yes?" Bogdashka moved out of view, then reappeared in the room beside Taissia. "You will be a good girl, won't you?"

"Leave me alone!" her daughter screamed, tightening in on herself. "I want my mommy!"

Bereft, Iskra cupped her hands over her mouth.

"I have been very patient, *kotyonok*."

Recognizing the words, the threat that hung in the air after them, she choked out a sob. "No," she whispered, clenching her fists as Bogdashka reached toward Taissia.

Terror scratched her daughter's face and fed a survival reaction that made her kick and scream.

Anger tumbled through Iskra. "No," she ground out. "Touch her and I will kill you."

But Bogdashka could not hear, and it did not matter. The old woman knew what Iskra would do to her. Knew what she was capable of doing.

"I will have to teach you how to behave," Bogdashka intoned.

"No!" Mercy gasped, turning away.

Iskra refused to hide. Instead, she watched—memorized—

Bogdashka sliding a needle into Taissia's thigh. Too familiar was the sting of that needle so many times in her own leg. She replayed it over in her head, vowing that Bogdashka had made her choice. Her choice to die.

"Iskra." Leif's voice was heavy with anger that mirrored her own. He turned to her. Caught her shoulders. "We'll get her back. This woman—"

She wrested free. "No."

He frowned.

Iskra knew what to do, what must be done. With or without them. She looked at the admiral. "You said they are at the Pearl?"

Manche considered Leif, then her, but didn't answer.

Leif angled around. "Listen to me."

"I defy you to say anything that will alter my course!"

"Tell them about the implant," Manche said, his tone flat.

Leif glanced down and to the side, as if unwilling to face the admiral or what he'd said. But it wasn't Leif the admiral was speaking to.

Mercy straightened, arms unfolding and falling to her sides. "I . . ."

"Go on," Manche barked. "It needs to be out in the open."

Mercy's cheek twitched. "When I was tracking the Neiothen RFIDs, I detected two signals here in the hub." She again crossed her arms, hugging herself. "I've confirmed that both of them were operational, but one was at a lower intensity." She chewed her lip. "It still is."

"Meaning?" Leif growled.

"Are you sure?" Cell asked, inching in.

"I've checked it every hour," Mercy said, her expression sorrowful. "I'm sorry, Leif, but your chip isn't inactive. There are moments where its receptivity is low for a short period, but it's strong for a lot longer."

"I knew that was a possibility—we all did," Leif said with

a sigh. Then his expression changed. Hardened. "Wait. You went over my head to Manche about this. So you think I've been turned? Is that it? You think I'm a Neiothen, that I'm just playing you?" He seemed ready to blow.

"No," Mercy said, her ache evident in her contorted features. "But—"

"You said two." Leif's thoughts seemed to bounce from one thread to another. "Two signals. Who was the other?"

"There's . . . only one now." She shrugged. "The second must've been Nesto."

"His death was confirmed ten minutes ago," Manche said.

"Un-freakin'-believable," Leif growled.

The nightmares just would not stop. Iskra ached, watching him discover that he might still be at the mercy of Veratti. His anger was raw and primal, mirroring what Iskra felt toward Bogdashka.

"She did the right thing," Manche said, his voice vibrating. "She detected a problem and reported it just as she should." He looked at the team.

"Agreed," Leif said miserably with a nod to Mercy. "Good job."

Mercy gave him a sorrowful, apologetic shrug, her mouth twisted with sadness.

"You're all heading to the Pearl," Manche barked. "But I need everyone in this room to understand: there is no way to know if the chief here is going to shoot them or you."

THIRTY-THREE

No matter what he did or tried, he posed a threat to those he loved.

The realization corkscrewed through Leif, twisting his gut and thoughts. No way he'd let Reaper go to the Pearl without him. But he had to admit, it scared him, knowing this thing in his head was still receptive to influence. To Veratti.

Their lack of knowledge about the implant's function created more questions—what was its purpose? To trigger the past? To activate what he'd been trained to do? Obviously it wasn't mind control in the truest sense, and that was the only reason Manche signed off on Leif being tasked to this mission with the stipulation that Reaper knew the truth and danger. The admiral had used more than a few colorful words about how they'd put Leif down if he fell out of line. There was also supposition that maybe the facility's depth would make triggering him more difficult or less likely. Maybe both.

"You okay?"

Leif glanced at his older brother, who'd be monitoring from topside. It was weird to see him here in the bunker. "Yeah."

"Knew you would be." Canyon's unwavering belief shouldn't surprise Leif, yet it did.

"Does Mom—"

"Think you're a thickheaded lout? Of course. You're a Metcalfe."

With a smile he didn't feel, Leif nodded—his appreciation

324

for Canyon keeping this between them, and for the familial ties that conveyed a lot without having to speak it. "Glad you're here."

Canyon grinned. "Wouldn't miss an op in the ocean."

It was nice being back on the water, this time aboard the U.S. Coast Guard *Seneca*, a medium endurance–class cutter, which headed away from the base and churned through the bay at a leisurely pace that belied the frenzy aboard. The slow crawl was crucial to allow the team time to get prepped and to convey the appearance of a routine patrol, not a race-to-the-finish mission to stop Ciro Veratti.

The last thing they needed was to tip off ArC, but for all they knew, the captain of the *Seneca* could be an ArC operative who'd already notified the underground facility of their intent and approach.

"Kind of strange," Iskra said as she tucked her arms into a neoprene dive suit, "being back here. With you. On the water."

"Better than *in* the water like last time." He glanced across the deck to where Andreas, Vega, Gilliam, and Huber were gearing up as well. Elvestad, Leif had learned, had died the same night Dru had, killed by the Gen2s. Manche had pulled in more than a few favors to get the Neiothen back in play. Especially Andreas, since he had more knowledge about the implant than any of them, as well as intel on the Gen2s. Not to mention his effectiveness against the latter.

"This is unbelievable," Culver complained as he helped Saito safety-check his dive equipment. "I could take every one of you every day of the year with all my limbs missing, and they sideline *me* for what amounts to a mosquito bite."

"The gunshot was close to your heart," Canyon noted from the Command station set up on deck.

"If he has one." Saito clicked his tongue. "Man, stop complaining and get healed so I don't have to keep doing all your work for you." He reviewed his weapons, the cartridges, and the round in the chamber. Though the weapons would work in the water, they'd have to chamber a round each time they fired.

"I feel your pain, Culver. I mean, it's a *submersible*," Cell said, emphasizing the word. "Even I'd be safe—"

"Doc said the pressure from the dive could cause complications with your wound," Leif reminded him. "Sorry, but you're too valuable to lose."

"Yeah, you didn't say that when you choked me unconscious." The words were muttered but imbued with more than a little resentment.

There was no way Leif could ever live that down. Shame had kept him from apologizing, but he knew he needed to. Friendship pushed him the ten feet starboard to where Cell stood with Baddar and Mercy, talking about what to do down there.

"Barc, I don't need a tutorial on hacking a Wi-Fi. I got this," Mercy huffed.

"Right."

Alisz bumped his shoulder. "Remember, this is what Nonna Kat designed her for," she said, deep admiration in her words.

His gaze hit Leif's, then diverted.

Though Leif hesitated, considered forgetting it, leaving it alone, he couldn't. "Purcell."

This time, the guy outright turned away. Showed his back.

He deserved that and so much more. "Cell. C'mon, man."

"Make sure Smiley is monitoring the gauges while you're working," Cell said to Mercy.

But Leif had never been one to be ignored. "Cell!"

"*What?*" His shout seemed to echo across the *Seneca* as he snapped around, his expression tight, lips thinned.

Surprised at the outburst, Leif glanced down, then pushed himself into his teammate's personal space. "I'm sorry." Finally met his gaze. "I'm sorry about Taipei."

"No."

Leif frowned. "What do you mean, 'no'?"

"I mean no, you're not doing this."

"I *am* doing this."

"No, no, you're not. It's too much like—'I'm about to die, so I'm clearing my slate to get into heaven.'" Cell moved around him as if he were a part of the cutter, not a person. "Sorry. Not giving you that Get Out of Hell Free card."

"Pretty sure only Jesus can do that," Leif teased, though he knew it fell flat. "That wasn't my intention, but why would that be so wrong? It'd say something about you that I wanted to set things right between us before I died."

"You're not dying," Iskra asserted.

"That," Cell said, pointing to her. "*She* is why I won't let you clear this offense, and it is an offense. When you come back, we'll talk, Usurper."

"Getting sentimental now," Leif taunted, feeling a knot loosen in his chest at the teasing. "Gives me hope."

"More like a hole in the head," Cell shot back.

At least he was joking. That said something, didn't it?

"Okay, ladies," Manche said as he crossed the deck. "So far, so good. Asset on the inside says there are several notable figures down in the facility."

"Which means Braun's intel was legit," Cell muttered.

With a clap, Manche said, "Alpha"—which was Baddar and Mercy in the submersible, staying in communication with Canyon, Cell, and Alisz on the *Seneca*—"you'll be visible on their radar almost as soon as you hit the water, but you have the script, and your pilot, Seaman Jones, will handle comms. Sound travels loud and fast in the water. If you stay quiet and let Jones do his work while you do yours, there shouldn't be an issue."

"Right," Mercy said, giving Baddar a worried look.

Smiley wasn't so smiley right now, focusing on their orders.

"Bravo," Manche barked, swiveling toward Leif, Iskra, Saito, and the four Neiothen. "Meet team Charlie, they'll be going in with you." He nodded to three operators standing nearby. "As you are aware, those fancy Neiothen devices that allow you to talk to each other without being heard by those outside the comms—well, they don't work so great three hundred feet below sea level. So once you're down there, you're on your own." His sharp-eyed gaze landed on Iskra. "Though your focus is on finding your daughter, I want eyes out. You know Veratti. You're likely to pick up on what's off faster."

Iskra inclined her head slowly.

"Okay." Manche clapped again. "Alpha, climb aboard the *Thoreau*. Bravo, you dive in ten." The admiral nodded and turned, then stopped. "Viorica, a word?"

Iskra looked to Leif, confusion and concern in her hazel eyes.

Though Leif gave her a reassuring nod, he wondered what the admiral wanted to talk to her about. Back at the hub, Manche hadn't seemed sure what to think of the beautiful operative. A protective instinct rose through Leif as she followed the admiral, who stepped into the wheelhouse. She followed hesitantly, and the door closed behind her.

"Viorica, I'm going to be blunt."

Unflinching, Iskra stared at the gruff admiral, a sense of defensiveness coating her muscles until they were pulled taut.

"I recognize that is a name you don't use anymore."

Protecting herself had always come first, and until she knew where a person stood in relation to her goals, she would not give them anything. So nodding to this man felt like a flaming betrayal. Yet she did.

"I'm using it on purpose." His eyes crinkled at the edges

and nearly vanished beneath his toothy grin. "If you catch my drift."

She did—he used the name of an assassin because that was who he wanted on the mission. Iskra lifted her jaw slightly. "I am not that person anymore."

"Well," Manche said with more of his gruffness, "I'm afraid we're going to need her eyes, ears, and skills. You see, there are several factors about this whole situation that don't exactly blow my skirt up."

Could this be said with fewer words? Because Iskra just wanted to get Taissia back.

"First, you're going in there with a brother that I probably know better than you do."

Iskra narrowed her eyes. He dared—

"I know." He raised a hand as he sat on a stool bolted into the deck. "You're blood, so you think that's stronger. All the same, I want your eyes on those men of his. I might trust Andrew, but I don't trust the Neiothen."

Did that include Leif?

"Second, I know you've worked with and for Veratti, and you have the skills to eliminate him." Thick arms folded over his chest, he gave her a hard look. "If you get that opportunity, do it. We'll cover you. Just get it done." He certainly did not mince words. "I don't take what I'm asking lightly either. You'd be doing me and this entire world a favor, so I'll do you one as well: my asset in the facility has put eyes on your girl."

Iskra's heart tripped, and she nearly lurched at him, demanding to know how Taissia was doing, what section of the facility she was in, how many guards there were. Instead, Iskra maintained her composure. Because she had an ominous feeling she was being baited.

"You don't seem excited. I'm a little disappointed."

"Disappointed that you cannot manipulate me to get what you want?"

"Manipulate? I just told you we know where your daughter is! How is that manipulating?"

"If it was not, you would have told me her location. In this, to me, you are no different than Veratti." She lifted her jaw. "So, Admiral, what do you want?"

"Smart girl." He grinned with those big white teeth. "I resent the comparison to Veratti, but you're right. I need more of those Viorica skills."

Already he asked her to kill Veratti. What else could he want her to do?

"I'm not happy about what I'm about to say, but"—he heaved a sigh—"it needs to be said. And there has to be a high level of trust."

"You do not know me beyond a name."

"I didn't say the trust was between you and me, though there is that." He rubbed his jaw. "What I know is that Viorica is associated with a hard focus to the mission, to seeing it done. To not letting *personal* feelings get in the way of mission success. Especially over blue-eyed SEALs."

"Leif." Her mind scrambled out of the wheelhouse, desperate not to hear what he was about to say.

He appeared contrite, sad. "He's compromised, Viorica."

Her heart gave a hard squeeze at his words, rejecting them.

"And if somehow they flip his switch again, he won't even know what he's doing."

"That is not true," she said, angry with him for twisting the truth to suit his agenda. "They can know and resist."

"Yeah." He sniffed. "Look how that turned out for Arlen Dempsey."

Iskra resented the mention of the Neiothen who'd killed himself right in front of Leif. "He was already having instability issues."

"Right." Manche roughed a hand over his face. "It's not like he took off and went hiking in the Sahara searching for answers. It's not like he nearly strangled his own friend to death—"

"He did not strangle Cell!"

He squinted at her. "I thought you didn't let personal feelings get in the way."

"And I thought you were an admiral who knew how to read a situation well enough not to make wildly inaccurate accusations." She drew her spine straight to draw a clean breath. "I will not work against Leif. And that *is* personal because, next to my daughter, he means more to me than anyone else."

"You love him."

She held her ground.

"And you'd do anything to protect him." He was suddenly very understanding. "So do me this favor, Viorica. Give me your word that you will protect Leif. Even if it's from himself."

THIRTY-FOUR

Cramped quarters was putting it mildly. Mercy had as much room to maneuver in the submersible as she might in a closet . . . with two guys. Correction: two Hulks. Seaman Jones was about six foot and must've been bored while deployed because his muscles were ready to explode. And then there was Baddar. The six-two, solidly built Afghan commando had more presence than the sea had water. However, and thankfully, Jones sat in the small cockpit, which was just the front of the long tubelike steel trap.

Yeah, not helping, Merc.

The rest of the submersible was gutted, save benches that lined the hull. They served as a backup in case Leif and the others got in trouble, but their primary mission was to dive and disable. In order to hack the underwater facility's Wi-Fi, she needed to be close enough to intercept it. Once the Wi-Fi was hacked, she'd upload her worm to disable ArC from launching Risen.

First, she loaded up her Kali Linux virtual machine and kicked off penetration testing tools to see what she was dealing with. She found an access point and attempted penetration. Failed. Huffing, she realized that repeater had been locked down. Of course, Veratti no doubt had multiple access points so that he could have access. She just had to identify which one wasn't locked . . .

And of course. First one was a fail.

She shouldn't be surprised, really, since Netherwood was able to implant chips in people's heads and not have them randomly trigger. Working, she noticed Baddar's chest swell into her periphery as he inhaled deeply, and eyed him with a smile. "Trying to distract me?"

His usual smile wasn't quite as bright. "Only if it work." His tone seemed a bit strained.

"Ah, you've been hanging around Leif too much already," she teased, trying another encryption to get past an access point. She wasn't sure how long she'd been working, but she felt the air thinning. Her ears popped.

"Looking good, Kitty," Cell comm'd over a surprisingly clear signal.

Mercy snorted. "Yep, smooth and deep." She attempted another penetration and saw it making good progress. Would this one actually work? Chewing her thumbnail, she studied the route of the code and the response from ArC's software. It wasn't happy. She wasn't happy. But how—

Baddar's leg bounced like a firing piston.

She angled away from his frenetic movement, but the edge of his tactical pants rustled against her jeans. Therefore her leg. Vibrating it raw.

Ignore it. Focus on the code.

Bouncebouncebouncebouncebouncebounce.

Ignore it. Find the right repeater.

Bouncebouncebouncebouncebouncebouncebouncebounce.

Mercy clamped a hand on Baddar's knee. "Stop!" She hadn't meant to sound harsh or slap him so hard that her hand stung. Or to yell. "Sorry." When his gaze leapt to hers, she startled at his wide eyes. "You—it's just . . . I need to focus."

Back to hacking. It was a frustrating trial and error. Since Veratti was going to launch this thing *any moment now*, they needed an access point that wasn't locked down.

C'mon, Merc. You can find it.

She shoved her hands into her hair, trying to tame her irritation. The cramped quarters definitely weren't helping.

"How we doing back there?" Jones called from the front.

"Excruciatingly slow," Mercy replied, not looking up from her laptop.

"You guys ever been in a sub before?"

"No," Mercy said, and since Jones could strand them on the ocean floor, she decided not to add that she likely never would be again.

Baddar's chest again swelled.

She slid him an annoyed glance, though she shouldn't, but it was really getting to her—not figuring out the encryption, bumping against locked-down repeaters, the tight quarters . . .

He shifted to the side. Away from her. What on earth was he doing?

His chest rose and fell raggedly. He stood but was too tall to fully straighten and thumped a broad shoulder against the hull. He hunched, turned. Whacked his head on something. Jerked to the side. Tripped backward onto the bench. Lost his balance.

"Hey!" Mercy frowned, looking at his brown eyes.

Wild. Panicked. He was sweating.

Recognizing his claustrophobia, she tossed her laptop onto the bench and caught him by the shoulders. "Hey. Baddar."

He shook his head, his gaze roving the hull, the cockpit, the hatch. For an Arab, he'd gone really white.

"Smiley." Mercy grabbed his face and tugged. When he resisted, she pulled harder until he faced her. "Baddar." When his eyes found hers, there was still a panic-struck distance. "Hey," she softened her voice. "You're okay." She nodded when it seemed like he was focusing. "We're here. We're okay.

Breathe." She deliberately started lowering herself, forcing him to sit back down. "Just breathe. We're okay."

"Air," he managed to say, his expression tormented and humiliated. "I can't—I can't breathe. It too small. Too big—I too big. Not safe. I was okay when first we come but no . . . no, I not do this. Too small. No air. I must—"

The words were a torrent mirroring the thrashing of his pulse. It broke her, seeing fear twist his handsome face. Dark eyes once so alive with smiles and congeniality were now haunted by intense fear.

"Baddar."

A smile. A huff. "Sorry. This not me. I am—air." His chest rose and stiffened. "I need air. I must have air." He started to rise again.

She had to distract him. Get his mind off their setting. But he wasn't listening. So Mercy moved in and pressed her mouth to his.

Baddar froze.

She kissed him again, framing his face with her hands, refusing to let him think about anything but her. Their kiss.

He was a block of ice, cold and stiff. She knew she hadn't overstepped—Baddar was crazy about her, but it was taking him a long time to respond. Or maybe he wouldn't. Was this the wrong tac to get him distracted from the confined space?

But then . . . he did respond. Boy, did he ever. His kiss was strong and powerful, urging and sweet. Then he slowed, his kisses more tender with a low, deep moan.

Still holding his face, she eased off and pressed her forehead to his. Realizing that hadn't just been a tactic. It was a promise that awakened something in her.

He smoothed a hand down the side of her face.

"Better?" she asked.

"Hate to break up the love fest," Jones called, "but we've got company."

UNDISCLOSED LOCATION NEAR CUBA

Thanks to the engine-powered assist of the SEAL delivery system after their drop-off, Leif, Iskra, and the rest of the teams made quick time.

"Bravo on approach," Leif relayed to Command through the comms. "Thirty meters and closing."

"Copy," came Canyon's steady voice from aboard the *Seneca*.

Eyes on the underground cave, the glow brightening as they erased the distance, Leif thought about Iskra. How she'd come storming out of the wheelhouse and stalked across the deck to him after talking with Manche. When he asked what was wrong, she said nothing was going right. Made some vague reference to everyone dying and then went silent. It didn't escape him that she'd started avoiding eye contact, leaving Leif with a pretty good idea of what Manche talked with her about—him.

Canyon had always said Leif was an overachiever, and admittedly, Leif had spent most of his youth trying to measure up to the Metcalfe military legacy and his brothers. Of course, he wanted to make his own mark, so he became a SEAL. It took one bad mission to get his head off-track, and he'd chucked it all away by joining the Netherwood project. Sad how much he could suddenly recall.

He tensed. Was the implant triggering? He hated knowing that thing was in his head.

When his device on his arm thumped, he released the handle of the SEAL delivery system and nodded for the others to do the same. "Bravo leaving the SDV now." After activating the remote that would deliver the vehicle back to the *Seneca*, he slipped off it and started swimming, scanning the cave opening and its lights. Expecting trouble—

"Eyes out, Bravo. *Thoreau* has enemy contact," Manche alerted. "We have negative penetration on the Risen program at this time."

Leif gritted his teeth as he descended, hoping Mercy changed that soon.

Shadows rippled below.

He retrieved his weapon and aimed in the general direction of the wavering light. Pops of light appeared at the cave opening, and he recognized them for what they were—shoulder-mounted lamps on the Gen2s. If they were bold enough to wear lamps, then they were confident in their abilities. Very confident.

"Enemy contact ten meters," Leif intoned as he targeted the nearest lamp and fired. "Engaging." He chambered another round.

Light winked out.

Water swirled around him as the enemy returned fire.

This felt like a sick game of Marco Polo. Leif kicked harder, ready to erase the distance and get on dry ground. Deal with these super soldiers with violence of action.

Vega and Gilliam were coming from directly above.

"Bravo," Canyon reported from topside, "we show ten enemy combatants closing in on your position."

Leif hesitated. *Ten?* He showed three. Where . . . ? His pulse jacked when he identified shadows spiriting toward them. Not slow like a swimmer, but fast. He fired and chambered. Fired and chambered.

A blow to his back thrust him forward. He twisted and caught a limb, only to sense a vortex of movement—legs. He jerked away, feeling as if he'd had a brush with death. Startled at their agility, he dove after the guy, then noted he was right on top of the cave opening.

His fear over Risen going online and Taissia down there forced him to act. That and his terror that his implant would activate. He aborted the skirmishes outside and went for the cave.

Something yanked him backward.

Leif thrashed against whatever held him but didn't make any progress. He reached behind him to find not a person, but a line. His tank had been harpooned, punctured. Which meant he was losing oxygen.

Crap! He eyed his O_2 gauge, then the cave. Was it close enough? Could he reach it without a tank? And once he got into the cave, how far or deep till he found air or dry ground? If anyone tried to stop him . . . well, it'd get interesting real fast. But out here, he had no prayer.

He surveyed the skirmishes around him. Iskra had somehow managed to kill her attacker, probably by getting a jump on him—she was fierce like that. A Gen2 and Andreas were making mincemeat of each other. The others weren't doing so well.

Amid a crimson cloud, Carsen Gilliam went limp.

Wasting time, Metcalfe. He jettisoned his empty tank and mask, kicking hard toward the opening.

Eight meters.

Five.

Twin shadows dove at him. Leif caught one, and the preternatural momentum of the Gen2 carried them toward the cave wall. Leif shifted, putting the super soldier in a chokehold and angling so that unusual force drove the man's head into the rock.

The Gen2 stopped fighting.

Leif kicked off the wall and surged toward an opening the size of a dump truck. Though the other guy came at him, Andreas diverted his attention. Leif slid through the cave opening and spotted a glimmering light—the surface!

Lungs burning, he swam for it. Felt the pressure against his temples. In his chest. With a shove, Leif broke the surface and sucked in a hard breath, taking in the cave.

Water pelted him. The telltale splats of gunfire forced him back under. Diving, he used slow, gentle movements to create as little disturbance as possible. Eyeing the shooters on the ledge, he waited until his lungs demanded relief. A shadowy corner lured him into its darkness to hide and maybe float to the surface, where he could snatch some air. He angled his head back and let his nose slip above the water. Drew in a patient breath.

A shape bobbed into his three—a body. He checked the face and twitched—Iskra! Was she dead?

She blinked. He made eye contact and held up three fingers. Then two. He gently raised his weapon and aimed at the guy on the right. Mouthed, "One."

They both fired.

A Gen2 got off a couple rounds as he fell backward.

Leif surged. Rushed the bank. Grabbed the Gen2's weapon and went to a knee at the entrance to the belowground facility for a quick look-see. It led down a tunnel that was half natural rock, half concrete. Cabling ran along the ceiling, providing a conduit for the intermittently placed lights. "Bravo Actual and Storm going in," he subvocalized.

"Copy," Canyon said.

"Speaking of storms," Cell commed, "you're not going to believe this, but there's a storm brewing. Came out of nowhere."

Leif's gut churned. What were the chances? "Meteoroi?"

"That's our guess," he said. "Weather was clear when we left dock."

"Bravo Five and Four going in. Bravo Three down," Andreas reported.

Huber. Leif winced at losing two people this early into the execution of the mission.

Glancing at the cave opening, Leif saw a member of team Charlie clamber onto the bank, the water, like some twisted miracle, turning red. "Charlie . . . Two . . . shot."

Vega appeared behind him, moving fast onto the cleft. "Seven inside as we—" He arched his spine as a harpoon pierced his chest, and he collapsed as several black-clad heads popped up in the water.

Andreas ducked behind a stack of crates and provided protective cover. "Go!" he shouted to Leif.

Turning, Leif shoved Iskra through the exit, hearing the pursuit of angry bullets. Weapons tight against their shoulders, they hurried down the tunnel with the daunting realization that ArC had cut their number of Neiothen in half before they even penetrated the building.

THOREAU SUBMERSIBLE, CARIBBEAN SEA

"I'm losing the signal!" Mercy cried as the submersible dove away from the facility to avoid projectiles.

"If I stop, they won't," Jones said. "Arrive alive or drown. Your choice."

Gritting her teeth, Mercy focused on an encryption, hoping, praying, *begging* this would be the right one. It was ridiculous how many she'd already attempted, but—

Without warning, she was pitched forward violently, throwing her into Baddar. He caught her, but she heard a loud crack. She gasped, searching the hull for a breach. Hands trembling, she removed herself and glanced at their pilot. "Did we get hit?"

"Depth charges," Jones called back. "They're searching for us, and that one was close."

"Searching?"

"Might want to finish your thing before they switch charges for missiles."

Right. Mercy retrieved her laptop from the deck—and gasped. "No!" Her screen was cracked. No, not just cracked.

Shattered. It looked like funky crackled glass. "I can't..." This was like trying to see coding through a sheet of ice. It was there, but next to impossible to make out.

"What's wrong?"

"My screen." A sickening sensation swirled through her gut. She was not going to be the one to fail the entire world. "It's shattered. I dropped it when we got tossed around."

"We have a system up here—"

"No, the Kali Linux virtual machine is on here." Panic crept along her shoulders and skittered down her spine as she thought of Leif and Iskra down there. In the cave. Facing off with Veratti. If she couldn't get this disabled, it meant they had to destroy the whole facility with Veratti and ArC inside, which wasn't terribly bad if it weren't for one thing: Leif and Iskra would die with them. And Mercy would not be the one to bury her friends in a watery grave.

UNDISCLOSED LOCATION NEAR CUBA

With the singular focus of finding Taissia, Iskra stayed close to Leif as he hurried to the hatch that separated the facility from the tunnels. Behind her came Mitre. As they approached the hatch, he and Saito covered their six. The four of them were the only ones who had made it out of the water.

Leif attached a box over the security panel. "Device attached, Topside."

"Copy." Cell and Alisz would work to remote bypass the locks. "Establishing link ... accessing now."

This was it—the point of no return. Once they went through the hatch, they would lose communication with topside and be on their own.

Leif cast her a glance that said he was thinking the same thing.

A definitive *shunk* rattled the hatch.

Leif trained his weapon on the hatch and commed, "Locks disengaged. Going in." He tugged the handle and eased back a safe distance.

The hatch lumbered aside with a painful slowness. Beyond it was a steel and pale gray passage that distinctly marked it as part of the facility, not the stone of the cave. A series of torches ran its length until a left turn junction. Beyond that, darkness.

As point, Leif crossed the lip of the hatch, taking Iskra's heart with him. But he was focused. Intense. Cheek to the stock as he cautiously advanced. Mitre and Saito sidled in behind her.

Whirp. Whirp. Whirp. A sound trilled through the steel passage. A grating, forbidding sound that announced their intrusion and warned they would soon have a lot of company.

Even as they sidled up to the corner, Iskra thought of Taissia, worried the alarms would force Veratti to flip the switch early—

"Bravo," Canyon commed, "we have a signal boost from the bunker. That may indicate Kitty has yet to deliver . . . Risen . . . live."

"Copy." At the juncture, Leif paused and used a snake camera to see around the corner. He used a penlike instrument to disable the cameras, then sent Mitre and Saito across to check the rest of this tunnel.

Mitre slid around them and crossed the open space into the unlit portion of the passage. She keenly felt the loss of protection on her six as he and Saito headed away from them.

With a nod to her, Leif banked left around the corner with a new intensity and urgency that drew Iskra behind him, knowing they all understood the danger to Taissia. To the world.

This passage was at least forty meters long with no door or exit. There was nowhere to go. They had no choice but to advance. Leif moved as if he knew where he was going. Was that the implant? Or had he seen something? Unease slithered through her stomach. Her nerves jounced as the end loomed closer and still there were no doors.

Relief struck when a gap presented itself. What seemed like a dead end was in fact a cross-shaped juncture. Passages banked right and left, and then another ten or twelve feet straight ahead were more doors.

They flanked the entrance. Using the camera snake again, Leif assessed their new path. About twenty feet long with three doors—one on each wall, two of them in recessed wells. A lot of concrete but no people. Corner-mounted cameras glowered down from both directions.

Leif disabled the cameras again, then motioned her to the right. Six feet down, that section ended in a door well. Anxious to find Taissia, Iskra started right, knowing Leif would follow, his back to hers to guard their rear.

Shouts sounded distantly. Or maybe just through the walls. She scanned around, trying to home in on the source, but it seemed to be coming from all directions, the steel carrying the sound heavily.

On her toes, she peered through a high-set rectangular window in the door. Darkness shrouded the room. A dull lamp sat to the side but did not cast enough light to see more than a few feet beyond that source of illumination. In the shadows stood a table with several drawers and a locked floor-to-ceiling cabinet. The far right was so dark it seemed black, making anything else indiscernible. Definitely no people. No Taissia. Defeat pushed Iskra back down, and she shook her head at Leif.

At her signal, he slipped to the juncture and cleared left, to be sure no threat had come down that first tunnel since they had left it. He advanced to the other side, toward the doors set in all three walls, this time with Iskra moving backward to watch their six.

This was too easy, too quiet. They should have encountered—

Shouts arose again, this time much closer.

She felt the soft bump of Leif and glanced back, seeing his raised fist. He pivoted and stepped back, planting his spine in the corner so he had a door on either side and diagonally across.

Iskra checked their rear again—and stilled as light swooned through the rectangular window in the door she'd checked a moment ago. The glow wasn't bright enough for a switch to have been turned on. Maybe a shoulder lamp? A torch? Light from another room?

She shifted to notify Leif, but he was clearing doors. He checked one, then rolled around to the next one, his movements quick, precise, determined.

Voices filtered through that far door, snatching Iskra's breath. That stern, forbidding voice. Bogdashka!

Iskra was gliding forward before she realized it. She chastised herself for leaving Leif, not signaling him. She knew better. But if Bogdashka was there. . . .

She again peered through the window. Halos fluttered across the room, spilling their illuminated hem across a small cot in the far corner.

Taissia! Her daughter lay with her back to the door, facing the wall. Men moved toward her. One shifted, enabling Iskra to see Bogdashka a step ahead, reaching for a sleeping Taissia.

Rage erupted. It took everything in Iskra not to scream and bang on the steel barrier. Whirling, she motioned to Leif, but he was focused on the final room. She spun back, a mother's determination carving a hard line through her restraint.

Iskra was not going to let them escape with her daughter, not when she was right there. Aiming at the lock, she fired—

careful to avoid the steel door and a ricochet. She kicked, but it held. Another shot and another kick. The door bucked free. Iskra rushed in, her weapon tucked firmly against her shoulder, only to find the trio already slipping through the other side.

She eyed the cot—empty. Iskra surged toward the door, firing at the retreating guards. One stumbled into the wall and collapsed.

Fury drove her into the narrow passage after Bogdashka. She sighted the second guard turning right and fired. He tripped and staggered, going to a knee, but then he pushed up and aimed at her. A shot pinged the wall.

Ducking, Iskra fired again and kept moving. At his slumped form, she checked the hall he'd been headed into. Empty.

She strangled her cry. Where was Taissia? Looking back the way she'd come, she caught a shadowy form struggling around a corner.

Iskra sucked in a breath. The guard had been a distraction! She raced back, narrowly avoiding a collision with Mitre, who emerged from the room. "I saw her!" She bolted toward a juncture and slowed, nearly skidding on the slick surface. She shouldered the wall. Peeked around.

Crack!

Iskra jerked back, smelling the chemical burn of the bullet that whizzed past her. Ducking, she rounded the corner. Sighted Bogdashka wrangling Taissia, who was thrashing in her arms, mouth gagged.

"Stop!" Iskra shouted. "Stop, or I will shoot."

"Don't be a fool," Bogdashka sneered, using her daughter as a shield. "You will not shoot. You could injure her."

"I would rather do that than let you have her one second longer." Iskra assessed Taissia—her mussed hair, eyes wild with terror. There was a small knot on her head, but no other visible injuries.

Bogdashka turned, apparently giving up on the door she'd been trying to access.

"Put her down," Iskra growled, advancing and ready to end this woman forever, "*Wilhelmina*."

Lifting her chin, Bogdashka gloated. "Took you long enough to learn who I was."

"I knew what you were from the very beginning."

"And yet," she said, hoisting a crying Taissia into a firmer hold, "you brought your daughter right into my home and *gave* her to me." She was eyeing something over her shoulder. Shifting backward. She pivoted toward it.

"No!" Iskra growled and shot low.

Bogdashka cried out, collapsing on a now-shattered knee, releasing her hostage.

Shrieking, Taissia surged toward Iskra with wild panic and desperation.

Iskra rushed at her daughter, weapon never leaving Bogdashka as she swept Taissia into her embrace. She struggled to remove the gag.

"Well, do it!" Bogdashka shouted. "Shoot her!"

Iskra scowled, confused. What did—

A shadow loomed over her. She started, then saw her brother and relaxed. "Mitre."

"Do it now!" Bogdashka growled. "Or Veratti will kill you."

Iskra's mind powered down, processing the information. Mitre. Bogdashka. Veratti. His weapon rising.

Clutching Taissia, she strangled a sob. "No," she breathed at her brother. "How could you?"

Mitre stepped into the light. "Very easily."

THIRTY-FIVE

Confident Andreas was covering Iskra and with Saito now covering his six, Leif continued toward the main operations area of the facility, if the increasingly heavy security measures and thick cabling racing along the ceiling were any indication. When a shot cracked the air, he shoved himself to the wall.

A head bobbed out of a door. Uniformed. Armed. Weapon up.

"Contact." Leif eased back the trigger. Delivered another man to the depths. He stalked forward, anticipating more engagement. At the door, he did a split-second look-see. Table and chairs. Vending machines. Break room. No threats.

They advanced, fingers on triggers, ready to neutralize, and came up on an elevator. Where were the stairs? He scanned the passage, swiveled back in the direction they'd come.

The door dinged.

Leif and Saito backed away, ready as the steel barriers slid apart and a volley of fire vomited from the elevator. He fired several shots into the elevator, though the enemy had stacked at the front corners. A body slumped out into the passage.

A swarm of black rushed from the elevator, and though Leif fired, he registered the tactical vests. Gen2s.

Pain exploded through his leg even as he sprayed at their knees. His knee buckled and shifted, his boot slipping in his own blood as he tried to take aim. Another round struck his arm. Shock riddled his limbs.

"Hold fire! He wants him alive." The swarm shifted, two men hustling to Saito, who was laid out.

Leif reached for his ankle-holstered gun, but blunt force slammed him into a wall. His head bounced, and the lights went out.

THOREAU SUBMERSIBLE, CARIBBEAN SEA

"Mercy," growled Manche, "you taking a vacation?"

"Can you read cracked code, Admiral?" she shot back, watching Baddar rigging an external monitor, by way of a tablet, to her shattered laptop. "This is not as easy as it doesn't look."

"We've lost communication with the team, and I don't want to lose their lives, too. Do you want that on your head?"

"I don't even want it on my pinky," she muttered, her sarcasm dark and perhaps tasteless. Which happened when she was pushed beyond reason.

"Ariadne," Alisz said. "They trained you for this. You can do it."

"Shut up," she huffed.

"Here." Baddar held up the tablet—now displaying her coding.

"You sexy man." Mercy grinned, shifting her gaze to the clear screen, and immediately the strain on her eyes relieved. "Okay, we're better off than I thought," she said to Command. "I think if I—" She sucked a breath, then laughed it out. "I'm in!" She laughed again, disbelieving how close she'd been when the screen cracked. "Yes, I'm in. Uploading the worm now."

"I think you doubly owe Baddar now," Jones said over his shoulder. "But I guess since you have to marry him, it's not going to be a problem repaying that debt."

She laughed, then frowned. "What?"

"That kiss," Jones said. "In Afghanistan, that's a very intimate gesture, only done between a husband and wife. I'm going to guess he expects to marry you now."

Mercy knew her eyes betrayed her startled panic when she whipped toward Baddar.

A blush spread through his cheeks, and though he tried to smile, it came out like a nervous waver. "We not live in my country," he said quietly.

Her thoughts vibrated at the idea, what he *wasn't* saying. Or that he wasn't arguing. Was he . . . ? Did he really . . . ?

No no no. "I can't do love and marriage right now. I have to save the world first."

UNDISCLOSED LOCATION NEAR CUBA

A sense of falling jerked Leif awake. His face hit a hard surface, and he rolled, groaning and pressing a hand to his temple. In front of him lay an unconscious Saito. His lips weren't blue, so he was still alive. Right?

"I'm impressed, Mr. Metcalfe."

Climbing onto all fours, he struggled to shake off the fog of unconsciousness. A roar of pain from the bullet wounds and pounding headache strangled his thoughts. But there was no mistaking who stood over him. "Veratti."

"Did you really think you would stop me, Mr. Metcalfe?"

"Didn't think—just did the best violence I could," Leif ground out around the thuds in his head. "I won't stop until one of us is dead." He pulled a leg under him and lifted his torso so he wasn't cowering like a dog. The world tilted and swayed, but he steadied himself.

"Is that what you told Director Iliescu on his yacht?"

Anger jolted Leif, along with outrage at what this man

had cost him and so many of those he cared about. "No, it's what we did to your men." He squinted around the pounding. "Heard there were extra body parts floating in the Atlantic. Think the Coast Guard had a strainer to pick them out?"

Veratti's gaze darkened. "You cost me a lot."

"You're welcome." Leif scanned his surroundings, trying to figure out what he could use as a weapon, since they'd stripped him of his. "You know what they say about payback. You cost me months of my life and the last four years looking for answers."

Veratti laughed. "That wasn't me, Mr. Metcalfe. If you had but asked, I would've told you everything."

"Only at the cost of my soul." Around the perimeter of the room were at least twenty men in black tactical gear, faces concealed behind black masks. "That's your currency, isn't it? Souls. You have plenty right here. I won't give you mine."

"That," Veratti said, "we had five years ago. Now you will see what we've done with it. And these . . ." He nodded to the Gen2s. "They are my enforcers. Counselors, if you will—helping people understand the importance and benefits of Risen."

"Benefits," Leif snorted.

"As you will see. We will all see." The prime minister stood proud amid a group of men in suits, all watching a screen where a series of numbers and names blipped, each addition nudging the lines of information up. It reminded Leif of the stock exchange, except with countries, not businesses. "How are we doing, Dhruv?"

"Good, sir," a man with jet-black hair said. "Risen is completely uploaded, and they're bringing it online. With the encryption and the level of sophistication, each country packet and component has to be brought online individually."

The same way they'd taken down countries and rearranged leadership.

Leif wanted to nuke this place. These suits were the men who'd assumed power in the wake of disasters and murders that had killed their predecessors.

In his periphery, he saw Saito's eyes flicker open, and he silently signaled him to stay still, quiet.

"Sir," an Asian man said from a computer, "I think . . . no, I'm positive someone is trying to hack the system."

Leif nearly grinned. *Do your stuff, HackerGirl. Kill this.*

"That's impossible," another man argued. "There are multiple redundancies and repeaters, and at this depth, they'd have to be—"

"In a submersible." Veratti's gaze struck Leif without question or confusion. "It's a shame we've had to hit it with a missile."

When Veratti focused back on his techs, Leif knew he had no time to panic. If Mercy had been taken out, his mission here was more important than ever. He'd have to blow this place—even if he went down with it.

He searched the room for anything flammable or explosive. Anything he could detonate. He eyed the cabling. But it was just him and Saito, who was awake now but not moving, waiting for Leif's instruction.

Needing a better perspective, Leif struggled to his feet. Feigning dizziness and more pain, he stumbled back a couple of steps.

In a fluid, graceful—but deadly—move, the Gen2s produced their weapons and trained them on Leif. Tension forced the suits to shift away, realizing they would be in the crossfire.

"Your guards are kind of twitchy, Ciro," Leif said around a faked groan, the heel of his hand to his head. But his ploy had worked. He was now within striking distance of the two nearest Gen2s, but better yet—they were focused on him. Not on Saito, who'd dragged himself out of sight between two waist-high vented systems.

"I would be careful, Mr. Metcalfe," Veratti snarled. "They are much faster and harder to kill than you."

"Sir, we have a problem," the tech said, his expression taut and concerned. "Sensors picked up several unfriendlies around the perimeter. Reports say they're setting explosives."

Veratti snapped his gaze to the Gen2s. "Go, before they kill us all!"

Man, that was a nice sound—fear in Veratti's voice. Leif had to find a way to create more of that.

The exfil of more than half the Gen2s was swift and quiet, like a whoosh of wind. Or maybe that was Leif releasing the breath he'd been holding. That announcement had evened things out a little. He liked these odds. A lot.

"Uh, sir?" the tech whined. "I . . . I think . . ."

"What?" Veratti growled.

The tech put his hands on his head as the screen blipped, went black . . . then the ooga-chaka baby splayed across it and started dancing.

"What is this?" Veratti demanded.

"A little Mercy." Seizing the distraction that filled the room with worried chatter and that annoying song from the '90s, Leif stepped back and drove his elbow into the face of the nearest Gen2, then snapped his fist hard and violently into the man's nose.

Even as he delivered that potentially fatal blow, he knife-handed the other guard in the throat. Gen2s might have better endurance or heal faster, but they were still human. They still needed air.

By the time he'd freed the weapon from the first man and fired off several rounds, he heard other shots—both the remaining Gen2s and Saito. Leif moved in an elimination arc through the Gen2s and suits, aiming for the system, the software. He wasn't discriminating. Suits cried or died.

The return volley of bullets forced Leif down behind a table, which he upended for cover.

"Mr. Metcalfe!" Veratti shouted. "I have something you want!"

The room fell strangely quiet, and whimpers thickened the air that was now rank with the metallic scent of blood. A side door whisked open, and Andreas entered.

Good. They'd settle this. Win thi—

In lurched Iskra, gagged and carrying a clinging Taissia.

Leif dropped back down against the upended table, gripping his weapon. Swiped a hand over his mouth, anger roiling. He'd tried. Failed. Again. Iskra and Taissia needed him. He wouldn't give up. But for now, the smarter play was surrender. So he could figure a way out.

Across the way, he noted Saito hunkering out of sight.

Leif slowly came to his feet, Gen2s taking a bead on him as another person entered, weapon trained on Iskra's back. Not Bogdashka but . . .

"Braun." *How?* "You were in lockup."

The admiral met his gaze evenly. "I convinced Manche he needed me onsite. Remember what you said? That Dru said to watch out for me?" Braun shrugged, giving him a nearly apathetic smile. "I think you misunderstood."

Like lightning, the moment in the Atlantic surged in Leif's mind, recalling the director's dying words. "Dru knew." He hadn't been telling Leif to *protect* her. "He was trying to warn me."

"She did not become an admiral through her good looks," Veratti mocked. "She is shrewd. Tenacious. Once Manche brought her down to Guantanamo, I sent a Gen2 in as a Marine to retrieve her."

"Pretty stupid, risking your men for her," Leif said. "I think you missed a memo: she's not that important."

"Maybe not to you. But to me—how do you think we got the American component?" Veratti was way too calm. "Risen

353

will be implemented in doses, since fear of the mark of the beast"—he laughed—"scares even the atheist into avoidance. But the gullible will accept it because they'll think—oh, this makes life so much easier. It removes limitations. I can get what I want—faster, better, easier."

Leif gritted his teeth, knowing how easily convenience drove people.

Veratti angled his head. "That's what you thought, was it not, when you joined Netherwood?"

"I wanted to keep my men alive."

"Yes! Easier to live without the weight of deaths on your conscience."

Leif forced himself to stay cool, his grip firm but light as he held his weapon in a low-ready position.

"It's a good thing you had our training," Veratti said with a laugh. "I saw the intent in your gaze when the ladies entered. You thought another threat was coming, so you were ready! Then"—he raised his arms—"it's your girlfriend. And Braun! Your implant increased your ability to process that information at an incredible speed and cut emotional entanglement in carrying out your job. Without that, you might have shot the lovely Iskra. Maybe her innocent daughter." He smoothed a hand over Taissia's head, who violently recoiled at his touch.

Fury thumping his rib cage, Leif wanted to kill him.

He noticed the way Andreas moved not into a tactical position to defend his sister or Leif, but closer to Braun and Veratti. The ArC mastermind nodded, and Andreas took Taissia from Iskra.

No. Leif's belief that they had a prayer in stopping Veratti slipped several notches.

Veratti noticed. "Yes, wasn't that brilliant? Having Andreas pretend to be such a loyal friend and advocate to Rutger, the disloyal imbecile. One would think killing Katrin might've kept him in line." He shrugged. "I suppose I cannot be right all the time. And neither can you eliminate all the newer models in this room."

"Maybe," Leif said, "but I've changed the odds a little." He toed one of the bodies on the floor.

"Perhaps." Veratti ambled toward Andreas. "But will you try to shoot us when there is such precious cargo in the way?" As he lifted the girl from Andreas's arms, Taissia cried out, but he held her fast.

I am the weapon.

Dru's dying words wafted through his mind. *"'Al'el must go to the deep and there yield a mighty blow . . . At last the final war comes. Al'el must . . . move fast . . . and use his mind . . . to wit and war. Blood . . . spilled . . . then so much more . . . raging soul delivers . . . lethal blow . . . back where it started . . . stands against those who reap. Facing . . . betrayal and danger, his blade has come, sealing . . . fate.'"*

Blood had been spilled—a lot. Too much.

Seeking the enemy back where it started—this facility.

Standing against those who reap—he'd thought that meant Reaper, but what if it meant those who cut and gather, just as Ciro had done, bringing the suits and Gen2s here?

But the blade . . . the lethal blow . . . Was this all a part of his lethal blow? *His.* He was Al'el. He almost laughed. This whole thing had been about his journey. Doubt existed—how could it not? But his confidence was bolstered by those words. His determination to give it his best.

A man spoke to Veratti, drawing his attention away for a moment. A suit in the corner nursed a chest wound. Another held his bloody arm. Suits wouldn't be a threat, but the Gen2s were. And with only Leif and Saito here, odds were pretty narrow for victory and coming out alive. Unless . . .

Iskra. His gaze landed on her tactical pants—in particular, her ankle. Did she have her knife? If she could get it, then cut the line . . . a spark was all they needed.

"Runt," came Cell's quiet voice in his internal comms. But how? They were too far belowground. "Mercy did us a favor—when the worm uploaded, she gave us a back door into their servers. I have eyes on you. The man working on the system."

Not wanting to betray the new voice in his head, Leif checked his periphery for the tech, who was hovered over a computer.

"I need you to kill that computer he's on. He's already found Mercy's worm. He's disabling it."

Understood.

He visually traced the cables coming out of the system. First—cut those. To do that, he needed a distraction. He looked to Saito. Gave signals to relay the message.

Saito stilled, confusion in his brown eyes, but then recognition flared.

Leif wanted a double measure of reassurance that they could kill this program. He glanced again at Iskra's pant leg and thought he could see the imprint of her knife there—surprised Andreas had missed it. How could he get her to understand?

Her boot shifted, snapping his gaze to hers. She gave the barest of nods.

His heart leapt a little. Man, he loved her. Loved her tactical mind. No doubt she'd been working out how to stop this, too. He made a deliberate visual line between her and the cables on the ceiling.

No nod, but intensity. Determination. Tight lips.

Verifying Iskra and Saito were watching, Leif lifted one of the fingers that braced the barrel of his weapon. *One.*

Two.

Saito erupted in a flurry of kicks, curses, and thrashing. Attention swiveled his way.

Leif snapped up his weapon and fired two rounds into the tech's computer as screams erupted from the suits. Agile

Iskra used a counter to shove off and leapt upward with a violent thrust of her knife against the electrical cabling.

Sparks flew.

A guard to his left barreled at Leif. He struggled to stay upright. Hooked the man's neck and spun him around into a chokehold. Used him as a shield and fired several times at the system for good measure.

The tech leapt backward, but not fast enough. Smoke and chunks of plastic and metal exploded. A bullet pierced his lower abdomen.

Instinct forced Veratti to turn away, thereby protecting Taissia.

Bent in agony, the tech clutched at his stomach and let out a strangled cry. "You idiot!" He gaped at the system.

"*No!*" Veratti roared, his eyes ablaze. "You can't!" He thrust the child at Braun, who missed catching Taissia as the girl slid to the floor and ran toward Iskra. "Shoot! Kill him!" he ordered Andreas, who swung toward Leif but then caught Taissia in mid-flight.

Braun aimed her gun at Leif.

"Admiral, don't! Don't make me do this." Leif peered down the stock at her. Through the earpiece Cell gave the abort command to the contingency team, confirming the Risen upload had failed. Relief checked Leif. They'd succeeded.

Now to exfil and make sure Veratti didn't surface again. Literally.

Braun's eyes glittered. "I've done a lot I'm not proud of," she said, her voice surprisingly thick with emotion. "Including helping Veratti for years, letting him sway influence to advance me up the food chain." She winced. "Dru found out, but he tried to play the game against me. You always wondered why he kept telling you not to dig."

A chasm opened before Leif, so many things making sense. "Because you were watching, reporting back to your master."

Her face contorted. "And in the end," she said, "I killed one of my closest friends. I let the future, Ciro's future, determine my course. I didn't listen to my own better judgment."

Veratti frowned at her.

There was intention in her eyes—the same intention that had been there right before she killed Nesto. Now grief was swallowing her whole, forbidding any other course of action. "I hate that he died thinking of me as a traitor." She aimed the weapon at her chin.

Leif lunged. "No!"

Even as their bodies collided, she fired.

They landed hard on the concrete floor. The sonic boom of the weapon exploded near his ear, the damage instant and excruciating. Despite it, he held Braun's wrist above her head.

Men slammed into him, and his wounded leg didn't appreciate the impact as others piled on, trying to intervene.

Prying the gun from Braun's hand, Leif saw Veratti rushing for a door. Fighting the two Gen2s pinning him, he managed to fire off a few shots at the escaping enemy. The weight on him lifted as chaos engulfed the room.

As he came to a knee, Leif silently thanked Saito for distracting the Gen2s with a few well-placed shots and took aim at the nearest super soldier.

A piercing, violent scream roared through the facility, debilitating him. Shoving him back to the deck and making him curl in on himself. Warmth slid from his ears and nose, plopped onto the ground in an eerie way amid the claxon.

Disoriented, he wasn't sure if the noise was in his head or if Iskra and the others could hear it, too. He wiped away the blood, and his veins swelled, pulsing hard and threatening to rupture. It felt like something was trying to get out of his head. Somewhere in the din, he heard hollow noises—shots. But his vibrating skull refused to release its agonizing grip.

The noise stopped.

Head still throbbing, Leif struggled for his bearings. Peered past tears marring his vision, through that door to the fleeing suits. Someone was aiming a device at him as he fled. The resonance weapon.

Enraged, Leif shot him. Saw the man stumble around, stagger over a hatch, and collapse.

Exhausted, Leif sagged for a moment, tried to shake off the thunder that now replaced the scream, then pushed up. But couldn't.

An arm hooked his, and he accepted the assist. Stood—and found Iskra at his side. Taissia propped on her hip. Instinct hooked his arm around her shoulders. He saw Saito in a fight with two super soldiers and rotated his girls to the side and fired, nailing a Gen2 in the back of the head. The other one shifted, startled by his buddy's death. That small break was enough for Saito to take control. Neutralize the enemy.

On the other side of the room, Andreas was a lethal machine, targeting the remnant suits who had bottlenecked at the hatch. Who was he really working for?

"We have to stop them." Leif's words sounded hollow, garbled—the resonance weapon and Braun's shot had damaged his hearing.

The body on the floor shifted.

Braun hadn't succeeded in killing herself. She rolled onto her back, weary red-rimmed eyes meeting his. He winced—the shot had sheared off part of her chin and cheek, as well as a chunk of her ear. But it seemed the bullet hadn't penetrated her skull. Her groan warbled through his aching ear.

Sad, Leif crouched beside her. "Alene—"

"Do it." She touched his weapon. "Kill me," she pleaded. "Please, kill me. You have to. I don't deserve to live."

Part of him wanted to grant her wish—she had betrayed

him, Dru—all of them, the entire world. She was the reason he hadn't gotten answers. But . . . she'd tried to kill herself instead of him. That said something, didn't it?

Boom, boom, boom!

Leif jerked up straight, listening, feeling. "What was that?" It sounded a lot like a structural breach.

"Runt," Canyon commed, "you have a problem."

"What's new?"

"About a million problems," Cell chimed in. "A million gallons, that is. One of the charges the contingency operators set accidentally detonated."

Leif almost cursed. "Move! That was a detonation!" He imagined water gushing into the hole the charge had created and frantically motioned Iskra and Taissia to the same hatch ArC had exited. "Go go go!"

Saito and Andreas followed her into the main passage system with hatches banking off every thirty meters. The nearest to the left—Veratti was ducking through it.

"Stop, or I—" Vibration wormed through Leif's boots and up into his knees as he hurried toward the opening.

"Wait," Andreas shouted. "Hear that?"

A roaring thunder came from the same route Veratti and his minions had taken. Suddenly, Veratti threw himself back through the hatch—right into their path.

Andreas swung out a hand to stop Leif and Iskra.

Leif felt the threat, too. Watched as one of the suits and a hobbling Bogdashka scrambled out of the same tunnel. With Veratti, they fought to close the hatch door. Screams turned to shouts—the other suits trying to get out as well. The trio pushed hard—the strength of the ocean struggling against them. It finally closed with a hard *thunk*. Face white, the suit spun the hatch's handle, locking it.

They stepped back, shin-deep in sea water. Veratti looked at Leif and his team, stricken. Stunned. Yet more focused than ever to live. To beat this. He threw himself to the right. The suit did the same.

"Stop!" Leif yelled. He fired—as did Andreas, coming up alongside him. The suit pitched forward into the foot of water, Andreas's bullet in his back.

Crack! Groaaaan!

Veratti trudged on, glancing up to find the source of the groan. A large steel pipe leapt from the ceiling like a swing arm and slammed him backward. Pinned him against the hull. His feral scream echoed in the tunnel.

Leif hesitated, then trudged toward the ArC mastermind.

The woman behind Netherwood fought in vain against the rapidly rising water. She might have had a chance if her knee hadn't been shattered.

"Bogdashka," Iskra yelled, clearly worried the woman was getting away. With the rushing water and the distance, she had little chance of throwing her knife effectively, especially with Taissia in her arms.

Andreas marched forward, seemingly unhindered by the rapids. With a cheek weld, he sighted down the darkening tunnel. Fired.

Screams mingling with Veratti's, Bogdashka sloshed into the murky water and didn't rise.

"The other hatch is flooded." Iskra eased back from the window in the closed hatch where the suits had been trapped by Veratti. Her expression was wan, telling him the ArC members were dead.

Leif battled the ever-increasing rage of swelling water—it was waist-high now—to reach the fallen pipe. He peered over its gray-painted hull.

Veratti, legs and hips pinned, gripped a rung attached to the pipe to keep his face out of the water. Frantic eyes found his. "Help me!"

"Let's go!" Andreas barked. "He's not worth it. Leave him."

A venomous howl filled the air around them.

Startled, Leif looked around. Started toward Iskra.

"You can't leave me!" Veratti shouted, his tone panicked yet angry.

Conscience pricked Leif. Iskra and Taissia were what was important. Braun. She had helped them in the end.

Part of him wanted to turn his back on Veratti. Walk out. Let him drown. It'd serve him right after all the lives he'd snuffed out, the good soldiers and sailors and Marines from around the world whose lives he'd ruined in the Netherwood project. The countries he'd altered or destroyed. Botswana. Angola. Ghana.

But . . . maybe this was why Leif had been in the Book of the Wars. In the painting. Not to dictate what happened, but to show that Leif was key. He could alter it. Change it.

Because he wasn't the man who left men to drown. Who showed no compassion. He wasn't a coldblooded killer. Even when they tampered with his brain and activated the implant in Taipei, he'd fought *not* to be that man.

No way would Veratti win this one, succeed in turning him into a monster.

"Saito, get Braun and get them out!" Leif started toward the pipe.

"Leif, no!" Iskra screamed as Saito and Andreas dragged her back through the hatch.

"Go." He met her gaze. "Get Taissia out. Before it's too late!"

Her screams pierced his willpower, and his comms piece erupted in shouts and orders to get out of the facility. To leave before it was too late. It was a painful cacophony against his still-aching ears.

Shouldering past all that, Leif crouched and gripped the pipe.

"Thank you!" Veratti had water and tears on his face. "I always knew you were—"

"Shut up and push," Leif bit out as he heaved. Nothing. Not an inch. The pipe was heavier than expected. The water wasn't helping, rushing in through the opening and fighting him.

"Leif!" Andreas barked. "Water's too high. We have to close the hatch."

Straining, Leif tried again. This time he felt it shift marginally. And it couldn't have been the force of the water.

He thought through his mental map. The water was coming from the direction of the first passages they'd used after entering the underground system. He was a SEAL. One with a longer-than-average ability to hold his breath and focus, thanks to the Neiothen enhancements.

He looked at the others. "Go! I'll meet you at the cave." He bent and hugged the pipe, trying to pull it free.

"No!" Iskra shouted.

Andreas glowered. "He's not worth your life."

Pretty much know that. "Get Iskra and Taissia to the cave!"

Common sense said to let Veratti drown, not save him. And wasn't that the point of salvation? The value placed on life, regardless of a subjective definition of worth?

When he heard and felt the thud of the hatch slamming shut, Leif's heart hiccupped. *Guess I'm committed now.*

"I'm not a good swimmer," Veratti said, shivering, head tilted back as the water riffled his hair.

"You don't have to be." With the water having nowhere to escape, the passage was filling fast. Leif tried again. Broke loose a stray piece of rebar from the damaged cabling and used it as a wedge.

Veratti let out a strangled cry as water covered his face.

Crap. Though Leif tried again, it was a no-go. Water to his shoulders, he took several quick, deep breaths to expand his lungs, then slipped under. With the added buoyancy of the rising water, he managed to shift the pipe. As he did, Veratti jolted and let out a silent scream. Sucked in water.

A red cloud plumed around him.

Leif wanted to curse when he saw that a supporting brace had speared Veratti's side. The ArC leader went limp.

Frustrated, Leif banged the pipe. Toed off and catapulted down the passage. He pinned his arms to his side and waved his legs, swimming hard.

A body rolled toward him—Bogdashka, eyes vacant, unseeing. But then, hadn't she always been, if she couldn't see the harm she'd done to so many young women?

He nudged her aside and continued on until he came to the juncture and vaulted to the left. Lungs burning, he focused on getting to the other side. As he rounded the last corner, he found the hatch closed. He sped toward it and tried to crank the handle, but it wouldn't budge. Again he tried, but a bubble of air slipped from him. His pulse thumped against his temple, reminding him he needed oxygen.

He banged hard on the hatch, then worked on destroying the lock mechanism, hoping it would disengage. No way he had enough time to double back. There were no options. There was little chance he'd be heard, but he prayed the others had made it this far. That they'd hear the warbling sound.

Though the glass cracked, nothing changed on the hatch. Once more, he tried the wheel.

No go.

He swam back the dozen feet to the juncture. But it was just more of the same. Something told him to return to the hatch, so he did. He banged again, telling himself not to panic over the building boulder-like pressure in his chest. At least Iskra got out. Saved Taissia. They'd have a good life. Reaper would watch out for them.

And wasn't that the beauty of friendship? You couldn't have betrayal without a sense of trust, without a bond that went beyond the surface.

A grunt freed itself, releasing air bubbles. Leif tried not

to stress. Felt his ability to hold his breath slipping. That first breath would drown him. He kicked and jerked on the handle, refusing to let go. Refusing to lose. To let Veratti get another one over on him.

Even as the grim possibility rose that he'd drown, that he'd fulfill the depiction of a flayed friend on a battlefield of betrayal from a book written thousands of years ago, Leif knew he'd done his best with what he had. He was okay with it. He'd found the answers. Found the truth. Found Iskra.

He took a breath.

Water slipped in. He trapped it in his mouth but knew he couldn't hold it any longer. He couldn't—

He choked a breath.

Water flooded him. Filled his throat. His lungs. He thrashed. Felt it drown his lungs. He groped for air, tried to find some. But instead he found more water, burning water. His vision ghosted, and he stopped fighting it. Trusted whatever God wanted to do. Even if it meant him dying.

Like a cannon, he felt himself falling . . . forward. Toward light.

I'm dying.

He fell hard. *So not Heav—*

His shoulder hit hard. He coughed and gagged. Cold, hard steel pressed against his palms. Blinked as something rushed at him and the warmth and beauty that was Iskra and Taissia enfolded him.

Oh, thank you, God!

Saito and Andreas hauled him up. He swiped a hand over his face and hated the burn that radiated through his throat and chest.

"Veratti?" Andreas asked, helping him down the passage. Braun trailed their group.

Leif shook his head as they slipped through a door he and Iskra had come through earlier. How had it not flooded? It was a tight, narrow passage, and all he could think about was how quickly it'd fill with water if breached.

They made it to a small room lined with lockers. "Grab gear and suit up," Andreas said.

"Taissia doesn't know how to dive!" Iskra said as they started removing dive suits from storage.

"Put a tank and mask on her." Leif shouldered into a tank, eyeing Andreas, who was gearing up as well. "Strap her to me." He caught Iskra's arm and eased in, whispering, "You trust him?"

Warily, she set Taissia on a bench as she lifted a tank and mask. "I think he does not want to die as much as we do not." She went to work securing the mask on Taissia, who was fighting her.

"We have to sedate her," Andreas said, handing Iskra a vial injector. "Two CCs."

Iskra punched to her feet, and they were both rattling in Bulgarian like a rapid-fire combat engagement. Finally, she shoved her hair from her face and knelt, said something to her daughter in Russian, then touched the needle to Taissia's leg and gave her the shot. She helped a crying Taissia lie down, then put her tank on.

"What was that?" Leif asked her.

Her eyes warily came to his. "I warned that if she died, he would, too."

That's my girl. Suited up, Leif checked Braun's equipment. Two minutes later, after more gear checks, they headed to another door, where they found the large, dark pool.

"See where the water is slightly lighter?" Andreas pointed to a spot in the distance. "That is the edge of the cave wall with sunlight on the other side. To reach it, we must go down and under a ledge. From there, rise. Follow me."

Leif took Taissia into his arms and tied her to his chest, so he could monitor her oxygen as they went.

I will rise.
I will rise.
I will rise.

It had a different meaning now. For Leif—he would rise. Iskra—she would rise. And Taissia—she would rise.

They slipped into the water and moved from the darkness into the light.

Epilogue

ARLINGTON NATIONAL CEMETERY, VIRGINIA

Each crack of the twenty-one-gun salute felt like a smack in the face as Leif stood stiff in his dress uniform, hands at his sides. He let his gaze stray to the chairs where Dru's parents were seated, flanked by Mercy on one side and Iskra on the other, Taissia on her lap.

It should be me in that box.

That thought, though borne of grief and love for a friend, disrespected what Dru Iliescu had sacrificed for Leif. For Reaper.

As the minister spoke of grief and a life lived well, Leif took in the team that had changed so much. Altered by losing members and nearly losing Peyton, who was now sandwiched between Iskra and Adam. She wore a thick scarf to ward off the cold, but also to conceal the scarring from the sniper bullet that had chewed up her chest and neck. Culver and Saito stood at his side as pallbearers, their expressions tight.

Cell stood on the other side, also serving as a pallbearer, his demeanor haunted. Seated among the hundreds gathered, Alisz Vogt had applied for asylum because other countries sought her for what she'd done on behalf of ArC. Veratti and Bogdashka were still in their watery grave with their creations. It would take months to excavate the collapsed facility. Nobody had seen Andreas since they'd reached topside, and somehow Iskra was at peace with that. Leif understood wanting to slip off the radar.

Marines went through the sharp, precise ritual of folding the flag, then turning it over to Admiral Manche, who presented it to Dru's elderly parents with thanks on behalf of a grateful nation.

As the bugler began "Taps," Leif let his gaze rest once more on the flag-draped coffin. Moments later, the family departed and the guests walked by, offering Dru one final farewell. When it was his turn, Leif pounded his SEAL trident into the oak, then laid a palm over it. "I will never forget what you did . . . and why you did it." His throat felt raw. "But we got them. Because of you. Thank you, Dru."

SIX MONTHS LATER
VOIDOKILIA BEACH, PELOPONNESE, GREECE

"In the shark-infested waters of the Caribbean, two prawns called Justin and Christian are discussing the pressures—"

"H-two-*oh no!*" Cell let out a loud groan. "Too soon, man. Too soon!"

"I don't know," Baddar said with a grin. "It is nice that he tells jokes again."

"No. No, it's not. His jokes are lame." Cell stood and took Alisz's hand. "We're heading out to do some sightseeing. See you losers later."

Leif laughed and gave Cell a salute, then stared down the beach.

It had to be Greece. The country where they'd officially

met—granted, in an armed standoff, both ready to kill the other. But for that vacation Iskra had promised Taissia, Leif insisted they return to Greece. It also wasn't too far from Istanbul, where he'd encouraged her to flee into the night with him.

Peyton and Adam were in the water, and this was the first time Leif had seen her without her arm in a sling. She'd never given the ring back, forcing Adam to add a wedding band and make it official. Not that anyone had to twist the big guy's arm.

Mercy's ooga-chaka baby virus that saved the world was classic, and the team had high-fived her over that. She and Baddar had done some hiking around the sights, then joined them here. They weren't yet talking marriage, but they'd become inseparable.

At the edge of the water, Leif sat with Iskra and Taissia, making sandcastles. They'd both vowed never to let the little firecracker out of their sight again. And Leif had heeded Adam's warning to "put a ring on that." He dug in the sand and framed out what looked like a book. In the center, he dropped the box, then covered it, his heart thumping harder than usual.

"What are you doing?" Iskra asked, shifting to look at him. She leaned closer, her long dark hair teasing his shoulder. "Is that a book?"

Leif smirked at her wrinkled nose. "Do you remember at the Pearl—the first time"—he squinted up into her eyes—"what you said to me?" He stretched out, giving his still-aching leg wound relief as he continued writing on his sand sculpture.

"Which time?" Confusion pinched her expression as she again looked at what he was building.

"Before you jumped into the churning sea."

A smile slid onto her olive complexion. "Letters of Marque."

"That's right. A special license to capture vessels of a nation at war, then basically a transfer of ownership."

Iskra seemed truly confused. "So?" She laughed. "Is this—"

"Go on." He pointed to it. "Break the seal."

With a bemused smile, Iskra dusted her hand over the book he'd made of sand. Buried in it, she found the package he'd wrapped. Drew it out. "What is it?"

"Open it."

She removed the butcher paper. "Shoes?"

He grunted. "No, that was the only box I had. Look inside."

She removed the lid, and her lips parted. Wide, melty eyes locked on his.

"I thought, since that thing brought us together . . ." He nodded at it. "Keep going."

She gently opened the leaves of the Book of the Wars, her mouth still hanging open, and found what he'd hidden. "A ring."

"You issued a Letter of Marque at the Pearl—and now I insist you make good on that special license." He slipped his hand behind her neck and drew her closer. "We were at war, you captured me, and now you have to take ownership."

"What if I don't want to?"

"Oh, it's too late for that." He pulled a folded paper from the book. "See, this is a marriage license."

She gasped. "But—how? They said—"

"When will you learn that I have powers?"

"Enhanced abilities," she corrected, stealing the words he'd always shot at the team.

"That too. After saving the world, a lot of people owed me favors. So I called them in. Your citizenship is official. And, apparently, so is our marriage. As of today. On this beach."

Tear slipped down her cheeks.

Leif faltered, his bravado lost. He swallowed, realizing that, with his nerves over his unofficial-official wedding thing, maybe he'd done this wrong. "Did I screw up again? I thought you wanted—"

"No—yes." She shook her head. Hands framing his face, she kissed him. "I never thought after Hristoff that I would find *this*."

Relief chugged through him as he slipped the ring on her finger. "Find? You captured me, woman!" He kissed her back. "I am, forever and always, your prisoner. You get me and a lifetime of bad jokes."

"I know where you can get a quick divorce," Cell called.

"Hey—you were supposed to be leaving!"

"Me or Iskra?"

Leif surged toward Cell, but Iskra called him back. "Hey, I thought you said you were my prisoner."

He dropped next to her. "Man, I feel the ball and chain already."

Iskra gave him a demure look and leaned in to kiss him.

As he took her into his arms, epiphany struck: the truth he'd been looking for hadn't begun to unfold when he'd taken matters into his own hands. It had started that day at Aperióristos Labs, when Iskra walked into that facility, took aim at his heart, and irrevocably altered his course. Far more than the Netherwood project ever had.

That was love. And it wasn't a ball and chain . . . it was an anchor that had saved him amid a storm rising, kings falling, and a soul raging.

Ronie Kendig is the bestselling, award-winning author of over twenty-five novels. She grew up an Army brat, and now she and her hunky hero are adventuring on the East Coast with their retired military working dog, VVolt N629, and Benning the Stealth Golden. Ronie's degree in psychology has helped her pen novels with intense, raw characters. Visit Ronie online at www.roniekendig.com.

Sign Up for Ronie's Newsletter

Keep up to date with Ronie's new book releases and events by signing up for her email list at roniekendig.com.

More from Ronie Kendig

On a mission to recover the Book of the Wars, Leif and his team are diverted by a foretelling of formidable warriors who will decimate the enemies of the ArC, while Iskra uses her connections to hunt down the book. As they try to stop the warriors, failure becomes familiar, and the threats creep closer to home, with implications that could tear them apart.

Kings Falling
THE BOOK OF THE WARS #2

More from Bethany House

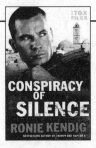

When an archaeological dig unleashes a centuries-old virus, paramilitary operative Cole 'Tox' Russell is forced back into action. With the help of archaeologist Tzivia Khalon and FBI agent Kasey Cortes, Tox searches for answers—and becomes entangled in a web of deception. As the team races to stop a pandemic, a secret society counters their every move.

Conspiracy of Silence by Ronie Kendig
THE TOX FILES #1
roniekendig.com

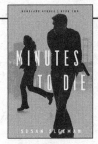

Terrorists have been smuggled into the country intent on unleashing a deadly attack, and FBI Agent Kiley Dawson and ICE Agent Evan Bowers are charged with taking it down—only, Kiley blames Evan for the death of her former partner and can't be in the same room as him. As threats ensue, the two are pushed to the breaking point in a race to save countless lives.

Minutes to Die by Susan Sleeman
HOMELAND HEROES #2
susansleeman.com

After one of her team members is murdered and the CIA opens an internal investigation on her, Layla Karam reluctantly turns to her ex-boyfriend and private investigator Hunter McCoy to help clear her name and uncover the real killer. With threats on all sides, Layla must put her trust in the man who broke her heart and hope they both come out alive.

Backlash by Rachel Dylan
CAPITAL INTRIGUE #2
racheldylan.com

⬩BETHANYHOUSE

You May Also Like . . .

When multiple corpses are found, their remains point to a serial killer with a familiar MO but who's been in prison for over twenty years—Special Agent Kaely Quinn's father. In order to prevent more deaths, she must come face-to-face with the man she's hated for years. In a race against time, will this case cost Kaely her identity and perhaps even her life?

Dead End by Nancy Mehl
KAELY QUINN PROFILER #3
nancymehl.com

When an accident claims the life of an oil-rig worker off the North Carolina coast, Coast Guard investigators Rissi Dawson and Mason Rogers are sent to take the case. But mounting evidence shows the death may not have been an accident at all, and they find themselves racing to discover the killer's identity before he eliminates the threat they pose.

The Crushing Depths by Dani Pettrey
COASTAL GUARDIANS #2
danipettrey.com

Brooke Danvers wants to learn the truth about her father's suspicious death, but she'll need the help of Luke Fereday, a National Park Ranger and her ex-boyfriend. Keeping Brooke safe will take all of Luke's skills, and falling in love with her will only complicate matters.

Standoff by Patricia Bradley
NATCHEZ TRACE PARK RANGERS #1
ptbradley.com

BETHANYHOUSE